C000124996

WHERE ARE YOU

SALLY BRYAN

Where Are You

Sally Bryan

This book is a work of fiction. Events, situations, people and places are all products of the author's imagination. This book contains pornographic scenes and reader discretion is advised.

First Printing, 2014

ISBN: 9781089692881

CONTENTS

For Pamela

That I would meet a genuine Napoletana while writing this book, set in Napoli, can only have been fate. Thanks for all your help and input.

WHERE ARE YOU

You entered my life when I needed a friend,
Bright eyes meeting mine from through the crowd.
I didn't know then you would change my whole life,
In only a year we had, more anyone else allowed.

You entered my life and showed me new ways,
My perfect companion, you breathed me new life.
The things we did, the memories we made,
Just so much promise and future so bright.

You entered my life when I needed you most,
Over my own heart, the power you held.
But like all good things, they must one day come end,
Then that day you left me, you felt compelled.

You entered my life and tore out my soul,
So now I write this as a final farewell.
Will I ever love again, bright eyes through the crowd,
Will I ever be whole, can I break your spell.

Part One

CAMBRIDGE

Chapter One

FATE

A nd still, approaching two days after *that* poem fell out from within the musty pages of some old and forgotten textbook, Erin convalesced in bed. Her aching heart, she hoped, would not take so long to heal this time around as it had when she'd first bled her soul into writing it. How long had it been, ten years? Perhaps even to the day. The universe did often play such tricks, with fate intervening in mystic ways to force one to consider the state of their life, to question whether changes should be made.

And at that point, it was up to the individual to act, or not.

Ok, so she was no poet. Erin knew that. But those words had poured from her at a time she'd felt most hopeless.

It had been during a rare couple of days off work and she'd merely taken the chance to sort through her old books, promote some to the living room bookshelf before taking the rest to the Salvation Army. Never did get round to that last bit.

Because the evil thing had fallen out and fluttered through the air sans ceremony. Such a piddling thing to confine an adult to bed. And she'd known what it was before it had even touched the floor, even though it'd spent so long out of her mind, like the books that gathered dust.

After forever staring at it, she'd changed her mind several times before finally, with the same care she handled the most delicate of her patients, picking it up from the floor, the masochist within winning out over the sane Erin she'd nurtured since writing it. The poem had been a way of saying goodbye, to forever put to rest the demon that was the damn Italian. Trouble in its purest svelte brunette form.

Why she'd read it, she couldn't say. Though reading it twice was pure madness and so she settled on just that, she was mad, or had been madly in love. At the very least, she was a masochist. And somewhere in that wardrobe, there'd be a box stashed full of all their old stuff. Soon she'd feel compelled to find that box, like how an addict would always return to what would ultimately destroy them.

By God, it ached. And so, two days later, she was still abed, curled up, large damp blotches covering the pillow, tissues strewn about the room. No empty dishes though.

It was true that life wasn't fair but what had happened to Erin ten years before had wrenched her very being from within. The mind finds ways of coping and the poem had been a part of that. But since then she'd cast the memories of Gianna, as much as possible, out from her mind.

She had to survive, after all.

But now they flooded back and as a consequence of switching off her phone, missing appointments and of apparently disappearing from the face of the earth; ferocious knocking now resounded against the front door.

It took a lot to fluster Erin these days, the composed girl she'd become, much thanks to *her*. But, as she had so recently discovered, the damn Italian still held power over Erin, even though she was not here.

And even though she'd not heard from Gianna in exactly ten years to the day.

SHE DREADED OPENING THE DOOR TO THE ANATOMY Building of Downing College. This was the University of Cambridge, after all, and once she entered, the next three years would have officially begun; she would be a student, a grown-up, at least officially, she'd be on her own. As the door drew nearer, Erin began taking smaller steps to gift herself some precious additional moments as a child, to gain composure.

She'd arrived in Cambridge only over the weekend, the memory of her parents waving as they drove away down the cobbles made her long for their embrace. Had this been one huge mistake? Who was *she* to leave home, to try make her way in the world when she was barely even out of school? She'd yet to even work a part-time job, take a holiday abroad or even date a boy for any longer than a vodka and cherry cola fuelled weekend at the skatepark. Indeed, there'd been times the crippling social anxiety disorder had prevented her merely visiting the local shops. The cognitive behavioural therapy had helped a little but Cambridge was next-level stuff.

Now, as she pushed open the door and the prominent carved oak creaked with age, a lump grew in her throat as her breathing came in short, sharp spurts. She entered and slipped her hands inside her pockets to dry them on the already damp tissues.

Erin had meant to arrive early, which was her way of avoiding all the inevitable stares that usually comes from being a girl walking into a crowded room but now, feeling the heat of so many bodies and seeing the large chattering clusters of so many students crowding the atrium, she regretted walking so slowly. It was the first day and it seemed everybody else had the same idea of arriving early.

Time stopped as countless heads turned to examine the girl, as anticipated, who was standing all alone. As usual, the male stares lingered longest, before turning back to resume conversations. That strangers could so easily engage in such casual talk was amazing to Erin, some groups genuinely looked like they'd known each other for ages, and how could she ever hope to imitate such behaviour when it was hard to even breathe? Was Erin truly the only one who struggled with this? Granted, today would be tenser than most but to see them, you wouldn't know it, and the thought of approaching one of the already formed cliques, to introduce her insignificant self was beyond terrifying.

Still blocking the door, three students pushed past and then she found herself shuffling aimlessly further into the abyss of what was a large anteroom connecting four lecture theatres, scrutinising the floor as she did. People's feet shifted aside, but she might have been imagining that, and when she finally dared tilt up her chin she found herself standing lost amidst several large groups.

Her extremities went cold, despite the rising heat, and she began exploring the mural above to distract her mind. Was it a mural if it was on the ceiling? Anyway, two horses were pulling a vicar in a carriage. Was he a vicar, or just a badly dressed man in robes? Dogs were running alongside trying to keep pace, perhaps hoping for scraps, and one of them looked like Auntie Jane's collie. Lower down, the sculpted wood-panelled walls reminded her where she was, a grand place of prestige and history.

By God, it was painful. She'd been told that people weren't really watching her, that it was all in her mind and that even if they did look, study and judge, then so what? Get over it. Don't be a prisoner inside your own head. But it was never as easy as that.

Was the black-haired ponytailed girl looking at her? Did she just say something to her friend? Maybe about how lonely the strange red-haired girl looked. How much longer could this unpleasantness continue? All Erin wanted was for the theatre to open so she could finally sit and occupy herself, to fade away, for the attention to be on some professor instead. At least he was paid for it.

Suddenly, the heat rose to some unbearable temperature, sweat pricked her forehead, her scalp itched, bringing an obscene urge to scratch, but what would people think if she did that. There was an overwhelming desire to run, to never look back, to get out, quick, to breathe cool air, to cry, to return home, to be with her parents. She hitched her backpack higher on one shoulder; half in an attempt to occupy herself for one solitary second, to remove some small semblance of pressure, and half because now, Erin was seriously contemplating flight mode. Indeed, her feet were already moving when…

From the far end of the atrium, a loud thud startled most of those in the immediate vicinity, there was another thump followed by what might have been a faint, wood-muffled groan and as the chattering began to recede, almost every single person in the atrium began diverting their attention toward the racket. Erin felt relief from the temporary respite wash over her like a cool breeze and peered through a gap in the masses to see the noise was coming from the other side of the fire door. A clatter, louder still, was followed by a pained yelp, prompting several sniggers until finally, one student tried helping by pressing down on the horizontal bar and from the inside, pulling the heavy door open just as a heap of long brown hair, a girl, found nothing in the way of her renewed effort at shouldering her way in. Announcing her

Cambridge arrival, she came in tumbling but worse still, the strap from her exceptionally large backpack caught on the doorknob, which checked her forward momentum and flung her back, momentarily lifting her feet off the ground as she came to land, not too unkindly, considering everything, on her back, the offending baggage taking most of the sting.

Erin's hand found its own way to her mouth as the entire atrium erupted into hysterics, a cup of water was thrown from one side to the other and several more followed. *Glad that wasn't me*, was all she could think, because death was far preferable.

The girl didn't die, though, but merely scrambled to her feet, "stupida porta del cazzo," she cursed, whatever that meant, though it was easy to guess, and threw down the offending burden, which was one of those large unwieldy things you see on travellers, broken, as the strap now was. Erin felt mortified for the poor girl but she barely even cracked a blush as she blew out air and examined her overcoat for tears.

For a while, everyone continued staring until, one by one, the hapless girl was forgotten as conversations resumed.

Erin allowed herself a chuckle. Why had she entered from the cloister anyway? How silly. Anyway, whoever she was would soon join everybody else in finding instant companions and the best of luck to her.

Now, where was she? Ah, yes, contemplating flight.

Erin turned her feet toward the exit but checked the movement when the blundering girl clocked her through an opening in the crowd. Maybe it was curiosity but for whatever reason, Erin could not bring herself to look immediately away, which was odd for her, and before she could send the signal for her legs to carry her out, for home and a job at the supermarket checkout, the newcomer nodded, of all things, as in, *I see you, just wait a minute*.

In one large swinging effort, she returned the backpack to her shoulder, unceremoniously shunting the two nearest lads as she did, before commencing to press through the huddle. Worse, she was even now heading for the only other girl still solo.

Through the shock and panic renewing, Erin noticed the girl was slender and half a head taller than any of the four girls she now skirted, with dark features befitting a typical Southern European. Spain, Italy, Greece perhaps? Certainly, it was that she was overdressed in a thick brown winter jacket that gave it away more than anything else, considering it was still September. Long brown hair flowed over her shoulders, which sprang to life as she bobbed between students, cutting a path through the mass, to where, only she knew, because surely she wasn't heading for Erin. She held her head high and bundled through another group, her large backpack clobbering nearly everyone in her way.

To live life with such an attitude was completely alien and Erin now watched the girl with a growing fascination. It wasn't that she was confident, whoever she was, but that she had a complete lack of spatial awareness, and possibly a case of ADD thrown in with it. Either that or she just didn't give a shit, as another boy grimaced when the bulk of her rig shoved him sideways.

The last few people wisely stepped aside and then, truly, the stranger was standing before her. Erin took an instinctive step back, glancing once over a shoulder for the person who'd obviously be standing there. But there wasn't anyone.

"Hi," the girl said, apparently not noticing Erin's painful uncertainty.

And then, having made eye contact again, Erin surprised herself further by not looking away. Either she didn't truly wish to run and there was something curious about this person or she was undergoing a mind stupor and her flight response would kick in any second but still, she held her gaze.

"Hello," Erin said back, realising she had nothing else to say. *Time to run! No? Well, look down to the floor, at least. Comfort. You know you want it.*

The girl gave a sudden and easy smile, bright-eyed and flashed a perfect set of white teeth. Two small dimples appeared on her cheeks.

How long had the silence been? The prior urge for flight intensified but Erin found herself fixed to the spot.

"Anatomy Building?" The girl asked.

"Um, what?"

"This *is* the Anatomy Building, isn't it? Please say it is. I can't face barging into another wrong lecture, that prof was pissed." The girl's accent was thick and Erin feared being thought stupid if she failed to fathom its crazy bouncing rhythm.

"Erm, I understood some of what you said, but could you talk a little slower please?" She squeaked, just barely audible to her own ears.

"Is this the … Anatomy … Building … of Cambridge University?" The strange girl rolled her *r's*, but spoke slower the second time and Erin now understood but still feared coming over as slow or stupid. Had there been a hint of sarcasm in the unduly strung out question or had Erin imagined it?

"Yes, this is the Anatomy Building." Erin had scoped out the place the previous night during a dry run, to arrive early, not that it made a difference in the end.

"Thank God." The girl's forehead was perspiring, maybe she was human after all, and would certainly benefit from removing her jacket. It was way too hot inside as it was. She glanced about the room, likely for someone more talkative, but for now seemed content to remain where she stood. She dumped the bag on the floor and there was the distinct rattle of cutlery, plates, maybe even a frying pan or two. She gave it a kick. "You're probably wondering but I arrived only thirty minutes ago, stupid English trains, and I couldn't get in the flat, hence most my worldly possessions..."

"Ah," Erin nodded, that explained some of it, perhaps. She knew the right thing was to try make small talk, ask the usual questions, fill the silence, which was beginning to stretch again, but neither did she wish to come over predictable. What would the girl think then?

"You're a quiet one, aren't you?" She made it sound halfway between a question and a statement and Erin wasn't sure if she was supposed to answer it or not.

"Always, yes." Great! Now her big secret was out the way, maybe the girl would go easy and Erin could retreat back to the realms of comfort that was silence and loneliness. Shyness really was a prison sentence, though largely a self-imposed one.

"Wow, you really are, aren't you." The girl took a step closer as her face softened. "Well, I don't bite," she held out a hand, "and my name's Gianna."

Erin took her hand and shook it, noting the cold feel to her skin, doubtless still acclimatising to the great English weather. "I'm Erin."

"*Erin*...hmm," she bounced once on her toes, "let me know if I sound like a chipmunk on caffeine and I'll slow down. My English isn't perfect but most of the time my mum can't even understand me, so she just ignores me instead. Can't blame her really."

Erin knew that to be a joke, so she smiled out of politeness. She tried placing the accent and when she couldn't, thought to ask but stopped herself just in time. It was such a mundane question.

"So where are you from?" Gianna asked.

Erin jerked at that, "oh, not far away."

"Where?"

"Oh, a town called Alnwick, up in the north."

Gianna paused, as though expecting more and when there wasn't, "and now you return the question to me."

Erin flushed. She wasn't being rude but she just couldn't understand why the girl was still talking to her when there was a roomful of people a lot more like she was, people who could string a sentence together for one, and engage with others. "I'm sorry, Gianna, where are you from?"

"That's ok, I can relate to your problem, by the way. My older brother, Marco, barely speaks to anyone but please, call me *Gia*. *Gianna's* way too much effort, whereas *Gia* means *already* in Italian which, as you've witnessed, I most certainly am not." Gia grinned and gave Erin a reassuring rub of the arm, which felt comforting.

"Ok, I will do." Erin paused, waiting for the answer, and when it didn't come, she chuckled.

"Hey, what?"

"You didn't answer the question."

"Hah, you're not so shy at all, are you? Looks like I had you all wrong." She grinned and flashed those bright eyes again. "I'm from Napoli or, as you English call, *Naples*."

"I've never heard of it."

"Really? I should be offended. It's in Southern Italy but we Neapolitans pretty much consider ourselves an independent nation."

"Why?"

"You'd know if you went." As if that was explanation enough.

Gia looked pretty much like the stereotypically attractive Italian girl. Her features were sharp, almost hawkish, with a look that warned against starting an argument. Yet her demeanour masked that *look*. It was almost contradictory. It was as though she was intimidating from afar, but the exact opposite once you were engaged in conversation and for the first time since stepping inside the building, Erin found herself almost able to relax and it was all thanks to Gia. Though deep down she knew the girl would tire of her and find some real people to talk with, sooner or later. Exotic women did not seek out the awkward mute type for friends but instead gravitated toward people more like themselves.

"I have to check though, because I see four theatres..." Gia waved her arms about to gesture the large room, "I assume not all these people are enrolled in the same course? There's too many."

At that, a group of students began filing into one of the theatres and Erin's heart screamed. She'd assumed everybody was part of the same course but, as it turned out, this was merely the atrium for the four lecture theatres and therefore, likely, four different courses. Would Gia even be enrolled in the same course?

"Well, I'm doing Physiotherapy. How about you?" Erin asked urgently, hoping this friendly girl would be joining her.

"Same." The Italian straightened in delight. "Looks like I've made my first friend."

"Really?" Oh, that sounded lame.

"Of course, unless you're thinking about running away and leaving me all alone?"

Erin laughed at that, genuinely, it was all she could do, and with it she felt a beautiful wave of relief flood through her.

And as the students began filing inside the impressive theatre, she made sure to sit beside Gia.

Because Erin had made a friend.

Chapter Two

FORLORN

"Erin, what the hell?" Ben half barged his way past as she opened the door in her dressing gown. "I hope you have a good explanation for this."

"I know. And there is. I've been ill, that's all." She closed the door behind him and braced herself. He had every right to be angry.

"What's the matter?" His eyes widened in a sudden burst of fear.

"Oh, just flu symptoms, but they're not as bad as yesterday. I think I'm on the mend." Erin pottered into the kitchen in front of Ben.

"Oh, thank God! Christ, you had me worried you were dying or something." He glanced over the accumulated mess, the dirty dishes and rubbish that gathered in the corner, most notably the used tissues that spilled out. At least they'd add credence to the story. "You should have told me. Do you have any idea how many times I've tried contacting you? Absolutely no response!" He threw up his hands. "What was I supposed to think? And the mess..." he gestured toward the dishes in the sink, "Erin, this is not like you."

"I'm sorry and I know. Sometimes when I'm ill, I just switch everything off and hibernate." She faced the window to avoid his gaze, another rainy day in Cambridge.

"Well, that's not fair, Erin. Babe, you knew full well I was up in Newcastle. How the bloody hell was I supposed to know you were ok? I had to leave early, and on my dad's birthday. Do you know how close I was to calling the police and having them check on you?"

"You're right. I've said I'm sorry. Can we just drop it, please?"

"Anyway, if you're ill it's best you get back to bed. I'll clean up down here." He filled the kettle. "Lots of fluids. Hot water with honey and lemon." He picked through the bowl of fruit on the countertop. "Ok, so you're out of lemons but limes will certainly suffice."

"That's good of you but I'm fine."

Ignoring her, he switched on the kettle, which began to boil as Ben rubbed at the faint bristles that were covering his chin. He really had been worried. "Since when do you *hibernate* when ill? That time in Alnwick, you spent the entire duration watching movies and begging for my attention."

Erin had to quickly think. "Well, that's the only time you've seen me ill. You were at your parents. Maybe if you'd been here..." he was good and she hoped the inquisition would cease. She wasn't in the mood.

Ben poured the hot water into a glass, mixed in a teaspoon of honey and began squeezing a lime. Several veins in his forearms pulsed as the juice trickled into the steaming glass. "This should make you feel better. I'll get you another in about an hour but I'll have to go to the shop first."

"Thank you." She took the glass, although she knew the bittersweet concoction would not cure her ailment, nor even abate it in the slightest.

"Really, this is not like you at all." He was referring to the refuse as he stooped to gather up the used tissues before stuffing them into the overflowing rubbish bag. He tied the ends and dumped the bag by the door. "I'll deal with it. Go to bed." His phone rang but he ignored it.

"Aren't you going to see who that is?" Erin asked, sipping the remedy.

"I don't care who it is, you're more important right now." He turned the phone off without even looking. "I'm probably wanted at work but it'll wait."

Ben was a couple years older than Erin's twenty-nine years and had met properly during the early days after Gianna's departure, when Erin had been at her lowest ebb. He'd been a true rock and they ended up in a relationship. That relationship had been off and on ever since. In fact, Erin had lost count of the times they'd broken up, only to get back together at some point in the future. He was an attractive man; tall with broad shoulders, dark brown hair and now, apparently, some stubble. Erin often noticed the looks he attracted from other women, which had been the cause of more than one of those break ups. Although Erin would readily admit, it was the lack of passion on her own part that had so often been responsible.

"Ben, you shouldn't neglect your duties, I can manage alone."

He waved a hand as if to dismiss her words, then pinched at his lower lip. "Erin, this isn't anything to do with me is it?"

She placed the glass on the countertop and went over to him. "Of course not. What would make you think that?"

"I don't know. I just had a feeling, that's all."

"As I told you, it's just the flu. I'll be back at work in a couple more days. I feel much better already." Erin lied, much preferring flu to her present emotional illness.

Ben opened out his arms and drew her into him, kissing

her cheek. "Great, because don't forget, you have the Relief for Heroes ceremony the day after tomorrow."

As if she could forget she was due to accept an award in front of a large gathering of peers.

"GAIT ANALYSIS, ANTI-GRAVITY TREADMILLS AND BOTH IN the first month, and pool running and tomorrow we're starting on knee fractures. I just can't wait." Much of the course modules would consist of group work, which Erin feared almost as much as the thought of having to give a presentation. But she'd have to grin and bear it, to push through the discomfort of being around other people, of being watched and judged. For Erin, university was about so much more than simply attaining a prestigious degree. She also needed pulling out from her comfort zone in order to grow as an individual.

Erin and Gia left the theatre amongst a crowd of students to emerge in the Downing College cloister, essentially a well-pampered lawn surrounded by arched corridors on all sides. Each college had a similar cloister and for centuries they'd served as places to meet fellow scholars, indeed, a definite sense of history radiated from every corner, stone and fountain. To think some of the world's best; Newton, Darwin and Hawking might have gathered to chat or eat at the exact same spot. Well, not *this* exact spot because this was Downing College, but the same spot at their own, more prestigious colleges perhaps, which was not the same spot at all.

"We must see the library," Erin squeaked while tugging Gia back toward the college interior, "the main library, that is, not all one hundred and fourteen of them, at least not yet, but we should definitely see the Trinity Hall library too, which dates back further than ... well, I'm sure you get it, hey..."

Gia resisted the pull and laughed. "Oh, Erin, you are such a nerd."

Shit! What had she done? She'd blown it, for sure. "What do you mean?" Erin asked with alarm.

"I mean you're such a nerd. Why don't you loosen up? If there's anyone I've met so far in this country who needs to relax, it's you." Gia pulled Erin closer in a gesture of comfort. "Of course, I don't mean it in a bad way but this is our first day at uni. We need to get drunk, like everyone else."

"Get drunk?" Erin yelped, not sure whether or not to be horrified. She'd partaken in alcohol in the past, most notably to get through giving presentations in the sixth form, and her father's minibar had proven invaluable, but she'd never once drunk socially, unless the skatepark counted and she wanted to forget all about that. The very concept of walking into a pub with the intention of getting drunk had one major drawback – Erin would need to be drunk in order to enter the establishment in the first place. A slight catch there.

"Erin, you'd fit in real great back home. You can probably guess why I needed to get away so bad?"

"But it's only eleven in the morning."

"I don't mean right now, silly." Gia laughed. "You really are a complete innocent aren't you."

"Oh, I'm not so sure about that."

"Let's get a coffee first." She pulled a face. "Over here, it tastes like dishwater but never mind, I'm sure I'll adjust." Gia didn't give Erin a choice and was already tugging her by the wrist. "And since you're such a nerd, we can discuss the course if it'll make you happy."

The Starbucks on the road that ran between Christ's and Trinity College had obviously been designed to accommodate students. The upstairs seating area consisted of long wooden benches with plug sockets for laptops, which apparently, at least a third of the students seemed to possess. They took seats with their coffees.

"So this is the famous Starbucks, is it?" Gia sounded unimpressed and grimaced as she sipped her Americano.

"You mean you've never been to one?" Erin was amazed it was even possible not to have visited a Starbucks in the year 2003. She, herself, had also only recently ventured inside one, but for completely different reasons.

"Not much chance in Italy, we don't have them." She saw Erin's gaping mouth and continued. "I know, hard to believe, but we'd only boycott it anyway, just like we did the fast food movement."

"That's good, I prefer a place with a little more soul, we should have gone to the small cafe outside Downing." Erin frowned but it was too late now.

"Well, how about next time? We'll do it then."

"Ok." There was going to be a next time? Erin was still amazed Gia hadn't yet ditched her for one of the girly cliques that had already formed within the main course group. There were some interesting young women there from all kinds of countries and they were already pairing off with some of the more attractive men, who were likewise from faraway and interesting places. Contrast Erin with ... well, the obvious. No, it was only a matter of time, that much was a law of nature.

"What? What are you thinking? You don't want to have coffee with me again?" She touched Erin's hand and smiled. "Am I really that frightening?"

"No, of course not. You're the exact opposite, in fact, but sometimes I..."

A shadow from in front interrupted Erin's flow and they glanced up to find a not totally unattractive male Starbucks employee collecting the used mugs. As he leaned over the table, he cast a shy smile down on Erin. "Hi," he said, flushing a deep red and scurrying away.

Erin smiled nervously and turned her head to avoid further eye contact in case he looked back.

Gia threw herself back in her seat and slapped her thighs. "Erin, he was very much checking you out." She barked and had to compose herself. "But I can see we'd need to work on the two of you. Perhaps if we locked you both in a room, you'd be talking within six months."

Erin found herself slapping Gia's leg and blushed, unable to meet her friend's eyes. "You're imagining it, Gia, he wasn't looking at me. Why ever would he do such a thing?"

"What?" Gia almost shouted, startling even herself. "Are you kidding? You're the stereotypical English rose, from that song ... I forget, but that's what I thought when I first saw you. Damn it, the name will bug me now."

Erin giggled. "What are you talking about? There's no such song."

"There is too." She leaned forward. "When you say *English rose*, the mind makes images of a pretty girl with red hair. She's always the timid, butter wouldn't melt type." She pointed both index fingers at Erin and winked. "Exactly what we have here."

"Stop teasing me, I am not." Although she knew she wasn't totally unpleasant in the looks department, Erin had never thought of herself as the pretty type. She simply didn't receive the same kind of positive reinforcement that some of the other girls constantly got from guys. A girl could only know how attractive she was from the attention she was given. But then, she also knew that avoiding social situations, like she always had, meant she also avoided opportunities to receive that positive reinforcement in the form of male attention. On the contrary, the negative reinforcement had been abundant, particularly at school with the endless mean names she'd been called for having red hair. Erin had never been able to work out just how large a part the bullying had played in her timidity. Was she shy and withdrawn because she was bullied, or was she bullied because she was shy and withdrawn? Either way, having a head like an out of control forest fire with its inevitable accompanying pale skin and freckles had not helped one bit and it was only more recently she was beginning to appreciate the way she looked, at least a tiny bit, as she was finally starting to grow into her features.

"What I think, is that you need to spend less time with your head in the books and more time getting out there, having fun and meeting people. You'd benefit a great deal and you know it." Gia took another sip from her Americano and her face contorted. "Damn, this coffee is foul."

"Yes, you're correct about all this."

"Of course, I am," Gia said, smiling to herself. "Wait, are you talking about the coffee or what I said before?"

Erin hit her playfully on the arm. "You don't understand what it's like though. Meeting people is just so terrifying." She shrank back into her seat. "I'm completely useless."

"No, you're not," Gia said, a little less playfully. "Just look at the way you're talking to me now. I'd never have known you were any different to anyone else."

"I don't know." Erin gestured between Gia and herself. "This just feels a little different."

Gia's eye's narrowed. "How so?"

Erin thought for a bit. "I don't know. I get good vibes from you, just a nice feeling. You're easy to talk to but then, you do most of the talking. You're comfortable in your own skin and it transfers to me."

"Well, I come from a very loud and crowded city, I'm used to having people around me. But really, I've noticed such a big difference in you already and we met only a few hours ago, so don't put yourself down like that."

Erin exhaled sharply through her nose. "Yeah, I kind of feel it too." *But as soon as Gia abandons me...*

The Italian grunted as she hefted her enormous bag onto the table. "Looks like we have a lot to talk about but I did promise we'd do some study."

After spending around an hour reviewing the first term prospectus, they left Starbucks and headed for The Baron of Beef which, while in the theatre, they'd overheard was one of the popular Cambridge hangouts.

Gia linked arms with Erin in a way that almost felt protective. "Cheap food and drink, apparently," she squeezed Erin a little tighter, "and don't worry, it's a friendly student crowd and I'll take good care of you."

Erin half felt like an invalid but merely being around Gia, at least for the time being, had a majestic effect on her confidence and she was surprised at how she felt only slight trepidation at the prospect of entering her first pub as a student.

Gia pushed the door open and as Erin stepped inside, she wondered if a slight haze fell over her vision. It's all in your head, she told herself, looking through the gathering of rowdy students to a table in the far corner. Her instincts told her to grab it quick and sit with her back to the wall where she could cower and make herself appear tiny.

Instead, Gia guided her to a different table in the centre, beside a particularly large and rowdy group situated around too many empty glasses to count. "Don't forget, this is my first English pub too. A couple of drinks and we'll be feeling relaxed." Gia waited for Erin to sit and then threw her bag over the seat next to her. "What would you like?"

"I think, I'll have a beer." Erin watched as Gia pushed her way toward the bar. The queue was four or five deep, which meant being alone for a while. Several students in the vicinity turned around to peer at the solitary girl, looking down at the table, fiddling with her bag strap. Her heart beat fast and her mouth dried up. Once or twice, Gia twisted around to check on her. Oh please be quick.

A few minutes later, she plonked down two large glasses of beer and took her seat beside Erin, close enough she could smell the rose petals. Gia's perfume was quite a contrast against the musky stench of unwashed students.

"You ok? You look a little flushed." Gia asked after taking a sip.

"Yeah, I think I could benefit from a little tearing of the band-aid," Erin admitted the obvious and breathed deeply. "You don't have pubs similar to this in Napoli?"

She shook her head. "We have bars, obviously, but they tend to be a lot smaller and more intimate." She gestured to some students, two of whom were standing on chairs debating something as part of a drinking game. "You'd never get away with *that* where I'm from. The locals would quote bible verses and frown you all the way toward the exit." Her face scrunched up in an animated and comical way. "Are they really arguing about Meet the Fockers?"

Erin sniggered. "I think the other guy's on the side of the original."

"An easy win."

"Do you drink back home?"

Gia almost spilt her beer. "We're not completely alien you know, Erin, we get up to all the same stuff as you do. I often lie about my age to get into bars and take alcohol to my friend's house."

"Why did you choose Cambridge?"

One corner of her mouth rose and her dimple emerged. "You don't say *no* to Cambridge, do you. If you're accepted then you take it." Her face saddened in contemplation. "The truth is, all my applications were in England, I wanted to come here to get away from the confines of southern Italy."

23

"Why?" Erin asked leaning closer.

"It's just way too conservative. A girl needs to travel and see what the rest of the world has to offer. England seemed like the exact opposite, so here I am, and of course, I wanted to improve my English too." Gia's face sprang to life, bright eyes sparkling. "And what about you? Why here?"

Erin shrugged. "Well, as you said, you don't say *no* to Cambridge. I studied hard and was lucky enough to get in." She thought of all the times she'd declined to meet friends, visit the pub or even go shopping like everybody else. The studying had paid off, at the expense of other things, like having a life. "So why Physiotherapy?"

Gia looked down at the table and for the first time, Erin wondered if she'd overstepped the mark. It was a simple and obvious question that perhaps she shouldn't have asked.

"Um..."

"I'm not being intrusive am I?" Erin asked, almost panicking.

"Oh no, don't worry about it. I guess it's because of my dad," Gia sighed. "When I was ten he was involved in a car accident and has needed physio ever since. I've witnessed the good it can do and I suppose I was inspired by it."

"I'm so sorry, I had no idea."

Gia smiled. "Well, how were you to know, you silly goose?" She patted her on the wrist. "I hadn't told you, had I? You really have to learn not to be so timid, especially with me, even though I find it kind of sweet."

Two male blurs approached and gestured to the spare seats. "You girls don't mind if we take these, do you?" The slightly taller of the two, with an unkempt beard and long curly hair asked while gesturing about the room. "Doesn't look like there's anywhere else to sit." The man spoke with a thick Scottish accent that needed a few seconds to figure out, while the crinkles on Gia's forehead signalled she was struggling even more with it than Erin.

"No, go ahead," Erin said, surprising herself by speaking up for the two of them.

They pulled out the chairs but for the time being, remained stood for the introductions. "I'm Mikey, this is Scruffy. It's not an ironic thing." The tidier of the two jested as he reached forward to shake their hands. They looked kind of similar, their contrasting styles masking the possibility they might be twins.

Erin couldn't help but grin as her eyes flicked across at Gia, still frowning in extreme concentration. "You're both from Scotland?"

"Was it the shaggy appearance that gave me away?" Scruffy held out his hand and Gia hesitated before reluctantly shaking it, followed by Erin. An audible snap fully complete with crunch and sheer pain washing over Scruffy's face preceded his cry of agony as his hand went limp. "Arghhh."

The entire establishment fell silent and even the group surrounding the pool table at the far side of the pub had stopped their game and turned to face the source of the agonised cry.

And then the haze fell, nearly clouding Erin's vision. Her fingers tingled as she covered her mouth. "Oh my God, I'm so sorry. What happened?" She didn't think her grip was strong enough to do damage but she couldn't deny feeling something break. Oh, poor Scruffy, what had she done?

Scruffy doubled over in agony and gripped his wrist, his face a contortion of suffering.

Mikey placed a hand on Scruffy's arm. "That sounded worse than the cycling accident." He shook his head at Erin, whose skin was turning even paler. "There goes his engineering degree. What did you do to him?"

Erin gaped, pleading silently to Gia, who'd already

stepped protectively in front of her. "I'm so sorry, I don't know what I did. I just shook his hand and I felt something break." The urge to crawl under the table and curl into the foetal position was overwhelming.

After milking it for a few more excruciating seconds, Scruffy slowly looked up, a wide grin stretched across his face, and then a crushed can fell out from underneath his sweater. He saw Erin's hopeless expression and commenced laughing, it sounded so evil, before grinding his double-jointed wrist around in its socket, which looked beyond gross. "Gotcha."

Erin sighed loudly, relieved, even though so many people were still watching. The heat rose to some unbearable temperature and she knew her face would by now be the colour of a flamingo. This was not the *tearing of the band-aid* she had in mind.

Gia leaned over to hit the pair of them with fists clenched. "You mean boys. That's the worst thing I've ever seen. Ever! How could you be so horrible?"

The two men were in such hysterics that manoeuvring to take the spare seats was a task and they almost knocked over all four glasses of beer as they did.

"And now you expect to sit with us?" Gia held out her arm to stop them but gave up at the futility of it. She rattled off some lightning quick Italian that unsettled Erin but not the guys in the least. Indeed, they appeared to be revelling in having embarrassed one and angered the other. "This is how you two boys go about meeting girls, is it?"

"I've never seen anybody fall for it so hard." Scruffy gestured between both girls. "I'm sorry, but you're both obviously freshmen, we couldn't resist and you," he tried stammering to Erin through palpitations, "you looked truly petrified."

"I have no idea what you're even saying," Gia yelled in retort, prompting yet more laughter from the two men, which annoyed her even further. She unzipped her jacket and threw it down on her seat. "It's getting hot in here all of a sudden."

It was the first time Erin had seen Gia without that damned thick winter jacket, which just went to show how much she was riled, and found herself spending more than a second inspecting her figure, as were both boys. Beneath she still wore a thick long-sleeved red sweater against the mild English early autumn and possessed a slim, athletic figure. Erin saw how her breasts stretched out the fabric and neither did they go unnoticed by either Scottish idiot, whose eyes were hardly subtle.

But Erin knew she'd have to support her friend now, even though she was far from the confrontational sort. "You should see a doctor about that wrist of yours, that thing you do can't be healthy." She glanced at Gia for approval and was pleased to receive a nod.

"Ah, come on, it was just a wee bit of fun. I'm sure you can forgive us?" Scruffy asked, pushing a thick clump of matted hair out from his eyes.

"I'll forgive you when you take a bath and get a haircut," Gia growled, prompting even more laughter.

"I take it getting your number's out of the question then?" Mikey asked, doing his best to sound serious but failing miserably as he blubbered out the words.

Erin twisted toward Gia and awaited her answer. Neither guy was unattractive and they both possessed confidence, too much of it, in fact, they were obviously friendly and might even prove likeable once the stupid wrist incident was forgotten. But how would Gia handle being asked for her number, even if it had been a joke? Or was it?

"I'd rather spend a night alone in the Catacombs of Rome, and I told my friend this was a *friendly student crowd*." Gia chided. "You ruined it!" Her demeanour no longer seemed to match her spirited words as her resistance slowly began to crumble and as she finally retook her seat, Erin definitely noticed her friend was blushing, though, that might have been the non-existent heat.

"Ok, listen, how about a peace offering? Let us buy you another drink and we'll call it evens," Scruffy offered. "Deal?"

Their beers were approaching the empty side but Erin hardly thought the peace offering necessary. She was more than happy to have met them; it would sure make for a memorable first visit to a Cambridge student pub, even if the situation that had transpired was a scene from her worst nightmares. At least the nosy crowds had gone back to their own business, which now included a lively tabletop debate about which college had the best boat team.

Gia hesitated but eventually nodded. "Ok then, we'll accept your peace offering, you may purchase us a beer."

Mikey was grinning obscenely as he went to the bar and left the three of them to attempt a regular conversation. Erin studied Gia's face, particularly the narrowing of the eyes and scrunching up of the skin between her eyebrows as she tried to understand the fast-talking Scot. She was an amusing thing to watch.

Mikey returned with four beers in pint glasses and set them on the table.

"Thank you, say, I think I was being harsh earlier, so for that, I'm sorry." Gia sounded more reasonable and restrained now. "You were only having a bit of fun at our expense and I overreacted."

"Aye, well, you survived it." Mikey agreed.

Gia leaned closer to Mikey. "How about we play another game?"

Mikey's eye flicked briefly over his brother. "Aye, what game did you have in mind?"

"Hmmm," she rubbed at her chin, exchanging glances

between the two of them, "if you can both hold your glasses against the ceiling using only a pool cue and keep them there for a whole minute, without spilling a single drop then..." Gia smiled at Mikey and slightly pushed out her breasts, "then you can have my number."

Mikey shot bolt upright in his seat and without even looking, jerked his chin at Erin. "And Scruff gets her number." He made a clicking sound with his tongue. "Hey, it's only fair, after all, besides, we wouldn't leave you out." He now made eye contact with Erin long enough to deliver a wink. She didn't know what to make of it.

"Deal." Gia agreed, knocking knees with Erin below the table. What was she playing at?

Erin's heart shot into her mouth. All she'd wanted was to have a drink with her new friend and now she was being pressed into going on a date with some guy called Scruffy who had a mangled wrist. One giant hurdle at a time, please.

Scruffy was tellingly quick to borrow two cues from the pool table and handing one to his brother. Exchanging bemused expressions, they positioned themselves, raising their drinks in outstretched arms and touching the glasses to the ceiling, which wasn't hard as they were both tall, before manoeuvring the cues into position at the base.

Both girls were standing now and Gia covertly bumped Erin's hip before instructing, "remember, you have to last a full minute without spilling a single drop."

"I hope you know what you're doing," Erin whispered in her ear.

Scruffy sniggered. "You could at least give us something hard." He shrugged in Mikey's direction as they positioned the tips of their cues against the underside of the glasses, taking a second to ensure everything was secure, and thus pinning them against the ceiling. Slowly, they began working their hands down the length of the shafts as their drinks remained fixed against the festering, brown stained plaster above until eventually, they had to squat awkwardly to hold the base of the cues in their opened palms.

"Are you sure this is it?" Mikey asked, confused. "A bit easy, ain't it? Shall I just take your number now?" He made a motion with his face to where his mobile rested on the table.

Gia grabbed her bag and coat before turning to Erin. "Let's go, babe."

"What?" Erin asked in disbelief and then laughed aloud, the realisation hitting her, a plan for revenge all along, as she yelped at both men, who were both unable to even move lest they be drenched by two full glasses of beer.

Scruffy and Mikey shot each other looks as the ball dropped, duped by a pair of female freshmen. "Alright, girls, fair play, but you couldn't help us out here, could you?"

Gia took Erin's hand, "now where would be the fun in that?" and then dragged her away toward the exit.

Erin couldn't help but glance back to approve of her friend's handiwork as the crowd began to gather around Gia's victims, still squatting, to cheer, take photos, pat foreheads and tickle under armpits, and she couldn't deny feeling bad for them ... but only a little.

In the moment, Erin felt invincible, like she could do anything and it was all thanks to Gia. Though, as the Italian squeezed her hand, they began running down the cobbled street in the rain and the adrenaline began to flow, she also took a moment to reflect on just how glad she was it wasn't her left in such a predicament.

Death might have been better.

Chapter Three

MEMORIES

Most of what Robert Smith; Founder of Relief for Heroes was saying had gone straight in one ear and out the other. Erin cursed herself. The evening was important; not just for her future career but for many of the heroes who'd made the journey; men and women who'd sacrificed so much. She owed it to too many people to be on good form tonight.

To more than three-hundred present, Robert had spoken for the last twenty minutes about the work his organisation carried out. Relief for Heroes was a charity that took care of the many wounded soldiers returning from the war in Afghanistan who were in need of care, home modifications to enable wheelchair access, artificial limbs or money to allow their loved ones to visit as they recuperated in centres across the country. Erin had become involved after picking up more and more physio clients with war wounds. They didn't encompass all her work, but unfortunately, over the years they had become a larger part of it. Erin disliked relying so much on money from the charity to keep her practice afloat and the truth was, she longed for the day she wouldn't need to see another wounded soldier who needed to learn to walk again.

The evening was a £150 per head meal with guest speakers and even a comedian who'd somehow managed to find the humour in having had both legs blown off by an improvised explosive device. Although Erin herself hadn't been required to pay the fee, on account of receiving an award for recognition, she had insisted on paying double, as had Ben.

"Not long now, I hope you're ok?" He whispered into her ear.

So far, Erin had imbibed only the one large glass of Lugana DOC, which had been more to dull certain memories than the need for courage. Despite everything, she was lagging behind the rest of the table. "I'll be fine." She squeezed his hand and wondered if he was more nervous than herself.

"And now we pay thanks to the many physiotherapists up and down the country who do such incredible work with us." Robert Smith continued from the stage. "Tonight we honour one such therapist, in particular, and to introduce our honouree, please welcome Sergeant Major Thomas Becker."

This was a surprise.

Tom struggled across the stage unaided, but he was doing it, and Erin could do nothing but applaud, knowing the difficulty he'd be having. Tom had sure kept this one quiet; she'd only seen him the week before when he'd barely managed a hundred metres over the course of an hour on the treadmill.

He shook hands with Robert and turned to the podium. "Ladies and gentlemen, I first became acquainted with the winner of this appreciation award when I returned from the war having lost the use of both legs. I fully expected to spend the rest of my life in a wheelchair, relying on friends and family for such things as going to the park or taking a shower..." He continued to speak about the treatment he'd received at the Cambridge Revival Centre, about how when he arrived he was a shell of a man, unable to even stand, and now, as witnessed by everybody present, he could walk unaided with his head held high. "I owe all this to one person and I'd like to introduce you all to this very special lady." He paused, "please welcome Doctor Erin Baker."

She stood, kissed Ben on the lips and made her way toward Thomas on the stage, squeezing him tight. "You are in big trouble, Tom."

He winked at her. "You deserve this, enjoy the moment." He placed a small, modest bronze medal around her neck that had engraved the simple inscription *Relief for Heroes*.

She pottered toward the podium and had to wait almost a minute for the applause to fade whilst gazing out toward the many large round tables overflowing with wine bottles ... strange faces ... flashes ... *she's not here ... you don't need her ... forget she ever existed.*

"Thank you, Sergeant Major, my friend Tom. I'm truly honoured to be receiving this award but I do so on behalf of all physiotherapists up and down the country who carry out similar work with our wounded heroes. I am simply one of their number and can take no more credit than any one of us."

Erin elaborated on the importance of what they did as well as the difficulties they faced and how the charity was helping overcome obstacles. There was still work to be done and many of the wounded would require therapy for the rest of their lives. She found Ben's face and smiled. "I must thank Doctor Ben Harper whose work in developing improved prosthetic limbs has done so much. Ben, you have been an inspiration, as well as my greatest rock throughout the hard times." She paused to allow the gravity of her words to make an impact, not just to those listening. "I also pay thanks to the many people who've helped along the way; my parents, Andy Atkins, Professor of Physiotherapy at the University of Cambridge and all the scholars and researchers who've contributed to the field."

Won't you even say her name? Go on, thank her. You owe it all to her. Stop being ungrateful. Ben won't mind. Go on, say her name! Say it! You'd be nothing without her, a checkout girl, still living with your parents.

She shook the fog away, they were all still gazing back, and managed to finish the speech without destroying her reputation or credibility. When she left the stage she muttered, "where are you?"

The memories, some hard but mostly fond, had continued to filter through Erin's mind in the days following the inconvenient reappearance of that evil poem. Events not thought about in so long, assumed forever forgotten, had struck her with the emotional equivalent of an out of control locomotive. Suppressing the smiles wasn't always easy and as Ben drove them home, she had to turn away as she recalled their first visit to The Baron of Beef and how they'd been told by the disciplinary board they had to return, to apologise to the landlord so they wouldn't be barred, which they duly did the very next day.

That incident had set in motion events that would define the rest of their relationship.

When they arrived back at Ben's countryside estate in Little Thetford, he gave her a warm embrace, "I'm so proud of you," before handing her a glass of wine. "You've come such a long way over the years, my lovely lady."

"That's kind of you." Erin questioned whether the lack of nerves she'd experienced was because she was permanently over the self-imposed prison sentence that was chronic shyness or because her present emotional state prevailed over everything else. Regardless of everything, sometimes it didn't feel like she'd changed at all. Outside factors she had no control over were still dictating her state of mind.

He took her hand, "how about we take the wine upstairs?" and led her to the bedroom. "Are you ok?" He asked with uncertainty. "You look a little glum considering the evening you've had." He loosened his tie and threw it to the chair.

"Yeah, I'm fine." She slipped out of her heels and dropped noticeably in height before Ben's stature, meeting his lips as he fiddled with the zip at the back of her dress.

"You're so beautiful." He slid the zip down with one hand while brushing her red hair with the other.

But it didn't feel right, not tonight. "I'm sorry, I don't think I'm in the mood right now. It's been a big evening." She stepped away and perched on the bed.

"I knew it, there is something wrong, isn't there?" He exhaled and paced over to the other side of the room, picking up his wine and taking a gulp. "You've not been right since you were ill, supposedly."

"I *was* ill, Ben, I had the flu." She hated lying to him but had little choice until she worked out what was happening inside her head. "I just don't feel my usual self at the moment." She pleaded, "could we just go to sleep?"

Ben crossed back over to her and lightly caressed the side of her face with the backs of his fingers. "It's your special evening so if that's what you'd like. But something's not quite right and I deserve to know what it is."

"The Pirate Society." Erin screeched, surprising Gia with her enthusiasm.

"It'll just be some overgrown teenagers who never got to play out their childhood fantasies. Besides, I hated the movie, it bored me to tears. Can you believe they're thinking of making another? Who would want to watch the sequel?" Gia plucked at a blade of grass, balled it up and flicked it at Erin, hitting her square on the forehead.

Erin slapped her on the shoulder and watched as she rolled onto her back, raising a hand to block out the sun. The cloister hummed and the lawn was almost filled with students lying back reading, eating, sleeping.

"Pirates of the Caribbean was awesome!"

"No it wasn't and I don't get the obsession with Johnny Depp either."

"You don't like Johnny Depp?" Erin shrieked, almost as shrill as when she mentioned joining the Pirate Society.

"Nuh-uh." Gia shook her head and plucked at another blade of grass.

"So, you're more of an Orlando Bloom kind of girl? I guess he's younger and way less risky, if you prefer playing things safe, which come to think of it, isn't you at all, as I'm finding out."

Gia nudged her with an elbow. "Don't make me flick more grass at you."

"Yes, miss." Erin lay down beside her and used her bag as a pillow. "So, who is your favourite movie star?"

"That's an easy one, Monica Bellucci." Gia rolled on her side to face Erin. "Oh my God, did you see her in Malena?"

"Malena? No, I've never heard of it, or of Monica Bel...who?"

"What? Then you have been truly deprived of great films and beautiful actresses."

"Ok," Erin said flatly. "Well, what's this film about?"

"It's about this woman, *Malena*, who everybody suspects is sleeping with the entire town, just because she's so damn beautiful but underneath the story is about how people always judge others based on looks or on hearsay, rather than actually getting to know a person before making a judgement."

"Oh, I see, and what happened to her?"

"The townspeople drove her over the edge," she said glumly. "But it all ends well ... kind of, anyway." She perked and touched Erin's arm. "Hey, you should come over and watch it. It's subtitled but I'm pretty sure you can read, right?" Gia absently gestured about the cloister, as if to suggest being at Cambridge was evidence she wasn't dumb.

"I can read," Erin gave her a playful slap, "and I'd love to. Just say when and I'm there." Erin paused as if expecting Gia to continue and when she didn't... "So that's it?"

"It? What's it?"

"I half expected you to say Brad Pitt or Colin Farrell or someone."

"Why?"

"Um, I don't know, I just pictured you with somebody rugged."

Gia rolled over, returning to her back. "We are *not* joining the Pirate Society."

Erin sat up and chewed her lip as she ran her finger down the list. "How about the Society for Gentlemanly Pursuits?"

"Oh, right, can you imagine me sitting around with a bunch of Cambridge toffs, drinking Scotch? That's a recipe for disaster, right there." She snatched the sheet from Erin's hand. "You, girl, need something that involves lots of people. The more the better and something not so dull and boring." She studied the paper for a while. "Harry Potter, No! Assassins Society ... oh, my God. The Let's Put Rocks in Size Order Society has your name stamped all over it though."

Erin snatched the paper back. "You are useless. Let me see. Ooh, how about the Tennis Club? I've always been pretty good playing against my brother." Erin had spent most of her life playing tennis, in fact, it was the one thing, other than studying she knew she excelled at. It had suited her well due to the solo nature of the sport and kept her in good shape at the same time.

"Tennis, silly, is a sport for loners and still in your comfort zone."

Erin pursed her lips and continued scanning down the diminishing list. "There's a Trampoline Club. I've always wanted to give that a try."

"Um, hello..." Gia said, pointing to her breasts. "Can you see me jumping up and down with these things? Now *that* is an accident waiting to happen. And besides, since when did the trampoline involve you being around a large group of rowdy students?"

Erin folded the paper as her lips turned down. "Well then, I guess we've exhausted our options."

Gia twisted in the direction of a large group of girls wearing black shorts and dark purple sleeveless club jerseys as they strode beneath one of the arches. They certainly drew the eye. "Where are they going?"

Erin shielded her eyes against the sun. "Um, I don't know, some kind of a sports club?"

Gia fell silent as she watched. "Just look at them, how happy they all look."

"You can get all that from how they're walking?"

"They're not walking, they're bouncing," Gia persisted squinting in their direction, "and shush you and tell me what their jerseys say."

Erin tried to read the black font emblazoned upon purple, not a great combination, and the sun was low and right in their line of sight but she already had an idea of what they were anyway. "No! Gia, no way."

"What? What does it say? Who are they and where are they going?" Gia rose to her feet, pulling Erin up with her, almost unable to contain herself. The bright sparkle in those eyes possessed strange powers when she smiled. "Damn my poor vision at a time like this."

Erin sighed. "It says C...U...B...C."

Gia shrugged, "which means what, exactly?"

Erin could have told a white lie, just a small fib, but the girl would only hound her mercilessly until she had her pound of flesh. "Cambridge University Boat Club. Or in everyday speaking terms ... rowing."

Gia didn't even respond but simply took Erin's hand and tugged her in the direction of the low arch where the rowers were still streaming through in numbers.

Erin resisted the pull but knew it would ultimately prove futile. "No, Gia, it's the bloody rowing club. It's world-famous. Are you trying to destroy me?"

The pest turned to face Erin and placed both hands on her shoulders. "You *need* this and I *want* this."

"But ... it's rowing. It'll be sooooo competitive and I might just accidentally end up in the bloody annual Boat Race. It's televised!" Even as she spoke, Erin could feel her resistance dissipating. After all, she couldn't say *no* to Gia and those big brown, magical, hawk-like eyes that demanded compliance.

"Trust me, you'll thank me when you're a glowing, confident woman who everybody looks up to as a model of just what's possible when you try."

Erin burst into hysterics and knew any further resistance would be a waste of breath. "You are talking such garbage." Her legs were pottering along the grass now, gaining speed, almost like she'd yielded all power over them to Gia. "You'd better look after me."

Gia stuck out her bottom lip. "Oh, how you hurt me with your mistrust."

THE DOWNING BOATHOUSE, WHICH THEY'D BEEN TOLD WAS brand new, stood underwhelming and apparently lopsided a few metres from the edge of the River Cam. Erin wondered just why the gathering of freshman rowers was taking place *outside* the expensive new structure, rather than inside where it would be warm, perhaps with tea and biscuits to go around. It was a criminal waste of facilities.

"We've become famous for our dodgy foundations, in case you somehow failed to notice. The river overflowed during construction and damaged the foundations, which is why we're outside. Can't take the risk, you see? They tell me that if we exceed capacity then to have the building collapse in on us will invalidate the insurance." The President, Professor Geoffrey something spoke to the large gathering of individuals stood around in shorts, shivering, looking miserable, and answering Erin's query. "But ne'er fear, dear scholars, future architects, scientists, Nobel Prize winners, because your numbers will soon dwindle, as they always do. You watch the annual Boat Race and yearn for the glamour, celebrity and prestige, which is why you're all here, don't think I don't know, but a single six in the morning start is usually all it takes to separate the fantasists from the athletes, and when the former have kindly left us to pursue the next novelty on their list, then we may continue the rest of the season from within the comfort of our new one million pound structure with its dodgy foundations, you see, we really do live up to our name as a *boathouse*." Someone coughed. "Oh, I see we have a swimmer already, bon voyage, gute reise, hyvä matka, fellow scholar, you shall be missed by all, I'm sure. Would there be anyone else? No? Did I mention the six in the morning starts? Did you ever try that with a hangover?"

Erin found herself rolling her eyes though Gia did not seem to notice nor even recognise the prof's dry eccentric wit. He eventually moved on to talking about the history of rowing at the university, about their rivalry with the Oxford Boat Club and how, most importantly of all, when considering the annual Boat Race held on the River Thames each year, Cambridge was leading their rival by seventy seven wins to seventy one for the men, or for the women, a very impressive thirty seven wins to twenty. Every time someone slinked off from boredom, he'd loudly proclaim it to a mixture of bewilderment and growing hilarity until it became obvious he was intentionally trying to reduce the intake. But if Erin hoped Gia would soon join the other stragglers, she was to be left disappointed.

There were sixteen boathouses situated along this section of the Cam, which belonged to the colleges and throughout the year various competitive events were held between them. The best crews from each boathouse would compete amongst themselves to decide who'd represent Cambridge in the annual Boat Race against Oxford. "We must maintain our lead at all costs, so your training schedule will be brutal. They will also be early. Did I say six in the morning? Ah, yes I did. But did I say that would be three times a week?"

The loudest murmur yet rose above the crowd and several more freshmen broke away as though their lives depended on it. Come first training session, there'd be nobody left at this rate but Erin understood. The club President was dispensing the harsh truth, in the hope of weeding out the time-wasters and less committed, of which, evidently, there were many. Rickety buildings aside, there were only so many spots on a boat, after all, and still no protest from Gia.

On the contrary, she was standing tiptoed to gain a better view of the speaker and frequently had to reposition to see beyond two large male students who looked like born athletes. No, Gia would yet drag them both into a boat at six on a cold rainy morning, wind, rain or snow.

The next morning, Erin woke to her phone vibrating loudly against her desk. At only a quarter past five, there were several texts waiting from guess who.

'You'd better be awake! x'

'This is it, girl! x'

'The new you starts today. x'

'If you have cereal bars, bring them. Meet you at the river. xxx'

The girl was insane, yet also exhilarating, which could only prove a lethal combination. What could possibly go wrong on a boat with a crazy Italian at six in the morning?

"Is chocolate Nutrigrain ok?" Erin asked as she approached Gia with the bar in an outstretched hand.

"Only one way to find out." She tore off the wrapper, snapped off half and jammed it in her mouth.

Erin yawned, "hey, you might want to go easy on that. There's that thing called indigestion."

"When the English start eating real breakfasts accompanied by thick, dark espresso then I'll take lessons from you." She shivered in the late September morning chill. "Damn, I'm missing home already."

Erin giggled, "this was all your idea and it's not too late to back out. You didn't bank on the English weather at all, did you?" Despite being stupid o'clock, it would have been a disappointment if Gia chose to back out now. Indeed, Erin definitely wanted to spend some quality time with her new and exotic Italian friend and although she wouldn't give Gia a big head, she was right about this whole boat club thing.

"I'll never get used to this weather."

Several tangles of students, having braved the early morning chill, mingled and chatted amongst themselves. As usual, it was Erin and Gia by themselves and Erin couldn't help but feel a pang of guilt that maybe, just maybe, she was preventing Gia from making other friends. A girl like Gia would find natural habitat in being at the centre of one of the cooler groups. It was only a matter of time, Erin reminded herself, so don't beat yourself up when it finally happens.

Erin kicked a pebble into the Cam. "You know, you can go speak to some of the others, if you wish."

"What?" Gia nearly gagged on her Nutrigrain. "What do you mean *I can go speak to some of the others?*"

"I just meant that I'm not keeping you ... I'd understand." Erin looked down at the gravel, plenty more pebbles to kick should the need arise.

"What the hell has got into you?" She snapped off a portion of cereal bar and held it up to Erin's face. "Eat this, you're gonna need it."

As it neared six, the gathering of freshmen slowly began to grow but it was obvious that now they'd had time to think about a few things, their numbers would be diminished even more. Who could blame them?

Further along the river, a small group were kitting up outside what looked like Corpus Christi College Boat Club, second or third-year students most likely, since they already appeared to be in the swing of things, and beyond them, three boats were using oars to prod their boats away from the bank. Ten seconds later they were gliding down the Cam, even though it appeared to Erin like they hardly seemed to be moving. It also looked like the only people awake at this hour were rowers. A serious business round these parts.

Gia scrunched up her snack wrapper and thrust it inside her bag. "You know what, you're right, we really should be making friends with some of the others," she motioned with her head to a knot of four girls closer to the boathouse entrance, "it's half the reason we're here, after all."

A shooting force from the pit of Erin's stomach shot into her mouth. Panic. But Gia was already walking towards them and all Erin could do was follow after her.

Gia found a small gap between two girls and inserted herself into it. "Morning, are you all here for the rowing?"

"Obviously." The taller of the women said with a slight sneer, her eyes seemed to narrow at hearing Gia's southern Italian accent, the skin under her eyes creasing. Erin recognised the girl from her first physiotherapy lecture.

"I'm Gianna and this is my friend, Erin." She gestured to the girl standing close.

"Hi." Two of the girls said together, while the shorter of the four stood unmoved. The taller glanced at Gia's oversized winter jacket and snorted, blanking Erin entirely.

"Oh, I'm sorry, was that your pig impersonation? You're very good, let's hear it again." Gia returned, quick as expected. Two of the girls had to look away to hide the fact they agreed.

"It's ok, Gia, let's go." Erin grabbed her elbow and dragged her away.

"Fucking bitches!" Getting on the wrong side of Gia was something not worth contemplating but to give her credit, she knew how to stand up for herself, that much was evident.

"I agree with you, honey. Thanks for trying anyway but I think we should stay away from them."

A woman emerged from inside and ushered the gathering toward the entrance. Although Erin didn't count them, she estimated the number to be at around forty, which would surely not invalidate any insurance claim should the building happen to implode under their weight. They were led into a large, plush ladies locker room, that Erin could swear was on a slant, and told to get changed. The woman gestured to several boxes along one of the benches. "Here are your uniforms. Purple with black shorts are the Downing colours. Make sure to collect a purple oar on the way out."

Erin found a quiet spot in the corner and keeping to herself, she kicked off her jogging bottoms and threw off the hooded top. She sensed Gia's presence somewhere close but was too preoccupied maintaining a speedy changing tempo to gauge her precise location. Erin usually sought a cubicle when changing at the sports centre for her tennis matches but these expensive new premises had no such facility. Changing in front of a large group of girls was one thing she'd only ever done at school and even then she'd usually arrive early so she'd be ready before anyone else appeared.

She pulled up the shorts, which were way too short for her liking and exposed nearly everything south of her cheeks. She then quickly slipped on the purple Downing College jersey, sleeveless to reveal yet more flesh. Great.

Erin turned around, expecting half the room to be changed and ready. They weren't and to her mind, it seemed like everybody instinctively glanced up to see how the uniform actually looked. At once, Erin felt her knee quiver as the haze threatened to seep down over her vision, to save her from the curious eyes.

"Whoohoo, look at you." Gia skipped over from along the bench in only her shorts and sports bra while holding the purple jersey against her side. In the fog, it seemed like the lush tanned complexion of Gia's face was matched everywhere else, her flat abdomen framed in a tiny waist set between broad hips and large breasts confined within the restrictive bra. She possessed that same impossible hourglass figure that was common to many Southern European women. Gia, perhaps sensing Erin's discomfort turned her away from the room's scrutinising eyes.

"I'd rather not," Erin mumbled, daring not look at her friend. The proximity was hard enough and there was no doubting the lack of material in the uniform had something to do with her self-consciousness. The contrast between their two bodies could not have been greater; her pale skin beside Gia's deep tan.

The Italian had no such apprehensions but then, why would she, despite having her torso almost on full display, and in the moment, her closeness was uncomfortable. Even barefoot, she stood a few inches taller than Erin in her trainers. "Don't be silly, you look great." She sounded convincing enough and looked Erin up and down, seemingly pausing at her legs, before taking a step back and finally slipping into her own jersey.

On the way out they collected an oar each from the hooks on the wall. They'd been told to grab a purple oar since that was the Downing colour but all the blades were purple, this was the Downing boathouse, after all, and Erin could only question the sanity of the supposedly educated people running the club. The oars came in two sections and the shorter handle end alone was more than half Erin's height. The cleaver end, so-called because it truly resembled a meat cleaver, towered over her. Outside, they were instructed to screw the ends together and the result was an oar almost four metres in length. It felt unwieldy, unnatural and stupidly heavy.

As Erin stood amongst the group of girls, shivering in the morning cold, she knew she'd still be tucked up in bed without Gia's influence. Despite the short term discomfort, the girl was opening up a whole new world to her, even if right now it was hard to appreciate it.

But if Erin was feeling the chill, Gia was suffering even more visibly as she folded her shaking arms to cover her midriff. Tiny hairs stood up on her arms and Erin felt the sudden urge to rub her hands over her friend's skin to generate some warmth. However, as soon as the idea entered her head, she dismissed it. Getting on a boat and finally doing some rowing would be welcome.

The Cam was now alive with activity as numerous boats slid past where they stood, propelled by long slender oars stroking the water in beautiful unison. The hardest part would surely be having eight boat members rowing at precisely the same force and stroke rate. Hardest part but for the early starts, of course. Erin watched with a keen interest as eight women in a longboat from Jesus College effortlessly glided past at speed, their cox issuing instructions and steering from the bow.

Five women, all athletic, lean and wearing Downing colours arrived and divided the group into five sets of eight; two male groups, two female and a mixed group. Gia was quick to see where the count was going and yanked Erin into a different position so they wouldn't be separated, a prospect not worth contemplating.

Each of the women took a group, found a space and spent some time warming everybody up with a bunch of bodyweight exercises. Then they were briefed on health and safety and taken through the basics and mechanics of rowing on a novice women's Janousek eight.

"Just get us on a boat already, it's fucking freezing." The tall girl complained from behind.

Gia turned around and gave her a scowl. "Shush."

"Don't you *shush* me." The girl retorted, loud enough for the instructor to hear. Erin recognised the accent as one of those real posh Home Counties dialects, the girl might have grown up on some royal estate somewhere, but Erin doubted Gia would recognise that. The fact she looked down on her, metaphorically as well as literally, however, was not lost on Gia.

"We're trying to listen to the damn instructor. Be quiet!" Gia growled, not intimidated in the slightest.

Erin threaded her hand inside Gia's elbow and guided her attention back toward the instructor. Gia patted Erin's forearm as if to show all was ok. The contrast of the warm hand on her chilled flesh did not go unnoticed.

Finally, the instructor, who would also be acting as cox, demonstrated entry technique. Gently lowering down into the boat as it rocked was terrifying but within a few minutes, the eight girls had taken positions and secured their oars into the locks.

Erin and Gia were sitting in positions four and five respectively, meaning that Erin was rowing port side and Gia starboard.

"Port side, use your oars to push off." The cox instructed and Erin, along with the three other girls positioned at even numbers pushed against the port with their oars. The boat edged off into the centre of the river just as another sailed past on the starboard side.

It was hard to believe the thing hadn't tipped over and Erin had to suppress the overwhelming urge to throw up into the Cam. She doubted she'd have been the first. How much traction could such a long and narrow thing possibly have? Most of the girls in the boat were far taller than the average eighteen-year-old, which would only raise the centre of gravity further, decreasing the boat's purchase on the surface and increasing the likelihood of nine women experiencing the cold water of the Cam. Paranoid thoughts, Erin knew, but she couldn't help it and neither did the other boats help when they whistled by and unsettled the water further.

Then the cox yelled, "and puuuullllllllll!"

Nothing much happened at first, timid as it now appeared everybody was, and the cox had to yell again. Erin pulled at the blade and was surprised at the strength required, straightening her legs as the seat slid back in its track, the resistance feeling like treacle. The boat hardly seemed to budge, the boathouse and trees to their side remaining annoyingly constant.

To Erin's front, Gia pulled her blade through the water and made a comically loud grunt as she did. Indeed, the boat was a strange combination of unladylike sounds, out of tune and timing as their strokes were almost entirely out of sync. It was no wonder the water felt so heavy. Erin changed rhythm to match that of Gia's and within a few strokes, the boat began to shift as she assumed the three girls behind were matching her own pattern. Erin couldn't help but stare at the musculature in Gia's back as she strained against driving the blade through the Cam. The Italian possessed the kind of lithe athletic figure that didn't come naturally but only through time spent in hard training and Erin wondered just what sport back home had gifted Gia with her toned physique.

"Well done four and five, perfect rhythm, keep it up." Yelled the cox. "Seven, speed up and take shorter strokes." The cox held a handle in each hand that she used to steer.

After twenty minutes, the cox used a wide arc to turn the boat around and then they were heading back the way they came, only this time against the flow of the tide. "That was your warm-up, ladies, you'll need to pull harder now."

Erin's view of the cox was completely blocked by the four girls in front; indeed her view consisted entirely of Gia's back and buttocks as she slid back and forth on the track. Small beads of sweat on her shoulders and arms glistened in the early morning sun as she gave her full concentration to pulling on the oar.

The cox yelled more encouragement as the boat glided through the water as if on air. The feeling of moving such a large object, so freely and at such high speed as part of a group of girls, acting as one single organism was like nothing else Erin had ever experienced. Her knuckles turned white as she gripped harder the handle, concentrating on the rhythmical movements of her body.

They arrived back at the boathouse where, as soon as they'd landed and pulled the boat from the water, the tall girl threw up into the river. One of her friends comforted her with an arm across the shoulders.

Erin couldn't help but giggle. "I can't say I'm upset about that one."

"I feel like being sick myself." Gia held onto Erin's shoulder as she stretched her quads and made small hops with her grounded foot, despite using Erin as a support post. The slightest scent of body odour mixed with peach filled the small space between them.

"Here, let me steady you, you're exhausted." Erin reached out and placed her hands on Gia's hips until she regained balance. They really were broad compared to her belly, which this close appeared even slimmer with so much sweat making the Downing jersey constrict and cling to her flesh. "There you are, done?" Erin released her grasp and felt the clamminess on her palms and fingers.

"Thanks, honey." She switched legs, which meant leaning on Erin with the other hand. "So? What did you think?"

"We're definitely coming back. It was so much fun." Erin again reached out to steady Gia's hips, even though on this occasion it didn't seem necessary. "I'm so glad you gave me the push." Trying something new was always hardest the first time. The unknown thoughts of walking through the door, not having any idea of what to expect on the other side was what had always kept Erin from trying out new things, from speaking to new people and making new friends. It was the fear of uncertainty. Now that she'd done it and enjoyed it, she wondered what she had been so afraid of. How many opportunities to improve her life had Erin missed?

"Oi, girls? Girls?" A loud voice boomed from somewhere on the river.

"What the heck?" Erin scanned the Cam to see who was shouting and when she saw who it was, a large breath of air escaped her.

Scruffy and Mikey were in a two-man scull, standing while making a *phone me* gesture with their hands. "You owe us your numbers."

Gia held up her oar to mimic the pool cue incident, as both girls broke into hysterics.

Chapter Four

MELANCHOLY

Erin smiled at the memory of their first time on a boat. It would not be their last. The next time they'd arrived at the boathouse they were praised by Hilary, one of the instructors who'd been cox that day, and told they'd been the only two girls perfectly in sync. Their effort had also been recognised, as well as their natural stature, which was perfect for the sport.

"You're both tall and have lots of stamina," she said after taking them aside. "We can either put you on a boat as two of the most promising eight from your year group. Or better yet, you can change to the double scull and row as a two."

It was an easy decision and both Erin and Gianna had given the answer together, Erin remembered with particular fondness. "We'll row as a two."

It had kind of defeated the initial objective of rowing to meet more people, but there and then, the decision was made to take the actual sport more seriously. Besides, over the following months, Erin and Gianna would meet many new people. Things were changing.

After spending several minutes gazing glassy-eyed into the photo of the two of them on the double scull, Erin locked it away in her desk drawer. She didn't know why she'd brought it to work, indeed she had no idea why she'd climbed into the attic to dig it out, it was far too painful to have facing her all day, beside the larger frame of her and Ben.

Erin sighed, "oh, Gianna."

She jumped as the intercom buzzed. "Doctor Baker, your nine-thirty appointment, Mr Prudhoe is here."

"I'm ready, send him in."

Yvette, Erin's receptionist held the door open as a one-legged man on crutches manoeuvred himself inside.

"Good morning, Glen, I hope you're feeling well enough to be taken through your paces today?"

"Give us your best, Erin." Glen had been flown back from Afghanistan the year before after shrapnel from an improvised explosive device blew his right leg off below the knee. He'd been Erin's patient for the last four months.

The session began by testing Glen's balance and posture with the crutches using gait analysis monitors. Then his balance without the crutches was monitored by use of a balance plate.

"All good so far." She picked up a medicine ball and stood a metre from him. "I'd like you to catch this."

He caught the heavy ball, barely flinching on his one leg. She then progressed to two, three and four metres; throwing the ball back and forth. The backrest possessed pressure sensors monitoring Glen's balance. "It'll take more than a ball to knock me off my foot."

Erin greatly admired the soldiers' spirit and had yet to encounter one who'd allowed his injuries to prevent him living a full life. "You're strong, Glen, strong enough to do away with those damned things." She gestured to the crutches, propped in the corner. "Are you excited for Friday?" Erin referred to his appointment to collect his new prosthetic limb.

"A little nervous but I can't tell you how much of a difference it'll finally make." He breathed deeply. "It'll be a big day, for sure."

"Hey, you'll do great, I know Doctor Harper personally. He's one of the best and he'll take good care of you."

He nodded. "I saw you at the Relief for Heroes awards the other week and when you mentioned him, I kind of guessed you were acquainted." He winked at Erin.

She hid behind her hands. "Oh no, was it really that obvious?"

He flapped a dismissive hand. "Someone's gonna be dating you, may as well be one of the good ones." He began spinning the medicine ball around on the end of his index finger. "And what he does for the Army of Angels ... Wow!"

"Army of Angels?" She'd heard of the charity, which performed similar work to Relief for Heroes.

"You know, um, well, my sergeant tells me he donates half his company's income to them." He must have seen Erin's mouth slacken. "Fuck, I've just put my only remaining foot in it, haven't I?" He straightened and his eyes flicked across to the crutches. "Shit, Erin, you couldn't just pretend I never opened my big mouth, could you?"

She took a step back, slowly shaking her head. "I honestly had no idea he was doing such a thing."

But when she gave it some thought, there had been clues. Apart from the nice house in the countryside, Ben didn't possess anything extravagant at all. He drove a twelve-year-old Peugeot hatchback, which Erin had often pleaded with him to scrap for something better. Not once had he ever whisked her off for a weekend in Paris or even Skegness; a subject which, along with his lack of apparent romanticism, had been the cause of many arguments. And nor did Ben have any real hobbies either, apart from his work. It wasn't like he collected expensive wines or paintings, or even owned a decent watch. In fact, there had been times Erin had wondered exactly what he did with his money, given that his company excelled in what it did. As it transpired, all along he was giving it away, to help wounded war veterans and keeping it all to himself.

"Erin?"

"Huh?"

"I was just asking if you wanted me on the treatment table?" Glen was pointing to where it was located.

"Oh, yes please."

He hopped over and positioned himself face up. "And by the way, congratulations on the award."

"Um, yes, thank you."

An hour later, while Erin analysed Glen's reports, she was interrupted by a knock on the door.

"Hi," Ben poked his head inside and entered, "I just thought I'd stop by and surprise you."

Erin leapt from her seat, ran over and embraced him. "It's very good to see you."

"I can tell." He squeezed her, pressing his cheek against hers. "Whatever has got into you, can you please keep taking it?"

"I will."

He kissed her on the lips then strolled across to the window, gazing out casually before turning back to face Erin with a broad smile. "It's such a lovely day, I thought I'd take you out for lunch. Yvette says you have a clean schedule until half two."

"That sounds lovely. Where exactly did you have in mind?"

"I don't care. Anywhere it's just the two of us."

She smiled and walked toward the cloakroom. "Two minutes, I'll just get my bag."

When she returned, Ben was sitting at the spare desk.

"Oh, sweetheart, not there, please." She dashed over and grabbed Ben's hand before tugging him onto his feet.

"What? There's nothing wrong with it, is there?" He swivelled the chair around on its axis, as if expecting it to break.

"No, nothing like that. It's just a superstition I have. You know how much I've always wanted to expand and take on another therapist..."

"Ah, and if I sit at his desk then it may never come true, right?" He took Erin's hand and pulled her towards the door.

"Something like that."

"You are silly, a superstitious doctor, but this is why I love you."

They walked along the narrow, cobbled streets of historic Cambridge with its five, six and seven hundred-year-old colleges, perfectly manicured lawns, bridges, endless coffee shops, vibrancy, toffs in capes, cyclists everywhere, distant ringing of bells and all teeming with students and tourists. No matter how familiar Erin had become with the city, she never grew tired of it. She'd often thought of it as the most beautiful place in England. The hometown she came from in the north, Alnwick, was also very beautiful, but Cambridge, despite the often painful memories had proven impossible to leave.

"You're in deep thought, aren't you," Ben said, catching Erin admiring some of the thirteenth-century architecture.

"I just love this place, that's all." She squeezed his hand.

"Do you miss being a student?"

She considered her answer. "They were some of the best times of my life. But there are certain things I'd do differently."

"Well, things are great now, right?" Ben asked with a hint of trepidation.

"Of course, I'm very happy." She said, casting a lingering glance on Downing College.

He perked up and Erin felt his arm relax. "There's not a lot I'd change, babe. We have our businesses in the city, lots of friends, our careers are looking fantastic but most of all, we have each other." He spun her towards him, clasping her in his arms and planting a deep, passionate kiss on her lips. When it was over, he pointed at the river. "Let's take a punt ride."

"Let's take a punt ride," Gia suggested, dragging Erin along by the arm and not bothering to wait for her answer.

"No, Gia, I can't." Erin tried to resist the pull, but as usual, found refusing this particular girl a task too difficult.

Gia eased up when they neared the end of the short jetty and twisted around to face Erin. "And why not? I know your schedule inside out. You have nothing better to do right now other than taking a punt ride with me."

"I don't know, it's just weird." She gestured with her head to the punt and the tour guide standing on the bow yawning.

"What? You know him?" Gia asked, alarmed.

"No."

"So, you've got no reason then."

"Well, no not really." Erin looked at the floor and shuffled.

"Because I know you're not afraid of the water, you row for the college, remember, but you won't take a punt ride with me?" Gia stepped away and raised an eyebrow. "What's going on, Erin?"

Erin sensed the challenge in Gia's tone. How could she

put this without sounding too much like an oddball? "It's really silly but when we row, it's just us two. There's a man there now." She gestured again with her head toward the man standing on the punt with a long stick and straw hat, minding his own business. "It just wouldn't be the same."

Gia doubled over in laughter. "Oh, you are so precious, not to mention a big prune, oh, you really would fit right in back home. I should show you around sometime." She straightened and rubbed Erin's arm. "But you are one eternally sweet lady."

"I told you it was silly."

Gia grabbed her hand again. "You're coming, prune."

"Good afternoon." The tour guide said, steadying the boat with one foot on the mooring.

They took seats at the stern, as far from the tour guide as possible where the confines of the punt forced their knees to press together. The man pushed off the dock and began manoeuvring down the river.

"Really, Erin, if it wasn't for me, you'd be stuck inside being your true self the whole time."

"Which is what?"

"A geek!" She nudged Erin's shoulder. "I knew what you were the minute I clapped eyes on you, which must be why I took such pity."

"You know I'm not a complete geek." Erin thought of their ever-improving times along the Cam in their double scull, the athlete she was making of herself and how *that* was hardly a stereotypical *geek* attribute. She'd show her yet.

"No, you're right and I wouldn't change you for anything."

Erin laughed and a large smile broke out across her face just as the punt startled a Kingfisher, majestic in its orange and blue plumage as it flew into the heavens.

"What?" Gia asked, angling her head back.

"Or anyone?"

"What do you mean?"

It was a difficult subject but Erin knew she could confide in Gia now. "You know what I am. And you're like ... just the complete opposite of me. You're just so confident and funny. I used to always wonder why you chose to hang out with me when you could be friends with anybody." Erin noted how Gia turned to face her with a glazed over, non-blinking expression, full of concentration. "Let's face it, I was a loser ... no, don't interrupt ... I'm aware I was absolutely hopeless and if you only knew how close I was from running away that day and forever turning my back on all this, on everything." She opened out her arms as if to encompass her entire life. "You could have been friends with anybody you chose and I'd still have been the girl who never spoke to anyone."

Gia took Erin's hand and began grazing the skin with her thumb. "Erin, I don't know what to say."

Erin sniffed, "so you can be made speechless." She moved her free hand over Gia's. "For a while, I kept expecting you to abandon me for some other group of girls and I'd go back to living in my shell."

Gia brought her free hand over so that they were now clasping each other's hands. "Erin, I want you to know that I would never, ever abandon you. Not for anybody." Gia's eyes shimmered with the formation of tears and she turned away blinking. "Damn you, look what you're doing."

The breath caught in Erin's throat. "I'm sorry, maybe I really am a nerd."

"No, Erin, it's the two of us who're the cool group, which is why there's no need to leave you for another."

The fact the tour guide had remained quiet was not lost on Erin. Perhaps he sensed the two girls weren't *that* type of tourist group, the type that needed long memorised stories about landmarks. They approached the famous Bridge of Sighs that connected St John's College over the river. It surely had to be one of the most beautiful bridges in the world, regal and splendid, and there were several punts filled with tourists gathered around as cameras flashed. Erin had heard there was also a *Bridge of Sighs* in Venice, in Gia's home country, but she couldn't imagine it being anything quite as impressive as this.

As they floated under the bridge, Erin knew she could leave the fears and anxieties that had dogged her entire life behind her. Beyond, where swans preened themselves on the water, the future came into focus, where she'd have the confidence to be herself. She would remember this moment and that it was Gia's hands she held. It had all been thanks to her, for giving Erin a chance, for standing by her when most would have given up, for pushing her, even when she fought against it.

The future would be easier now. She'd have somebody to go out in the evening with, somebody to row away the semesters, a friend with whom to talk when she had problems, but most of all, she had somebody she could simply look forward to getting to know.

"What do you plan on doing after you graduate?" Gia asked, releasing Erin's hands and twisting to face her.

"I've given it some thought but not come to anything concrete. All I know is that I want to do something in physio. How about you?"

"Did I tell you I have an older brother in the Italian army?"

"No." Erin wondered if this was a change of subject or a long story about what she intended to do after graduation. "I mean, I knew you had a brother, but you never said he was in the army."

"Well, he's serving in Afghanistan with the International

Security Assistance Force. It seems like every single time we speak he tells me about how one of his battalion friends has been injured. You don't hear about it when someone gets an arm or a leg blown off, only a few seconds of airtime when a soldier gets killed. It's a real fucking scandal."

Erin felt her eyes widen. Her fiery Italian friend had said the *f* word too many times to count, it never did take much but she'd never heard Gia this passionate about anything before.

"Here we are on your right..." the tour guide gestured with an arm to one of the most iconic scenes in all of England, so he did have a tongue after all. Erin had been so engrossed with Gia that despite facing the landmark, she'd completely failed to notice it. "This is The King's College of Our Lady and Saint Nicholas in Cambridge, or simply *King's College* for short. Established in 1441 by King Henry VI, it contains the world's largest fan vault, a style of architecture typical for the period and..."

Erin folded her arms and gave the man her best scowl. He must have got the message because he ceased talking and turned back toward the river. Erin felt bad for not being a better customer, but his timing had been appalling.

Gia continued with a little more composure. "Anyway, these brave people are in great need of physio. For the rest of their lives, they'll need it. I just feel like I need to do *something*. I have many friends in the army and..." she clenched her fist so that her knuckles turned a strange shade of white for her.

"It's ok, I understand." Erin placed her arm around Gia's shoulders and pulled her close.

Gia exhaled softly through her nose and smiled. "You're supposed to be the erratic one here."

"No, actually I tend to be consistently quiet." Erin

squeezed Gia tight, her head nestling comfortably upon Erin's shoulder.

Erin held her friend as what seemed like the first winter's chill of the season bore down upon them. The punt continued to drift along the Cam, nearing the point they'd have to disembark. Erin closed her eyes and lost herself in the perfection of the moment, wishing it could last just that little bit longer. Quiet sniffles announced Gia was crying and Erin rested her cheek against the top of her head as peach pleasantly pervaded her sinuses. Erin could not recall a moment she'd felt closer to another person.

"I think it's such a wonderful and noble idea," Erin said, breaking the long silence.

Gia pulled herself out from Erin's embrace. "What is?"

"I ... I assume you're planning on opening some kind of physio or treatment facility for wounded soldiers?"

Gia's eyes clouded over and for a moment seemed lost in thought. Finally, she focused fully on Erin. "Yes! Yes, you are right." She moved to arm's length, her hands on Erin's shoulders. "And you should join me."

"What?" Erin hissed. "I should join you?"

"Yes! It would be so perfect. Erin, you are my best friend in the entire world and when we graduate we should go into business together."

Erin thought back to the split-second decision she'd had to make about rowing with Gia on the double scull. That had been easy and turned out to be the best decision of her life. Making the choice to go into business with her best friend would be nothing like that but the decision was plain and simple regardless. Indeed, it was a total none brainer. Owning her own business had always been some far off, unobtainable goal but with Gia then anything was possible. They'd both be doing what they were trained to do. What was there to think about?

"Ok." Erin couldn't believe it. "It's a deal."

"You're serious?"

"Yes! Yes! Yes!"

They opened their arms and embraced.

And to think Erin had wanted to avoid this punt ride.

Chapter Five

SURPRISE

A clicking sound wrenched Erin from her thoughts and her eyes regained focus to find Ben snapping his fingers in front of her nose.

"And welcome back to planet earth, Doctor Baker." He gestured to the Cam. "Really, Erin, I didn't think you were *that* afraid of the water." He laughed. "It's such a beautiful day, I just thought it'd be special." He pointed at the punt. "I know you've never been on one of these things but there's really nothing to worry about."

The tall, stripy topped, straw-hatted, long stick holding tour guide faced away with his head bowed, like he was hardly fussed whether he picked up the fare or not. Honestly, where did they find such people? It was amazing how ten years made so little difference. The pay was about what one might expect for such low skilled work, most of the guides were students who either really badly needed the money or didn't need it all, and only toiled the things as a means of meeting foreign women on holiday. Erin, being with Ben, might not have provided adequate motivation for such an individual.

Erin sighed and conceded, "ok, it'll be nice." Though it

would be an experience she could do without, considering the memories of her only ever punt ride along the Cam. But come on, Erin, that was an age ago, get over it! She had a fantastic guy who, for whatever reason, was crazy about her, and here he was finally doing something romantic. The least she could do was put her faith in him and actually dare to enjoy the moment.

Just try not to think of Gianna.

"Two, please," Ben told the man while steadying Erin's hand as she stepped in the punt. "Easy, there, careful."

The mute tour guide actually bothered to nod his head but did not so much as say a word in welcome. It really was the rudest thing Erin had ever come across.

"What is with that guy?" She asked, loud enough for him to hear. "No tip for him."

Ben took his seat beside Erin. "Give the man a break, it must be exhausting pushing this thing around all day." He dipped his fingers in the water. "And *you* need to cheer up."

"Yeah, you're right, I'm glad you're here and this was a nice idea."

The punt pushed away and began its journey along the Cam. At the point where Erin remembered seeing the beautiful rare Kingfisher, only ducks quacked now and did so beneath a shower of bread thrown from a flock of tourists. That Kingfisher had been symbolic of the hope she'd felt that day, losing herself in its beauty as it flew into the heavens. She'd since discovered that ten years on, the Kingfisher population was dwindling alarmingly. Ok, so this punt ride would not be the same, but Erin wouldn't take it out on Ben.

You're thinking about her, aren't you? Even now. While you're with Ben. He doesn't know, does he? Go on, why don't you tell him, he won't mind. You're a fish. Better on the water than anybody. He's done all this, for you, but you're thinking of her. Ungrateful bitch! No wonder she left! You don't deserve him, just like you never deserved her.

She snapped out of her trance, Ben was also being uncharacteristically quiet, fidgeting with his hands, once even rubbing his palms over his trousers as he stared at the far off river before it could disappear on the bend. Erin covered his hand with hers. The silence was palpable and the tour guide, if he could be called such a thing, missed every landmark and opportunity to bestow upon his customers fun facts or anecdotes. He even remained dumbstruck as they slithered under the Bridge of Sighs, surely a cue to impart any knowledge, if any was known. The combination made for a silent tour, save for the ducks, which was not altogether unwelcome in the afternoon sun.

"Are you ok?" Erin asked. "Shouldn't you be pointing out the various wildlife and launching into long rambles about your favourite birds right about now?" She pointed at on overhanging tree. "Look, a bearded tit." She said, giving him a nudge.

"It's a Greenfinch." He nudged her back. "How could you possibly get the two mixed up?" Well, it had been Ben who'd told her the Kingfisher population was in decline.

"Ok, so it's a Greenfinch. I'll remember that." She gave him a mock salute.

Ben chuckled under his breath, then again wiped his hands on his trousers.

"Those things'll need drying off if you're not careful." She'd not seen Ben this nervous since the day she met him. "It'll soon be over, and I bet you won't make this mistake again, right?" Ben was one of the most self-assured people she'd ever known, in fact, being around him so much over the years had influenced her own demeanour; it was hard not to take little bits away from people you spent time with, admired and adored. It was Ben's calming face she thought about when the haze threatened to appear, which these days didn't very often happen.

The punt slinked toward King's College, the familiar chapel with the adjacent Clare College in her line of sight. What was unfamiliar, however, was the large marquee on the Back Lawn. Term time and graduation had finished for the summer, yet a large gathering lingered on the bank. As they approached, the meaty smell of barbecue ignited her taste buds. A large table contained row after row of drinks. Somebody was having a party.

"I didn't know you could hire the Back Lawn for a private party." She twisted and glanced at Ben, who in turn looked away with a smirk. "Hey, you, don't ignore me." More people were now standing in a line along the bank, someone called out and then even more came running down from further up the lawn. Strangest of all, they were all waving at Erin.

Then Beethoven's 5th symphony, one of Erin's favourites, became more and more audible the closer they neared. Then she saw the five-piece orchestra. "Oh, my God." Erin's mouth gaped as a middle-aged couple began waving insanely. "Ben, what the hell are my parents doing here?" She scanned the rest of the faces. "My brother, Cousin Louise. Ben, I know these people."

What was happening? Was she dreaming this? Could Erin possibly dare hope a certain somebody else might be amongst the faces?

"Ben, what is this?"

The tour guide jammed his oar into the water, bringing the punt to a stop parallel to the gathering. She was mere metres from the cluster, faces she recognised, and nearly all with such dopey expressions she'd never seen. The whole thing was so surreal, and the weirdest part was that nobody was saying anything, which almost made it seem like time itself had stopped.

She stood and needed to grab the backrest for support as she turned to face Ben. He'd better have some answers.

Ben lowered himself to one knee...

And brought out a small, opened box with a very large ring.

"Ben?" It wasn't the full-on haze that threatened to make a long overdue reappearance, but she did feel lightheaded. This was different. The blurry tour guide standing on the bow had now also turned around to face her, though any further details she could not make out in the moment.

"Erin, ever since the moment I first saw you, all I wanted to do was hold you close and never let you go. To my eternal stupidity, I've let you go too many times over the years and each time, I realised I could not live without you. Now, I never mean to let you go ever again. I love you with all my heart and want to spend the rest of my life with you ... Always." He took ahold of Erin's hand. The clicks of cameras from everywhere were one of the small details that made it through to Erin's consciousness, though nothing much else was clear at this moment. "Erin, will you marry me?"

She blinked several times. It took a few seconds but the blur began to recede as clarity returned. The tour guide had stepped off his perch and gradually moved into Erin's focus, taking photo after photo. An answer was needed quick.

"Yes." She pulled him up into an embrace. "Of course, I'll marry you."

"We have a *yes*!" The tour guide announced to the guests as he threw his straw hat into the air.

Erin turned to glare at him. "Scruffy?" Her face broke into a grin, her eyes glazed over, this time with tears. She punched her old friend on the arm. "I cannot believe you."

THE FIRST THING ERIN DID AFTER STEPPING ONTO THE Back Lawn was scan frantically for Gianna. It was only natural, after all, that maybe, by some miracle, she'd be there, lounging under a parasol, drinking a cocktail, probably causing trouble. The gathering was a mixture of family and friends from past and present. It wasn't so unreasonable to hope that maybe the most important person who'd ever existed could have been there too. But she wasn't. And Erin was glad. Not because she didn't want to see her, because Erin's heart truly ached for her, but because she'd just agreed to marry Ben.

It was a lot to take in, on top of everything else, and she'd have to process everything later on.

"How did you manage all this?" Erin's legs were still wobbling but of course, her fiancé was happy to act as a support.

"Oh, you know, when you have contacts..." he flapped a hand at arguably England's most iconic scene as though it had been no bother at all, "two postgraduates with businesses in the city. Things can be done." Apparently so, even when neither of them were graduates of King's or Clare College, the buildings of which encompassed this stunning classic English setting. The Back Lawn was the large area of grass as seen on all the postcards of Cambridge, between the river, King's College and Clare College.

But more than how he'd secured the location, Erin had really wanted to know about how he'd managed to assemble all her friends and family without her knowledge. That appeared lost on him, though it was still a monumental achievement, an act of stealth.

Erin spent the first twenty minutes moving quickly from guest to guest, telling them how incredibly overwhelmed she felt that they'd made the effort to be a part of her engagement. Her parents, brother and cousin had travelled the 264 miles from Alnwick to Cambridge. After making quick pleasantries to acknowledge their presence, Erin promised she'd spend more time with everyone on her second way around the gathering. It would take some time.

"I know what you're thinking, you have that preoccupied look on your face." Ben squeezed her hand. "Yvette agreed to lock up at the surgery and will be down shortly, so don't be worrying about returning to work."

"Looks like you thought of everything. I truly am quite overcome by all this." She pulled herself closer into him. "You must have gone to an incredible amount of effort."

"It wasn't all easy and I was quite justifiably worried your cousin wouldn't keep quiet." Ben glanced over at Louise, his future cousin-in-law, who smiled and walked over holding a glass of champagne.

"You're not keeping that ring from me any longer. Let me see." She wrenched Ben and Erin's hands apart and went in for a closer look. "Oh, my God! I'm not even guessing at the cost."

"Oh, Louise, it's not all about the money."

"I know but we all dream about this day, the ring too, of course. Have fun today, ok?"

"I am having fun, honestly, I am. It means the world to me that you've made the journey." There had only been a couple of times in ten years that any family member had bothered making the trip south. Usually, it was Erin who returned home to Alnwick to visit the family. She spotted the mobile bar with spruced up bartender waiting patiently behind. "Why, it'd be rude not to."

"What would you like?" The man had to speak louder because the five-piece orchestra began with Edvard Grieg's Morning Mood.

"I'll have a glass of white wine and a lager for Ben."

"We have Peroni and Pinot Grigio?" He poised with the

bottle over a glass, the label stating it was from the Lombardy region. Hmm, both Italian.

"Ok, that'll be fine." Was there nowhere to hide? Why, even now, was she being reminded?

Across the lawn, Erin made eye contact with Scruffy. She'd never have thought on the day she met the character that he'd end up becoming one of her closest friends, one of the mainstays of her entire time in the city, a link to the past. In the early days, it had hurt to be around him because of the connection to *her* but after a while, it became easier, once she'd forced herself to forget the damn Italian, by any means necessary. Now, with everything since that bloody poem resurfaced, she worried that being around the guy would prove too difficult. She hoped not but there was only one way to find out.

"Ben, did you meet my old inconvenience from Cambridge?" She elbowed the Scot in the ribs, clean and immaculately groomed as he now needed to be for his engineering role. How things change. "This is, um, Scruffy."

"Scruffy?" Ben frowned. "There must be an ironic twist to that, surely?"

Erin was quick to intervene. "Oh, Ben, don't give him an easy opening."

Scruffy shrugged, all innocent and completely convincing. "She always had it in for me did that one. No matter what she says about me, just ignore it. The nickname does indeed have an ironic twist, as you can see," he motioned with his hands in an elaborate gesture, indicating himself, "I'm the very image of a well-groomed and respected man of repute. In fact, I'm considering running for President of the Alumni."

Erin grit her teeth, knowing he was having too much fun with this.

"She does get things wrong from time to time," Ben conceded with a nod.

"As do we all, good sir."

Ben squinted, "now I can place you ... I know you as Stewart, don't I? You're the chap I spoke to on the phone last week. Your description was rather vague and for a moment I worried we were on the wrong punt." Oh, no. It was rapidly turning into one of those surreal conversations that can only come from two very different parts of a person's world colliding in the same time and space and it would be a lie if Erin were to say she felt comfortable. Worse, Ben was now reaching out to shake Scruffy's hand but Erin was ready and exceptionally quick to yank it away.

"Perhaps not the best of ideas." She clasped her fiancé's hand in a protective embrace, where it would remain, but it was funny hearing Scruffy referred by his proper name. She'd only discovered what it was herself a couple of years ago. "You must excuse Scruffy, he has a bad wrist." She said, matter of fact, and then grimaced after realising the connotation. The bastard could do it to her without even making an effort.

Ever the gentleman, Ben made no indication of even noticing. "Oh, I'm sorry to hear that." He jerked his chin at the river. "Didn't you just punt us here all the way from the Quayside?"

"Like I said, whatever Erin says about me, you should just take with a pinch of salt." The idiot paused for effect. "And I never once asked her out on a date."

Ben's head lolled back in laughter and Scruffy took the split-second to pull a hideous face in Erin's direction. Her hand balled into a fist.

"You must have some interesting stories," Ben remarked, jovially. "How exactly do you know each other?"

Erin jumped in before Scruffy had the chance to open his mouth. "Our group were all part of the Cambridge Boat Club." It was as detailed an answer as she wanted to give. She wasn't lying to Ben, per se, but she was being extremely measly with the details, which to many would have been just as bad. The last thing she needed was to be reminded of the bloody Boat Club. It was history. In fact, the last time she'd even rowed was with Gianna, her trophies and medals were stashed away in the attic and the rest of her photos and memorabilia were someplace she didn't even know about, possibly the landfill, committed back to the earth. All part of the process. Ben was faintly aware she'd rowed during her freshman year and that she'd even been considered gifted at the sport, the internet existed, after all, but she never spoke of the subject if she could get away with it.

"Ah, yes, I always regretted never giving it a try," Ben said to Scruffy. "Rowing is so quintessentially Cambridge. Cricket was more my thing, orienteering at a pinch but with work and everything, I never got chance to commit myself entirely to any one thing. It's one of my biggest regrets." He turned to Erin. "You really don't speak much of your rowing days, babe." Then back to Scruffy. "What boat did you row?"

"Well, technically, because it was a two-man boat and we each *rowed* with two oars rather than one; it was considered *sculling* rather than rowing." Although Scruffy's answer was detailed enough, it was delivered with little enthusiasm, quiet and with no animation, which was in contrast to how he'd conducted the rest of the conversation. Like Erin, he had his reasons for not wanting to discuss the subject, and like Erin, she knew, he would not want to elaborate upon those reasons. At least not at a party.

"Isn't that what you rowed, babe?" Ben asked his fiancée. "Sorry, *sculled*."

Scruffy was quick to interject on Erin's behalf, knowing how she'd feel about the subject, bless him, and did so while sounding even more downcast than before. "We were all part of the larger Boat Club. We rotated boats and crewmates."

That was a lie and Scruffy tightened his lips as he turned away to glance absently at the river. The subject needed dropping at once. He turned back and tilted his empty glass. "Time for another, I think. Would anyone like anything?"

Erin motioned to the half-full glasses she and Ben held. "I think we're fine for the time being, but thank you, Scruffy." She squeezed his shoulder. "Hey, we'll arrange to have a drink real soon, right?"

"Aye, we will. Just let me know when." Scruffy turned away, looked left and right, then trudged off toward the bar.

"Did I say something wrong?" Ben asked. "A truly wonderful chap but by God, did he just flip in an instant."

Erin took a breath. "You weren't to know, honey. He sculled with his twin brother. He battled with depression and … well, he wishes he could have done more."

"Oh, Jesus Christ." Ben ran a hand through his hair. "You should have just kicked me. I'll drop the subject of rowing from now on."

"Hey, you weren't to know."

"No, you're right." He brought her in for a hug then released her, exhaling loudly. "This is supposed to be a bloody engagement party. Where's that photographer?"

They continued working their way around the guests; Erin's parents, Ben's parents, several friends from both their courses, even Sergeant Major Thomas Becker made an appearance, unaided by walking sticks. "He improves more and more every time I see him," Erin told Ben.

Shortly after, the orchestra began with Four Seasons by Vivaldi. Great, even more hard memories to battle through. And to think it was supposed to be a day about looking to the future. Erin finished her next glass of wine before the symphony had even finished the first season. Although she loved classical music, listening to Vivaldi had proven difficult over the years.

A familiar man was strolling across the lawn in the direction of the marquee. "You invited my old professor?"

"Of course, the more people I get to show off my fiancé to is all for the better." Ben nodded in the direction of the approaching man, "now, tell me quick ... what subjects should I avoid?"

Oh, as long as you don't somehow mention Gianna then all will be well. "He'll be a little touchy about the Boat Race last weekend, so just avoid any mention of that." Erin referred to the debacle that was Oxford demolishing Cambridge by eleven lengths a few days before; a victory the size of which had only been surpassed thirteen times in the race's 160-year history.

Ben straightened and muttered. "I think I can manage that."

"Free drink, free food and free drink again, Erin, you've done well for yourself." The professor held out his hand to Ben. "I'm Andy, nice to meet you."

"You too, I'm Ben, but I feel I'm the one who's done well for himself."

"Yes, I read about your prosthetics company in one of the physiotherapy rags they make me contribute." He winked at Ben.

"Oh, thank you very much, Andy," Erin thrust her hands on her hips, taking mock offence and nudging Ben, "and I don't know why you're smiling."

"I'm sorry, babe." He looked back to Andy. "I'm glad you could make it. It means a lot to us both."

"Well, I only live in the city and it's cheaper than going out to eat but free drink aside, Erin was one of the finest students I've ever had the pleasure of teaching." It was nice of the professor to say so. The truth was that after her freshman year, she plunged herself into learning all she could about physiotherapy, more so than was necessary even for

Cambridge. She needed the distraction. "Oh, and congratulations on your award from that charity, it was well deserved. I'm sorry I couldn't have been there but I heard you gave me a mention. Really, there was no need." He waved a dismissive hand but Erin could tell he was pleased.

"Honestly, Andy, you've been one of my biggest inspirations and by far the most likeable don in the faculty." She said with complete sincerity.

"Really, how much have you had to drink? Speaking of which," he twisted toward the bar, where apparently, Scruffy was still standing, "I should probably make a start getting tanked up. Oh, dear God, that fellow looks awfully forlorn. Is he in the right place? Who is he?" He turned back to Erin. "Maybe I'll wait a bit." His eyes changed focus to stare over her shoulder. "Oh, bloody ducks on the Back Lawn, of all sacred places, they don't half crap all over the grass. Bloody things have no respect for the poor caretaker."

Erin glanced sideways at Ben, as if to confirm that *yes, the professor is exactly as eccentric as I told you.*

"Speaking of ducks, did you ever find out what happened to that friend of yours? Damn it, what was her name now? The tall one, Italian was it? Pretty thing with the attitude, talked back constantly. You don't forget a girl like that." Oh shit. Please Andy, please stay quiet. "Oh, that'll bug me forever. You remember, the one you were permanently glued to. What *was* her name?"

"Um, I'm really not too sure..." Erin noticed Ben turn away from the ducks, his interest piqued.

The professor spoke to Ben. "I'd never have put the two of *them* together. They were not exactly what you'd call one and the same but for whatever reason, they got along famously and..." he was about to say more but became distracted by the sight of two ducks strutting into the marquee. "Damn bloody things think they own the place ...

well, that was, until she vanished ... and all without a word to anyone ... oh, I pity the poor groundsman, is all I can say."

Erin didn't need this. Not now. Why could she not escape it? Ever since that confounded poem ... she'd been as miserable as the day Gianna disappeared. There'd been the overwhelming therapeutic need to write the thing at the time, to spill out her emotions on paper, but by God, she should have cast it to the flames straight after.

Were strange forces pulling the giant strings of the universe, forcing these events and coincidences to occur all within a short space of time? If so, why? What *was* the universe trying to tell her? Because all Erin knew for sure was that she needed to forget the damn Italian, otherwise, she would never be happy.

"Andy, I think the bar is free now."

Ben's eyes narrowed. "You know what, I think I actually very vaguely remember that girl. Wasn't she..."

The professor, who'd turned toward the bar, whipped back on Erin. "Anyway, that's my cue." He pumped Ben's hand and hugged Erin. "And don't look so worried, girl, you're supposed to be celebrating a wonderful thing. Don't be afraid, just go for it!"

"DON'T BE AFRAID, JUST GO FOR IT!" PROFESSOR ANDY Atkins told the seminar. "You knew today was coming. You've had all bloody Christmas to prepare for it. Quite honestly, I'm shocked at how unprepared most of you are. It's almost enough to think you were at Oxford, not Cambridge. *Here*, we do things right."

He approached Gia lying supine on the therapy table. Erin stood beside her. They both wore cycling shorts and t-shirts. The professor spoke low enough so only the two of them could hear. "Well done, girls, you're about the only two in this entire rabble who's taking this bloody thing seriously." He glanced around with dismay at the rest of the group, wearing a mixture of jeans, hooded tops and some garb he could in no way ascertain; most students had the look, and stench, of inebriation upon them, not to mention Christmas overindulgence, the shame, though ultimately no harm as long as they were not rowers for the faculty, otherwise it was their own lives they were wasting. "I understand some of you will be nervous about having to touch your friends but there's really nothing sexual in it, Gavin, are you listening to me? If this is what you're intending to do as a career then you'd better get over your reservations fast. If you wanted to do a half-hearted course then you should have applied for Oxford."

The professor continued ranting but much of it went through Erin's head as she stared down upon her friend, lying in front of her, in tight clothing. The pink t-shirt she wore had the word *Bella* written in red writing. Despite being on her back and wearing restrictive material, Gia's breasts were trying their hardest to push out that tight pink t-shirt.

"Um, I have to be honest with you, Gia…"

"Will you just get on with it! Put your hand under my knee, lift it and bend my bloody leg." Since when had Gia started using Englishisms such as *bloody*? Erin would have asked but did not want to be accused of stalling.

It didn't help that this was the first she'd seen of Gia since returning for the new year. That the first class back was 'hands-on' hardly made it easier either. Things were simpler before.

Something had changed over the holidays.

"WILL YOU PUT THE BOOKS DOWN." GIA GRABBED THE copy of Orthopaedic Physiotherapy from Erin's hands, slammed it shut and dropped it to the floor as though it was some book on crochet or knitting. It landed with a thump. "Really, your nerdiness is over the top sometimes. I leave for Italy in six hours and you'd rather read about isokinetic dynamometry? I'm truly hurt, Erin." She placed a hand over her heart in exaggeration.

Erin frowned and took a sip from her coffee. "I'm sorry, I'm more than happy to talk normal stuff." The truth was that even though Erin looked forward to returning to Alnwick for Christmas, she had no idea just how she would occupy her free time without Gia. The totality of the last three and a half months had involved her in some way or other; from the large to the small, from being study buddies and rowing on the double sculls to shopping for groceries and almost getting banned from popular student bars. "Are you looking forward to going home?"

Gia rolled her eyes, made snoring noises and dropped her head to the table. "Booooring." When she brought her head back up, she was staring beyond Erin and scowled at something.

"What?" Erin twisted around. The Starbucks employee who was gathering up the used cups, caught Erin's eye then quickly looked away.

"I'm telling you, it's every time we come here, he checks you out every single time." Gia collapsed back in her seat and folded her arms.

"Does he? I've not noticed."

"Because you always have your head in a book." Gia looked beyond Erin again, who continued facing front. "If he thinks I'm letting him take you away from *me*, then he can think again."

"Nobody can take me away from you," Erin said deadpan

and sipped more coffee. "Well, say *hi* to your madre anyway." She paused to watch Gia, who was still holding her gaze over Erin's shoulder. Honestly, what did it matter if he stared at her the whole time? Erin was far too busy studying, rowing and amusing a full time best friend to add a boyfriend to the mix. "Gia?"

She started, "yes?"

"Can I ask you something?"

"No, of course not. What?"

"Did you mean what you said the other day? About showing me around your hometown?" She saw Gia's eyes widen and spoke quickly to fill the gap. "It's just that I've always wanted to see Italy and you live so close to Pompeii."

"The other day?" Gia asked with narrowed eyes and a tilted head.

"Yeah, you were pretty blasé about it. It was on the punt, you said you'd show me around sometime. I thought it was just a joke, you don't remember half the things you say, including this." Erin sensed the heat rising and looked down to the safety of her vanquished muffin crumbs. She gathered a few errant scraps and scooped them into her mouth.

Gia reached over and touched her arm. Erin wasn't expecting it and jumped from the sensation. "Erin, you are welcome to come and stay with us whenever you like. You're my best friend, you silly goose." Gia sat back and laughed.

"What?"

"You had that *the whole world is about to come to an end* expression on your face. It's so cute. I'd missed it. Haven't seen it in a while."

"Otherwise known as *the haze*." Erin sat back. "And thank you. I'd really love to come and visit sometime. And of course, you're welcome in Alnwick anytime you like. The castle there is the one used in those two Harry Potter films."

"Oh, Erin, you really do have the worst taste in films."

Gia's face perked. "And you, missy, were supposed to come over and watch Malena."

Erin's eyebrows raised of their own accord. She'd still not seen where Gia lived. Living in the flats within the Downing campus had meant stricter rules on guests. "You mean you actually remember inviting me to watch that?"

Gia spoke so much and usually so quickly that there was no way on earth she could possibly remember even a fraction of the things she rambled on about, even the more important things on any given day were routinely forgotten, such as the time they were supposedly training. "Erin, I had my mother post it over from Italy especially so we could watch it together."

"Wow, ok." It looked like Erin had underestimated her friend.

"You know, you should give me a little more credit."

Erin nodded. "Yes, you are absolutely correct. And I guess I should say *sorry*." She held Gia's eye contact, wanting it to sound sincere.

"Hey, that's cool, it really is. There's no way *you* can offend me." She held Erin's gaze. Gia always carried a certain intensity, a mysterious force that emanated from the eyes and when they looked at you like that, it was as though she was looking into your very soul. Not surprisingly, it was Erin who broke first by looking down into her cup from when the silence persisted for a few uncomfortable seconds. "So, this haze ... tell me what it's like." Gia finally broke the tension.

Erin breathed. "Well, I've had it for as long as I can remember. It's not some metaphorical thing, an exaggeration or something I made up. Coming from a practical or evolutionary viewpoint, I think it happens as a kind of self-defence mechanism. Although it's really not. It's brought me more harm than good over the years by preventing me from growing out of it. It's the equivalent of curling up into a ball and hiding in the corner, only, I'm still standing, but everything else gets blotted out."

Gia focused fully on Erin. Those eyes. "Does it still happen?"

"The thing is, it always happened when I was nervous. My vision would blur, my palms would sweat and my body would shake uncontrollably. Ever since we've been hanging out, you kind of took the pressure off, simply by being there and deflecting everything. But at the same time, you never allowed me to take it easy. By God, Gia, but you've pushed me harder than anybody else has ever pushed me in my life and we've only known each other a few months." Erin paused to consider her answer. "In all honesty, I still see fog clouding my vision but it's further away and it doesn't bother me as much. I guess I owe you an awful lot."

"Hey, if it wasn't me, you'd be friends with somebody else."

"Oh, I'm not so sure about that."

"Yes, you would. You're a lovely girl and *I'm* the one who's lucky to be *your* friend."

Erin thought back to her first day at Downing. She'd never know for sure if she would have actually run away that day, to ruin her entire life and career, before Gia stumbled into her path. "We're lucky to have each other."

The Italian exhaled then slapped the tabletop. "This film won't watch itself. It's either now or after the new year?"

Erin grabbed her bag. "Now!"

ERIN LOOKED OUT FROM GIA'S GROUND FLOOR BEDROOM window. "You mean your room actually looks out onto the cloister?"

"Yup, not a bad view at all. We get free run of the place too." Gia shuffled through her things, searching for the DVD.

Erin recalled the day they'd met, how Gia had entered the atrium through the fire door and caused quite a fuss. It all made sense now. "You found it?"

"Not yet, I know it's amongst all this junk somewhere."

The room was a strange contradiction. It had the usual high ceilings and traditional style as the rest of the college, with a tasteful view over the lawn that together should have bestowed an upmarket feel, especially considering this was student accommodation. It was the drab Ikea furniture that brought the tone down; that and all the clothes Gia had strewn about the place, giving the entire room a pleasant peachy scent.

"Nice to see you keep your room as consistently messy as your mind." Erin teased. "I'm sure Malena is buried somewhere." She stepped toward the bed, trying not to tread on any clothes.

Gia threw sports leggings airwards. "Somehow I get the impression your bedroom is the exact opposite."

"You would be correct, although the rest of the house looks pretty much as you'd expect, like your average filthy student accommodation." The perils of having to share with other freshmen.

Erin took a seat on the edge of the bed, there was nowhere else to sit and the TV was positioned directly opposite. She took the time to glance over the walls, which Gia had adorned with several posters of extremely well-toned female athletes. From the looks of them, they were Italian sprinters, swimmers and one of a beautiful woman who held what looked like a pole vault. Strange, but there were no posters of male athletes. Italy, of all places, would be sure to have oodles of hot masculine men in skin-hugging spandex.

"I'm just curious, but what sport did you play back home?" Erin asked.

"I *played* swimming." She said on all fours, shifting through the mess on the floor. "Why?"

Erin pictured Gia's toned physique as she heaved on those heavy oars, a body she aspired to possess for herself. "Just wondered."

Gia found a padded envelope sandwiched somewhere between a heap of sweaters. "Found it! Prepare to be amazed and to fall in love with Monica Bellucci." She really did like this actress.

"Um, ok."

"One minute..." Gia left and returned a few minutes later with two glasses and a bottle of white wine. "If we're going to do this, then we're doing it properly." She closed the curtains, shutting out the afternoon light and enshrouded the room in darkness. She poured wine into the glasses and dived back onto the bed.

Erin, still perched on the end, felt a foot rub against her lower back. "Yeah?"

"Jump back, silly, and relax, you're blocking the view."

"Sorry." Erin leant backwards and manoeuvred her way up the bed until she came parallel to Gia with her body upright against the backrest. She had to reach across Gia to take her wine from the bedside table.

The movie began and Erin was immediately transported to the stunning town of Noto in Sicily, which was like somewhere out of a medieval fantasy world. Then, in some nightmare scenario for Erin, Malena began striding through the town, as every single head, male and female, turned to gawp at the sight. The men fell over themselves to get near her, to open doors or pull out her chair. This, in turn, gave the women a serious case of the green-eyed demon, staring daggers at the woman. Beauty was both a blessing and a curse but you couldn't help but feel sympathy for Malena because she didn't ask for any of the attention, it came looking for her and in reality, she was beautiful on the inside too. She loved her husband and was distraught when he left to fight in the war and didn't return. When the allies pushed the Germans out of the town, the townswomen took the opportunity to ruin her. They cut off her hair and publicly whipped Malena.

After two glasses of wine, Gia repositioned herself to lay flat on the bed, propping her head on Erin's lap. She did it in such a natural way that Erin didn't think anything of it, although she did wonder where to put her hands; her left was pushed off her lap and now hung at her side, while her right was caught between her belly and Gia's head.

Malena left town to escape the persecution and then her presumed dead husband returned, only to find his wife had vanished. He received a tip-off as to her whereabouts and went in search, but not before first having to endure lies from the townspeople as to what his wife was 'really' like and what she had been doing while he was away fighting in the war. The film ended when both Malena and her husband returned to Noto, hand in hand, walking through the streets with their heads held high. For Erin, it was the epitome of courage and something she wished she possessed herself.

"What did I tell you?" Gia sat up and turned to Erin. "You're crying?"

"Am I?" Erin wiped a sleeve across her eyes.

"Yeah, pretty much, wussy." Gia smiled. "I got over crying for Malena after something like my thirteenth viewing, so I can understand. You do get desensitised to it."

"She was just so brave." Erin sniffed.

"Beats the hell out of Harry Potter, don't you think?"

Erin snorted a globule of snot from her nose. "Oh God, how embarrassing." She hid behind her hands as Gia collapsed sideways in laughter.

"I got a full-on view of that," Gia said through the hysterics.

"It's not funny, I tasted wine through my nose."

Gia curled into a ball as she descended into a fit, her Italian browned face turning almost red. "You ... sure ... you sure know how to ruin a moment."

"Oh, I did not." Erin took out a tissue and blew her nose.

Gia pushed herself up, tears flecking at the eyes. "Look what you've done to me." She said, pointing to her face.

"We're quite the pair but at least I'm crying for a real reason."

Gia brought her hand toward Erin's face. "Here let me just..." Erin wondered what she was about to do, her head backing an inch away out of instinct, and then Gia's thumb wiped away an errant tear from Erin's cheek. It was a nice gesture and one that only Gia could have done without making Erin feel uncomfortable, "...got it. That would've bugged me otherwise."

"Um, thanks."

Gia moved into a cross-legged position, facing Erin as she sat against the headrest. "So what did you think of Monica Bellucci?"

Erin thought about her answer. "She's a fantastic actress and she played the part very believably. If she could move me to tears, then I guess she did a good job."

"Blah blah blah. But what did you think of *her*?" She tilted forward from the hips, so close that the peach intensified. It was as though Erin's opinion mattered a great deal to Gia.

"I'm not too sure what you mean?" Erin pulled her feet into her body and wrapped her hands around her knees.

"I'm asking you, Erin, what did you think of Monica Bellucci?" She spoke slow and in monotone, those big, brown hawkish eyes demanding full attention.

"What did I think of her? I just told you what I thought

of her." This wasn't so funny anymore. What was she getting at?

"No, you didn't. For all your qualities, you can be painfully slow sometimes, Erin." She still held an expression of total seriousness, which after thirty seconds was a record for her. When would her face crack and return to laughter? Gia began rocking her body gently to-and-fro, her hands clutched together in her lap. Was she aware she was doing it? It was the most vulnerable Erin had ever seen her friend.

"I can be painfully slow?" Erin's breathing increased in volume as her heart pounded away in her chest. "Gia, is there something you're trying to tell me?"

"Argh, I don't know ... I mean yes ... I'm not sure." She ran her hands over her face and shuffled about on the bed. "I mean, I've not told anybody about this but I ought to be able to tell *you*, shouldn't I?"

"Tell me what?"

Monica Bellucci, the posters on the wall - Was it related to *that*? To women? Now that she took a second to think about it, Erin had not once heard Gia talk about any guy she had a crush on, ever. In fact, she seemed to show a complete indifference to men. Even more, she actively deflected them, not only from herself, but from Erin too. When she'd wiped away Erin's tear moments earlier – What was that?

But no, Erin had not known a single gay guy or lesbian her entire life. Surely, her best friend was not a secret lesbian this whole time? But even if she was, would Erin have even known?

"My God, Gia, you're serious, aren't you?" Erin felt the urge to comfort her, to show something, any kind of gesture in support, but something stopped her. If this was what she suspected, then what could she possibly say? It had all come from nowhere and Erin felt truly stumped, and to make matters worse, the silence had now protracted for a painfully long time. "Gia? Gia, speak to me."

"I can see it in your eyes." She tilted forward again, her voice wavering. This was so unlike her, the eternally confident Gia. "You know, but you won't say it."

"Why can't *you* say it? I'm your friend." And then Erin realised, no matter what it was, even though it would be a shock, it still wouldn't matter. "Gia, I promise you, whatever it is, I'm here for you. But I need to hear *you* say it." Erin reached over, finally, and took ahold of Gia's hand, her fingers sweaty and hot. "And I think you need to say it for yourself too."

Gia took a deep breath. "Ok, here goes." She looked down, took another breath, then met Erin's eyes. "Erin, I think I'm... No, let me say it differently." She shuffled again. "Ok ... I like girls." A single tear trickled down her cheek and this time it was Erin who wiped it away. Gia laughed, part in relief, part because of the beautiful gesture. "Oh, God, please don't say you hate me."

Erin pulled her forward into an embrace and felt Gia's ribcage shaking as she broke into a cry. "Of course, I don't hate you, I'm so proud of you."

Wow! Was the one word that came to mind. There was so much Erin wanted, needed to ask; how long had she known? Had she ever kissed a girl? Or more? Was Erin really the only person who knew? Who did she have a crush on? What would happen when her family discovered the truth? But all those questions would wait. All that mattered at this moment was that she held her friend.

Gia packed her bag in silence, having left the task to the last minute. Erin helped by picking up as many of her clothes from the floor as time permitted and folded them into neat piles.

"Are you taking your orange hoody?" Erin asked, feeling the need to fill the silence.

"I don't think I'll be in need of a hoody in Napoli, even in December." She smiled then turned back to the suitcase. "But thanks."

"Are you sure you're all right?"

"Yes, of course." She continued cramming items into the case. When she finished packing, Gia opened the top drawer beside the bed. "Before I forget." She handed Erin a small, wrapped present.

"Thank you," Erin said. She'd already given Gia a framed photo of them both sat in the double scull with their oars raised in the air. She'd been certain to ensure Gia had packed it.

"Not to open before Christmas."

"Of course and that goes for yours too." Erin noticed a lump in her throat. This wasn't goodbye, but it sure felt odd. Was it because Gia just came out to her, or was it merely because she wouldn't be around for the next month and Erin had no idea what she'd do with herself? "Here, let me get that for you." Erin took the smaller of the two bags.

The taxi pulled up outside Downing just as they arrived on the street.

"Text me as soon as you arrive. Let me know you're safe." Erin said, dropping the bag to the floor.

"I will," Gia dropped her bag and opened her arms.

Erin fell into them and gave her a squeeze.

"I know what you're thinking, but I'm fine, so please don't worry about me, ok?" Gia said, releasing Erin. "Sorry, I kind of went a bit weird before."

"Oh, I understand entirely, don't be silly." Erin pulled her in for another hug. "I'll miss you like you won't believe." She felt Gia rubbing her back then Erin brought her back to arm's length. "I'm so proud of you. Have a great Christmas and I'll see you in a month."

"Miss you already." Gia positioned her lips to kiss Erin on the cheek.

Instead, Erin shocked herself by kissing Gia on the lips. They both froze, wide-eyed. What the fuck did she do that for? "Sorry, I just thought that ... Never mind." Oh, fucking, Christ. She stepped back and noticed Gia's eyebrows dip and then the Italian was climbing inside and slamming the door.

As the car drove out of sight, Erin stamped down hard onto the cobbles. "Stupid idiot! Why did I do that?"

ERIN DECIDED TO REMAIN BACK IN CAMBRIDGE FOR A WEEK before heading north for home. She occupied herself as best she could, given that Gia was sunning it up in Napoli and in the meantime, Cambridge had succumbed to the usual English winter weather. It hadn't snowed, which at least might have been pleasant, and the morning frost preventing training on the Cam for all but the most hardcore of rowers. Erin decided there wasn't much point in double sculling with nobody to make up the duo.

As the week progressed, Cambridge, with its twenty-five percent student population gradually began to resemble a ghost town as thousands of scholars scattered to every corner of the UK, Europe and even the world.

With little better to do, Erin headed to Starbucks, ordered a coffee and hit the books. Isokinetic dynamometry. She snorted, "damn it."

A girl, two tables over, scowled at Erin as she blew her nose. At least now she could learn about the subject without the major distraction that was Gia. After twenty minutes, Erin closed the books. It just wasn't the same.

It was a five and a half hour coach ride north and throughout, Erin found herself checking her phone, over and over again. Why hadn't Gia texted to let her know she'd arrived home? Erin remembered specifically asking her to take the trouble to make the text. It was nothing more than the polite thing to do, wasn't it? After a week she was unlikely to send the text now but Erin couldn't help but check her phone anyway. The words, *'text to let me know you've arrived safe,'* weren't just a figure of speech, were they?

Regardless, there were a million other subjects Gia could have texted about, but hadn't. How much longer would this coach ride take? Erin needed a distraction.

She typed into her phone, *'Hi, babe, just checking you're ok? Haven't heard from you since you arrived'.* So much for a distraction. Her finger hovered over *send.* "I'm so silly." She muttered under her breath and deleted the message. "On second thoughts..." she turned the phone off completely and stuffed it at the bottom of her bag, out of reach.

The present from Gia rested at the top of the bag. She took it out, ran her fingers over the paper, shook it. Some kind of a DVD boxset perhaps? Should she open it? No! She'd promised Gia she'd wait until Christmas day. Gia wouldn't open her present before Christmas day, she was probably not even thinking about it, running her fingers over the paper, shaking it and now, oh, God, even sniffing it. What the heck. Erin thrust the present back in the bag, zipped it up and heaved it into the storage compartment.

What else was there to do? Isokinetic dynamometry? Nope, she'd already tried that. *Gia, why had you not texted?*

The week before Christmas, Erin played tennis with her brother nearly every day. Her aerobic capacity had improved a great deal, allowing her to play longer without feeling tired. Although she still couldn't beat her brother, he did comment about how she'd improved, which was funny considering she hadn't even played the game in three months.

"Obviously, all that aerobic work in your little boat has given you some kind of transference." He said, prodding her with his racket. "Perhaps by the time you graduate, you'll be able to beat me."

She replied by swiping his arm with her racket.

On Christmas morning, the first thing she did was text Gia. '*Hey hun, Merrrrrrrry Christmas :) I hope you liked the present?*' Having an actual reason to finally make the text made everything so much easier.

She rolled out of bed and grabbed Gia's present. She'd made it, which was an achievement in itself. She tore off the paper, revealing a plain box. So it wasn't a DVD boxset. She carefully opened the box and slid out a photo frame.

"Oh, my God."

It was a framed photo of the exact same image Erin had given Gia. They were sitting in their double scull, smiling at the camera, oars raised above their heads, big gurning smiles plastered across their faces. She closed her eyes and clasped the frame against her heart. "This will go on my bedside table. Remember to take it back to Cambridge." She said to herself.

The excitement of Christmas day; lots of great food, giving out and opening presents, as well as being around her mum, dad, brother and grandma all acted as a distraction from Gia. Kind of.

When she found herself checking her phone every few minutes while the family were sitting around the dinner table, she knew something was wrong, not least with Gia, who still hadn't replied, but also with herself.

There were other things to occupy her mind on this of all days. Yet, just like many times before, since Gia left for Italy, after coming out as a lesbian, there was only one thing in

Erin's thoughts. Damn that Italian. *The damn Italian.* Erin sniggered with a mouthful of turkey and sprout.

"That's funny to you, Erin, is it?" The look mum gave was awful. "Your grandma's hip operation postponed again?" That's one way to bring a girl out from a trance.

Erin almost choked on her mouthful. "What? Oh, no. Of course not." She reached beyond her brother and rubbed her gran on the arm. "I'm so sorry, Gran, I was just thinking of something else. There's nothing funny about your hip op."

"That's alright, love, I'm not offended." She took Erin's hand and gave it a squeeze before turning back to the rest of the table. "I says ... she's been on that little telephone she carries around the whole time ... not seen her off it once." Gran announced to the rest of the table. It wasn't quite the truth, a bit of an exaggeration actually, but Erin didn't want to contradict her sweet grandma. "I says ... she's got herself a fella' down at Oxford."

Oh, God, not this. "Cambridge, Gran, I'm at Cambridge." From the corner of her eye, her mum and dad smiled and leaned forward.

"In my day we went straight from school to the factory. Did I tell you I made the seats in them Spitfires?" She cut off a tiny chunk from her turkey, from a plate that was far too full for her appetite.

"You did, Gran."

Her brother took a swig of champagne and swilled it around in his mouth, making a disgusting sound that annoyed everybody. "She hasn't got a boyfriend. Who would find *her* attractive?"

Oh, very mature. "Thanks for that, Stephen," Erin said, who'd been thankful gran had somehow managed to connect the subject of a potential boyfriend at 'Oxford,' to when she built planes during the war. Now, Stephen had deliberately returned to the one subject Erin wanted to avoid.

"Do you have a boyfriend?" Mum asked, coming straight out with it.

"No, mum, if I did, I'd have told you."

"So I was right then," Stephen said.

Erin ground her teeth. "Yes, you were right, idiot." Without even realising it, she took out her phone and checked the screen. Nothing.

"See, again. All these gadgets young people have these days and I bet she wouldn't even know how to use a washboard," Gran said, apparently monitoring Erin's every move.

"Mother, washboards became obsolete years ago. *I* don't even use a washboard." Erin's mum said. "And Erin, it's rude to be on your phone at the dinner table."

"Sorry, mum."

Erin's mum softened her expression. "Are you certain there's no boyfriend? I'm sure you've had lots of offers?"

Ok, from now on, no more checking the phone around the family. "I'm pretty sure, mum," Erin said, noticing her mum's unhappy expression.

"She'll have lots of boys courting her," Gran said, as though Erin never spoke.

On Boxing day, Erin took the two German Shepherds to the grounds around Alnwick castle. A thin layer of snow covered the grass, which the dogs took pleasure rolling around in. The fresh country air lifted her spirits, at least temporarily, until Gia popped back into her head.

She'd had a good friend once, in primary school. Erin and Nancy Turner, aged seven, had been inseparable. She remembered crying for days when her family moved to New Zealand. One day Nancy was at school, the next she was gone, and it had been left to the teacher, Mrs Reed, to break the awful news. Thinking back, Erin wondered what effect that incident had on the rest of her life. What was the point in making friends, if they could vanish without a trace and all for reasons you couldn't understand at the time. She decided it was most probably a contributing factor to her underdeveloped social abilities.

But no, the present situation was nothing like that. Gia had only returned to Italy for Christmas and Erin would be reunited with her in a little over two weeks. If only she'd text to tell Erin how her Christmas was going, how she found her present, how the family were and if she missed Cambridge. All would be well then.

Why had she kissed Gia on the lips? Was *that* the reason she was being ignored? Erin had no idea why she'd done that other than it just felt right at the time. She reasoned that she wanted to show solidarity with Gia and demonstrate that her being a lesbian didn't change anything, that she still thought the world of her, but instead Erin had managed to turn it into easily the most cringe-inducing moment of her life. By acting differently, by kissing her on the lips instead of the cheek like they always did, Erin *had* demonstrated that her being a lesbian *did* change things.

Damnit. What a mess.

Erin whipped out her phone and sent a text, '*Hey, I'm guessing you've been ignoring me because of that awkward moment before you jumped in the taxi. Just wanted to say sorry.*'

Ugh, but how many texts had she sent Gia and all without receiving a single response? Half a dozen perhaps?

As Erin turned in for the night, she grabbed the framed photo from the bedside table and gazed into it. "Damn you, girl, what are you doing to me?"

ERIN PLACED HER HAND BELOW GIA'S KNEE AND LIFTED IT from the table as she slid the foot inwards toward her buttocks.

"Finally. That wasn't too hard, was it, you silly goose." Gia lay back with her hands clasped behind her head, so casual she might have been on the couch watching TV.

"Um, no, I guess not." Erin returned the leg to the straightened position and repeated the manoeuvre several more times. To describe Gia's skin as *smooth* would have been an understatement. Had she just waxed them?

Most of the other students were scratching their heads or making jokes to delay having to touch their course mates. An awkward silence prevailed, broken only by the occasional cough or by the professor's feet as he stepped between physio tables. Gia's knee cracked.

"Somebody needs to loosen up." Erin joked as she increased the range of motion at both Gia's knee and hip joint, bringing the knee fully into her chest.

"And I thank you for that." Gia was watching Erin with focused eyes that were almost unsettling in their intensity. She tilted her head as her eyes narrowed. "Since when did you start wearing makeup to seminars at nine in the morning?"

Erin had indeed risen a few minutes earlier to make time to apply some makeup and all for reasons she wasn't so sure about. "Um, no reason, I guess." She'd also worn her hair down but if Gia noticed that, she made no mention it.

Erin eased the knee into an extended position as the hip joint remained flexed, gauging where the hamstring muscles would become stretched. Her hand remained pressed down on the back of Gia's knee as she pushed it toward her chest. No matter how much Gia's knee straightened, Erin felt no tension. "By God, girl, you are flexible." She rubbed the back of Gia's thigh, expecting to feel resistance in the form of tightening muscles, or some sort of nerve or muscle pulsing. Nothing, and Erin wondered if she was doing it right.

"It was for swimming. Flexibility is important. It helps your range of motion and increases stroke length, which obviously helps propel you through the water." She jerked her chin at Erin's hand. "Keep going, you'll see."

Erin ran her hand further down Gia's leg toward the ankle, keeping the other hand clasped around the knee joint. "Ok, I'll go slow." She pushed down on the ankle and straightened the leg as far as it would go. Erin could swear her fingertips were tingling from the soft sensation of Gia's tanned flesh.

Gia's foot was now shoved back almost behind her head, and all without the slightest sign of discomfort.

"Unbelievable! You're a contortionist."

"Not a contortionist, just very flexible."

Erin took Gia through a range of positions for the legs and upper body, then the professor signalled for everybody to change over. Erin took position lying supine on the table, clasping her hands in front of her solar plexus as Gia surveyed the body in front.

Gia sniggered, "I'm making you nervous? You've just been getting down and intimate with me, girl."

Erin felt the shiver run down her spine. The room was air-conditioned and she wore only cycling shorts and a t-shirt, but still. She was about to have her lesbian best friend's hands run over her bare flesh. "I'm not nervous, it's just the cold." Why was the air-con even switched on in mid-January? But she knew it was a fib and she most certainly did feel apprehension. There was the small matter of the messages Gia had ignored over Christmas and the New Year.

"Sure, but your body and face tell a different story," Gia said as she slid a hand under Erin's knee.

Erin trembled from the sudden warm contact then rolled

her eyes and unclasped her hands, not wanting to make her nerves appear too obvious if she could help it. She didn't know where to put them, so they just hung limp at her sides. As usual, Erin's body language had given her away and Gia had become accustomed to reading her.

Gia manoeuvred Erin's knee toward her chest and returned it to the supine position. She repeated the action several times, pressing firmly against Erin's thigh with one hand. It felt warm against the cold. Gia repeated the same action as Erin had done, straightening the knee joint and feeling the hamstrings for any signs of tension. Erin watched her friend, seemingly engrossed on her anatomy as she pressed fingers against specific areas, searching for tight spots. As Gia eased the leg back further, Erin felt the tightness in her hamstring.

Gia grinned, "and there it goes, gotcha."

"Yeah, I'm feeling that." And probably a bit more. Was it the damn cold or the damn Italian?

Gia rubbed the hamstring, searching for the area with the greatest tightness, then began massaging it with her fingertips.

Wow, even through the discomfort, that kind of felt nice. Erin closed her eyes and concentrated on deep, rhythmical breathing.

Erin didn't see Gia lean close to her ear and whisper, "I got your messages."

"Ouch!" Erin cried as the tension shot through her leg.

Gia leapt backwards, smothering her mouth to save from laughing. "Sorry, sorry, that's my fault." She waved to the professor, who merely shook his head. She took hold of Erin's leg again and eased back into the stretch.

Erin had pushed herself halfway up on one arm, her eyes staring daggers at Gia. "You got my messages?" She whispered with a seething edge. "You got my messages? And you didn't think to reply? Do you have any idea how worried I was? You could have been lying faced down in a ditch for all I knew." She looked about for any sign of eavesdroppers but the other students were far too engrossed in their present uncomfortable predicaments.

"Hey, relax, I only got them last night."

"What?"

"I arrived back in Cambridge last night, switched on my phone and found your messages. Very cute." She grinned wide and genuine at Erin. "I probably should have written down your number though ... my bad."

"What? You mean, you didn't take your phone with you?"

"Of course, not. It's my English phone. I use my Italian phone back home. I should have said, but I was kind of preoccupied with other stuff if you remember."

"Yes, I kind of remember all that." Erin winced as Gia moved forward with the stretch, prompting Erin to lower herself back down into the supine position. All that worry and distress for nothing, a simple misunderstanding. Erin felt like a complete idiot.

"You're a silly goose." Gia's diaphragm began to shake from something she was finding humorous. "You went kind of crazy in those last two, didn't you?"

Oh, God, but she couldn't be referring to the drunken New Year's messages? Erin vaguely recalled sending at least one but couldn't remember the exact content. "Um, remind me."

"A few too many expletives to be repeated by *this* polite Italian lady." Well, at least she smiled, signalling no offence had been caused. "But like I said ... very cute."

"Oh, my God." Erin covered her face. "I can't even look at you."

"Hmm, well, if it makes you feel any better, honey, I feel the exact same way," Gia teased.

Erin slapped the table. "Right, that's it, you'd better show me what's on your bloody phone." Erin exhaled deeply and muttered into her hands. "No more drunken texting for me. What an arse I am."

Even more so considering that in her inebriated and emotional state, she'd deleted all her messages.

❧

"You tidied up?" Erin gawped with amazement at the pristine room. "I mean, you can actually see the floor now." It took all of thirty seconds to walk from the lab to Gia's bedroom and all without having to step outside.

"That's why I never called last night, I was busy with all this..." she gestured about the room, "it took hours. And just continue with your cheek if you never want to see those messages."

"I'm sorry, I'll be good." Erin stood bolt upright as if standing to attention while she watched Gia plucking the phone from the top drawer. "But, only hours? Are you sure? I'd have thought it'd take a decontamination crew a full week to clean that mess."

"Right, missy, that's it." Gia grinned and slipped the phone inside the pocket of her cycling shorts. "You've really overstepped the boundaries this time. Where's that mute girl I grew to love?"

Why did Erin have to goad the girl? She'd known it would result in some kind of a response, a challenge and ultimately having to attempt to take possession of the phone by physical means. The only alternative was backing down and damn it, she needed to know what she'd written in her drunken stupor.

And there Gia stood, a couple of metres away, arms folded across her ribcage, a defensive posture that begged to be challenged, breasts stretching her pink t-shirt, legs exposing ample flesh, long and slender, leading up to those cycling shorts and the phone-sized bulge protruding so temptingly from the material.

Why would she do this, unless she wanted Erin to try and take it?

Erin swallowed, "you know I need to see what I wrote you, right?" She prayed Gia would succumb to reason and give her the bloody phone so she could see the damn messages. Yet at the same time, for some reason she couldn't even begin to fathom, Erin also felt the desire, the need to be closer to this girl, this beautiful Italian girl who'd been in her thoughts one way or another for the entire holiday period.

"Of course, I can see how badly you want it." She stood on her toes and twisted around ninety degrees, bringing the phone that little bit closer and tempting Erin to make a move.

Instead, Erin found herself gazing at Gia's buttocks, pert and high in those black shorts. Was Gia doing this deliberately? Was she trying to provoke some sort of a reaction from Erin? "Please, Gia, don't make me do this. You know I can take you." It was a lie, she knew and so too knew her thumping heart but joking was by far the best method of defusing the tension.

"How badly do you want it?" She hissed more than spoke, almost like she was trying to be seductive, but what would Erin know about that? Was she still even talking about the phone? And, God, those eyes, big and brown, with pupils dilated, which transfixed anyone who stared into them, like Medusa, but instead of turning to stone, Erin felt her legs turning to jelly.

"Gia, um..."

"...I'm just messing with you." She delved inside her pocket and tugged out the phone, tossing it to Erin, who somehow managed to catch it despite being in a trance. "There you go, enjoy. I'm off to take a shower." She pattered away and closed the en-suite door behind her.

For a while, Erin remained still.

What the heck was that?

Feeling light-headed, she sat on the bed.

That situation had so very nearly escalated, in fact, she'd been seconds away from initiating a play fight and all to get ahold of the phone, which could only have meant half-molesting the girl in the process. Would she really have gone through with *that*? Deep down and in the moment, Erin had *wanted* to touch her. Erin had wanted to feel closer to Gia and she couldn't understand why.

Her hand shook as she scrolled through the inbox, there were more messages than she remembered sending.

The final text read, '*You are being very mean by ignoring me but I want you to know, I forgive you. You are my best friend in the whole world, I think about you all the time and I love you to bits. Happy new year xxxxxx.*'

Oh, crap.

Chapter Six

BECOMING

I n the passenger seat of Ben's Peugeot hatchback, Erin had been asleep most of the journey back. She hated that car and found sleeping in the thing impossible, which was why Ben was surprised that despite the amount of alcohol she'd consumed at the engagement party, she'd propped her head in the gap between the headrest and window and fallen asleep. When he saw this, he'd pulled over to remove his jacket and positioned it beneath her head before resuming the journey home.

With an arm draped over Ben's shoulders, he carried Erin into the house. At the foot of the stairs, he unpropped her arm and cradled her in his arms. He took a breath and braced for the journey upwards.

"Oh, hi, you." She sighed and began stroking his face while he struggled up the steps. "How'd we get here?" She nodded off again.

"Sshhhhh, I've got you, my beautiful fiancée." He gazed into her face, so peaceful, graceful, delicate, perfect. He loved her more than life itself. Everything he did was for Erin and now he would spend the rest of his life with her.

He'd spent weeks preparing the perfect proposal. And it *had* been perfect. He almost couldn't believe he'd pulled it off without anything going wrong, although Stewart had been a close call. Even Erin's cousin had not given the game away, though Ben had been careful only to let her in on the plan at the last possible moment. Louise was nothing like her cousin in that regard. Where Louise was mouthy, materialistic and shallow, Erin was contemplative, spiritual and layered. Even now he was still figuring her out and he doubted he'd ever know her fully, and that, Ben thought, was a good thing.

Ben had taken note of the quantity of alcohol Erin had taken throughout the evening and had even been alarmed by it. In the ten years he'd known her, he'd never once seen her drink so much but he could forgive all that because, after all, she'd just agreed to be his wife and it was only once that you became engaged to be married.

Still, Ben couldn't help but feel jilted, which was perhaps putting it mildly. They hadn't had sex in weeks, ever since Erin had caught the flu, and he'd hoped that tonight, of all nights, he could have shown her just how much she meant to him. One more night of celibacy, even if an important night, hardly mattered in the grand scheme of things. Although he missed being physical with Erin, he loved her regardless and was more than willing to wait for this blip, whatever Erin was battling with, to resolve itself. They'd had their problems in the past. This was merely another hurdle to cross. They'd get over it together and that could only make them stronger.

She roused as Ben's foot struck the second flight of stairs, her long red hair flowed over his arms. She was so beautiful. He'd loved her since the moment he first saw her and now he could scarcely believe they'd be together forever.

She muttered something unintelligible, followed by a sweet high-pitched sigh. "Where are you? Gi ... where are you?"

"Shush, my dear. I'm right here. Go to sleep."

"SIXTEEN SECONDS, ERIN. SIXTEEN SECONDS! KISS GOODBYE to Fairbairns." She was referring to the May competition where boats from all seventeen colleges would be competing along the Cam. As always, there wasn't a great deal expected from Downing with its purple colours and moon-touched president. Even their boathouse was built on rancid foundations, which Gia repeatedly joked would prove a pertinent metaphor. At least, Erin assumed she was joking though truthfully, it was hard to tell.

"We can reasonably expect to finish in the top three or four if we can knock ten seconds off that." Erin heaved herself out from the double scull and onto the gravel path. "Though there's no shame in finishing somewhere in the middle, Geoff would still be pleased with that." She watched as Gia pulled herself out, catching a sneaky glimpse, as she always did, down her top.

The weather was improving now, which meant Gia had switched from her usual fully clad sportswear to shorts and t-shirt. The Italian had finally accustomed to the English weather, even though she still complained about it, but for Erin, it was proving more and more torturous by the day, especially as the mornings became warmer, the quantity of sweat Gia produced increased and ever more layers were discarded. The other day she'd trained in only her sports bra and poor Erin had delivered such a terrible performance that the damn Italian had made her wrath known.

"Top three or four? Top three or four? Somewhere in the *middle*?" Gia sounded aghast and scowled at Erin, an expression that hurt. "Is that why we do this every day, Erin? To finish with the losers?" She threw her oars onto the grass.

"Sixteen seconds from last year's winners ... that's a fucking mountain. How long till Fairbairns?" She approached the double scull and bent over, grabbing the rear handles.

Erin stood, as she always did, at least for a couple of precious stolen seconds. But by God, Gia was shapely. Erin neared the front handles, crouched and together they heaved the boat from the water. "Six weeks," she confirmed, almost as an admission of defeat. She wanted to win Fairbairns as much for Gia as for herself. They'd both put months of early morning training sessions into this thing.

"Well, there's always next year." Gia dismissed as they carried the boat above their heads back to Downing Boathouse. The one problem with that plan was that the advanced team finishing times were far superior to that of the novices; sixteen seconds would become twenty-four next year. Maybe the year after that...

Ahead, another double scull was blocking the path, Erin could see because it was lying horizontally across the ground. There were also two pairs of feet with their accompanying white legs along with black and maroon striped shorts, some other boat club, though, above that, her view was impeded owing to having her head inserted inside the boat's seat cavity. They stopped and Erin heard Gia grunt with irritation.

"Girls, we finally meet again." Came the invisible Scottish accent. "And this time you can't run." Two men laughed.

They brought their heads out from the boat together and placed the bulk of the scull's weight upon their shoulders, a position that could not be held for long. Two men, each holding a pair of long oars, with grins even longer, if that was possible, were standing behind the boat, arms folded. Erin recognised them from her first day at college, though she couldn't remember their names. She'd seen them a couple of times since on the river but had never spoken to either.

"Now's not a good time," Gia spoke for them both. "In fact, there'll never be a good time."

"Hey come on. If we can let bygones be bygones then surely you can too?" The one who Erin remembered could disjoint his wrist said. What's more, he was now holding his hand out to Gia. "Friends?"

Gia laughed and lowered her end of the boat to the ground, prompting Erin to do likewise. "You must think I have a short memory."

"You're right," he retracted his hand, "and because your memory's so great, you'll recall, the two of you owe us a date." He smiled a cheeky grin. One had to admire his confidence and sheer brazenness. "One minute ... was the amount of time you said we had to maintain that hold. Well, I'm here to tell you we kept our side of the bargain, and considerably more besides."

Gia leaned forward squinting. "I'm sorry, what did you say? I'm having trouble understanding you."

Erin knew she should probably interject and say something but Gia was still way better at dealing with these things than she was. Besides, it wasn't like she was suddenly into men and would go along with this whole date idea, unless her sense of honour was so strong that it overcame her sexuality, which was doubtful. Either way, surely any impartial judge would consider any deal made in a pub many months ago to be null and void.

"We were watching you on the river." The less hairy of the two spoke, "I don't know if you noticed," he pointed sarcastically to the ten and a half metre long lump at his feet, "but we happen to know a thing or two about the double scull."

Gia's expression softened slightly from the scowl she'd held since disembarking, to a mere pout. "And?"

"Girls, you're talking to last year's Fairbairns' winners."

The tidy one gestured between himself and his comrade, and Erin still couldn't tell whether or not they were twins, just brothers or not related at all.

"You won Fairbairns?" Erin squeaked.

"Aye." The unkempt one confirmed with a proud grin. "You both have great stamina and we can see how much effort you put into your training ... but your technique could do with some fixes."

"Really? And you two nice fellows just happen to want to help us out?" Gia asked sarcastically as she crouched to grab the boat handles again. "And all out of the kindness of your hearts?"

"Look, I think the four of us really need to start again. I'm Scruffy, this is my twin brother Mikey. We row for different colleges but in the same category, which should make us enemies as far as things go around here but we'd really like to help you out because you clearly have potential."

"I'm sure you've noticed but in Cambridge, rowing is serious business," Mikey added, "plus you proved your worth back in September. I'll never forget that day. Let's get changed and meet at The Baron of Beef and we'll take you through how you can improve and maybe, just maybe win at Fairbairns." He saw the sceptical, squinted eyed look Gia was still giving him. He showed his opened palms. "It's not a *date*. We genuinely want to help."

"Sixteen seconds," Erin muttered under her breath.

Gia sighed, "fine, but no funny stuff."

"It wasn't an easy thing to overcome." Scruffy shifted in his seat and shielded his eyes from the spot that had become infamous from when two female freshers had embarrassed two second-year males with a pair of pool cues.

"We still get called names and the other week a group of students wanted their pictures taken with us on the same spot." He smirked, thankfully seeing the funny side. "The landlord is thinking about mounting a plaque in commemoration."

"You have to admit, you both deserved it," Gia remarked, taking a sip of beer. "Though we had to return and apologise."

"We had a message on Hermes saying we'd be disciplined if we didn't come back." Erin referred to Cambridge's internal email system. "Obviously, someone recognised us and didn't take too kindly to the prank."

"Aye, yeah, we did deserve it," Mikey flapped a hand, "but we're still living the damn thing down. Never mind. We know not to cross you two again." He clinked glasses with Erin and took a large gulp.

"So, you really won the Fairbairns' trophy in your freshman year?" Gia asked. "Tell us your secrets."

"The most important thing you already do." Scruffy leaned back in his seat and gesticulated freely with a hand. "You get up early every day and make it to the river, no matter the weather. You put in the hours ... that's the most important thing. Conditioning yourself."

"But it's the little things, and there are many of them, that make all the difference in the world." Mikey looked at Gia as though she was the most beautiful woman on earth. If Erin was being truthful, it bothered her and it bothered her a great deal. Mikey's enlarged pupils, his body language that mirrored Gia's and the constantly stolen glances whenever he could get away with it all spoke of his infatuation.

"How can you tell if you're not out there on the boat with us?" Erin asked, trying to take Mikey's eyes away from Gia's chest and exposed arm flesh, if only for a few seconds.

"We don't need to be out there when we can watch from Corpus Christi Boathouse," Scruffy said, "and, speaking from an engineering and bio-mechanical point of view, there are certain small tweaks you should be taking advantage of." He sniggered to himself. "They obviously don't teach this at Downing, which explains a few things."

"Yeah, all right," Gia waved a hand in defeat, "they can't even rid Downing of the sewer stench, so what's your advice?"

"First, you need to switch positions." Scruffy pointed to Erin. "You're slightly less powerful than your Spanish friend, so you need to let her sit at stern and set the rhythm."

Oh great, so now Erin would be staring into Gia's back the whole time, trying not to drool over her rear end as it slid to-and-fro along the track. Distraction much?

"Your oars will have fractionally less resistance and that one thing alone will knock a couple seconds off your finishing time and I promise, you'll notice the difference right away." Scruffy took a sip from his beer. "We noticed your oars weren't leather patched."

"Leather patched?" Erin asked. "Is that to stop that awful rattling noise?"

Mikey laughed, "not just the noise but because your oars are moving around within the locks, you're wasting energy, which means you're having to make compensating corrections each and every time you make a stroke. Again, it's minute, but it adds up."

Over the next hour; Mikey and Scruffy took Erin and Gia through a range of techniques, strategies and tips, some of which might have been interpreted as borderline cheating if only everybody 'in the know' wasn't already doing it. The standard foot straps were made to a one-size-fits-all, causing smaller feet, typically found on women, to move about due to the slack, thus wasting more energy. The advice was to punch in more holes to tighten the hold around the feet. Erin thought she saw a light bulb turn on above Gia's head when she heard that one. They were also advised to clean the underside of the boat before taking it out onto the Cam. "Leaves and all the other crap that gathers underneath will only create more drag."

They saved the best, most obvious, yet most underutilised tip for the end. "It never fails to amaze us," Mikey began as Erin and Gia leaned forward, "nobody *ever* warms up! I'm sure you've experienced how it feels to be completely knackered after only a few minutes of work? That's because you didn't warm up. Your cardiovascular system needs time to gradually build-up to full working capacity, just like a motor in any vehicle in the world. If you go all-out, full pelt straight away, then obviously, you'll fatigue quickly. But if you warm up before getting in the scull then you can go hell for leather from the starting pistol and maintain the same rhythm the entire race."

Erin and Gia turned to face each other, the realisation hitting them together. "On race day we jog on the spot before entering the scull, right, babe?" Gia said.

"Aye," Mikey winked, "while the rest just stand around freezing their bollocks off."

By the end, both girls were itching to get back on the water.

"Tomorrow, six in the morning, let's see what difference all this makes." Gia glanced from Erin to Scruffy. "Thank you. But I'm Italian, not Spanish."

"My apologies," Scruffy held up his hands in a gesture of mock surrender.

"I know I promised I wouldn't. But with you sitting here, so close, I just can't resist." Mikey brought out his phone and placed it in front of Gia. "May I have your number?"

Erin straightened against her seat and took a sudden interest in her own phone. Gia was into girls; she liked boobs, smooth and hairless skin as well as the sweet smells that accompanied *girls*. Surely, she wasn't about to give Mikey her number. Please, please, please, God, no. She wouldn't do that, would she? Erin couldn't stand the thought of a hot, charismatic athlete's naked body writhing on top of her friend. It wasn't just that it would feel almost like a betrayal; Gia, after all, had come out to Erin during a moment when they'd both really connected. It was just as much that Erin was still coming to terms with her own feelings for her best *friend*. She hadn't admitted them to herself yet, simply because she didn't know.

"Hey, didn't you say we were going to revise for the practical this evening?" Erin tugged on Gia's arm, trying to distract her from the two men. She could thank her later. "We'd better get a move on."

"What's the rush?" Gia resisted the pull and with a fleeting glance at Erin, turned back to Mikey before taking his phone from the table. "I don't give this to just anybody, you know."

His face lit up, even though he tried not to show it.

Even his brother seemed impressed, surprised even. "Looks like I owe you five quid." Scruffy slid a fiver across the tabletop.

"Cheers."

"What's that for?" Erin asked, unsure whether or not to be angry.

Scruffy hesitated, "it's just that I thought Gia was, you know..." his body jerked and Erin could have sworn Mikey had kicked him beneath the table.

Gia gave Mikey back his phone. "Best you call after this week though. Like she said, we have a practical examination on Friday."

Scruffy held a clenched fist to his mouth and coughed. After waiting a few seconds, and Erin still hadn't taken the hint, he coughed again.

"Give me your bloody phone," Erin said, holding out her

hand before punching in her number while trying to see what, if any, reaction Gia made.

The Italian was indeed watching Erin with what might be described as a faux smile. "You know what, Mikey, on second thoughts, ring me Saturday."

"Look what I did." Gia made a drumbeat on the makeshift treatment table she'd obviously spent at least twenty minutes cobbling together. Bless her, she looked so proud of herself.

"Wow, Gia, I'm really not sure what to make of it." Erin stared with uncertainty at the desk that had been pulled away from the wall. On the surface, a layer of cushions that had to have come from the common room couch overlapped the edges on all sides, but that was ok because Gia's chair was propping up one end, whilst her suitcase, tipped on its side, held up another. Over everything, she'd draped a blanket. It was almost enough to disguise the obvious health hazard. "I suppose it'll do, I think."

"It'll do? I'd like to see how anyone else has bettered this." She skipped around the thing to press a button on the CD player, a second later nice soothing sounds began playing through the speakers.

After a short while, it sounded familiar. "What is this?"

"You mean, you've never heard it?"

"No, I mean, I have, it's definitely very famous but who is it?"

"Vivaldi." She closed her eyes and gently swayed her head as the violin came to the fore. "This particular piece is Four Seasons." She gracefully glided toward the treatment table and gestured for Erin to climb aboard. "Lie back, relax and enjoy because it lasts for a while."

Erin stared at it whilst contemplating the least hazardous way of mounting the thing. Eventually, she just hopped up and tried to relax as the desk creaked.

Gia brought over a book at an opened page and set it down on the desk beside Erin's knee. "Comfy?"

"As much as possible."

Gia rolled up the cuffs of Erin's shorts, sliding them up as far as they could go. Her leg let out an involuntary jerk as cold fingers grazed the inside of her thigh, followed by a shiver when Gia applied a few drops of oil to the area.

"Quadriceps tendonitis..." Gia slipped her hand beneath Erin's knee and pressed softly as she used her fingers to feel just above the joint for the tendon. Then she began massaging across the fibres with her fingertips. "I'm not hurting you, am I?"

"No, you can go as deep as you like." Erin lay back, closed her eyes and listened to Vivaldi, concentrating on the feeling of Gia's fingers pressing, stretching and massaging the tendon as well as the muscle positioned above. There was nothing sexual in it, but it was still a thrilling experience. Erin's knee was lifted off the table and then she felt what had to be Gia's own knee below it, propping her own up. The tendon was pinched hard as Gia flexed Erin's knee. "Hmmm." Erin hummed a little too loud as the tendon stretched enough for her to feel it. Four Seasons changed rhythm, which had to mean it had gone into summer, or was it autumn? It didn't matter. The highs, the lows, the emotion of classical Europa at its most beautiful filled Erin's world. And Gia's touch.

A solitary tear ran down Erin's cheek.

She knew it.

She'd suspected it for a long while but now she was sure. She was in love with Gia. She felt safe around her, comfortable and free. What's more, she felt alive in her presence, like Gia was the very air she needed to survive. A year ago, Erin could never have imagined she'd be as close to another person as she was with Gia. She wasn't simply the best friend a girl could ever hope to have, she helped Erin breathe.

Gia's phone vibrated and she dashed away from the table, jolting Erin back into reality. She turned the music down so Erin could hear what it was. "A text from Mikey ... God, he's keen. He says, he'd like to meet Saturday night."

Erin sighed and turned away to wipe the tear from her cheek. As she dropped her feet to the floor, she felt the slickness that had developed between her legs. There was no mistaking that or what it meant.

Gia fired off a reply, threw the phone to the bed, turned the music back on and returned to the table. "Your turn, babe, you'll find the muscle becomes more pliant after a few minutes. Damn this bloody cold." Gia took her position, lying back on the table and closed her eyes, losing herself in Vivaldi.

Erin took a moment to collect herself before she rolled up the cuffs of Gia's shorts, exposing her thighs, long, smooth, toned and Italian browned.

But damn it, what was the damn Italian playing at with Mikey? Erin would need to have *the* conversation with Gia. And soon.

The problem was that Erin did not know if she possessed the courage needed.

How much could a person grow in one year?

Chapter Seven

DECISION

E rin took a small sip from her beer and checked her watch. The Snug Bar was situated depressingly close to Downing, but it was either here or The Baron of Beef, which Erin had not been inside since Gianna's vanishing act and according to Scruffy, neither had he since his brother's death.

"Hurry up, you loser," Erin muttered to herself just as her tall, apparently ironically named friend opened the door and began scanning the clientele. She raised a hand and he came bounding over.

"Sorry I'm late, can I get you a..." he saw Erin already had a drink and stopped, "never mind."

She stood and they hugged before taking their seats. Scruffy removed his jacket, slung it over the back of the chair and snapped his fingers at a young barman who happened to be passing.

"Um, Scruff, I don't think they do table service here."

"Nah, it'll be fine," he winked then turned around to meet the eye of the barman. "Evening, I'm Chief Running Tab.

Keep stopping by this table every fifteen or twenty minutes and I'll make it worth your while."

"No problem, sir, can I get you anything to drink?"

Scruffy nodded in the direction of four girls sat two tables away. "How about something to make that lot look more appealing."

Erin buried her head in her hands and gave serious consideration to kicking him beneath the table. "Just get him one of these." She raised her Corona to the barman. "It never gets easier does it." She said to him as the barman walked away, realising the meaning of her words were ambiguous.

"Are you talking about your present situation or being in my company?"

She smiled, he got it. "Both."

"It's been a while since we've done this. You're normally too entrenched in your work to bother with your old university mates. So tell me ... if I couldn't already have guessed by your overall demeanour on your happy day," Scruffy said, referring to the engagement party, "but there's clearly something wrong. You're not happy, are you?"

"I know, it's been a while," she shrugged, "and I can only apologise but you're in my thoughts, believe it or not." Erin paused and waited for the barman to place Scruffy's drink down and walk away. "So how's work?"

"You're avoiding my question."

"I'm postponing answering your question." She'd thought through what she wanted to get off her chest and how she wanted to say it but didn't think she'd had anywhere near enough to drink yet. "How's work?"

He exhaled and took a sip from his beer. "Bloody politics always gets in the way. We could come up with the best wind turbine design on earth but if the government already has contracts with some other company then we can kiss everything goodbye. Everybody suffers then. We have people looking into whether certain bastard government ministers have shares where they shouldn't. Not that they'd be *that* stupid but you'd be surprised. More likely some distant uncle has a few thousand bought, which of course makes it a lot harder to nail the fuckers ... or some old school friend," air escaped his mouth and Erin sensed his frustration. "Best not get me started." He took a long pull from his beer. "I mean, every time you drive by the bloody things, they're never working, no matter the wind."

"I agree with you." Erin sat back, happy to listen, happy to delay.

During the next hour and three drinks each, they spoke about work, Scruffy's bachelor status and Cambridge's rank in the elite universities of the world; that since the days when they were students, Cambridge had improved in the Quacquarelli Symonds World University Rankings. "We're still lagging behind Harvard but at least we're ahead of bloody Oxford, even if they did beat us in the bloody Boat Race this year." That, however, depended entirely on which ranking system you looked at. Sure enough, some even scored Oxford ahead of Cambridge. To that, they both agreed those ranking systems should be ignored, since whoever put those lists together had obviously been to Oxford. "Or more likely he has no education at all."

The topic eventually switched to Erin's recent engagement party. "How did he find you?" She'd been trying to figure that one out ever since the event.

Scruffy shrugged, "he emailed and when I didn't respond, he phoned."

"No, but I mean, how? How did he know about *you*?" Given that she hardly ever spoke of anything that connected her life to Gianna.

"I don't know. I mean, he's *your* fiancé ... he's supposed to know you, isn't he? Maybe he went back a few years on your Facebook profile. No, wait, you're not even on it, are you. Erin, when are you going to join 2014? Anyway, where there's a will, there's a way. But it was a pleasure to be a part of it. He's a lovely guy. I'll just always regret never having had my own wicked way with you." At least the alcohol was finally kicking in. It was needed.

Erin's eyes glazed over. "He is ... he is a lovely guy."

"And there it goes again! You keep doing that look." He sat forward, wanting her to take notice.

"What look? What do you mean?"

"It's nothing short of a *guilty* expression. Like you're thinking of something else." He took a long drink from his beer. "Or someone else. And I have a feeling I know who it is." He paused, gaging Erin's reaction, which had remained as indifferent as she could force. "So, since you're on the verge of destroying the lives of two people, one of whom I happen to care deeply about, I think you'd better tell me everything that's on your mind. And no more stalling."

Erin exhaled deeply. "Well, I think you're right when you say you '*know who it is*.' Who else could it be?" She braced herself for her upcoming admission.

"She made an impression on all of us, not least of all Mikey."

"Scruffy, I just don't know what to do. It's been *ten* years. Why is she still in my thoughts? She doesn't deserve to be in my thoughts. Not like this. Not now when I should be settling down with Ben. But I just can't get her out of my head. Ever since that fucking poem..." her voice cracked and was thankful for the brief respite when Scruffy interrupted her.

"Poem? I never had you down as a poet."

"I'm not really. It was pretty bad, but it was truthful."

"Read it to me."

"No way. I think considering the mess I'm in, I could do without anybody seeing *that*." She noticed how her hand was trembling around the beer bottle as she brought it to her mouth. "That damn Italian."

He leaned forward, then back again. "Did you ever find out what happened to her?"

"Only what we knew when she left."

"And you've done no further research? You've not tried contacting her?"

"I put her out of my mind for many years. That was the whole reason for writing the poem, for some closure. I just never banked on it fluttering back into existence."

"Fluttering?"

"Never mind. Of course, back then, with the internet in its infancy, social media not existing; stalking a girl from a different country just wasn't that easy."

"But you've looked now?"

"I haven't been able to bring myself to do it." What if she was still so insanely attractive and Erin was stuck at the other end of the continent unable to do a thing about it?

"So you don't even know what her present situation is?"

"Or if she's even alive. For all I know she's married with kids."

"Or maybe she's dreadfully unhappy and waiting for that perfect person to walk back into her life. That's if you can find her." He pointed at Erin to add emphasis to his next point. "That's if you *want* to find her? The fact we're even here now suggests to me you've been giving this some serious thought, or at least I hope you have."

"Thought?" Erin unleashed an uncharacteristically loud cackle. "I haven't been able to think of anything but. Poor Ben, I've never lied to him but I've been, let's say, *economical* with the truth lately. No, wait, I did lie about being ill." She ran a hand through her hair. "Ugh, this is all such a mess."

"Like I said, he's a good man and he too deserves to be happy. But I don't see how *you*, in your present state of mind can settle down and be happy with him. You'll only end up making you both miserable."

"I know. I can't in all good conscience marry Ben with such a large and unresolved hole in my life."

Scruffy paused, allowing the gravity of what Erin had just said to sink in; not just in his head, but hers. "So you really have thought this through then. I'm guessing you must have felt under pressure to accept his proposal because of the grand gesture and everybody being there?"

Erin breathed, "if only he'd proposed a year earlier. Things could have been different."

"Aye, maybe. Or perhaps all this would have remained festering beneath the surface." He took another sip from his drink and hardened his expression. "What if nothing comes of this? What if you do find her and she's fat, ugly or has been taken prisoner in some Italian convent and she's living out her life as a nun. Then could you still marry Ben and be happy? Would it even be fair by him that he's second best?"

"Yes, you're right."

"I'd hate to see you burn all your bridges but you need to also decide if all this is fair on him."

"Of course."

He smiled, "and if you do burn them then I'd be more than happy to pick up the pieces." It was a welcome light joke given the seriousness of the last few minutes. "This question might be a bit simplistic but I have to ask..."

"Go on."

"Are you a lesbian? I mean, do you consider yourself to be a lesbian?"

She hesitated and was about to speak when...

"You see, if you even need to think about that."

Erin sighed. "It was never really as black and white as that. I never put a label on it. I mean, I never used to think of girls ... women in that way. At least not before Gianna. She changed everything for me. It was the *person* I was in love with. And I thought she was in love with me."

"Do people who're in love disappear without saying a word?"

"Not really."

"I'm not trying to put you off, I'm just trying to make you see clearer." He opened out his palms. "She left, never said a bloody word to anybody and nobody over here has any clue as to the reasons."

"Exactly, Scruffy."

"Perhaps there was a family disaster or something."

"Or maybe she realised she wasn't a lesbian." She said monotone. That possibility was a new scenario she'd not before even considered, Scruffy was doing too good a job at making her see this from new angles. "Maybe ... after ... maybe she felt pressured by me ... about..." she couldn't continue down that path, the hurt, that all along she'd meant nothing to Gianna, or worse, that after they'd ... she'd been disgusted by...

Scruffy laughed. "Yeah, or maybe Mount Vesuvius erupted and buried Napoli under twenty metres of ash." His certainty as to Gianna's lesbianism came as a comfort, which in itself said an awful lot to Erin. Still, she wanted clarification.

"You truly believe she was a lesbian?"

"Twenty metres of fucking ash!"

"Hey, don't laugh, that actually happened."

"Oh, I'm fully aware of Pompeii."

Erin hesitated. "Can I ask you something?"

He grabbed his beer and found it empty. "You want to ask about Mikey?"

Erin smiled sadly and softened her eyes. "Do you think Gianna leaving had anything to do with what he did?"

"No!" He didn't even need to think about it, which came as a great relief. "Mikey had his problems, always had, but the damn Italian was not one of them." He mirrored Erin's forlorn smile. "To give the man credit, he lived a full life without any regrets. If Mikey had your problem, there's no question about what he'd do. He wouldn't live another second not knowing what could have been." He stared into his opened hands. "I only wish I could emulate him in that regard."

"So you're saying I should find her?"

"It can only be your call. I'm saying Mikey wouldn't have lived with not knowing. But there's one thing you can be one hundred percent sure of..."

"What's that?"

"Any one of us could die tomorrow." Scruffy tilted his head and straightened when he saw the tears pouring from Erin's eyes.

"I have to find her," she sniffed, wiping at her face with a sleeve.

Scruffy shuffled uncomfortably. "Good God, girl, not this." The barman walked by and Scruffy placed a hand on his arm to stop him. "What does the tab come to, mate?"

"Eighteen pounds, sir."

Scruffy delved into his wallet, pulled out some notes and placed them in his palm as he went to shake the barman's hand. "Keep the change."

Erin's eyes widened as she braced...

THE CREWS LOOSENED THEIR BODIES, MOBILISED SHOULDER joints, stretched quads, psyched themselves with private rituals, or else shivered in the afternoon breeze. Erin had done all that several times already.

She glanced down the starting platform and regretted it instantly. "Why the fuck is there a crew from Oxford?" She cried out to nobody in particular, glaring at the two impossibly tall girls wearing the distinctive all-black colours of their rival educational institution, like black was supposed to be intimidating. Erin stared in amazement at their muscular physiques and then with distraction as they underwent some bizarre pre-race ritual that involved slapping each others' shoulders in fast rhythm. Clearly, it was all designed to terrorise their competitors. Even the name of their college, emblazoned on the black sounded wicked, "Oxford Wolfson?"

"Erin, it's not like you to swear," Gia said, taking a break from her on the spot jogging, jaw almost hitting the floor. She rubbed Erin's arm in an attempt to calm her nerves. "Ignore them, let's just concentrate on our own performance, that's the only thing we have control over."

"Yeah, I know that, but still … Oxford shouldn't be here." She had enough trouble with the thought of racing the six other Cambridge boats, all of whom had the fastest qualifying times to make the final, one of whom they'd earlier trailed by nearly two whole seconds in the semis. That Downing had mistakenly made it this far had surprised quite a few people already and just as Erin dared hope they had an outside shot of at least winning silver, two wolves materialise as if from thin air. That they were here now, for the final, could only mean they'd been granted automatic qualification and Erin made a mental note to endeavour to discover just who was responsible for such an outrageous decision. A complaint would be submitted Monday morning. By now, some of the other crews had noticed too, and word passed down the line that the two wolves had won the Oxford equivalent of Fairbairns', the Christ Church Regatta, only the other week and had thus come to pit themselves against whatever Cambridge had to offer. All in the interest of friendly relations between the two, you understand.

Using their passes, Scruffy and Mikey had come to see them on the starting platform that had been erected over the river outside of the Jesus College Boathouse, who every year hosted the Fairbairn Cup. Erin and Gia had drawn lane four and now, with all eight boats in position, it was time for Scruffy and Mikey to make the near two-mile bike ride downstream to the finish line. They'd been helpful in carrying the boat into position and just as helpful in scrubbing its underside before applying their magic leather patches to the oars. They were a loan and good luck gesture.

Mikey pecked Gia on the cheek, "see you both at the finish line," and waved without looking back as the entire platform lumbered from his shifting weight.

Erin stopped her on the spot jogging. "What the heck was that?" Her words came out a little louder than intended and the Oxford crew, all the way down in lane one, gave her a funny look. But more to the bloody point, were they pecking now? Was this yet one more new development in the ever-changing tale of Gia's sexuality? More shit to adjust to and she'd still not come to terms with them having had their second date a few nights back.

"What the heck was what?" Gia asked, checking her descent into the boat as her long tanned leg strained to steady herself.

Um, let's see, you're a lesbian but boys are smooching with your cheek. "Mikey kissed you?"

"Um, yeah, so what? He kissed you too."

"No, he didn't!"

"Oh, but his brother did."

"Um, hello, no he didn't!" And Erin thought *she* was the one who'd been distracted by everything.

"What do you care, Erin?" Gia stood and faced her, peaches winning out over the fishy river smell. "How'd your date with Scruffy go the other night? Huh? You want to talk about that?" The same night, coincidentally, that Mikey and Gia had been feeding the ducks along the Cam, Erin and Scruffy had gone bird watching along the same said river.

"He showed me a Kingfisher nest. How'd yours go?" Erin asked, half turning her head, but maintaining full concentration.

"To be honest, Erin, that's none of your business." She half manhandled Erin aside in an attempt to enter the boat, her touch sending a shiver down Erin's spine, but then she stopped, irritated. "You, Erin! You enter first. You're behind me!"

Erin scanned across the other lanes and saw that everybody else was already in position. "Shit!" Almost slipping, she quickly embarked, taking her seat and fastening the straps extra tight using the new punch holes Scruffy had skewered into them using a nail. But by God, Gia was frustrating her right now. But *this* was the time to focus.

Gia secured herself in position and twisted around. "This is it, babe." Despite everything, she still managed to give Erin a smile and nearly melted her heart as she did.

Seven months of intense training all came down to this moment. Their bodies had undergone almost unbelievable changes. Erin had dropped five percent of her body fat and could now see her abdominals. Erin had noticed, many times, how Gia's calf muscles had started to pop when she wore heels. They were both highly conditioned and physically prepared. However, when it came to the all-important *mental* preparation, that was a different matter entirely. This would be their first proper competitive final and Erin had never experienced pressure like it. Against better sense, she glanced at the other boats and there was barely a girl competing that could not be described as extremely athletic, Amazonian, even, particularly those black-clad Goddesses in the Oxford boat in the end lane. She scrutinised them a second longer than the others as they whispered tactics.

Was nobody else nervous, edgy, panicking, about to throw up? Or was Erin the only one?

Then something unthinkable happened.

Erin's periphery vision disappeared into a haze of darkness. No. Not now! Please God, not now. She wanted, needed to do this for Gia, her friend who she loved. Her hands quivered around the oar handles, the leather patches doing their job in preventing the rattling that would otherwise give her away, her foot straps carrying out an identical job below. Her heart beat in her throat, the feeling of drowning almost preventing her from breathing. Then the haze crept into her frontal vision so that all she could see was Gia's back, in front of her.

"Gia, it's happening," Erin stammered, "I can't see very well."

She twisted around, wide-eyed. "What? Oh, my God, you're shaking."

"Two-minute warning." A voice echoed over the intercom system.

"I'm not sure I can do this. I'm going to let you down real bad, I can feel it."

"Come here." Gia wrapped Erin in her arms as much as the restrictions of her position would allow before speaking low enough so nobody else could hear. "I'm so proud of you for getting this far, honey, it makes no difference what happens today. No matter where we finish, I'm here with you, and we're doing this together. We win or lose together."

"Yes ... together."

"Ignore everybody else. It's you and me, alone. Just another training session on the river. The two of us, quiet, in a boat, doing what we love." She pulled away to look her in the eye. "With *who* we love."

"One-minute warning. All crews, standby."

Erin blinked, the fog in her immediate vision had succumbed, leaving only a grey cloud enveloping everything that wasn't the two of them in their boat. Erin kissed Gia on the cheek. "I think I'll be fine. Let's do our best." She released Gia and watched as she turned back to face the front. Her beautiful, lush tanned back would be what Erin would concentrate on. That and her stroke rhythm.

"Crews ready..." the starting cannon blasted and the girls were out of the blocks.

Nothing outside of her narrow field of vision existed. Her smell was limited to the fishy odour that drifted up from the river, mixed with her own sweat. All she heard were the rhythmical splashes of blades striking water, interspersed by Gia's grunts with every heave of the oars. The heavy drag of pulling blades through water was all she could feel, making her muscles ache. The taste of sweat on her lips as it ran down her forehead. Above all, she concentrated on the sight of Gia, her rhythm and pace as she drove the sculls through the river, the muscles in her back as they worked against the resistance, her pert buttocks as they slid to-and-fro on the seat.

Somewhere above, the clouds parted to reveal blue sky. Almost immediately, Erin's field of vision grew wider. To the right, three boats inched further away as Erin and Gia established a gap. To the left ... Oxford ... neck and neck, though the view of them was partially blocked by the two boats in between, their screams, audible over the water, was proof to the effort they gave.

But none of that mattered, Erin had to concentrate on herself.

One hundred metres to go.

Her arms and legs, her entire body was on fire as her cardiovascular system struggled to break down the impossibly high build-up of lactic acid that threatened to soon bring a stop to her moving so much as another inch. Just when she thought she could not take one more second of agony and had to collapse where she toiled, they began inching in front, bit by minuscule bit, though in truth it was impossible to know, as Oxford continued seething so close, stubbornly on their flank.

Fifty metres.

One stroke it seemed like they were ahead, the next it didn't. She had to stop, she just had to, she couldn't go on, not even for one more second, the lactic acid had reached her fingertips, her head, the aches, the pain, it was like nothing she'd ever thought possible. Gia was still there, screaming with every agonising pull. Erin concentrated on Gia, the sweat streaming down her back, how was she doing this?

Twenty metres.

Her entire body shook, her legs had no more thrust left, she was spent. Only sheer adrenaline, that and the love she held for Gia pushed her on, just that tiny bit further, no matter the torture. She dared glance left, Oxford were right there with them.

Ten metres.

Erin screamed as she gave everything for the final two pulls.

Something flashed, the photo finish timing system.

Erin had to prise her fingers from around the oars and felt the sting as she did, her palms were raw. Gia collapsed backwards into Erin's lap and opened out her arms. Erin leaned forward to embrace her incredible partner, sweat on sweat, their chests heaving together as they struggled for every breath.

When they sat up, they saw they'd drifted to within a few metres of Oxford. The two black-clad women paddled closer to shake their hands. "Fuck, you two gave us a run. Do you have any idea who won?"

Nobody knew but it was either Cambridge Downing or Oxford Wolfson, nobody would debate that. They all fixed their eyes on the big screen and awaited the replay. Clare and Jesus colleges were only now crossing the line and something must have happened to Trinity along the way because they were nowhere to be seen.

The screen displayed a still from five metres out and then commenced in slow motion. Oh, it was painful to watch.

"Wow, it's close," Gia mumbled, taking Erin's hand and coming to their feet. How could they remain seated at a time like this? "We did our best, babe, so whatever happens, I'm proud of us."

"I know, we couldn't have done any more than that." An understatement.

It truly was close and whoever was operating the software had to zoom on the points of the two boats using a split-screen as they approached the dotted line. One metre out and Erin still couldn't guess who had it and the images had to slow down even further. The frame stopped when the first boat touched the dots.

By the length of a grain of rice, there was a winner.

"Downing." The voice crackled over the speakers.

Elation.

All Erin thought to do was plant a smacker hard on Gia's lips – Sod it – She held Gia's face, pulled her close and kissed her and judging by Gia's bright-eyed expression she wasn't exactly expecting it but neither did she draw back. Erin pulled away, saw Gia's big smile and then finally became aware of the spectator's cheers. It was as though a switch had been flipped and her senses had returned to their full working capacities.

This was what it meant to be alive.

"Are we jumping in?" Gia was giddy beside her.

"Of course," Erin took her hand.

And together they leapt into the Cam.

AFTER WATCHING SCRUFFY AND MIKEY'S EASY VICTORY IN the male double sculls, Erin and Gia had departed for their respective student dwellings. The Fairbairns' Ball would begin in only an hour and Erin still had to get ready.

She didn't know what to expect, other than collecting a medal and hanging out with other rowers, perhaps with a nice spread, lots of alcohol and a few photos. It was everything else that a big fat question mark hung over. Possibly, technically, in all reality, could this potentially be labelled Gia and Mikey's third date? Ugh. Then she realised that possibly, technically, in all reality, this could potentially be *her* third date with Scruffy too.

She knew she really ought to put a stop to it. Scruffy was a dear, adorable man, but to see him naked, Erin most certainly did not have that desire.

No. The one person she wanted to see naked was her best friend, who right now was at home dolling herself up in God only knew what, waiting for her prince and saviour of our Fairbairns to collect her in his carriage and take her to the ball.

Ugh.

Erin slipped on her black backless halter neck dress. It was the one she saved only for very special occasions because she knew it attracted the kind of attention that usually made her uncomfortable, for it clung to her figure, emphasised her curves and pushed up her breasts. Yes, it was a work of brilliance, "and you *will* notice me Gia, lest I doubt your whole bullshit *coming out* story." She was muttering to herself now, a new development, while pinning up her hair, exposing a long neck and delicate collar bones. She didn't often make such an effort but when she did... "Damn it but we could be so perfect for each other, if only you'd bloody look at me that way." She sprayed on some perfume. Ouch, but she looked good, she looked different, in fact, certainly not the shy and reserved type and indeed, to see herself looking like this was to *feel* more confidence than she'd ever known, she felt powerful, even, in her femininity. "I'm just sorry for you Scruffy, you're an innocent victim in this. I don't like it but what choice do I have? Damn it, Gia, but look at what you're doing to me. And it's *you* who's supposed to be the bloody lesbian."

Her phone vibrated and the text said, 'I'm outside. Hurry, looks like it's about to rain.'

"Shit." Rain was one thing she did not need right now so she grabbed her clutch and dashed out the door.

Scruffy was standing halfway between the front door and the taxi. "Oh, holy shit!" His mouth very nearly hit the soon to be rain soaked floor. "I mean, oh wow! You look like, Holy shit!" To give Scruffy credit, when donning a tux, he scrubbed up reasonably well.

Her heels clip-clapped on the cobbles and she worried about slipping. "Yeah, yeah, I guess I should make an effort more often, right?"

Scruffy didn't respond but when she entered the taxi she could definitely feel his eyes burning into her rear end. He piled in straight after and closed the door. "Jesus College Boathouse," he said as the taxi rumbled down the cobbles.

"So, is your brother collecting Gia?"

"Huh? Oh, yeah, I guess so." He was still distracted and less than subtle with the way he was turned bodily into her on the backseat.

"Do you know if they're already there or if we're likely to arrive first?"

He shrugged dismissively, "well, you'll find out in a few minutes, won't you," his response was most uncaring, almost infuriatingly so.

"Has Mikey told you what Gia's wearing?"

He laughed, "no, why ever would he do that?" He shook his head and smirked.

"But she's gone to a lot of effort, right?"

"Aye, well she's celebrating tonight, isn't she." He was not so subtly gazing at her breasts, at the small heart-shaped pendant that hung between them. When he turned to look outside the window, Erin's hand on his shoulder brought his attention back.

"Do you know if they've kissed?" She held her breath for his answer.

He scratched his head. "You're full of the questions tonight, lass. How about you pause for breath a wee bit, maybe take on some oxygen, I hear it's essential for survival."

She punched him on the arm. "Tell me!"

He rubbed his arm and sniggered. "Do you really think Mikey and I discuss that shit with each other?"

Erin grunted and turned away folding her arms.

As it turned out, Gia and Mikey had arrived first. They were standing over by the drinks table, both holding glasses of Champagne while Mikey leaned into her ear and gesticulated elaborately with a hand. Gia was squinting deeply, suggesting that even now, she was unable to understand a bloody word of it.

But the moment Erin's eyes crossed over Gia, she felt her

heart leap into her mouth. Because, in the words of Scruffy, *Holy shit!*

She was wearing an impossibly tight red single strapped cocktail dress that emphasised her Mediterranean curves which, from the side bestowed Erin with a torturous view of her buttocks, yet it was her breasts that completely drew the eye, as they stretched out the fabric obscenely while somehow still managing to maintain an elegant look. Few women could pull that off. The single strapped nature of the dress exposed the tender flesh of one shoulder, while both arms remained uncovered, her tanned skin complimented perfectly by the red. The dress ended at her knees which, Erin knew, would be a problem with so much leg on display, especially considering she was wearing heels. Erin was beginning to wonder if she had a leg fetish. *Holy shit,* indeed.

But then, Mikey looked ok too, tux, which might also be an issue should Gia prove herself that way inclined after all, because, let's face it, Erin had yet to be convinced either way.

Sensing two looming figures in her periphery, Gia's eyes passed in Erin's direction, who was still standing hopeless by the door. Without so much as an acknowledgement, Gia turned back to Mikey, her face remaining entirely unmoved the whole time.

What the fuck? Um, hello?

It wasn't until a full two seconds later that her attention shot back to Erin, her head jerking back, eyes wide. A second after that, Mikey followed her lead, realising the rest of the group had arrived and he beckoned them over with a hand.

This was it, Erin's big entrance, the one she'd played over several times in her head. "Good evening, Mikey," she said as he kissed her cheek, "you're looking rather dapper tonight, exceptionally polished, in fact, I'd say you're a credit to your boathouse." Feeling Gia's intense gaze, Erin glanced easily at her and tried to sound as blasé as she possibly could. "Hello,

Gianna, you look nice." *Nice* being as neutral a descriptor as she could get away with.

"Hello to you too, Erin." Her voice remained surprisingly monotone for the usually expressive Italian.

Erin turned back to Scruffy. "Let's get ourselves a drink, shall we?" She held out her elbow in some overly showy way for Scruffy to link with, for the two-metre walk to the drinks table.

"Aye."

They set off, one step then two, and she made an attempt at checking over her shoulder to see if Gia was following their movement but unfortunately, Scruffy's lumbering mass was flush in the way. "Champagne, champagne, champagne."

"You sure you're all right?" Scruffy glanced back at his brother and shrugged.

Erin took a sip from her glass, "what do you mean?" then another.

He was still looking at the others. "Is that really the girl you just won the Fairbairns' Cup with or...?" She shoved a glass in his hand. "I don't know ... you sure you're all right?"

"I've never felt better, Scruffy." She finished her glass and grabbed a second. "I think I'm just nervous about the medal ceremony. I don't usually like being the centre of attention, even for a second." Well, it was the half-truth.

"Aye." But he bought it fully.

A steady trickle of dolled up people continued to enter, some of whom Erin recognised from the race, her college or Downing Boat House until the low jazz being played over the speakers became drowned out by the hum of so many conversations. The evening was only thirty minutes old when word passed around that at least three of the coxed eight gold medallists from the 2000 Olympic Games in Sydney would be making a surprise appearance. This prompted several committee members to descend into a state of near hysteria, which included a VIP area being hastily assembled in one of the rooms.

"There goes their evening." Scruffy had to turn bodily away to hide his grin and Erin had no need to ask who'd spread the stories. Maybe if she'd been keeping a better eye on him rather his brother's date... Honestly, it was the rowing equivalent of spiking the punch.

When it was finally announced the medals would be presented by a one Solomon Smythe-de la Haye, Treasurer of the Jesus College Boat Club, and not multiple Olympic gold medallist Sir Steve Redgrave, as had been the chatter making its way around the venue, a very audible groan made the man check his step as he walked onto the platform. The poor fellow then had to honour each of the very underwhelmed winners from each class and event.

Erin and Gia had their photos taken together while holding up their medals, and then a few more standing with the Oxford runners up. To see the two Goddesses again, up close, was to wonder how in the heck they'd managed to scratch a victory. It was the story of hard and consistent work overcoming natural advantage, which Erin took for a very valuable life-lesson. Mikey insisted on having a group photo of the four of them together and so Erin, Gia, Scruffy and Mikey posed in front of the trophy cabinet, each raising their medals while the subdued treasurer took the photo.

For the next twenty minutes, while taking advantage of the buffet, they had numerous people congratulate them on their victories. "It looked to me like you took that final bend a bit wide ... could have avoided that tense finish altogether ... knock a few years off the end of your rowing career, what?" Solomon Smythe-de la Haye spoke with an accent one might expect from reading his name on the guest list at a royal wedding. He shrugged, "could be worse. Trinity capsized after ten seconds and the poor girl's sworn never to row again. You two, however, if you keep doing what you're doing, could well go all the way, maybe even to the Olympics if you're intending on carrying on with it, which I truly hope you will." He inflected upward the final word to make it sound like a question.

"Yeah, just one problem there, I'm Italian," Gia admitted, bursting his Olympic bubble.

"Ah, pity that." He sighed deeply and rubbed his eye. "Oh, dear, I don't think there's any way around that. Oh well, there's always the Henley Royal Regatta, not quite the same but the next best thing, no doubt. Aim high."

After he left, Erin realised Gia had not answered his query. Was she intending to continue rowing next year or not? Erin knew for sure that she most definitely *did* want to continue. It had enriched her life in many ways and there was no telling how far she could take it. She really wanted to ask Gia for confirmation of her intentions but there was still an unusual awkwardness existing between them and quite honestly, it was beginning to irk. Erin was well aware they'd barely spoken a word to each since she'd entered the boathouse over an hour ago, other than a few one-word answers to mundane questions, and it was now getting to the point of causing distress despite, Erin knew, that she was at least half responsible for it. Even receiving the medals she'd wondered if she was invisible and had therefore treated her scull buddy the same. No, something was not right and the longer it persisted the worse Erin began to feel. How the boys hadn't yet picked up on it was anyone's guess but then Erin had once read that men lost up to ten percent of their intelligence when their minds were on the obvious, which might have gone some way to explaining their apparent blindness. The worst part was that tonight ought to have been a celebration of their incredible achievement against all odds, as well as the height of their friendship up to this point.

Instead, they could barely even look at each other and it was so far beyond awful that Erin was surprised she'd not yet broken down in tears.

"It doesn't look like Sir Steve's turning up, Scruff," Mikey smirked as he slid an arm fluidly around Gia's midriff.

Gia momentarily placed more weight on one leg, then shuffled back to equilibrium while making brief eye contact with Erin as she did, her face remaining poker, but more to the bloody point, Mikey was advancing, and Erin could do nothing but watch mortified as he laid on his smooth moves. Even now, his hand was stroking the crease of flesh above her hips.

Scruffy startled Erin, "oh, cheer up, that was a funny gag."

"Oh, I'm sorry, I was on another planet there." Erin shook away the fog and not so smoothly wrapped her arm around Scruffy's waist. She noticed Gia's head jerk ever so slightly in surprise, though Scruffy was more than happy with the gesture and in return began rubbing Erin's hip through the thin layer of black halter neck dress. What had she started?

Gia gave Mikey a sideward glance, before turning her attention to Scruffy. "It was kind of funny, if not a little juvenile." She wrapped her arm around her date, the sides of his mouth turning subtly upwards.

"Well, they're only twenty. Let them have their fun. There'll be plenty of time for being prudish and boring after they graduate." Erin said while making a point of giving a supportive smile to Scruffy and patting the top of his hand as she did.

Gia's eyes narrowed as she visibly tugged Mikey closer. "So you're finally speaking to me are you, Erin?"

"I was not under the impression, *Gianna*, that I was not speaking to you." Erin clumsily shuffled closer to Scruffy and wondered if Gia's eye had flickered at the use of the full version of her name.

Scruffy glanced at his brother and gave a small shake of his head. "Honestly, I wish I'd never made the bloody joke now."

"You've not been speaking to me all night, and you know it!" Gia retorted.

"Well, *you* have not been speaking to *me*!" Erin defended, prompting Gia to gawp open-mouthed at Mikey, as Erin took the brief opportunity to steal a glance at her cleavage. There wasn't a great deal of breast on display, at least not from above, it was more *through* the damn material where they expanded the fabric outwards that was proving a distraction.

Gia made an extravagant spectacle of dropping her arm that was tightly gripping Mikey's side and instead grabbed his hand before interlinking her fingers in his. "You called me *Gianna* the moment you entered, you silly goose. You've never once called me *Gianna*." She whispered something in Mikey's ear and the sides of his mouth curled into a near demonic grin, displaying his Scottish pearly whites.

Erin clenched her fists, not realising that...

"...Ow." Scruffy yelped, rubbing his side.

"Sorry," she said, not bothering to look at him. She released her arm from around Scruffy's side and grabbed his hand, mimicking with the fingers what Gia had done a few seconds before. "And you've never once..." she checked her words just in time. You coward, Erin, but now was probably not the time to accuse Gia of never showing any interest in her, at least not of the sexual kind, "...never mind." Instead, she reached across her body in some truly awkward gesture, placing her opposing hand on top of Scruffy's as he held hers.

"Do you even know your date's *real* name, Erin?" Gia smiled with satisfaction. "I mean, it's usually the first thing you ask, you know, out of politeness."

Erin froze. She didn't have a clue, and looked to Scruffy for help but he just shrugged.

"Mikey," Gia began as she pushed out her breasts to some agonising degree, "let's find a nice table in some quiet room and have our first proper smooch."

Erin's jaw nearly hit the floor as she squeezed Scruffy's hand painfully tight, feeling him wince. "Scruffy, let's get out of here." She headed for the exit, only to be yanked back.

"Enough!" Scruffy demanded, throwing down Erin's hand.

When she turned around, Mikey had also discarded Gia. "Do you really think we can't see what's going on?" He drained his champagne and slammed the empty glass down to the table before turning on his date. "Gia, who do you think you're bloody fooling?"

"What?" She hissed, wide-eyed, like a fox caught in the headlights and dared not look at Erin or Mikey.

"The other day, feeding the ducks, all you bloody spoke about was Erin. Erin this, Erin that. I didn't think it was possible to make a connection between feeding ducks and Erin, between going for sushi and Erin, but somehow you bloody managed it. Erin, Erin, Erin, all the time, bloody Erin." He made a *talking mouth* gesture with his hand. "And then on the way here ... *What's Erin wearing?* Like I'd have a bloody clue. *Have Erin and Scruffy kissed yet? What does Scruffy think of Erin?* Blah, blah, blah."

Erin gaped at her in disbelief, not yet knowing what to think of the tirade coming from Mikey's mouth. Was he drunk? Her knees were shaking, "I think I need to sit down."

"And you..." Mikey pointed to Erin. "I've been stood opposite you most of the bloody evening and I've lost count of the times you've ogled my date. Quite honestly, you're more perverted than I am." He chuckled to himself, though it wasn't funny. Well, not really.

Erin looked at the floor, taking a sudden interest in some hardened chewing gum stuck to the carpet. She wondered how long it had been there. Months probably. Why did the cleaners not scrape it up? Was it even possible to remove squashed gum from a carpet after it'd been trampled over hundreds of times? Was it getting hot in here?

"Oh, Mikey, I've had the exact same from this one," Scruffy said from somewhere close and Erin made the logical assumption he meant her. "*Can we stay close enough to keep an eye on Mikey and Gia.*" He mimicked Erin's Northumbrian accent and to be fair, he had it down. "*I'd like to see what Mikey and Gia are doing. Gia would love to see this Kingfisher nest. What does Mikey think of Gia?* And you..." he turned his attention to the Italian, "I know my date is hot but if you keep staring at her breasts like that, you'll stare a hole right through them."

Now it was Gia's turn to take a sudden interest in what appeared to be some other piece of gum. Really, what did the cleaners even do around here?

"Here," Mikey delved into his pocket and pulled out his wallet, "here's your fiver back, plus another five. Looks like you won the fucking bet."

"Aye, winning five quid has never been so fucking painful."

"What bet was that?" Erin squeaked, finally looking up, but daring not look at Gia.

"That *she* was a lesbian," Mikey said, pointing to Gia.

"But neither of us thought *you* were one as well." Scruffy nudged Erin's shoulder.

Talk about ripping off the band-aid. Ouch.

A silence carried for a few long, painful seconds, before Mikey exhaled deep and spoke. "Look, girls ... this is *your* special day. Maybe you should both be enjoying it *together*."

Scruffy added, "maybe those two Oxford girls are single."

Mikey hugged Gia, whispering something in her ear, then kissed her on the cheek. "We're still friends. You ain't getting rid of us."

Scruffy pulled Erin in tight and whispered, "go for it. Make yourself happy. I'll see you on the Cam."

The men grabbed a glass of champagne each then stepped towards the other side of the room to disappear within a large group of rowers from Corpus Christi.

Gia had turned a redder shade of brown and they made brief eye contact before breaking it. It was still awkward but then they both laughed together, which was an incredible relief of tension. "I missed you." Gia came in for a hug and it felt like heaven. The boathouse was beyond hot, not to mention busy and loud. "Looks like they caught us." The Italian sighed as she pulled away and her eyes never looked so beautiful as she managed to hold Erin's for a couple of seconds longer. "Are you ok?"

It was weird, like a huge crushing weight had been lifted. "Well, that I wasn't expecting but yes, I'm quite all right, thanks."

"Let's go for a walk."

"Was that the truth back there, what Mikey said?" Gia asked.

"Um, I guess he did catch me a few times staring at your breasts." Thank God for alcohol. "I tried to be subtle, I really did."

"Yeah, me too." Gia sighed. "They were really into us. Both of us. I feel bad."

"Yeah, me too. I love those guys, but if it's not right..." Erin trailed off. "So, what about the rest of what he said?" Erin slowed her already slow stroll, turning inwards slightly. "Did you, um, talk about me when I wasn't there?"

Gia laughed, matching Erin's pace on the path alongside the Cam. The twilight cast a serene glow over the river as several geese skidded across the water. It was a miracle it hadn't yet rained. The smell of the imminent downpour was present in the air and it would only be a matter of time before the heavens opened. "I think you already know that I was. And you were too? You were talking about me?"

"I think I pissed Scruffy off with it all." Erin cringed. "Oh God, he must think I was the worst date ever."

"If it makes you feel any better, you have strong competition for that title."

Erin kicked a pebble into the river, the splash was satisfying. "Why'd you give him your number then? If you're into women, then you shouldn't be giving your number to guys, especially if you're aware they have romantic intentions."

"Oh, Erin, you know, for a Cambridge girl, you really can be an idiot sometimes." Gia softly bumped her hip.

"As I'm discovering." She hesitated for a moment. "You did it to make me jealous, didn't you?"

"It's not that I wanted to make you jealous. Damn it, girl, I wanted you to get a move on. Granted I could have chosen differently but they were both there at the time and they just kept pushing. Ideally, Mikey would have had nice shiny long red hair, big round boobs, soft smooth skin and be my best friend as well, but damn it, I wasn't going to wait forever for *you* to decide if you liked me that way."

Erin was overcome with the sudden need to stop walking, her legs felt weak anyway. "Do you really mean all these things?" Assuming Gia had sent the signals, how had she missed them? Was she really that slow? Granted, Erin had not been exposed to the same level of socialisation as most people her age but if Gia had been interested in her all this time, then she well and truly missed all the signs, or had been too much inside her own head to have noticed. Despite all Gia had done for her, in the end, Erin's introverted nature had obscured so much of the outside from her consciousness and had very nearly succeeded in preventing the coming moment from ever happening.

"Come here." Gia turned to face her, tenderly took her hands and pulled her closer.

"What?" Dear God, what was she about to do?

"Close your eyes." Gia raised Erin's hands to hold them snug between their breasts.

"Yes," Erin hissed, closing her eyes. Nothing happened for a few beats as the tension built, though she was completely aware she was holding both Gia's hands, the soft sensation of her flesh heightened in the blackness. Then the beautiful scent of peach grew stronger until finally, she felt Gia's lips touch hers. She was so gentle, nothing like Erin had expected yet at the same time, exactly what she'd hoped. Gia squeezed her hands and Erin responded in kind. Their tongues connected, slightly at first, then a little more. It was Heaven.

Gia pulled away, releasing one hand, but keeping hold of the other. "Does that answer your question?"

Erin needed a moment to gather her coherent thoughts. "No, um, I mean yes. Definitely yes." Erin giggled and then Gia did the same.

Then the tiny patters of rain began flecking the Cam and a thousand drops created as many pretty swirls, forming the distinctive patterns on the water. Then came the sound as the intensity increased and Erin felt the summer rain's warmth on her skin. Gia's hair seemed to darken a shade as it absorbed the wetness, yet she just remained there and held Erin's gaze as lines of water streamed down her face.

"We can't run, not in our heels," Erin said as she pulled Gia along the riverbank in the direction of the city.

"I don't think it makes any difference now anyway. Besides, it's kind of nice." She glanced at Erin's dress as it constricted from the intake of water. "You look hot when you're wet."

Erin blanched. *Ditto*, she thought, ogling Gia from the corner of her eye, the already tight cocktail dress clinging ever harder to her curves, particularly her breasts which led the way along the Cam.

Gia's hand felt like silk against her own clammy skin. Erin's chest, tight almost to the point of suffocation. Her senses were heightened many times to the extent she could hear rain hitting rooftops far into the distance, yet at the same time, she was oblivious to the same sensations. Her skin was cold, evidenced by the many goosebumps up and down her arms, yet her heart pumped blood at some obscene rate.

There was so much Erin wanted, needed to ask Gia, but couldn't for the life of her remember any specifics at this moment.

"Your hand is shaking. Do I really make you that nervous?" Gia asked.

"Not usually, but I'm kind of taking it as a good thing. It's not bad nerves. You seem your usual self."

"Erin, if only I could describe to you how I'm feeling right now."

Erin's heart soared. Then she remembered one important question she'd had on her mind. "When are you heading back home for the summer? Will it be immediately after the exams or will you stay behind for a bit?" They passed under a tree, granting temporary respite from the rain, not that it made any difference to their already saturated forms.

"I'll have to go back at some point, I miss my mum and dad but I'd miss you just as much if I was away for a full three months. I'll probably remain in Cambridge for half the summer and return to Napoli for the other half."

That was all Erin needed to hear. "Well, that obviously means I'm sticking behind too then. But I should definitely take you to Alnwick." She sprang on her heels like an excited child as they stepped out from the tree's shelter. "We have a holiday home in the Lake District. We could spend a week there, just the two of us." Erin hoped she wasn't thinking way too far ahead but she just couldn't help herself. She couldn't stand the thought of being parted from Gia, even for a few days.

"I'd love to. Yes, we should definitely do that. Perhaps also you can come to Napoli? You're always talking about visiting Pompeii."

Erin could almost feel herself vibrating with excitement. What a summer it would be, just as soon as the exams were over in two weeks. Being freshers, the exams wouldn't count toward their final grades but they both wanted to give their full effort regardless.

"I'm sorry about earlier, you know, about calling you *Gianna* and trying to make you jealous."

Gia laughed. "If it wasn't for that little stunt we may not be holding hands right now." She swung their arms with a little extra momentum for emphasis. "It's just funny that in the end, it was *you* and not me who brought this about. You're braver than you give yourself credit for."

"Well, it was kind of both of us, with a little help from those pesky twins."

"I guess we got tired of waiting for each other," Gia said as they neared Downing. "I'm curious ... how long have you felt this way about me? I know for sure I was pretty much just your best friend for a long time."

Erin knew the answer, though still gave it some thought. "My feelings for you definitely developed over a period of months. You're my best friend in the whole world and I just feel alive when I'm with you. But if I was to attribute a single event to it, then I'd say I realised my feelings over Christmas. When you weren't around, I just felt empty, like a part of myself had been taken away. And you..." she squeezed the soft flesh of Gia's hand, "you had me all worried when you never replied to me. It felt like I'd lost you and it was unbearable. I guess you can say that absence really does make the heart grow fonder."

Gia laughed. "You really are one corny girl but I totally love it." They stopped outside the entrance to Gia's Downing College residence, the thin fabric of their dresses along with their hair having absorbed as much rain as possible, their skin slippery with moisture.

The moment was conspicuous by the tense silence that permeated the air between them. Like *this* was the moment something was supposed to happen, but didn't. It always happened about *now* in the movies, at that moment when you and your date arrived at the front gate. The reality, as Erin now discovered, was not like the movies. She looked at Gia and froze, wanting so badly to kiss her; long and slow, then hard and serious with all the passion she could summon.

"So..." Gia said, letting go of Erin's hand. Damn, but this was awkward.

"So..." Oh, this was bad. "I'll see you around..." No! The night could not end now. This was their special night.

"Unless..." Gia said, a small glint of panic in her eyes, panic that filled Erin with hope.

"Yes?" Please, please, please.

"I had another Vivaldi CD sent from home. Perhaps we could..."

"Yes!" Erin shouted, cutting her off, startling both Gia and herself. "I *love* Vivaldi."

Gia's lips smushed together as she suppressed the laughter. "Ok, well, let's go inside then. Besides, you need to get out of that dress..." Gia said, slurring the final word as though she'd not thought about what she was saying. She looked down then back up but avoided Erin's eyes. "What I meant was ... you're all wet and ... ugh, it's not good to be in wet clothes." She looked away again, rolling her eyes and stamped a foot on the ground.

Erin grinned and totally took pleasure in her friend's slip of the tongue and subsequent discomfort.

Gia saw the smile, "ok, I'll shut up now," she squeezed Erin's hand, "but you're such a meanie."

Erin returned the squeeze. "Let's go inside." And listen to Vivaldi and kiss some more.

They entered the flat and Gia closed the door behind them, threw her bag to the desk and sauntered across to the CD player. "Make yourself at home."

Erin slyly applied the chain to the door before placing her bag beside Gia's. She watched her as she flipped through a stack of CDs. Those legs, the curvature of her calves that sent Erin over the edge, even from a distance, her wide hips in that rain-soaked red dress gifted her with an impossible hourglass look, her slim waist, sculpted from hours and hours gruelling on the Cam gave way to breasts that Erin had spent so long imagining. How would they feel to touch, to caress, to have in her mouth? When would the bloody music start? Say something. "Nice to see your room still tidy." Lame, so bloody lame.

"Thanks."

Finally, the unmistakable sound of violin trilled from the speakers, blending with the pelting of rain against the windows. Gia closed the blinds and smiled at Erin from across the room, her dark hair wild and unkempt. After a few seconds, she asked, "can I get you anything?"

"No, thanks, I'm good." An annoying apprehension took form, like it was expected something was supposed to happen, but wasn't. If it hadn't been for Vivaldi's double-stop trills, the silence might have been uncomfortable but damn it, someone had to make a move here and clearly, the alcohol was wearing off. Erin took a seat on the edge of the bed and made brief eye contact with Gia as she did.

"Here, let me get you a towel." Gia delved into a drawer and pulled out two towels, she moved closer and placed one in Erin's lap.

Erin watched as Gia half turned away and patted her arms, neck and hair. Erin did the same from her seated position, though she still felt wet to the core. "Are you ok?" Erin asked.

Gia took a perch on the window ledge and glanced up with a slow intake of air. "Yeah, I think so." She opened her mouth, as if to say something more, but stopped herself.

"Maybe I should go," Erin said, standing. It pained her to leave but if it wasn't happening then it wasn't happening. These things should happen naturally, shouldn't they?

"No!" Gia moved away from the ledge. "I don't want you to leave." She took a step closer while her hands fidgeted in front. Again, there was something she wanted to say.

"What's on your mind?"

Gia came closer and took both Erin's hands. Finally, that touch and the comfort and feeling of wholeness that came with it. "I just get the impression you think I've *been there and done that* and have tonnes of experience with this." Gia was actually nervous, very nervous. For a change, it was *her* hands that felt clammy and not just because they were wet from the downpour. She took a deep breath, her breasts heaving against the tight confines of the dress. "Just because I've known for a few years that I like girls, doesn't mean I've..." she hesitated, "got experience. Remember where I'm from. Things are different there."

Erin's eyes glazed over. "You mean ... you've never been with another girl?" Wow, she really did have her friend all wrong. But it felt nice. Really nice.

Gia shook her head. "I'm not saying this because I feel

the need to make a big confession or anything. Well, I guess maybe a little bit. The main reason is, I just don't want you to be disappointed. I may not live up to your expectations."

Erin could not believe what she was hearing. She wanted to wrap Gia up in her arms and never let go. "I have no expectations whatsoever. And you already know my lack of history with girls, but then again, we are both only nineteen." Erin just wanted to be with her, to feel close to her and to hold her. Using each other's bodies for practice could be fun. "I was actually afraid myself that I'd disappoint *you*."

Gia took a step back and looked Erin up and down. "Babe, I don't think you and that body are going to disappoint me." Her eyes feasted on Erin's breasts in a way that was totally convincing.

Erin giggled and closed the gap as though her life depended on it, wrapping her arms around Gia's shoulders. "You are such a pervert."

They locked eyes, their smiles faded, Gia's pupils dilated, peaches filled the world. Their lips met and Erin explored the inside of Gia's mouth with her tongue while clasping hands down Gia's sodden midriff. She grazed the edges of her breasts with thumbs before her hands came to rest on Gia's shapely hips.

Erin felt Gia's hands around her back, searching for the zip. "Here, it's at the side." She moved Gia's hand to the zip and then felt the cool air on her flesh as Gia ran the zip down the length of the dress.

"Get me out of this thing," Gia demanded as she turned around.

Erin hardly needed telling twice and she tugged the zip down the length of Gia's back, exposing her deeply tanned flesh. As the dress hit the floor, she stepped out from it, revealing herself to Erin in only a matching red lace bra and underwear. The breath left Erin in a giant involuntary exhalation as she gazed upon, and lusted for Gia. Her true form was all Erin could have imagined and more.

Gia coughed, then nodded to Erin, still wearing her own dress.

"Whoops." Erin pulled the dress over her head, ruffling her hair. They'd frequently seen each other in only bra and underwear in the boat club changing rooms but this felt very different. And then the enormity of what was happening hit Erin, as they both stood facing each other, almost naked. Erin had wanted this for a long time, but now it was about to happen, she knew it would forever change things between them.

"Are you sure you want this?" Gia asked, as though she could read Erin's mind.

"Yes, I'm sure. I've never wanted anything so much."

Gia reached behind Erin's back and fumbled with her bra strap. After a few seconds, she rolled her eyes. "Well, I've never done it from this side before."

"That's fine. Take your time." Erin reached around the back of Gia for her bra strap. She found the hooks almost immediately and then both bras fell to the floor. "Oh, fuck."

Gia laughed because Erin's response had been completely reflexive. "So you like what you see?"

Erin brought her hands up, seizing Gia's breasts and feeling their weight. "Now *that* is what I'm talking about." She could scarcely believe the words came out from her own mouth.

Gia wrapped her arms around Erin's waist, lifted her from the ground and plonked her on the bed as she came to fall on top. Their lips clashed again, red hot passion stirring within them, their breasts crushing together. Erin ground upwards with her hips, rubbing her pussy against Gia's thigh, a deep guttural sigh escaping from inside. Gia moved her hand in front of her thigh and caressed Erin's most erotic part through the thin layer of underwear. "Holy crap, you're soaking."

"Am I?" Erin panted, not quite knowing what else to say. Guilty as charged. Erin needed the underwear removed. She wanted Gia's caresses on her true, without obstruction. She moved a hand down and tried to remove the barrier but Gia's hungry body prevented her from gaining any purchase. "Gia?"

"Oh." She realised what Erin was trying to do and so Gia slowly slid Erin's underwear down the length of her legs. "I think that's a little better." Gia pressed her knee against the inside of Erin's thigh while spreading the other leg apart with her free hand.

Erin tried to gauge Gia's reaction as she gazed at her damp folds. Did she like what she saw? Without realising, Erin brought her hands in front of her solar plexus, suddenly full of self-doubt. Then the sides of Gia's mouth curled into some devilish grin, her teeth shining as did her bright eyes. "Gia?"

"I want you." She hissed and then slid a finger inside, the invasion filling Erin's entire soul as she exhaled short, sharp breaths.

Erin closed her eyes, desiring only to experience the heightened sensations to their full. She felt another finger enter and her back arched as she reached back for the bedpost. The feeling of being stretched by the girl she loved as Gia's fingers worked away inside her, sliding slowly out and delving back inside over and over sent Erin into a near frenzy. Her legs widened further as Gia pressed down harder on her knee, she was close.

And then Erin exploded as her buttocks lifted off the bed, her head light, a haze, but a good one, clouding her vision. Erin had been so hungry for Gia, that hadn't taken long at all. When she opened her eyes, Gia was already beside her. Erin pulled her hard against her perspiring body. "Gia ... that ... was..." she couldn't finish the words.

"There was other stuff I wanted to do too," she said. All in good time.

"I guess you just really turn me on." Erin panted. "Your turn." Erin wasted no time sliding down Gia's body. Although it actually felt like it was *her* turn all over again. She covered Gia's breast with a hand, pressing, caressing firmly while she ran her tongue over her nipple. Gia bucked and then Erin felt a hand running through her hair. She kissed her way down Gia's toned belly and then Erin's eyes were level with her glistening folds. Erin's legs ran off the end of the bed to gain a better angle and she gripped Gia's legs and pulled her closer before pushing her feet in towards her buttocks, bending her legs. Erin gazed up at Gia's most intimate of parts, saliva building in her mouth as though she'd not eaten in days. She breathed in Gia's natural scent. This was it. After experiencing Gia's essence, Erin would forever be a changed woman.

She ran her tongue once over the entire length; from her opening to her clitoris, tasting raw Gia, her pre-juices now on Erin's tongue. Gia shivered, a silent moan coming from somewhere deep inside. Erin covered Gia's clit with her mouth, running her tongue over, across and around, feeling the bud with her tongue, sucking, nibbling and tasting. Gia shuddered and hissed something unintelligible in her native tongue. Erin felt the bud swell in her mouth as more blood rushed to the area and then Gia's breathing increased in speed and depth. Gia's back arched as a hand reached out and grabbed Erin's.

Silence for a second, the calm before the storm, then Gia's entire body tensed and juices gushed from her opening as Erin collected the nectar with a hunger.

Erin leapt back on the bed, wanting to be close to Gia and

shuffled herself level. They held each other tight, panting, gazing into the other's eyes. Erin had never felt closer to another person. She wanted to stay like this forever.

Gia kissed her hard on the lips. When their mouths parted, Gia pressed her forehead against Erin's. "I'm going back down." She whispered, then vanished out of sight as Erin's entire body shuddered in ecstasy.

Chapter Eight

ACTION

S mack.

The ball hit the wall and rebounded in Ben's direction. He unleashed an almighty crack and the ball smashed against the wall with a brutal force.

Erin missed the rebound. "Bloody hell, what has got into you?" She picked up the squash ball and prepared to serve. "Is this some kind of power record you're going for? I pity the poor guy you're thinking of when you strike the ball like that."

It had been meant as a joke, only, to Ben, it wasn't so funny.

He scrutinised her form in those shorts and squash jersey; her sport sculpted legs that ended at that backside, tight and perky. Breasts that pushed out against her top, taunting him with agonising frustration.

How long had it been? How long since he'd taken her, had his way with her, experienced her.

If he'd wanted to return Erin's comment with a joke of his own, nothing came to mind.

She half bent forward, threw the ball up, stretched and

155

struck the sphere against the wall, groaning from the sudden exertion, a sound Ben hadn't heard in too long.

The ball rebounded and Ben almost snapped a string, or seven, as he hit the ball with all the force his body could muster.

Erin missed the rebound. "I think that's game to you. Lunch?" She tossed her racket across the court and it came to land on the heap of sports bags and discarded layers in the corner.

"I was thinking..." Ben began as he wiped the sweat from his forehead with the inside of an elbow before slipping the racket back inside its sleeve.

"Yep?" She came closer, her scent, her sweat, her body sent Ben insane.

"We've never been abroad together."

"And you're only just realising this?" She propped her hands on her hips and sighed. "The amount of times I've mentioned this to you."

He shook his head as though he'd not heard. "I think it's time we went for a romantic break somewhere, see some sites, have some fun." And get that spark back and fuck each others' brains out.

She allowed her smile to slowly build, they were getting somewhere, finally. "Well, I think you already know my opinion on that."

"I'm doing this for you, my fiancée." As well as for his sanity. "I was thinking," he continued as he rammed his discarded sports jersey into his bag, "there are some wonderful castles in France, vineyards, history, culture, food. I've always fancied Bavaria too, or Austria, Switzerland, all those mountains, all that fresh air..."

"Italy!" Erin cut him off.

"Italy?" He rubbed his chin. "Hmm, I've always fancied

the thought of Venice. I've heard Rome's a little too busy but Florence would be nice. Lots of art."

"Napoli!" She said with conviction. "I've wanted to see Pompeii for a long, long time now."

"You have?" Ben wrinkled his nose. "Ok. I've not heard much about Napoli to be honest with you but the Amalfi Coast is supposed to be splendid. That's if we don't get run off the road and killed by one of the local drivers."

She hesitated, the smile of a few seconds before dipped and she turned away to begin rustling through her bag. "I've an old Cambridge friend who lives in Napoli. It'd be rude not to drop in and say *hi* while I'm there." She continued bundling her sports gear bagwards, not looking up.

He grabbed his bag, stood and shrugged. "Well, it's not every day we pass by Napoli, so you may as well take the opportunity if that's where we're going." He'd doubtless find something to occupy himself. Better some old cathedral than the reminiscences of two women. The very thought of it filled him with boredom.

"Napoli it is." And in those words, as her eyebrows rose higher than he'd ever seen them, it was as though something had returned, a spark in the eyes the likes of which he'd not seen since before that fucking flu took hold.

"Napoli it is," he agreed and found himself striding for the door.

It was odd, very odd. Kind of like taking your seat in a public place and realising you had no clothes on, just a weird feeling that could not be explained. She knew it and everybody else could see it.

"Where's Gia?" Rebecca asked. "I don't think I can ever

remember a time I've seen you without her glued to your side. Or vice versa."

Erin laughed, more out of politeness than anything else. "You know, I'm really not sure. I should probably text her." She whipped out her phone, flipped it open and that was the moment the professor chose to enter. Damn it. This particular professor was not afraid to shout at people he saw on phones during lectures and Erin could do without being centre of attention, especially considering her shield had taken it upon herself to skip the day's first class.

And that really was strange because neither of them had missed a single lecture, seminar, practical or anything else the entire year. They were model students. But being May, they were mainly covering old ground in preparation for exams next week. Oh well. Most likely, Gia had decided to sleep in and skip the first lecture with the grumpy prof and Erin could hardly say she blamed her. If anything, it was a compliment. In fact, she'd half thought about doing the same thing considering that, after they'd had sex for the first, second, third and fourth time only the night before, it had been something like three in the morning when they'd finally fallen asleep.

Still, Erin reflected, Gia might still have texted to let her know she was staying in bed a few more hours.

Erin had only left Gia's flat a couple of hours before and now, she pictured her beautiful face and relived their tender kiss before she'd departed. Erin had needed to go home because she had no desire to arrive for class in the same dress and heels she'd worn at the Fairbairns' Ball because, well, for obvious reasons. Gia had seen her to the door from where they'd smooched for at least ten minutes. Next time she'd make sure to prepare so she could shower and have breakfast with the girl she loved, rather than stealing out at some early hour to avoid the dreaded *walk of shame* through the crowds of Cambridge commuters. Talk about attention she didn't need. *Just remember Gia's kiss. You'll be together again soon.*

After the lecture, Erin brought out her phone to make the text. "Great, no battery." Staying the night at Gia's, she'd not had chance to charge the bloody thing.

She considered knocking on Gia's door during changeover and dragging her out of bed but thought better of it. She had no desire to come over as being completely desperate for the girl. Granted, they'd had sex only the night before, something she was still trying to get her head around, but although she wanted to be with her right this very minute, she knew it was probably best to give her at least a little bit of space. "But no more than a few hours," she muttered under her breath as she took a seat next to Rebecca, feeling naked and exposed.

At lunch, Erin took her sandwich onto the cloister, making sure to walk by Gia's window on the way over. The curtains were still drawn from the night before. She giggled to herself, "that girl is in big trouble." But then again, they really had gone to town on each others' naked bodies and only very recently, which had been mere hours after exerting themselves like never before during the Fairbairns' race. Erin still felt drained from that and could have quite easily spent the next week alone in a dark room had her body not been lit with all kinds of wonderful sensations. Chemicals, she knew. It was love. She'd sleep eventually, that was certain, even though she'd gladly forgo it tonight for some more hot passion with the most beautiful woman in the world.

When the final lecture finished, it was three in the afternoon and Erin would not wait one more minute before giving Gia a piece of her mind and if necessary, her body too.

She arrived at the door, knocked and waited.

No response.

She knocked again. Where was she? "Get up you lazy bum!"

Erin pressed her ear against the door but could hear nothing from inside.

After checking the kitchen and common room and finding neither Gia nor anybody else, Erin decided to head for home. Usually, it was only a ten-minute walk or double that if she was chatting with Gia. Presumably, she'd gone grocery shopping and, not being able to get in touch with Erin due to her phone being out of battery, they'd missed each other. No matter, Erin would get her eventually, that much was inevitable. *There's no escape for you.*

When Erin arrived home, she immediately plugged her phone into the power cable from when she commenced tapping it against her knee. "Come on, come on, come on. '*Welcome to Nokia.*' The display finally said.

Her heart fell to the pit of her stomach. Zero unread messages, which was an impossibility even on a bad day. What was that girl doing? Playing some kind of a game? No! That wasn't Gia. And definitely not after they'd cleared up their misunderstandings and given themselves to each other.

Erin fired off a quick message. 'You ok, hon? Missed you today xxx'

It was quickly followed by another. 'Please get in touch, hon, let me know you're ok.'

She waited all of thirty seconds, "sod this," then found her number at the top of *recent contacts*, and pressed the *call* button. The phone rang, which was a good thing, she'd soon pick up.

The longer it rang without her answering, the more Erin's eyes began to sting. That was a new sensation for her and one that was unaccompanied by the familiar haze. Erin's heart beat through her chest, or was it her stomach. Her skin felt numb. And why could she feel a pulse in her head?

Where was she? What was she doing? Who was she with? Why wasn't she answering?

Erin tried to occupy herself. She forced down some food, merely for sustenance rather than pleasure, then cleaned her room, though sitting down to do any study would require more concentration than she could possibly summon right now.

No, she had to return to Downing and bang on Gia's door until she showed her face. Man, did that girl ever have some explaining to do.

And then, ten minutes later, Downing was where Erin found herself. Her knocks turned to bangs, which soon became kicks.

A female student in dressing gown emerged from the room next door. "What's with all the noise?"

"Do you know where Gia is?" Erin knew she sounded rude but in the moment, she didn't give a shit.

"Who?" She was foreign, like all the students bunking at Downing, and squinted, most likely because she usually wore glasses.

"Um, your neighbour? Gianna De Luca, the girl who lives here, the Italian one." Cambridge?

"Oh, Gianna," she rubbed at her eyes and didn't seem in the least offended at being spoken to like she was stupid, "I haven't seen her in a few days. Normally see her making breakfast. All that Italian stuff. But I do tend to *hear* her every day. Slams the door. Loud girl. Bit like you." She smiled, disappeared for a moment then returned with a suitcase she used to wedge open her door. She stepped closer to Erin and stared at Gia's door as though doing so might provide an answer.

Erin shook her head and sounded impatient, "when did you last *hear* her?"

"This morning, around the usual time. Um, nine o'clock? Maybe a tad before." She raised her eyebrows. "We could check her milk."

161

"Check her milk?"

She plodded down the hallway in the direction of the kitchen and Erin followed behind. "Yeah, I know when she leaves because she always slams the door. I like her. Who needs sleep anyway?" They entered the kitchen and opened the fridge from where the girl pulled out a two-litre plastic carton of skimmed milk. The girl tutted. "She goes through one of these a day. Usually starts an argument if anybody uses her milk, so she draws this line and signs each one. I like her." She showed Erin the crude line drawn along the very top of the carton, save for an inch or so, the amount required for a cup of coffee.

"Shit," Erin hissed.

"Usually, at this time in the evening, the milk should be at about this level," she pointed halfway down the carton, to where nothing but whiteness showed through the transparent container, "and there'd be a half dozen little Gia squiggles but we've been known to drink it anyway and just replace what we take with water. She never notices." She returned the milk and closed the fridge door. "Not talking to me so dumb now, are you?"

Erin felt her eyes glazing over.

So Gia had left early, most likely between having her morning coffee and turning in for class. She hadn't returned, not even for lunch.

Erin had an idea so she thanked the girl and ran back to Gia's door. She decided to call her again. Erin recalled the Christmas debacle where Gia had left her phone in the flat. If she'd returned to Italy due to some emergency, or whatever, then her phone would still be in the room and Erin might just hear it ringing. She dialled.

Strange. It went straight through to the answering machine, which meant that at some point between Erin's last call and now, either the battery had died or - Gia had turned her phone off.

Immediately, the tears streamed down Erin's face, uncontrollable oceans of tears. She found herself unable to breathe and needed to get away, quick, but her legs began to shake, so she leant against the wall for support.

Why had Gia turned off her phone? Why did she not want to talk? Had they last night overstepped the acceptable boundaries of friendship? And had Gia panicked and fled? Or was it because Erin had been terrible in bed and Gia wanted an easy way out? No! Surely not that. None of these things were Gia.

It was possible, still slightly conceivable that Gia was in her room ignoring all calls, though Erin also had to consider the likelihood that she was in some bar with a girl or some sleazy guy but none of those were Gia either. Not knowing was the worst part. Whatever the truth of the matter, at best, Gia was being intentionally evasive. At worst, Erin shuddered, not even willing to consider *those* possibilities at this moment. And not for as long as possible.

When Erin began hyperventilating and the haze was almost blinding, she stumbled from the building and wandered alone into the night.

DESPITE THE EVENTS OF MONDAY, ERIN HAD STILL ARRIVED at classes Tuesday and Wednesday with the expectation that Gia would be there, red-faced and apologetic, possibly with some monstrous hangover and one heck of a story to tell. When that never happened, the enormity of what was possibly unfolding began to dawn on Erin.

She'd sent a hundred messages over the few days following

and tried to ring her just as often. Gia's phone always went straight through to voicemail.

After Erin had harassed Maria, Gia's neighbour, as well as the rest of her dormitory mates for information and failed to turn up any clues, Erin then asked around all their usual haunts.

The boat club had not seen anything of her and neither had Mikey or Scruffy. When Erin told them she hadn't seen Gia since Monday morning, they insisted on going to the police to file a missing person's report.

"Basically, we need to get inside her flat," Mikey said. "Maybe she trapped herself inside the bathroom."

"Hey, it happens," Scruffy placed a reassuring hand on Erin's shoulder.

Once the police report had been filed, progress stepped up several gears. The police didn't seem worried, which was reassuring, because students going missing was a regular occurrence.

Scruffy was trying his hardest to make Erin feel better. "When I was a fresher, I got so drunk that I woke up the next day to find myself drifting down the Cam in an eight-man coxed boat, which was strange because we row double sculls."

It was Wednesday evening when the Downing residence warden opened up Gia's room for Erin and two police officers.

The first thing that stood out was the mess. When Erin left, the room had been tidy, save for the bedsheets and Gia's dress, which had spent the night crumpled on the carpet. Now there were clothes strewn all about the floor, the drawers had been pulled open with much of the contents scattered about the immediate vicinity. Her Fairbairns' winner's medal lay randomly amongst the mess. At first glance, it looked as though she'd either gone insane and trashed the place, or had been robbed.

"Her mobile phone's here." The police officer said. "She must have left in a hurry."

Erin perked at the discovery; so Gia had not turned off the phone but Erin had most likely exhausted the damn battery with her constant harassment. "Oh no, not necessarily. If she's returned home then she'd have left that phone here."

"If she's returned home, then she's wasted a lot of people's time." The officer said.

Erin folded her arms. "I agree with you and there's nobody more than me who wants to give her a piece of my mind."

"Are you sure she's never done anything like this before?" The officer asked.

"No, never. This is not like Gia at all."

The other officer had been searching through Gia's drawers and shelves. "There's no sign of her passport."

Erin thought out loud. "But if she's gone home, wouldn't she have packed more clothes?"

"Is her bag around?" The first officer asked.

They found her large backpack, still with its broken strap from when she'd very nearly pulled the door off, but there was no sign of her smaller bag, the one she took to the boathouse.

A few minutes later, they were in the warden's office reviewing CCTV footage. From the cursory look inside Gia's room, it was beginning to appear that she hadn't been dragged off or kidnapped, but that she'd left in a hurry. This hypothesis was confirmed when the camera by the front door had filmed Gia running out the building with her training bag slung over one shoulder. The time stamp on the footage read 08:50.

Erin breathed deeply and felt some relief, but still didn't

quite know what to make of the news. The important thing was that Gia was safe but considering everything, she'd still fled without so much as a word to anyone.

The officer radioed through to the station and within ten minutes they received confirmation that Gia had boarded a plane from London Gatwick to Naples International Airport on Monday mid-afternoon. "Are you sure she didn't say she was travelling home on Monday?" The officer asked, looking down on Erin as though she'd wasted several hours of their time. "You students with your chit-chat can easily miss important details."

Erin chose not to answer his patronising question.

"You'd be surprised by some of the *missing people's* reports we have to file." The other officer sounded happy. They'd solved the mystery and all without any dead bodies. Their hands were now washed of it all.

One mystery had indeed been solved and most importantly, Gia was safe. The next mystery, though, was why in the bloody hell she'd fled in such a way? Something must have happened to make the girl run off like that and Erin just hoped it wasn't her who'd frightened Gia away. The best course of action, especially considering that stupidly, Erin had no way of contacting Gia in Italy since she only possessed her University of Cambridge Hermes email address as well as her UK mobile phone number, was to wait for Gia to contact *her*.

It had been a miserable few days but thankfully, it was now over, kind of. With the new information, and after giving the whole thing some thought, Erin began to feel a little more optimistic, mostly because one thing was obvious - She'd soon be back. Gia had made her home in Cambridge, exams were next week, she had rowing to train for and most importantly of all, she had Erin.

It hurt that Erin wasn't worth the courtesy of a *goodbye,* or of any explanation whatsoever, but as long as Gia was safe then Erin could relax and continue with her studies.

Gia would return and then things would pick up where they left off.

In the grand scheme of their lives, nothing had changed.

Chapter Nine

SUMMER HOLIDAY

No later than two hours after deciding on going to Napoli had Ben booked their holiday. She had to hand it to him; turned out he was keen on travelling after all. It also appeared he was keen to get away fast because the old romantic had booked the trip for the very next morning. "He must really want to see some scenery," she muttered to herself as she opened up her browser.

Because of the short notice, Erin had little time to prepare, pack, cancel appointments and, as her fingers created a trail of sweat over the touchpad, find out how the damn Italian could be located.

She opened Google and typed in 'Gianna De Luca Napoli.' There were several listings under that name but the one that stood out, according to her LinkedIn profile, was the Gianna De Luca who operated as a small independent physiotherapist, not far from the centre of Napoli.

So, she still possessed her birth name, ten years later. Interesting. "Hang on, Italian women keep their family name when they get married." That much was true. So there wasn't much, if anything, she could take from that.

Erin scribbled down the address of Gianna's practice, as well as her contact number on a scrap of paper and buried it in her bag. She remained motionless for a while and then began tapping the desk with her fingers, leaving small round moisture dots on the wood. What did Gianna look like these days? Was she still the strikingly beautiful girl she'd fallen in love with? She clicked on Images but unfortunately, nothing came up other than, rather bizarrely, some horrifying artwork and a map of Napoli. Google Images could be so random.

She sat and thought for a while longer. They were leaving tomorrow morning. Erin could hardly just breeze unannounced into her surgery, grin obscenely and say, "*surprise, here I am, remember me? I'm that girl who took your v-card.*" No, doing something so rash would inevitably turn into a disaster, not to mention convince the girl she'd made the right decision in fleeing in the first place. Probably best to at least give Gianna some warning that she was in town and that if she had chance, she'd stop by for a coffee. Ugh, but it felt like arranging a first date, except the other person had no idea about it. At least sending an email in advance would come over as being less stalkerish. What were the stalking laws in Italy?

After pottering for a while about the office, she decided to send the message via LinkedIn rather than by email. First of all, Erin did not possess her actual email address. Second, at least in her own head, Erin could just reason that she accidentally chanced upon Gianna's profile in her professional network the day before she just so happened to be travelling to Napoli. All just a coincidence, see?

Erin clicked 'Send a message' and after fifteen minutes, finally typed:

Hi Gianna,

I hope you remember me?

I also hope you are well and happy. It's been a long time. It just so happens I'll be passing through Napoli for a few days from tomorrow. I thought it'd be nice to grab a coffee and have a catch-up? How is Friday for you? I'll drop by your practice around mid-morning. If not, then that's cool.

Ciao,
Erin.

.

She toyed with the idea of adding kisses but decided against it. After reading through her words for the fifth time, she clicked 'Send message' with a clammy finger.

"Done. No going back now."

She shut down the computer and began to pack.

THE NOT SO FUNNY THING WAS THAT ERIN HAD ALWAYS expected that one day, Gia would abandon her. The vision had always been that Gia would simply stop talking to her and start hanging out with other, cooler and more popular girls instead. It had happened many times throughout secondary school so why would university be any different? However, that Gia would abandon her by skipping the country altogether and ditching her entire life in Cambridge without so much as a word, Erin had not expected. Was she really that bad? Had she really deserved all this?

As the weeks wore on, exams came and went, rowing

competitions were never entered, girly chats never occurred and life itself seemed completely pointless.

It had gradually dawned on Erin that Gia would not be returning when she'd missed all her exams and failed to hand in any course work, even though posting it from Italy would have been an option. When Erin checked the noticeboard, scrolled down their group's exam results and found a whole row of zeroes beside Gia's initials, she knew her friend had failed the year and would therefore not be permitted to progress to year two.

"She's not coming back." Erin hissed, the truth finally hitting her as once again, she began hyperventilating and staggered out from Downing College, the same building that was becoming increasingly difficult to be inside.

Her main regret – That she never got to tell Gia she was in love.

That was six weeks and two days after she'd last seen her.

At three months, Erin finally opened the curtains, revealing a section of the Cam they'd so often rowed along. She stared at it for an unknown while, blinked away the tears and slipped on her trainers. "Must do *something* today."

She opened the front door, stepped onto the cobbles and pottered in the direction of Starbucks, her backpack filled with physiotherapy books. When she arrived she ordered a coffee, averting her eyes from the spot they used to sit at the opposite side of the room. She took a book from her bag, found the page and settled down for some reading.

"IS IT REALLY HER?"

"I think so," he said, rubbing his chin, but he couldn't be sure.

"When'd you last see her?"

"Not sure. It's been a while. A few months, perhaps?"

"Where's her dyke friend?"

"How should I know. And don't be so cruel."

"Come on, she's a dyke and you know it."

"Most probably, yes."

"Which means that *she* is probably a dyke too." He gestured with his head to the girl sitting over by the window, which meant that if it was her, she wasn't in her usual spot. The girl looked sad and on edge, as though she didn't want to be there, or anywhere else for that matter, like she was truly uncomfortable in her own skin. "It's pointless wasting your jizz on that one." He placed an arm around his colleague's shoulder. "You should think about someone else when you tug yourself off, someone you have a chance with."

He closed his eyes and rubbed his forehead. "Will you stop. You're supposed to be offering encouragement."

"Ok, fine." He gestured again with his head toward the solitary girl, reading what looked to be a huge volume on physiotherapy. "She looks soul destroyed, whoever she is, but if that's the type you go for...?" He held up his hands. "On the other hand ... if that is the todger dodger then this is the only time she's *ever* been in here without her cock block," he sniggered, really struggling to keep it together, "which means it might also be the last. So don't chicken out on this one, right?"

"Shit." Every bone in his body shook. His throat, dry like his present run with the ladies, hurt when he swallowed. His hands, covered in coffee odour, mingled with the sweat that pushed through his pores, creating a disgusting residue over his fingers. "Shit, you're right, this could be my only chance."

His friend patted him on the shoulder. "So don't fuck it up. I'll want a full report when you're done." He walked back downstairs. Like *he'd* ever approached a girl cold before, when no alcohol had been involved.

He teetered in the girl's direction just as a large woman pulled out her chair, blocking his path and forcing him to leap sideways. It unsettled him and he had to take another second to collect himself. It seemed like everyone was watching, could read his thoughts, but he dismissed that lunacy. His legs were holding at least, a bonus. Where had she been lately? She was the only thing that made working here, with Jambo, tolerable, that once every few days he'd get to see her and her absence had very nearly pushed him to throw in the towel. But by God, she was beautiful. He'd thought that since the moment he first saw the girl. That long, slender body with boobs that drew the eye worse than a street mugging. Her smile that lit up the otherwise drab Starbucks. Her grace as she walked, like the very heavens cleared a path for her. Best of all, that long silky red hair he dreamed of pressing his nose against, inhaling her smell, sent from the heavens. There was no way this perfect Goddess could be a lesbian. God would not be so cruel. At least he prayed.

And then he found himself standing before her and time stopped and nothing else existed but himself and this girl. If he got sacked for doing this then so be it.

She glanced up from her book and he hesitated. Was it even her? Where was that spark, that life, that thing you just couldn't put words to? Behind her eyes, it was like something was missing. Maybe it wasn't...

"I'm sorry, I thought you were somebody else." He was almost relieved to have been let off the hook, yet at the same time devastated this wasn't his infatuation and that finally, he was speaking to her. He turned around but she held up a hand, there were scratches over her skin.

"You're that guy who always looks at me, aren't you?"

Busted, you fool! No, wait. It *is* her! "You, um, you look really different."

"Is it the shaved head, by any chance?" She asked with a raised eyebrow.

"Yes," he rolled his eyes, "but there's something else, I don't know, anyway, it doesn't matter..." My God but he was actually speaking to her. He took the seat opposite and was relieved to look up and find her still there. She hadn't bailed, at least yet. Perhaps he could draw confidence from that. She still looked amazing, even with an egg for a head, which was saying something. He'd never normally look twice at such a girl but this Goddess had been in his fantasies for so long and now he was actually speaking to her, alone, without her friend, or whoever she was, he was damned if he'd let a tiny thing like the fact she no longer possessed the red hair he coveted from stopping him at least getting a date. "What's your name?"

"I'm Erin," she held out a delicate hand. Both were scratched.

He took it and held on for longer than was polite but he didn't give a shit, and neither did she seem to mind. And if she noticed his sticky, coffee smelling mitts then she showed no sign, which was saying something about her, because he was sweating and he did indeed stink. Not just looks but this girl, *Erin*, was sweet too.

"I'm Ben, it's nice to meet you."

THE WHITE WALL WOULD SOON CHANGE COLOUR IF SHE stared at it any longer. Using her sleeve to wipe away a tear, she took out her notepad and opened it to a blank page.

Then began to write.

The words flew, or rather spewed, from her, like they'd been in her heart for weeks, months, fighting to escape. The poem took a mere five minutes to complete, by which time it was almost entirely smudged with tears.

When it was done, she decided against reading it. What was the point? It was out of her and now she should probably burn it.

"This is *goodbye*, Gianna." Referring to the damn Italian as her full name had been a way of distancing herself from the girl recently. It might have helped, at least a little.

But no, why go to the trouble of burning it when she could simply consign it forever to the blackness? And so, she reached for her copy of Orthopaedic Physiotherapy and placed the poem inside where the book fell open, at the section entitled 'Isokinetic Dynamometry' before slamming it closed. The stupid book was no longer required reading anyway, so there was no chance of the poem ever resurfacing.

She stood, placed the book at the back of the wardrobe, closed the door and returned to her desk.

She picked up her phone and scanned down the list for that guy she'd met today in Starbucks. He was kind of nice, friendly, reasonably attractive and it was most definitely what she needed right now – A fucking distraction.

"Hi ... yes, it's me ... what? ... Why would you be so surprised? ... I said I'd call ... Ben, wasn't it? ... How'd you like to go for a drink? ... No, not tomorrow, how's tonight? ... Great! ... No, not The Baron of Beef ... don't know it. Do you know The Snug Bar?"

Part Two

NAPOLI

Chapter Ten

WELCOME TO THE MADHOUSE

They say you can't truly know a person until you've lived and been on holiday with them. It had taken all of three minutes, from pulling the rental car out from the airport and onto the main road, for Erin to see a new side to Ben.

"What the fuck? Did you just see that lunatic?" He shouted as what looked like a helmetless twelve-year-old on a scooter swerved in front. "Oh, it's just a matter of time, my friend, it's just a matter of time." Several more near misses with scooters, some with up to three people riding them, occurred before we even entered the city centre, a mere two miles from the airport. There were also incidents with three hatchbacks, a truck, two heaps he couldn't identify as well as several pedestrians. "Seriously, what the fuck? Why bother having traffic lights if you're not going to use them?"

Sure enough, the lights were a total waste of power and metal. When Ben had the audacity to stop at the first set, the car behind honked relentlessly before finally deciding to reverse and overtake, but not before giving the finger.

Although Erin sympathised and dreaded the thought of

driving in what resembled a madhouse, she was still surprised to see this calm man banging his opened hands in anger against the steering wheel, swearing at the top of his voice and generally poisoning the atmosphere. ·

"Fuck! And you wanted to come *here?*" He glared at her, daring to take his eyes from the road for all of half a second.

Indeed, if this was the city Gianna had been born and raised then it might have gone a long way to explain her lack of volume control. It was a pity Erin never got to see Gianna drive, for that might have been an interesting experience, but then again, it was probably for the best.

"The fucking noise," Ben grunted and flinched as a scooter pulled up beside the stationary car. Sure enough, the constant hooting and honking of car horns permeated the air to the extent that one might be forgiven for thinking there was a war on. It was a far cry from the relative tranquillity of Cambridge.

"Hey, try not to let them wind you up. We'll be at the hotel soon and then we can relax. Carry on, straight ahead." Erin tried to sound reassuring as she followed the map on her phone.

"We've got a bond on this thing, if you don't recall." He patted the wheel then twisted to find a sunglasses-wearing teenage girl perched on a scooter right beside his opened window. A dog was sitting on the deck between her feet and she carelessly propped an elbow on the car roof as she waited for a path to clear through the traffic, though the road and pavements, yes, the pavements, were so dense with vehicles that she made no attempt at squeezing through the cracks. Even a scooter could not get through. "Hand off the car, hand off the fucking car." He closed the windows and hastily turned on the air-circulation system as though it would save his life.

When the hotel was located, the next task was finding a

place to park and after driving around the block three times, which took a horrendously long time, Ben finally opted to park illegally, in the centre of the road between two opposing lanes. Ordinarily, and in any other city in the world, this might cause problems but then, not incorrectly, Ben said, "everybody else is doing it," before straining against the weight of his suitcase.

Upon entering the Grand Hotel Santa Lucia, Erin felt her blood pressure drop immediately. The place wasn't large but it was air-conditioned, thank God. Most importantly of all, the constant din from the outside was, for the most part, dampened. The noise could still be heard but instead, it sounded like a crowd cheering in some far-off football stadium, rather than actually being inside the stadium. Cars whooshed down the street, which gave the constant sound and feel of the wind forcing its way through the opened door, augmented only by the higher-pitched whiz from the scooters.

The concierge took one look at his guests, smiled in sympathy, gestured with his arms opened wide, then spoke. "Welcome to the madhouse." It was all enough to assume he took pride in it.

"And you're not joking, which is the funny thing," Erin wiped her forehead.

"Welcome to the Grand Hotel Santa Lucia." His smile remained as he dropped his arms down to his sides. "Now, the first thing I need to ask is … do you have a car?"

It wasn't a strange question to ask up front, it was more in the way he said it. Ben answered with a guarded tone. "Yes, a new rental, why?"

The concierge breathed in and linked his fingers in front of his chest. "I'm afraid you'll have to accept the very real possibility that your car has probably already been stolen, or at the very least, has been broken into and had its entire interior stripped." Well, that didn't take them long.

"What the fuck?" Ben ran his fingers through his hair and dashed from the building.

"Honk your horn outside and I'll open the gate," the concierge shouted after him. "You see that, through there?" He gestured for Erin at a small rusted hovel of a car through a window at the side of the desk. "I paid seventy euros for that piece of shit. Nobody ever touches it, apart from countless other vehicles, of course, but they hardly count. I absolutely love it! If you can get through a single day in the city without a scratch, you'll be the first ever to do so. Let me warn you never to rent or buy a new car in Napoli. In fact, I'm surprised you weren't told."

He checked Erin's reservation and handed over the keys to the room. Ben blasted the horn and the concierge pressed a button that opened an electronic gate. Thankfully, it didn't look like the car had been touched, yet.

Ben returned as what had to be an eighty-year-old porter arrived to take the bags. His uniform consisted of smart black trousers along with contrasting t-shirt emblazoned with a thick black stripe running diagonally across.

"Bit of an odd uniform?" Erin remarked, raising the pitch at the end of the sentence to make it sound like a question.

"That's not his uniform. You'll see many of those t-shirts around Napoli, so the police think we're wearing seat belts behind the wheel."

"Why?" She asked.

"They make a law saying we must wear belts ... We find a way around that law."

Oh, Gianna. This is home? Did she really give up beautiful, peaceful Cambridge for this place? She'd better have her reasons and they'd better be bloody good.

"Breakfast is between seven and ten, check out on your

day of departure is no later than ten." Outside the hotel, a car smashed into the back of another, and then the horns started. Erin's skull hurt, the concierge didn't flinch. "I hope you enjoy your stay."

THE STREETS OF THE HISTORIC CENTRE OF NAPOLI BUSTLED with life, crammed in between narrow walls that were built long before the population had exploded. *Crammed* was one word to describe the entire city but especially the historic centre.

On Spaccanapoli, that Erin remembered Gianna referring to on numerous occasions, literally meaning *split Napoli*, dividing the entire historic centre down the middle; street performers stood every few metres apart and vied for the attention of paying tourists and locals. One red-faced opera singer tried and almost succeeded in being heard above the crowd.

Erin and Ben had been exploring for the last hour and after having worked up an appetite had chanced upon what turned out to be one of the world's most famous pizza restaurants, Il Pizzaiolo del Presidente.

"It says they changed the name in honour of Bill Clinton's visit in 1994." Ben read from the English section of the menu, the back of which displayed a photo of the former President eating a slice of pizza, sitting not far from where they were.

"You know, I heard pizza was invented in this city," Erin said, watching Ben's genuine interest. For all the oddities of this city, they'd always have that claim. Gianna had often boasted of Napoli's pizza, how it was the best in the world by a long, long way and how she missed not having *proper pizza* in England.

"I can't wait to try it," he glanced around the busy

restaurant and caught the eye of the waiter, who came over and took their orders.

Erin's face softened, "I know you must probably think I'm insane for choosing *this* place over some of the others but..."

"...But *'it's a central hub for the Amalfi Coast, Pompeii and other places'* ... I know. Plus your friend is here." He sipped his wine and raised his eyebrows in appreciation. "But I don't think my blood pressure can handle being here for any more than a couple of nights, I already feel like I've knocked several years off my life." There was nothing wrong with his blood pressure but Erin could sympathise nonetheless.

"It's a, um, interesting city," she placated him.

"Now, *that*, it certainly is. But sure, it's beautiful and would be more so with fewer people and less noise." He smirked and shook his head. "Those bloody scooters, they are everywhere. Like flies you can't shake off."

"I don't think this city was built with cars in mind. It's a very old place."

He reached across to touch Erin's hand. "I'm sorry I lost my temper before, you know it's not like me. I'm not used to this kind of thing. I was taken completely off guard by the, um, locals."

"Hey, it's ok. I understand. You handled it very well considering ... but you got us here in one piece." Erin sipped her wine. "What do you suggest with regards to your blood pressure?"

Ben answered right away. "It's probably best you visit your friend as soon as possible and then we should take the car along the coast, preferably north and find a peaceful hotel overlooking the Tyrrhenian Sea. Sound perfect or what?"

"It does." She kept her smile even as her heart thumped with her next thought. "Then I'll pay her a visit tomorrow."

Tomorrow.

Chapter Eleven

GIANNA

She pressed her ear against the door, the muffled voices audible but not comprehensible. Why was he still here? "Just pay your bill and leave," she whispered against the wood for the third time.

Vedetta's voice grew more desperate. Gianna would have to intervene soon. She always preferred keeping the physio side separate from everything else, particularly having to ask clients for money because it looked more professional when her receptionist took care of that. And damn it, she *was* a professional. Or would be if some of her clients would allow it.

Finally, Gianna opened the door and stepped into the reception. "Signor Costa, is there a problem?" She noted the look of apology, mixed with relief on Vedetta's face as she slumped back in her chair.

"Yes, there is. I keep telling your assistant that I will pay next week, but she refuses to believe me." Signor Costa, in his mid-forties, stood with the aid of a stick, the sweat trickled down his bare arms and hairy neck to disappear beneath a white vest that was almost transparent with perspiration.

"Could you pass me Signor Costa's account card, please?" She held a hand out to Vedetta, even though Gianna already knew the standing of this particular account. The man cleared his throat as she pretended to read the details from the card. "Signor Costa, you booked in for a block of six treatments, which entitled you to the discounted rate of five hundred euros. The discounted rate is only applicable when you pay up front in advance. We've already allowed you to defer your payment several weeks."

"Yes, I know and I told the lady I'll pay *next* week." He waved a hand to dismiss them and half-turned toward the exit.

"Signor Costa, you've just had your sixth treatment."

"Sixth? That was my fifth."

Vedetta shook her head and squeezed the fleshy area of skin at the top of her nose.

Gianna waved the card at the man. "Signor Costa, we keep thorough records. That was your sixth treatment." She knew this oaf was playing her for a fool.

The door opened and the rattle of the bell distracted everybody for a brief moment. "Excuse me." Vincenzo entered and took a seat, squeezing all the air out from the sponge before opening up his newspaper.

"Signor Costa, that was your sixth treatment. You should have paid six weeks ago, you kept on deferring and now you must settle your account." Gianna could feel the heat rising within and had to dig deep to save from giving the man the full force of her temper, which would not have been a good idea.

"You see this?" He bounced the tip of his stick on the floor, threw it up into the air and caught it half way down the shaft. "This stick ... which after six visits, I *still* need to walk, to get to my car, to visit my mother, to take a shit." He pointed the stick's handle in Gianna's face, she held her ground but only just, the tip mere inches from her nose. "If your treatments were worth the money, I wouldn't need this confounded thing anymore."

Vincenzo placed a closed hand against his mouth and forced out a dry cough. Gianna waited for the hacking to abate before continuing.

"As I told you from our initial consultation, Signor Costa, you'd require more than a mere six sessions before you became fully recuperated. The body does what the body does, but you'll require treatment for a while yet before you'll be walking unaided."

"Well then, I'll pay when that happy day arrives." He jabbed the cane's handle against the bulk of Gianna's shoulder, forcing her to step back.

The phone rang in the treatment room, which could only be the obvious person, and Gianna tried not to be distracted by the sound.

Vedetta interjected. "Signor Costa did not book in for any more treatments, Dottoressa De Luca."

Gianna could only watch forlornly as Signor Costa hobbled toward the door. "So that's what you're going to do, is it?"

Vincenzo, an absolute brute of a man, stood and glanced at Gianna with a raised eyebrow. She knew why. He was asking permission to intervene. She shook her head and silently mouthed the word *no*.

Signor Costa flapped an arm to dismiss Gianna. "That's what I'm doing." And then the door slammed after him.

"I'm sorry, Dottoressa," Vedetta sighed, visibly shaken, "I really did try."

"I know you did. It's ok, you did your best." Gianna handed the card back to her, blew a few stray strands of hair from her eyes, smiled at Vincenzo and gestured toward the treatment room. "Let's go in here."

The large man plodded past her. "You must enjoy losing money, Dottoressa."

She closed the door behind them just as the phone silenced. "Vincenzo, what can I do for you?"

He gave her a funny look as though it was obvious why he was there, then paced about the surgery, picking up a small ornament of a man in the sprinting start position and studied it. "How are you, Dottoressa?"

"As well as can be expected." She stood upright by the window and rested the fleshy part of her arm on the ledge for support.

"How's your moth..." he stopped himself, closed his eyes and exhaled. "Don Sabbatino sends his regards and he hopes business is going well?" He replaced the ornament and continued pacing the room. His grey shirt had become untucked where his gut pushed it out at the front. Grey truly was the worst colour to wear on such a hot day, the damp that originated from his armpits stained both his flanks horrifically. All Gianna could focus on, though, was his slicked-back hair and pockmarked face. On realising she was treating his question as a rhetorical one, he continued. "It's that time of the month."

"Well, why else would you be here?" She shuffled behind her desk and opened the safe at its side, pulling out a bundle of notes. She threw the money down to the table and hesitated before speaking. "This ... this is most of it." Her thumbnail ascended to her teeth.

He took the money and flipped through it. "Only most?" He closed his eyes and shook his head. "Dottoressa, I'm not sure I can even look at you right now." His eyes flew open as he rushed a handkerchief from his pocket, pressed it against his snout and rasped a painful cough from his system. The ends of the handkerchief flared as it struggled to contain the force from his throat.

Gianna threw up her arms just as the phone began ringing again. The caller ID said *Agata*. Gianna lifted the receiver then pressed the *end call* button before leaving it to rest on her desk. She'd pay for that later.

Vincenzo recovered from his ordeal and screwed up the sodden handkerchief before thrusting it back in his trouser pocket. "You know how Don Sabbatino wants you to succeed but you're not making it easy on yourself." He shook his head again and appeared genuinely sad.

"You saw what happened out there. Times are tough. I'm doing my best." Gianna thought forward to the inevitable consequences, though in reality, she was more concerned with expelling the odour after Vincenzo left. Were there faint lines of steam drifting up from his neck? She squinted for a better look and decided there probably was.

"You're five hundred short. Don Sabbatino has been very accommodating towards you. You know he has."

"I know he has and I appreciate his kindness."

"But you understand that if word were to get out that one of his clients had taken bad council and refused to pay then it wouldn't be long before others took advantage of his good nature. I want you to know that it pains me." He looked like he was in enough pain already, despite adding more to his burden.

"If I don't have it then I don't have it. So go on, do what you have to do." She took a small step toward him and folded her arms, trying and probably failing to look defiant. All she wanted was the oaf gone so she held her stance and waited for him to act.

"Maybe there's another way, Dottoressa," he took a step toward her, "Signor Costa was it?"

Her arms fell to their sides. It was obvious where this was going. "What about him?"

He took another ornament from the shelf and pretended

to pay it interest. "You know how Don Sabbatino insists on looking after his clients."

"No!"

"All I need is an address, Dottoressa, and I'll recoup the money from your client."

To be fair, it was tempting, especially after the boor's conduct before. "I do not give out confidential client details."

"If Don Sabbatino was here now, he'd beg you." He did sound sincere and Gianna could see this was hard for him. "Can you really call him a *client* if he's never paid you a single dime or morsel?" He just didn't get it. Breaking the guy's legs to get the money he owed kind of defeated the object of visiting a physiotherapist in the first place but Gianna very much doubted that Knuckles saw the irony. "It's your call," he said, sliding out from his belt what looked like a foot-long iron tube.

She didn't have long to think about her options. She could set the oaf on Signor Costa to recoup her five hundred euros and be done with it. At worst, she'd lose a client who refused to pay and have his being crippled further on her conscience. But this wasn't why she came into physiotherapy, to see the people she was supposed to be helping get beat up by the Camorra. In truth, she'd feel far better administering that beating to Signor Costa herself.

"Please, Dottoressa, all I need is an address."

Gianna sighed. "I can't do it, Vincenzo. Do what you have to do."

He clamped his eyes shut and sighed but when he opened them he was a different man and struck through the air what Gianna now saw to be a cosh. Two narrower cylinders snapped out from the larger outer pipe to form one long iron baton that he gripped in a plump hand. "You may wish to step back." He plodded toward the ceiling lamp above the treatment table and reached up before pulling it down on its arm, the shirt tucked into the back of his trousers came loose to expose the matted grey hair above his crack. He positioned himself and twisted to Gianna. "I want you to know that this pains me deeply." Then he struck the light, shattering a million fragments of glass over his face.

His first reaction, much too late, was to shield his eyes with a chubby forearm. He staggered back, in obvious torment, while still maintaining an outstretched arm, as if even now he was searching for something to strike. To give the man credit, as blood from his eyes poured to the floor, he took it as well as any gangster could. Glass shards were sticking out from his face and neck where they'd penetrated the pockmarked flesh. The bulb from the skylight would cost a couple of Euros to replace. The mess on the other hand...

"Oh my God, Vincenzo, are you ok? Here, let me help you." Gianna rushed forward but was rebuked by his warning hand.

"Don't come close," he urged, poising with the cosh, his grey shirt morphing red. He unleashed an almighty hacking cough lasting several seconds, though on this occasion not troubling to bring out the handkerchief.

"Vincenzo, you need an ambulance," she called, backing away against the window.

"Just stand back!" He approached the monitor that was hooked to the electrotherapy short wave diathermy. The first swing with the baton missed, the follow through almost sent him tumbling over but he regained his balance and senses enough to make a much better second attempt. Gianna saw the spark as the cosh smashed through the monitor's glass just as the large man shot backwards across the room, crashing against the floor several metres away. The monitor would cost considerably more to replace.

Gianna unplugged the offending piece of equipment then opened the door to reception.

Vedetta was already standing, telephone receiver grasped ready in hand. "Another ambulance, Dottoressa?"

"Thank you, Vedetta."

Twenty minutes later, Vincenzo regained consciousness as the paramedics dropped him on the stretcher. They'd required the extra help from both Gianna and Vedetta to carry out the lift, the blood over his face having dried to an insane crust, his eyes menacing like a creature from the folklore of some long-extinct backward culture, and good riddance.

"I'll be back in three days, Dottoressa," he croaked and spat out a tooth, "and Don Sabbatino will require a late payment fee of five thousand Euros."

Gianna sighed and turned to the paramedic. "Will you make sure he recovers well?"

The ambulance pulled away, only to immediately find itself trapped within a dense mass of stationary vehicles. It would be a while before poor Vincenzo arrived at the emergency room.

Gianna turned to Vedetta, "so, how's your first week going?" She could only smile in apology.

Gianna returned to her desk, found the receiver still off the hook and replaced it. The phone rang within five seconds, the caller ID flashing *Agata*.

She collapsed forward against the desk, enshrouding herself in darkness, exhaled and braced for a few precious seconds before having to answer. "Agata."

"Why didn't you answer?"

"Hello, Agata."

"You hung up on me!"

Gianna took a long breath. "I'm very busy, you know this."

"Who are you with?"

"Nobody, Agata, just clients."

"It's that bitch, isn't it!"

"Agata, I keep telling you, she's my receptionist. There's literally nothing for you to worry about." And Gianna would be damned before she'd allow the paranoid woman to scare away another employee.

"I saw an ambulance outside your surgery."

"What?" She almost leapt from her chair and subconsciously turned to glance out the window. "Are you spying on me?"

"You didn't answer!"

Gianna exhaled and slumped back into her seat. "Why did you want me? Is it even important?"

"When can I see you?"

How about never. Gianna paused, hoping to find the courage to rid herself of this woman. "Um, I have a window tomorrow morning, if you're early. A quick coffee but then I have clients." Not to mention the small matter of finding five grand. Perhaps escaping to Cyprus might be a better option.

"Great." Well, that sure changed her tone. "I'll be over early tomorrow morning. I can't wait to see you. Ciao."

Gianna replaced the handset, thankful for the conversation to have ended. "Bathroom," she muttered to herself.

It was whilst washing her hands that she caught sight of something unsightly in the mirror. "Oh, no you don't." She moved closer and squinted. Another fucking grey hair. "I'm twenty-fucking-nine!" She yanked it from her scalp and flushed it down the toilet.

She grabbed her panino from the refrigerator, slumped down at her desk and called through to Vedetta. "How long until my next appointment?"

"A little under twenty minutes, Gia."

That wasn't long at all. "Thanks." She unwrapped the panino, prosciutto crudo, opened her mouth and jammed a large portion within. An almighty smash from somewhere close raised her buttocks a full inch from the seat. The usual car horns followed by shouts and screams. How there were so many collisions in a city that didn't move was beyond her.

"Email..." she mumbled and opened up the laptop before signing into Libero. Nothing but the usual Nigerian scams and suppliers trying to sell physiotherapy consumables with the occasional work enquiry sprinkled in. She took a bite from her panino, deleting the crap from her account. "Penis extensions, thanks but no..." and a LinkedIn alert from Doctor Erin Baker.

A chunk of ham was pulled down the wrong pipe and she shot to her feet, hunched over the desk and gasped as she struggled to induce a cough. Her eyes watered, a thick coating of mucus built in her throat and her face turned red. She heaved from the pit of her stomach and managed to fire a ham projectile half way across the room.

Close call.

She dabbed a tissue against her eyelids and took a long drink of water, clearing away the built-up mucus. She wrapped the panino back in its foil and placed it in the desk drawer. Then she took her seat and rearranged the papers that were haphazard on the desk. "What the fuck?" She glanced outside the window, endured a few moments of noise from without and thumped the desk. "Fuck! Fuck! Fuck!" She froze, still unable to face the laptop screen and found her fingers were tapping a rhythm against the touchpad. Her heart beat hard as sweat built over her forehead.

"Erin," she hissed. "Sweet, beautiful Erin."

She sat still for a few more minutes, settling herself, Erin's face, her smell, her oar grunts, her ears, and braced as she clicked on the alert. She held her eyes closed tight, breathed deeply, then allowed them to open.

"'*I hope you remember me?*' ... Of course, I remember you." She breathed and continued. "'*I also hope you are well and happy*'

... Not really, Erin ... *'It's been a long time'* ... Yes, it has. It's been too long ... *'It just so happens I'll be passing through Napoli for a few days from tomorrow'* ... What?" Gianna was unaware of just how hard her hand was gripping the edge of the desk. "Wait, tomorrow? When did she send this email?" She checked the date on the alert. "Yesterday! She's here now?" She made a strange yelping noise as she straightened and found that her foot was tapping against the floor. Must read on. "'*I thought it'd be nice to grab a coffee and have a catch up? How is Friday for you?*' ... Friday? What day is today? Shit! Mental block. It's Thursday. Fuck! ... *'I'll drop by your practice around mid-morning. If not, then that's cool'* ... Of course, it's cool, you silly goose." She sighed deeply and dabbed again at her eyes and cheeks.

Erin – The one who got away.

Gianna had never been able to decide if their finally getting together the day before she had to leave was a blessing or a tragedy. In truth, it was probably both, but it *had* been horrific timing.

Erin – The sweetest, most beautiful person she'd ever known. And Gianna had known at the time, as she'd known in ... how long? "Ten years? Fuck, where does it all go?" She'd known just how much her leaving would hurt Erin. Worse, that as the months and years elapsed, she had never been able to bring herself to contact her first love. And the longer she left it, the harder it became until the time arrived when she no longer possessed the kind of courage she once had.

But now Erin was reaching out to *her*. "Why? I don't deserve this. I don't deserve you, Erin."

Erin.

Gianna had so often reminisced with affection the many memories they shared in only their short time together. "A little under eight months." She whispered to herself, despair descending over her mood. The late-night study sessions where they'd talk about everything *but* physiotherapy. The physical practices and Erin being too nervous to touch her. The rowing; she gasped, "rowing." How she missed it, just her and Erin together in a boat, rowing down a beautiful river. How Erin would always bring an extra cereal bar in case she'd missed breakfast. The way Erin's tired morning eyes shot to life at the sight of her. Their first and only nervous night, where they'd fumbled around together, not quite knowing how things worked, that she'd replayed in her mind, over and over, where they finally got to be with each other. Erin's smooth skin, supple breasts, her smell, taste, that smile that few ever got to see, indeed, seemed reserved only for her.

Gianna had been the most important thing in Erin's life, she knew that, and now after everything, how could she possibly face her?

And there existed the problem.

Just how, exactly, *could* Gianna face Erin? "Tomorrow." How would she react to being near her again? What would she say to her? How could she explain running away like she had? Did she possess the strength and courage to meet Erin? Gianna was not the same person she'd been ten years before. She'd taken far too many knocks since then and it had affected her in so many ways.

Gianna was on the verge of turning grey. Lines had started to appear below her eyes but worst of all, she was no longer the svelte athlete Erin would remember her as. "How can I meet with her? I bet she's still so beautiful." She knew it was her ego taking over and she still possessed a great ego, even now. It was a thing common to many women, Italian women especially. To have been beautiful, only to lose it, would only take on a new apprehension when meeting old loves. But none of that would have mattered to the Erin she knew.

And there, on the computer screen, the thumbnail image of Doctor Erin Baker.

She hovered over it, daring to click it.

All she had of Erin's physical appearance were in her memories, having left her photographs in Cambridge.

She clicked on the image and her head swirled as the photo enlarged.

"Just as I remember you, my English rose."

The most beautiful girl in the world.

Tomorrow.

Chapter Twelve

TODON

TODAY

A nd there it was.

Fisioterapia di Napoli stood on the corner of a busy crossroads in what had to be one of the more rundown areas of Napoli, just outside of the historic centre, about a fifteen-minute walk from the hotel.

Even now at ten in the morning, with rush hour supposedly over, vehicles still remained for the most part stationary, crowding the intersection. Rush hour never ended in this city. The usual blaring of horns that enshrouded her added to something else that clung to the air, something that Erin could not fathom. It was a constant tension, like something was about to happen and she couldn't figure out if it was the atmosphere from this part of the city, or from what she was about to do.

Ben had left the hotel a little before Erin, in search of cathedrals, city walls and ancient monuments. As soon as the door closed behind him, Erin's nerves had been shot to pieces, combined with heavy heartbeats, nausea and all manner of other bodily stimuli serving to remind her that today would be big, even potentially life-changing.

Now, she'd been standing, warily, across the road for five minutes, though it was probably longer, staring bleary-eyed at Gianna's building. She'd made it this far, all the way to Napoli, after so much deliberation, heartache and emotional time spent. But those final few steps, she knew, would be the hardest.

So, she decided instead upon a quick espresso, perhaps not the most suitable of beverages, but she needed it anyway. It was either that or a whisky shot, which would hardly impress Gianna at a quarter past ten in the morning.

She had a reasonable view, through the traffic, of Fisioterapia di Napoli from her table on the street outside the café bar. The gentle breeze brought with it all manner of rubbish to stir around her feet.

She finished her espresso and regretted not getting something larger. "No more stalling, Erin." It was time to make a move.

Why was she putting it off? Had this all been one terrible mistake? One big emotional misadventure.

Surely, if Gianna had wanted to see Erin again then she'd have made the first move and probably would have done so years ago. It was true that Erin had received no response to her email but then again she'd stupidly forgotten to bring her European plug socket adaptor. Her phone's battery had vanquished its power sometime during the night and she'd yet to purchase a new adaptor in Napoli. It was entirely plausible that Gianna had emailed in the meantime, wasn't it? She remembered framing her initial email in such a way as to have come over relaxed about the whole meeting; it was no biggie if Gianna couldn't attend because Erin was in town anyway.

"Oh stop stalling, Erin, and get over there."

She grabbed her bag, stood and took a large breath of air.

And then the door to Fisioterapia di Napoli swung open and Gianna stepped outside.

IT HAD ALL HAPPENED SO FAST AND GIANNA HAD YET HAD the time to process the fact that Erin had contacted her and was even now pottering about the city. One moment she was checking her emails and the very next day she was due to meet the most important person who ever existed - After ten years.

Everything else that was happening in her life, the crap, hurt, pain, infatuated women, debts to the Camorra, had all taken a back seat to this. To Erin.

It was true that this had all come from nowhere and she knew Erin owed her nothing and Gianna most definitely did not deserve this visit but she'd made an effort anyway. How could she not?

Despite all the changes she'd undergone since last seeing Erin, Gianna still possessed that same monstrous ego, the same that had tried to talk her out of this meeting. She chuckled as she looked in the bathroom mirror, "that'll never change."

She'd visited a friend last night to have her hair cut and dried, with special instructions to pluck out all the greys, and to burn them if need be.

"I hope my English is still good." She hadn't spoken the language in years other than with that one American client with the hip replacement.

Erin had not stated exactly when she would arrive but now it was approaching ten in the morning, there was a certain feeling of imminence, as though something was about to happen, like someone very special was close by.

Then Vedetta's muffled voice was just audible, though not exactly comprehensible, through the door and over the traffic.

There was a pause, which Gia used to concentrate on her

breathing and then a knock resounded against her office door, sending a flood of electricity through her every vein, her hands clammed up as sweat pricked at the skin's surface all over her body.

She stood and patted down her dress. This was it. Good luck, Gia. "Come in."

Agata thrust open the door. "Excuse me?" She asked, barging inside. "Why are you talking English?"

"Shit!" What was *she* doing here? Why now? Please, not now!

"You're not happy to see me?" Agata demanded, her look mirroring Gianna's own. "You said *shit*!"

But there was no time for pleasantries, not today. "I don't have time for this, Agata, I have clients today."

"No, you don't!"

"Excuse me?"

"You told me yesterday, you have a window this morning. A quick coffee, you promised."

"Did I?" Shit, she really *had* promised.

"And your eleven o'clock, Signora Rossi..."

"Yes?" Gianna asked with narrowed eyes.

"She's not coming."

Gianna folded her arms. "And how would you know that?"

"Because she's me," Agata smiled, as though she was doing Gianna some great favour, "so now we can spend some time together."

Gianna exhaled an involuntary breath. How many of the other *no shows* had Agata been responsible for in the three months since they met in that gay bar? Anyway, she didn't want to think about *that* now, she needed Agata gone and fast. "A *very* quick coffee, Agata." Gianna grabbed her bag. "Let's go!" She rushed toward the door but could hear no footsteps in her wake. Hand gripping the handle, Gianna looked back over her shoulder to Agata, still stood there, head bowed. "What's wrong?"

"You're always so mean to me." Her face screwed up as the waterworks commenced in earnest.

This was not what she needed right now but seeing the girl there like that, and being at least partly responsible for it, Gianna's soft spot came to the fore. She hated having a soft spot, especially now. She gave Agata a hug, not too tight. "Hey, that's not true." And it kind of wasn't. Ugh, what a stupid mess. She made soothing sounds for a few seconds, then tried to gently prod Agata toward the door, who plodded along for three small steps before stopping.

"I just want you to love me like I love you," she moaned, grinding to a halt.

Aah, ooh, not the conversation for this minute. Ordinarily, now might be an ideal time to break things off and put some real distance between them but if Gianna were to do that now then the situation could only descend and that would steal *time*. Gianna did not have time. She hated doing it but in the moment, what alternative had the woman given her? "I do love you, you know this," she tugged the pest toward the exit.

"But you're not *in love* with me," she wailed, again applying the brakes.

Gianna could now feel no small quantity of panic building inside her. It wasn't merely from being forced into *this* conversation and *now*, whilst Erin was potentially minutes away, but ultimately, one could only be judged by the kind of people around them, by the company they kept, likes attract and such. And whilst this Neapolitana may have been attractive, with her long dark hair, clear skin, slender legs and breasts that were small, shapely and pert, the woman had persistently demonstrated her instability, which truly saying something for a Neapolitan lesbian. The way she so frequently materialised in the most random of places suggested something a little worse than mere possessiveness, though making fake client appointments was something new entirely. How had it ever come to this? That Gianna had fallen into such company, and what's more, despite knowing better, had kept it. Had her confidence really taken *that* much of a beating?

No. *That* conversation would need to happen soon. Just not now. "You know what, I've been thinking about this a lot recently but I really don't think that *here* is the place to discuss it. Let's go get that coffee over the road and talk about *us*." Gianna held out her hand for effect, plastering on the most convincingly genuine smile she could muster.

"Ok," Agata wiped away her tears and took Gianna's hand.

Then they left the surgery.

THERE SHE WAS.

After ten years – The damn Italian.

Grey clouds whirled in Erin's periphery, a thing that hadn't happened in so many years, time slowed, senses heightened, her skin tingled yet she didn't notice any of it. Neither did she notice the grey clouds receding, though much of the environment remained blotted out.

Gianna, if that was truly her, in the centre of Erin's focus, had clearly changed. A lot.

Though she would always be beautiful to Erin, Gianna had lost much of what had been the initial attraction. The flowing, silky dark hair that used to bounce with her every step or shake of the head was now shorter, had gained some curls and lost its former vitality. The energy she possessed of old had given way to lethargy, evidenced by the way she stepped, formerly with long confident strides that were hard to keep up with, now she absolutely dragged her feet. Indeed, Gianna had gained weight, lots of it, and even now ambled sluggishly through the stationary traffic – In Erin's direction, no less. But what was more; a tiny, minute detail that had taken a while to register, Gianna was holding hands with another woman.

"Shit!" Erin found herself almost rooted to the litter-strewn pavement before she could snap out of her semi-trance and back up, away from the café bar, towards a nearby street vendor. She had a good view of Gianna, through the passing pedestrians as she pretended to be interested in some tech magazine, or was it finance?

Erin studied Gianna, the source of her present melancholy bordering on depression, with scrutiny. Should she approach and say *hi*? No, of course not, she had company, and it really wasn't how Erin had envisaged her big reunion, having to share it with somebody else, least of all with a slender brunette who was even now holding Gianna's hand while looking at her in the exact same way Erin used to.

Gianna and the woman took seats at the same table Erin had been settled at only minutes earlier. The tall, attractive brunette took Erin's chair and pushed aside her spent espresso cup with the back of a hand before leaning inward toward Gianna with a carefree elbow on the table and a hand propping up her face.

It was an odd feeling, finally seeing Gianna so close, not just after ten years, but after the last few weeks where little else had occupied Erin's thoughts. The strange thing was, that even now, even after everything, it almost seemed like the completely natural thing to do, to simply step forward, approach the girl and announce her presence, almost like they'd never been separated and a part of Erin wondered just how easily they'd be able to fall back into the old routine of ease, comfort and familiarity.

Erin's senses were indeed heightened, still, in this most surreal of experiences, the minute noises in the distance amplified, yet conversely unnoticeable at the same time. It was almost as if a spotlight from the skies shone over Gianna and magnified every small detail, blanking out everything not inside the light. Unfortunately, the other woman was occupying that same light and Erin captured the same details and particularities about her.

The worst thing – Gianna was happy - And although Erin knew she should have been happy for her, in the moment, there was nothing but numbness.

They were engrossed in conversation, Gianna speaking with the same kind of animation she always had when trying to drag Erin out to some bar or sports social. In a way, it was comforting that some things remained constant. Gianna smiled as her companion rubbed her arm and she reached across the table to take the woman's hand, leaned over and then whispered something that had a magical effect as the woman straightened and grinned like a smitten schoolgirl while she twirled tassels of long brown hair between her fingers. In fact, to the prying eye, it looked like love and whatever Gianna had whispered, it must have been special, reserved for her only.

"The worst thing?" Erin muttered to herself. No, it wasn't *the worst thing* that Gianna was happy. It was the *best* thing.

Erin replaced the magazine in its rack and took one final look at the damn Italian, she who'd changed everything, and breathed as her eyes welled with tears. Only, this time, in a strange way, they were tears of joy. Gianna was happy. And it was time to let this *thing*, this fantasy go forever and find happiness for herself, happiness with the one man who loved her like she had once loved Gianna. Erin prayed that one day she could love Ben the same way.

Closure.

It was done.

"It's time to let it go," she smiled and breathed and it felt so relieving, "it's time to get on with your bloody life."

And without even looking back, Erin walked away.

AFTER PROMISING TO MAKE PLANS TO SEE AGATA WITHIN the next couple of days, Gianna watched with relief while, finally, she strutted off down the street. "Ugh." A necessary evil. Gianna would apologise for leading her on when she next saw her and would definitely break things off. Definitely.

How long had that coffee taken? She checked her watch, "twenty minutes." Well, it could have been far worse.

Although stupidly, Gianna had sat with her back to the surgery, she'd been mindful to check over her shoulder at regular intervals, just to ensure she didn't miss a certain English rose, not that she knew what she'd have done had Erin entered whilst she perched there drinking coffee with Agata, but still.

But the moment she returned to the surgery, Gianna knew her vigilance had failed. She knew because she could feel it, that Erin had been in the very same room only minutes before, her presence, and with that could only come the devastating loss of having missed her.

Then Vedetta confirmed Gianna's fears. "You had a visitor."

It was all Gianna's fault, she knew, as her stomach twisted. She should have told Vedetta that if anybody visited whilst she was out, then they should be locked inside the store cupboard until her return. "She left, didn't she." Gianna sounded completely defeated. The one and only opportunity to see Erin again, her pretty face, to answer her questions, to let her know it wasn't because of her, to make things right; that one opportunity had slipped through Gianna's fingers.

Vedetta reached over her desk with a small padded envelope, "she told me to give you this."

Gianna took it and unknowingly caressed the paper, "did she say anything?"

"Just that she was sorry to have missed you. And she said '*good luck*.'"

Gianna needed to sit down, but she also needed to know, "how did she look?"

"Um, it's really hard to say." She paused, trying to find the words. "She didn't stay long, maybe ten or twenty seconds. But she seemed happy."

Gianna closed her office door and took a seat at the desk. Deflated, dejected, devastated.

She carefully unsealed the envelope, knowing that this would be the last thing she'd ever have of Erin. It was the last thing she'd ever deserve of her former friend.

And when Gianna removed the contents, all she could do was weep. It was a symbol of her greatest friendship and greatest achievement. Something she'd received on her final night in England, something she'd always regretted not taking the time to salvage.

Erin had returned Gianna's Fairbairns' winner's medal.

Chapter Thirteen

ONWARDS

"Y ou know, once you learn to block out the traffic and the noise, the crowds and the rubbish flying around all over the place, it really ain't that much of a bad city," Ben said while breaking off a section of croissant and cramming it in his mouth. The breakfast dining area hummed with conversations from a dozen languages. "Even the sight of a million pieces of laundry hanging from windows, balconies and across the streets has a strange charm to it." He dabbed his forehead with a napkin. "But with this heat, I don't suppose there's much need for tumble dryers."

Erin was traipsing her arm over his shoulder, leaning into him and asked as a joke. "So you'd like to stay here a bit longer then?"

"Oh, good God, no chance." He laughed, then smiled when his laughter set Erin off. He placed a hand on her cheek and lightly guided her lips to his. Erin sank into the kiss, despite the restaurant being full, which was most unlike her and so Ben didn't pull away until he could no longer forego saying, "I don't know what has got into you, but I like it."

She hummed. "Can we get away from here? Away from

208

this city ... see Pompeii ... the Amalfi Coast." Erin spoke lazily while gazing into some imaginary horizon.

"Of course, I'm with you on that one." He gazed into that same horizon. "We'll do all that and then take the car up north. Rome, Florence, Lucca, Bologna, Milan, Verona, Venice." He spoke the final destination with finality whilst topping up their coffee and then a sudden thought came to him. "Oh, I forgot to ask. How'd it go with your friend yesterday?"

Erin didn't flinch. "My friend? Oh, she was out. Never mind," she took a long gulp from her cup.

Ben shuffled and appeared slightly irritated, "kind of a shame that. Oh well." He downed his coffee in one go then stood. "Right, we've got a long day ahead. Drink up. Get ready. We're leaving!"

"Yes, sir." Erin stood, grabbed his hand and they made their way up the stairs.

ON SATURDAY, GIANNA STAGGERED INTO WORK, PUFFY-faced and exhausted. She'd managed to steal a couple hours of sleep but no more and that was only after finally resolving what to do the next day.

It wasn't much of a plan but she had to do something and now she fired up the computer, logging into LinkedIn and replied to Erin's email:

Hi, Erin...

I'm so sorry I missed you yesterday, I'll never forgive myself for not being there. I don't know if you're still in the city, but if you are, please, please, please stop by my surgery. I'd love to see you again. I feel like we have so much to talk about.

Sorry for everything.

Gia xxx

.

Sure it sounded a little too whiny for her liking, in fact, it very much matched her mood in the moment, but she really wanted Erin to know how sincere she was.

Gianna sighed into her hands. "Oh, you're so brave Gia, sending an email when that shy girl you abandoned came across the continent to see you."

Being unable to sleep, Gianna had arrived at the surgery two hours early. Vedetta hadn't even arrived yet, but throughout the next hour, Gianna checked her email every few minutes whilst trying to clean, organise her schedule or else simply potter aimlessly about the room. "Reply, damn it!"

She tapped her fingers, went to the bathroom, tapped her fingers some more. "Ugh, I have to do more." Or else it would drive her insane. Erin was somewhere close by and all Gianna could do was stomp about her surgery, tapping her bloody fingers. "See! You think about her for a few minutes and you're already resorting to Englishisms." There was one other thing she could do. "I'll send another email." But this time to someone else. It would be a long shot but maybe this other person knew Erin's itinerary.

She expected at least a small amount of abuse from Mikey but she had no choice. Gianna had made sure to remember Mikey's email address for when the time came to get back in touch with and grovel to Erin. His name plus year of birth at Hotmail. Easy. She sent the email:

Hi Mikey,

I hope you're ok. I know it's been a while but I don't need a hard time over it right now. I need to know where in Napoli Erin is staying. Can you help me?

I'm sorry for everything but help me out and I'll explain all.

Gia xxx

PS: Do you have her mobile number?

.

But it still wasn't enough. There was also that idiotic brother of his. "What was his name?" She tapped a pen against her skull. Scratchy? Scratty? Shabby? She smiled, "Shaggy!" She'd simply replace Mikey's first name with *Shaggy* and hope it reached the guy.

So, she forwarded the same email to Shaggy and breathed. "You brave girl, Gia."

After an hour, several espressos and still no responses, Gianna kicked the desk and rolled across the floor on her chair. "Will one of you reply to me!" The scattergun technique never usually failed so miserably.

Gianna had grown used to having life-changing matters taken out of her control and the frustration of being so helpless was one of the things she hated even more than the gridlock in the city. This was another one of those occasions and she felt completely impotent. She really wanted to do more but without any information, what could she do? Stalk the city in search of her? Napoli was a city of almost a million people, the third largest in Italy. The chances of passing her in the street were miniscule. And that's if she was still even in the city. She could visit all the major hotels and demand to know if Erin was staying but that would take a long time and she very much doubted they'd willingly give over guest details to some crazy lady.

"If I was Erin and I was in Napoli for one final day, where would I go?" She tapped the pen against her skull, harder and harder.

The front door slammed, announcing the arrival of Vedetta.

Erin leapt from her seat.

It was time to shut up shop, give Vedetta the day off and drive the twenty-five kilometres to a very special place.

Chapter Fourteen
POMPEII

The modern town of Pompeii had grown out from the ancient city, still partially covered in ash. Because of this and to spare any confusion, the ancient city had been renamed Scavi Pompeii, meaning *excavations*. To Erin and Ben's great relief and to the Italian people's credit, they had kept the two separated. Ben had often complained about how the English cared little for their ancient heritage, even saying that had Venice been in England, they'd have paved over the canals to make roads. Perhaps an exaggeration, but there was no denying that Italy took great care of its monuments and culture.

Erin hated to think that the main reason for travelling to this part of Italy had turned into an anti-climax. The truth was that a day later, she felt confounded. Sure, she was pleased to know that Gianna was safe, happy and was achieving her dreams as a physiotherapist, yet at the same time, not being able to speak with her and to find out *why* was a huge disappointment. On balance, because Erin could now put this whole strange and unusual episode of her life behind her, the trip, so far could be judged a success – The rest of Erin's life was still to come.

The one completely weird aspect, even for the usually level-headed Erin, was the bloody poem that fluttered back into existence. Why had it resurfaced ten years to the day since writing it if it wasn't fate? Did the universe pull such strings, only to lead you down dark alleys, corners and dead ends? Or were there other reasons behind the events of the last few weeks? Erin fancied herself a pragmatist and did not readily believe in fate - But ten years to the day? Which also just happened to be the day she'd met Ben. Maybe the whole reason for everything had been to solidify her relationship with him? If that truly was the reason, then the universe was probably laughing at her right now given that she was presently in Italy and not the English countryside, but then, perhaps, this was what she had really needed, to be certain, if that is what she now was. Besides, at the very least, Erin was now fulfilling a lifelong ambition of visiting Pompeii.

"I was just so completely unprepared for how big this place is." She brought her mind away from fantasy and back to reality.

"It's enough to make you wonder how it was possible for it to remain undiscovered so long." Ben squeezed Erin's hand as they negotiated the crooked, uneven cobblestones.

Indeed, Pompeii was easily the size of Cambridge city centre and it would take many hours to view the dozens of ruined streets that had been painstakingly emptied of ash over the decades, though not to see every single crack and corner would be to deny Pompeii justice. It was, after all, unlikely that Erin would ever return.

There'd be much walking and the sun beat down hard. Erin slipped off the cardigan she wore over a flower print summer dress, revealing her pale flesh, nimble body as well as other assets. She caught Ben glancing across at her breasts and she squeezed his hand in acknowledgement. She'd been punishing him a lot recently, through no fault of his own, and frustrating him greatly. That punishment would soon end for him.

The ruined streets were narrow and cobbled with weeds sprouting from between the cracks. The parts of Pompeii that might have been thought more upmarket even had sanitation. Back in the day, Pompeii would have been considered far ahead of their time, a city of the future, only, fate had different plans.

At the entrance gate, where they'd paid their admittance fee, the queues had been quite long but inside, due to the sheer size, Erin and Ben would often go several minutes without passing any other tourists.

The many hundreds of stone-built homes lined up and down the ancient streets were free to enter and Ben chose one particular house, for no reason specifically, and pulled Erin inside, the temperature dropping noticeably in the shadow. He pushed her against the stone wall, using the back of a hand behind her head as a cushion, the other cupping her breast as he pressed his lips against hers. His tongue entered her mouth and clashed with her own, his hand pressed harder against her breast and she felt herself wilting.

After a minute Ben pulled away, clasped her face in his hands and spoke in a low husky voice, "that's just a taster of what I'm doing to you tonight, my sweet fiancée."

She panted in rhythm with her heart. It *was* time to end this dry spell and to end it tonight.

But not before spending some considerable time exploring these ancient ruins.

IT WAS MID-MORNING WHEN GIANNA ARRIVED AT SCAVI Pompeii, queued with impatience, paid her money and finally rushed through the turnstiles. She hadn't been to the theme park in five or six years and the place had been unbearably huge even then. Now, with more ash having been removed, several more streets and monuments would have been uncovered, doubtless making it even harder to find an errant English girl who most likely wasn't even here. Indeed, the ancient city was so large, that even with the good fortune that Erin was wandering aimlessly around, it would be by no means guaranteed they'd cross paths.

Gianna breathed and took her bearings whilst staring at the long ruined streets before her, a sprinkling of tourists spread throughout. It had been an effort merely walking from where she parked her car in the new city to the Scavi entrance. Now she could well be walking for most of the day, sweating, dishevelled in the sweltering heat. How would *that* look on the off chance she did happen across Erin? Hair plastered to her forehead, red and worn out face glistening from perspiration, the strong stench of body odour antiperspirant would be working extra hard to fight. It was by no means ideal, but if need be, Gianna would return the next day and the next in the vain hope of finding her.

Though Gianna had to be realistic, because deep down, she knew, even though Erin had always wanted to visit Pompeii, it was highly unlikely they'd bump into each other, but Gianna had to do *something*. Besides, simply by being here, she felt closer to Erin, not that *that* mitigated much of the guilt she still felt many years on.

How had it ever come to this? That the most important friendship she ever held, with the most wonderful, adorable, beautiful and sweet person she could ever imagine, had disintegrated in such a way that now, she had to resort to the forlorn hope of searching for her amongst the ash and weeds that sprung out from the ground, praying that for once, the heavens sent some good fortune instead of the misery and torment to which she'd become all too accustomed. The ache of loss that had grown inside over the years had exploded in the last couple of days and all because Erin had re-emerged, but within that ache were planted the seeds of something else. Could Gianna dare to hope?

Gianna, having had the rare opportunity to see Erin once more, to embrace her and then stupidly allowing that chance to slip away, wanted nothing more in the world other than to explain everything to the girl she had once loved. Though Gianna had to concede that even if this day brought nothing else and failed to reunite her with her old lover, at the very least, she'd have time to resolve matters within her own head; not that she needed to, really, because she was *here*, and willing to go through *this*, which had to count for something.

Gianna struggled along the cobbles, remnants of ash still filling the gaps between. Street after ancient street, within the houses, without the houses, she searched as the sun burned like it only could in southern Italy.

A large gathering of tourists mingled in an opening that gave view to Mount Vesuvio in the vista. It was the perfect setting for photographs of the ruins and their maker, which loomed so menacing, and still active, on the horizon. Gianna ambled amongst the groups, families, couples and solo tourists, scrutinising each and every face like a madwoman. Occasionally, she'd hear an English accent or see a long red mane and would frantically rush over in that direction with a renewed enthusiasm, only to be disappointed.

"Ugh, why?" Gianna stopped and gawked aghast at the Autogrill restaurant chain that since her last visit, they'd built into one of the ruined buildings. "Disgusting." She shook her head, eschewed her principles and entered regardless.

It wouldn't take long to scope out the vile globalist

restaurant chain. Around fifty people sat around a number of tables, enjoying lunch. Gianna purchased a bottle of water, took a seat and spent a few moments regaining her energy and composure. Sweat patches gathered down the flanks of her blouse, "ugh...attractive," she mumbled under her breath as she fanned her face. She pressed the chilled plastic bottle against her forehead and paid particular attention to the people entering. This was the only restaurant in Scavi Pompeii. If Erin was here and wanted to eat, she'd have to visit Autogrill. But after a few minutes, sitting around and doing nothing made her feel restless because what if Erin had already eaten and was even now walking around the ancient city, minding her own business, admiring old rocks like the complete nerd she doubtless still was.

As Gianna stood, she winced from the sharp pain that shot up from her foot. "Damn blisters already?" And she'd only been searching a few hours. She removed her trainers and rubbed her feet for a few minutes before limping from the restaurant.

The sun still baked down and with the majority of ruins being single-storeyed, precious little shadow was offered. There were now more tourists than before, many whom Gianna noticed gave her strange looks as she checked them over for signs of red hair.

Was this really going to work? Or had Gianna simply been overcome with the emotion that only the return of Erin could bring? Maybe Gianna deserved punishment, even more than she'd already experienced, for lacking the courage to either return to England or initiate any sort of contact with her in the years since. Gianna had time to ponder such questions as she lumbered from one ruin to another, it was all she could do.

Maybe she didn't deserve to find Erin. Maybe Erin didn't deserve to have any of Gianna's misfortune rub off on her.

Maybe Gianna should leave the outcome in fate's hands. If she was meant to find Erin then she'd find her and if not, then it was clear that fate had deemed Gianna unworthy of Erin's friendship.

The amphitheatre emerged up ahead. Situated in the far corner of the ancient city, it was one of the main attractions of Pompeii and the oldest surviving Roman amphitheatre anywhere. It was kind of ironic that only a few years ago it was completely buried beneath ash. Gianna entered the tunnel and emerged in the arena to find various scatterings of tourists, some taking seats in the tiers, others standing in the centre of the ring looking outwards at the remarkably intact structure. Low murmurs from a dozen conversations drifted over on the gentle breeze and Gianna needed only a matter of seconds to know that Erin wasn't among them.

"It's hopeless." Gianna's legs wobbled up the steps towards the upper tier from where she all but collapsed on the stone. At least the view was decent but all she could do was survey the tourists again as the sun burned into the back of her neck. "This is just not going to work," she conceded. If she was ever meant to see Erin again then it would have either happened the day before or sometime during the last five hours of toiling around Scavi Pompeii. Fuck, but if she was meant to see Erin again, then the ideal time would have presented itself at some point over the last ten years. Fate – Sometimes it just wasn't meant to be.

The amphitheatre possessed two entrance tunnels, which led either up the tiers or straight into the arena. Gianna now sat directly opposite one of those tunnels, with a clear view of light on the other side. Two groups exited through that tunnel whilst the other, directly below where Gianna sat, concealed itself from her line of sight. Another group disappeared from her view and Gianna could only presume they too were leaving the arena through the tunnel directly below.

She laughed to herself, "something I said?" Or did she really smell *that* bad after the day's exertion? Oh well, the peace wasn't unwelcome.

It was kind of eerie though. One moment there were a few dozen people loitering within, enjoying the monument, the next, they had all disappeared.

Gianna sat back against the step and stretched her arms out across the stone. After hours of walking, she appreciated the respite and deemed that after regaining her energy, she'd begin the walk back to modern-day Pompeii and her Fiat 500 left parked outside a mobile phone store. "Things would have been so much simpler back then." And being buried alive beneath a wall of red hot molten lava didn't sound so bad.

She focused on the arena and imagined the gladiatorial combats, public speeches and plays of years gone by. She flecked back her dampened hair and felt it flop back against her face then took a sip from her now warm bottle of water. The silence was so calming, even the gentle breeze was audible against the stone.

She saw the shadow first as it crept in from the concealed tunnel, the amphitheatre design restricting any structural shade in its totality. The solitary shadow grew longer; the head, body then legs stretching out along the arena's grass. "Great, there goes the peace and quiet."

A light breeze swept through the ancient structure and the grass swayed rhythmically in its wake. The head emerged, long red hair blowing in the wind to reveal a long, slim and fragile neck. The tall girl emerged with her back to Gianna and wore a striking summer dress printed with flowers. Her pale skin was doubtless burning in the sun as she made small lilting sweeps with a hand fan. Then the girl's head tilted back as she admired the upper tier to her fore.

Gianna sat slowly forward, barely able to breathe or form any coherent thought. Her mouth gaped as if preparing for some massive involuntary intake of oxygen to the brain – And heart. Her eyes widened, time stopped.

Without knowing it, Gianna was rising to her feet, her tired legs finding renewed enthusiasm. She floated down the steps, unable to take her eyes from the woman, not even for a second lest she disappear like some dream.

Was this real? Gianna pinched her arm. This *was* real.

Then, her feet scraped against the stone and the woman, startled, whipped around.

Seeing someone approaching her, the woman's first reaction was to take a step back.

Gianna descended the final step and landed on the grass, metres from the woman whose body, which had twisted fully to meet Gianna, stood in contrast to her feet, which still pointed the other way.

The woman was stunned, open-mouthed, her hands dropped to cover her solar plexus. Her eyes opened wide, almost to the point of fear as her skin, clear and perfect, losing blood, whitened several shades, even in this suppressing heat. The fan fell to the grass.

All Gianna wanted was to embrace the woman, for she knew, Erin was having an anxiety attack – The haze.

Erin, her body out of equilibrium, stooped sidewards.

Gianna arrived just in time to steady her, placing her hands around Erin's waist. "Ti ho preso." Gianna rolled her eyes and smiled, how silly. "I've got you."

Erin straightened, regaining her balance and composure, though the realisation still hadn't struck. Slowly, her expression of shock eased as her pupils diminished in size and finally, one side of her mouth rose into a delicate smile. She averted her stare, for a few seconds gazed down at the ground, shaking her head. Then she laughed, "Gianna."

"Erin," Gianna said softly, pulling her into a tight embrace. There was only one thing she needed to say more than anything else, "Erin, I'm so sorry."

"Babe, let's head back to the car and get to Amalfi." Ben squeezed her hand and gave a half-hearted pull in the direction of the exit, somewhere off to the south. "We'll find a nice hotel and eat some Italian food." He panted, perspiration shined on his forehead and his light blue shirt was stained dark down both sides.

"Oh, but we've not seen the amphitheatre yet." Which was kind of a big deal. "It's the oldest amphitheatre in the entire Roman world."

"As you've said numerous times." He smiled but tugged harder. "I'm starving and feel quite weary from all this walking." Once in the car, it would only be an hour's drive to the Amalfi Coast. "Now, babe, we've done what you want, it's about time you played fair and show a little consideration for your travelling companion," he said with just enough good humour that he didn't sound like a complete dick, although *he* was supposed to be the one who enjoyed old structures.

"Ben, no, not yet." She threw down his hand and noted his shocked expression as his head jerked back. "You know full well how excited I've been to see this place." She opened out her arms to encompass the ruins all around them. "I'm not going to leave, never to return, having missed the bloody amphitheatre." Erin began wafting the fan a few inches from her face, a movement that distracted his eye.

He guffawed, not quite knowing what to say. "Look, it's been a great day, but we've been walking for hours."

"Ben, if you're hungry then go back to that Autogrill monstrosity and buy yourself a snack." She pointed somewhere in the general direction of the restaurant. "We can meet back at the exit in half an hour."

"Fine," and with that, he turned his back, threw up a petulant arm and stamped away without another word.

Erin shook her head. "Bloody men, always thinking about their bellies." The damn amphitheatre was a matter of fifty metres away, so close they could see it, and he couldn't have even spared a few minutes to finish the visit with a climax. "Fine, you go and leave me then," she mumbled under her breath.

Erin stomped in the amphitheatre's direction and it required only a matter of seconds to forget the previous altercation with her fiancé as she neared the jaw-dropping wonder. It wasn't the largest of the ancient arenas but considering the pummelling it had taken almost two thousand years ago, it certainly was one of the most intact. The dozens of arches that maintained its structural integrity were remarkable, the intricate designs within the brickwork, fully visible.

A gaggle of tourists trickled out from the larger central arch. Obviously, that was the way inside and she smiled politely as they walked past, though they appeared largely in some kind of a trance, their eyes unblinking as they stared straight ahead in silence. How strange, but then, doubtless they'd been walking miles in the heat.

Through the archway, Erin could now see the interior; the grass that had grown on the inside and part of the tier at the far end where the top of the arch did not restrict her line of sight. As she walked through the tunnel, more and more of the tier became visible until she emerged on the inside. A relieving breeze swept across from the side, lifting the hair from her shoulders. When it abated, the contrasting temperature from the stifling sun was more apparent than ever. Erin continued stepping into the centre of the empty arena, her long shadow cast out in front. She stopped and fanned her face, admiring the finery, the detail, the fact that many modern-day constructions still used this same basic design.

The silence, interrupted only by the gentle breeze rebounding from the stone, created a serene and almost surreal atmosphere of peace, almost like the city had never been discovered, as though Erin was the only person alive.

A scraping from behind - She was not alone.

Her heart thumped from the report, providing her brain and muscles with a burst of blood and oxygen to deal with the threat. Erin whipped around and the outline of a figure materialised by the bottom step before her brain could fill in the details.

Erin recoiled as the woman stepped closer, heading straight for her. The confines of Erin's sight focused primarily on the approaching figure as swirling grey clouds closed off everything in her periphery. The large figure glided, as though assisted by some supernatural force, or maybe the enormity of what was unfolding played tricks with her mind. The woman smiled, as if trying to reassure Erin that all was perfect in the world, like how the spirit of an ancestor might comfort a child. Erin didn't know her mouth gaped, just as she couldn't control her arms that moved to cover her belly. Her eyes opened wide, not believing what they were seeing as a dizziness manifest in her head. The air went hot and cold at the same time, her fan fell to the floor.

The haze – A big one – Ten years in the making.

Erin swooned but the woman rushed forward and caught her around the waist.

"Ti ho preso." The woman smiled and rolled her eyes. It was as though nothing else in the world existed. "I've got you."

Erin straightened and managed to place a steadying hand

on the woman's shoulder, holding her eyes for as long as she dared – It couldn't be. This couldn't be real. How was it possible? It must be a dream. Except, Erin could feel the warmth of the woman's hands and the piercing hawkish glare of her eyes.

Erin couldn't help it, she broke into a smile, still unable to form any coherent sequence of words. She forced herself to blink, still expecting that this celestial moment would dissolve, to evanesce like so many dreams. It didn't. She shook her head and allowed herself to laugh. What else could she do? "Gianna."

"Erin," Gianna whispered and brought her into a tight embrace, for how long, it was impossible to know. "Erin, I'm so sorry."

Erin sniffed, her tears were falling over Gianna's bare shoulder.

This *was* real, it was *now* and would probably be the defining moment Erin would remember her entire life.

She slowly pushed herself to arm's length and looked Gianna up and down. "Gianna? How? Where how come you?" She laughed, breathed and took a few seconds to regain her wits, stealing a shy glance or two at Gianna's grinning face, who still had a hand clasped tight around Erin's wrist. "Gianna, where did you come from?" Erin finally managed to stutter with a half semblance of logic.

"It's a miracle I found you." Gianna rubbed her hand up and down the length of Erin's arm. This most certainly *was* real. "You English don't answer your fucking emails," she dabbed a hand to her mouth, which was more apology than she needed to give.

"Oh, my battery is dead and I forgot to bring an adaptor and I still haven't got round to buying a new..." Erin shook her head. Who the fuck cares? "I just can't believe it. I came to see..."

"...You came to see me yesterday but..."

"...But I saw you with somebody..." Erin shook her head, "I don't know ... a friend, a client, family member. But I didn't want to interrupt if you were busy so..." Erin reached forward and grabbed Gianna's hand. It was then she realised her entire arm was shaking all the way from the shoulder socket, though the grey clouds had largely receded.

"I would have always made time for *you*." Gianna shook her head. "But *she's* nobody, don't worry about it. How long are you in Italy? What do you do now? How is everything in England? Are you still living in Cambridge?" Gianna paused, stamped on the ground and caught her breath. "Ok, don't worry, plenty of time to answer my stupid questions."

"You can bet I have a few of my own." Erin's smile dropped momentarily but quickly returned. "I've missed you." *That* was an understatement.

"We have so much to talk about." Gianna's head shook minutely from side to side as she pressed her lips together, the faintest hint of something shimmering in her eyes. She shook it away and stated as a matter of fact, "you must be hungry."

"Are you kidding? I've never been hungrier." Erin beamed and motioned with her head while speaking with a downcast tone. "There's that Autogrill place..."

Gianna jumped in with an immediate answer, "not a chance are we eating there," and pulled Erin in the direction of the south tunnel, "in modern Pompeii, there's a much better place."

What should have been a fifteen-minute walk took considerably longer, the turnstiles at the exit giving way to modern life. They spoke mainly about Napoli, the culture shock and differences between this place and Cambridge; small talk almost in its totality. Erin wanted to save the important subjects for when she was sat facing Gianna. She needed to look her in the eyes when the Italian explained herself and for her own reasons, Gianna had thus far not volunteered it either.

Erin flapped a hand at the turnstiles. "I just hope you don't disappear when we walk through those." It was meant only half as a joke.

Gianna hesitated before speaking, evidently noting the gravity of Erin's remark. "Erin, we will have *that* conversation but for now I want you to know, I'm not going anywhere."

The heavy gates clunked as they walked through in single file. Erin panicked as she had to let go of Gianna's hand, almost like passing through to the other side might bring a change to them being reunited. But no, Gianna was still there, facing Erin, waiting for her to catch up until they were both no longer in the fantasy world, but reality.

And then reality hit. "Erin?" Only a few paces away, Ben was leaning against a lamppost. The skin above his nose crinkled and his head was tilted as he approached. He noticed Gianna, obviously, and raised his eyebrows toward Erin. "Hello?"

"Oh, hi, Ben." Erin glanced from Ben to Gianna and back. "Ben this is the friend I told you about, Gianna."

Ben took a breath and a beat before finally extending his hand to her and Erin hoped Gianna didn't notice his small gesture of irritation, because she certainly did. He was annoyed and from his point of view with good reason. Ben wanted to get away from the area, to move on, have dinner, have a bloody holiday. "Pleased to meet you." He shook Gianna's hand but continued staring at Erin whilst he awaited the formalities to continue.

If Gianna had been surprised Erin had travelled to Italy with a man, of all things, then she showed no outward signs, of that or anything else, save for her usual pleasantness and remained poker-faced as she shook Ben's hand. She wasn't stupid; she'd know what Ben was to Erin and if she expected that her old friend had spent the last ten years pining over her then her ego was about to take a knock.

Regardless, it was an uncomfortable introduction to have to make and she continued watching carefully for Gianna's reaction as she spoke, "Gianna, this is my fiancé, Ben."

She made a small pause and one nostril seemed to flare slightly, but that might have been Erin's imagination. "Hi, Ben, it's nice to meet you." For the most part, she gave nothing away and Erin decided there wasn't an awful lot that could be taken from it, other than her own discomfort.

Ben, on the other hand, straightened, puffed out his chest, raised his chin and almost appeared like he was squaring off against her. But he couldn't possibly remember Gianna, Erin's lesbian best friend, could he?

"We were about to grab a bite to eat, Ben, if you'd like to join us?"

"Oh, I'd love to join you," he said, reaching out and taking Erin's hand.

"So, you both took the same course at Cambridge?" Ben folded his arms and leaned back into his seat.

Erin could already tell he didn't like her and that this wouldn't be easy. No, in fact this would be damn right painful. For Erin, Ben had no right to ask the kind of questions that might lead to Gianna having to explain why she left Cambridge. As harsh as it sounded, Ben had no right to find out those answers at the same time as herself and the truth was that in the moment, Erin resented his presence. And that very fact bothered her because she accepted the legitimate grievances he'd have right about now. But Gianna was Gianna and when it came to *this* girl, because the rules were often thrown out, exceptions had to be made.

"We did indeed," Gianna confirmed whilst dipping calamari into a small dish of salsa sauce.

"I was on the verge of suffering another major haze attack back on day one," Erin recalled whilst smiling at Gianna.

"You were about to run, weren't you?" Gianna chuckled with a mouthful of squid.

"And I probably would have too, knowing how I was back then." Erin noticed Ben's grimace, probably from Gianna's lack of table etiquette. It was nice to know she still ate like a pig. "If it weren't for this girl, I'd most likely have jumped on the very next coach back to Alnwick, hidden in my room for a few months and then taken a job in a cave somewhere."

"I saved you." Gianna gave a quick sticky squeeze of Erin's hand below the table before bringing it back to claw another piece of breaded squid.

"You most certainly did save me." Erin agreed and beamed.

Ben checked his watch, sipped some water and stared at Gianna. "Well then, I guess I have you to thank then, don't I." He said, more rhetorically than as an actual question. "You were both rowing partners?" He asked Erin, "you never speak of this to me."

Erin held up a finger as she finished working on the chewy squid. Couldn't he have asked something about Italy, Napoli or where best to get pizza? She swallowed. "We were indeed rowing partners yes. We even won a medal at Fairbairns' for finishing first place, although it was a bloody close run thing."

Gianna perked and patted her handbag. "Oh, I got the medal, by the way. I always regretted leav... I mean, I always wondered what happened to it."

Ben was about to say something but Erin cut him off. "I kept it safe. Along with a few other things stuck at the back of the wardrobe." She glanced at Ben, "you don't know fatigue until you've rowed in an event like that," then back to Gianna, "lactic acid in the fingertips ... remember? And those two Oxford girls?"

"Of course. Oh, those demons pushed us the whole way."

"I could swear one of those two popped up at the Beijing Olympics ... Annabel something, I think she was called, rowing in the quadruple sculls. Did you see? They took silver. And when we jumped in the river? And do you remember the photo finish? Oh, I was ever so nervous."

Gianna slowly shook her head and smiled. "How we beat those two, I'll never quite know."

"So why did you quit?" Ben asked with squinty eyes, which gave him an uncommon sceptical look. Considering he'd been hungry, he hadn't touched much of the food. They'd ordered a whole array of interesting appetisers at Gianna's recommendation. "I mean, you obviously enjoyed it very much and even won medals in your first year. So why did you give up?"

Erin could easily have had her choice of sculling partner in the second year but rowing with some girl who wasn't Gianna had been a thought too appalling to contemplate. "I just got a little bogged down with work, that's all." She fiddled with her napkin and again, she hated lying to Ben but he was, intentionally or not, asking things which would only lead to the inevitable '*why did you leave?*' question, to which he did not have the right to ask and find out the answer to, at precisely the same moment as herself, Erin reiterated in her head.

"Really?" Ben's eyebrows elevated from a low squint to a much higher position on his head. "You spent most of your second year watching me play cricket for hours on end, getting drunk on the pavilion." It was a little bit of an exaggeration, but he had a point, sort of.

"What's cricket?" Gianna asked, saving Erin from the difficult question. "I've heard of it, I think, and might even semi recall seeing the boys tramping about in strange padded uniforms, but it's not a game we play here in Italy."

Erin smiled at Gianna and considered how great she was for saving her from having to answer awkward questions. She understood, even now. And Erin still couldn't believe she was actually sat next to Gianna at a table in a restaurant in Pompeii. Every minute since she walked into that amphitheatre had been a blur and she hoped she'd be able to recollect those precious moments later on. Erin looked on at Ben and awaited his answer, with a raised brow of her own, which soon changed to a scowl when he didn't.

Ben exhaled and commenced... "Cricket is the Englishman's baseball," he finally said, "though make no mistake, cricket was invented long before..."

Gianna nodded politely along and listened intently for several minutes whilst she fixed up cuttings of bread with cheese and ham or sun-dried tomatoes before cramming them in her mouth. "I shall have to watch it sometime." She said, this time covering her mouth with a hand. "Are you using this?" Gianna took her hand away to point at the butter beside Ben's plate.

"Go ahead," he said while averting his eyes from the churned up mess in Gianna's mouth, "though you'll probably find it the most tiresome experience of your life," Ben said deadpan.

"How are you enjoying the food, Ben?" Erin nodded at his plate, which contained a few assortments he'd hardly touched.

"I think I've lost my appetite."

Erin suppressed the urge to kick him; now wasn't the time or place. Instead, she turned to Gianna. "You must know all the best places to eat in Napoli? We went to that Presidente place the other night."

"Il Pizzaiolo del Presidente?" Gianna stuck out her tongue and made a mock *being sick* sound she brought from somewhere at the back of her throat. Ben wasn't amused. "You don't want to go there. The pizza is terrible. I'll show you the best pizza in Napoli, it's called Sorbillo." Gianna tilted her head. "Really, Erin, you need a tour guide."

"And if it's the best pizza in Napoli then that probably means it's the best pizza in the world, right?" Erin asked, doubting Gianna would remember the reference.

She straightened against her chair, gaining a few inches in height as her face exploded to life, "of course." Wow, ok, maybe she *did* remember. "Erin, you have to let me show you Napoli *tonight*." Gianna turned fully toward her, intercepting her hand as it was reaching for a slice of bread.

Erin unleashed a ten year confined grin. There was not one thing she wanted more but there was just one problem, which killed her to say. "We're supposed to be heading off to Amalfi. We already checked out of our hotel in the city." The underwhelming words felt like drowning.

Gianna pulled the face of a child who'd had her presents stolen on Christmas morning; a feeling Erin could relate to herself. "Well, that's just fucking shit!" Gianna sat back with a thump and either accidentally or deliberately, banged her knee against the underside of the table, unsettling the water carafe and spilling no small amount from Ben's glass. Whether intentional or not, it had the effect of impressing upon everybody else her displeasure as she glared her dissatisfaction at Ben.

After several seconds, Ben, who was still sitting somewhat stunned, spoke. "Maybe, we *could* check back into The Grand for a couple more nights." He watched Erin as he said it, and though cautionary, there was the faintest curl from his lips and softening of the eyes at seeing the joy splash over his fiancée's face.

"Perfetto, perfetto, perfetto." Gianna beamed, clapping her hands.

Ben wasn't stupid; he'd most likely know Gianna's sexuality simply by having been around her for a few minutes, if indeed he hadn't known before. And if, as Erin had thought, that Ben suspected the level of their previous friendship, then he showed no sign of it now, giving consent to his fiancée having a night on the town with a lesbian. This also meant more time in Napoli for him and less doing what he wanted to do. He'd hate returning to Napoli and Erin felt a pang of guilt wash over her, but Gianna was Gianna and exceptions had to be made. Erin would be sure to make it up to him during the remainder of their time in Italy.

"Thank you," Erin smiled and squeezed his hand.

Ben squeezed back but his eyes remained focused on Gianna. "So, how's business?"

"Business? Business is good, thank you, Ben," she nodded a few times, "we're on the up," then gave a thumbs up.

"Any boyfriend, husband on the scene?" He absolutely asked and to Gianna, it probably seemed completely innocent and with genuine interest but Erin knew better and either he wasn't sure and was digging for information, or was deliberately, yet incredibly subtly, being insulting, which wasn't like Ben at all.

Doubtless, they'd be having *that* conversation soon.

Chapter Fifteen

BACK TO NAPOLI

I t had been an eventful drive back to Napoli. The gradual increase in those pesky scooters began around five miles from the historical centre, raising Ben's blood pressure to new territory as they, some with up to four people on board, swerved in front at high speed. How four people could appear so comfortable on a scooter was beyond Erin's comprehension. Ben had learned to ignore the traffic lights once inside the city but he did stop once at a crossing strip, which was when an old man in a small Fiat tried to shunt the rental forward just as a young family were crossing the road.

"There goes the fucking bond, right there." Ben turned around and flipped his finger out the back window. "It's finally happened, babe, I'm just surprised we lasted this long."

Erin tried to sound soothing, "Ben, settle down, it's only money."

"You *knew* I wanted away from this fucking city." He slammed his open hands against the steering wheel. Napoli really did bring out the worst in him.

"Well then why did you suggest coming back?" Not that Erin was complaining.

"Because, *Erin*, you backed me into a fucking corner." He shook his head and scowled into the rearview mirror. A line of four scooters squeezed through the small gap beside the car, causing Ben to wince. "You and that Genie, whatever her name is."

"Gianna," she turned to face Ben, "and you *knew* I wanted to see her."

"Did I? You barely seemed bothered you'd missed her the other day."

"Well, I *was* bothered. She was probably the best friend I ever had. We have the rest of the trip to see some sites but I want to spend a little bit of time with her first."

"To be honest, Erin, I'm beginning to wonder just what your *friendship* entailed." He actually went there, whilst staring straight forward into the back end of a battered Citroen.

It looked like Ben was trying to force *that* conversation to take place here and now but Erin just wasn't ready for it yet. "And what's that supposed to mean?"

"What do you bloody think it's supposed to mean?" He asked, rhetorically. "How stupid do you think I am?"

"I think you need to say what's on your mind, Ben," Erin said, looking straight forward, hoping he wouldn't. Not yet. Why had she thought she could take this trip with Ben and avoid the issue? It was bound to come up but now the subject was introduced, the genie was out the bottle and dancing around, Erin wanted to stuff it right back in there. The entire situation was about to get so fucked up and somebody Erin cared for deeply was about to get hurt.

But then, to Erin's surprise, Ben said nothing. Instead, he just turned on the radio and some awful Euro-pop began blaring from the speakers.

Sometimes it was easier to ignore problems than confront them.

Erin wiped away a few tears and reminded herself that this whole trip was for Ben's benefit as well as her own. She needed to know if she still truly felt anything for Gianna and if not, then and only then could she put this whole matter to rest. Was Erin being naïve in believing that after all that, things could be perfect for herself and Ben?

A short time after checking back into the Grand Hotel Santa Lucia, Erin set out in the direction of the Quartieri Spagnoli, or Spanish Quarter. Gianna had warned her it was the rough area of town, but that she'd be perfectly safe. "The Camorra are under control, so there's nothing for anybody to worry about."

"Um, thanks, I'll bear that in mind." Erin had said as they departed separately from Pompeii.

Just as with many other areas of Napoli, if it hadn't been so overcrowded, with back to back traffic both on the roads and parked along every spare inch of pavement, making walking anywhere a huge challenge, then the Spanish Quarter might have been stunning. Unfortunately, the persistent cacophony of horns and car engines was far worse here than anywhere else Erin had so far experienced in the city. The streets were formed into giant grids, similar to the present-day American system, though Erin guessed that the streets had been this way here since the Romans. Although the streets were reasonably wide, the buildings on both sides were dominated by large balconies that hung precarious, almost into the road, giving a claustrophobic false impression of being trapped in a restricted space. Laundry hung drying from many of the balconies which, along with uncountable hanging plant pots, even further added to the confinement. It was almost hard to breathe as fumes from both car and scooter congealed thick in the air. Erin could not imagine a European city looking more in need of modernisation, but it was still beautiful in its own way and to lose it, whatever *it* was, would have been a tragedy as it was like stepping back in time at least two hundred years. "Well, it would be if it wasn't for all the traffic," Erin mumbled as she waited for a long line of scooters to whizz past before she dared cross the road.

And there was Gianna's building, as unimpressive as any of the others, sandwiched somewhere in the middle of a long row of conflicting structures. Many of the buildings had been painted all manner of colours, but Gianna's was the only one in a row of nine that made do with the colour of the original rendering, which crumbled in large patches and gave it a filthy, haphazard appearance.

Erin scanned up the list of names by the buzzer to find 'De Luca' faded in pen near the top. She pressed the button and within a second the door clicked.

The first thing Erin noticed as she stepped inside was the fusty smell, most likely from the age of the building, heat and lack of air conditioning. But as she ascended the stairs, large green blotches of mould stretched across sections of wall where the paint had stripped and crumbled to the floor, which was probably another contributor to the smell. Loud music boomed from somewhere in the direction Erin headed, a noise that was becoming familiar – Euro-pop.

Erin stopped outside number 41, small pricks of sweat from the climb in the heat moistening her forehead. She composed herself, breathed and knocked on the door.

Gianna pulled the door open within a second and was already beaming at her guest. "Hi." She wore a long robe, her hair damp, doubtless from the shower.

A light cool breeze from inside splashed over Erin's face, bringing a welcome relief. "Hi."

"Well, come on in." Gianna held the door open. "Make yourself at home. I still have to get ready but I shouldn't be long."

Erin stepped inside, the flat noticeably cooler than the

approach. The open balcony doors brought in a light breeze from the outside. "I see you've reverted to your old ways," Erin joked, referring to the clutter that was piled in almost every available spot. Clothes hung from doors, were heaped over the backs of chairs and in mounds on the floor. Boxes were stacked four high in places, some overflowing with fabrics, papers and other artefacts. It took a moment for it to register, but all this couldn't possibly belong to Gianna.

"I've had all this stuff ever since my mum died," Gianna shouted above the music. "I'll have to go through it all eventually."

"I'm very sorry, I didn't know." Erin had to raise her voice, wanting to step closer to her, only to find a few too many obstacles in the way.

"That's ok, you weren't to know. We have a lot of catching up to do." Gianna gritted her teeth and squeezed her eyelids closer together as she stomped onto the balcony. Erin watched with bemusement as the Italian grabbed a broom, conveniently positioned, leaned over the far side, bending her body precariously over the rails toward her neighbour and struck the wooden shutters with the brush end. "Vaffanculo! Fate silenzio! Quante volte devo dirvelo?" She shouted whilst banging some more.

Erin couldn't guess as to what she'd said, and probably for the best, but a few seconds later the music died and Gianna, red-faced, stamped back inside. "I was thinking I could show you Intra Moenia in Piazza Bellini tonight," Gianna said as though the previous minute hadn't happened.

Erin tried to stifle the laughter, but couldn't.

The skin around Gianna's mouth slackened as she took offence. "What are you laughing at?"

"Oh, you just never change." Even now, there was always some sort of a calamity wherever Gianna happened to be present, the girl was truly cursed, but the entertainment was so wonderful.

"I have noisy neighbours, alright." Gianna thrust her hands onto her hips and stuck out her bottom lip. "And I really don't think that's anything to laugh about." She smiled and clapped her hands together. "I'll just throw something else on. Please, make yourself at home." She walked into what Erin assumed to be the bedroom and tried to close the door, the clothes which hung over the top preventing it.

"I'm in Gianna's flat," Erin whispered as she trod about the room, just as muffled shouts in Italian came through the wall.

In the far corner, furthest away from the balcony, a small opening which had been obscured from Erin's view by several stacked boxes became visible as she manoeuvred herself around. It was the only part of the flat she'd seen that wasn't filled with clutter. Erin gasped and her hand moved toward her mouth as an empty feeling built in her stomach.

In the corner of the living room, built into the wall was a dedicated section with several portraits of a young man. The largest showed him wearing army fatigues in the desert. In other photos, he was dressed in school uniform with some highlighting extremely picturesque vistas. He bore a striking resemblance to Gianna; the same hawkish eyes for one. "Her brother." An army tag and chain rested below one framed photo and then Erin saw the crucifix, several candles spread out at intervals as well as an image of what had to be the Virgin Mary. "It's a shrine." Spread wider were photos of what must have been Gianna's mum and dad. Erin stepped back as that empty feeling grew. "Poor Gianna." Had Erin found her answers? She hoped Gianna would confide in her at some point.

Erin took a seat on the couch just as Gianna emerged from the bedroom. She wore a knee-length black skirt and white blouse, which left everything to the imagination, including her wrists. She looked down to the floor and fidgeted with her cuffs as she manoeuvred through the living room to stand in a small gap several metres from Erin. "I, um, I'm ready, if you are."

Erin swallowed, the lump that had formed in her throat announcing its presence. She felt the urge to give Gianna a big hug, not only because of what she'd possibly just discovered, but also because, Erin could tell, Gianna was uncharacteristically self-conscious. She guessed this was because Gianna had lost much of her old confidence. Sure, she didn't look the same as she used to, but Erin didn't care about that. Erin stood and was about to open out her arms just as the shouts from through the wall jolted Gianna into action.

She grabbed a heel from the floor and commenced striking it against the plaster. "Taci, taci, taci, taci." She shouted, still clobbering the wall. "These people will drive me insane."

Erin smiled and grabbed her bag.

PIAZZA BELLINI, A TEN-MINUTE WALK FROM THE SPANISH Quarter was certainly one of the more picturesque spots Erin had seen of Napoli. The large square was surrounded by municipal buildings, some of the city's more upmarket hotels and even a cathedral in one corner. In the square's centre, a large fountain spouted water close to a drop surrounded on all sides by railing. Erin and Gianna stood by the rails and stared down into the ancient construction that was probably a bathhouse built into the old city walls.

"It's amazing how long some of these old Roman structures last," Erin remarked.

"Greek."

"Excuse me?"

"This wall is Greek. The ancient Greeks founded Napoli long before the Romans."

"Bloody hell!" Erin's mouthed gaped. "Just how much is buried beneath the ground in this city?"

Gianna smiled, nodded toward Intra Moenia and threaded her arm inside Erin's as they set off at a stroll. "In all honesty, probably most of it. Napoli is an archaeologist's dream."

Intra Moenia was situated centrally on the east side of the square with a large canopied seating area directly in front of the main entrance. "It's adorable," Erin said, feeling Gianna's squeeze on her elbow.

The outside wall, completely green from the ivy cladding made Intra Moenia stand out from all the others. Dozens of hanging flower baskets added to the greenery, even the canopy interior was like entering a garden.

The evening gave a mild and welcoming breeze in the last remnants of the day's sun as tourists and sightseers with backpacks were gradually replaced by tourists and locals in evening wear as they ventured out to eat at one of the city's more classy restaurants.

They took seats at the only empty table, closest to the square, and Erin could not imagine a more beautiful place to finally be alone with the damn Italian.

When the waiter came, Gianna ordered two Bellini cocktails and gestured with a hand toward the vast open Piazza Bellini. "What else could be fitting?"

Erin stared at Gianna. She'd thought about this very moment for a long time and now it had actually arrived, her mind blanked out. She was certain the conversation would flow eventually, just like it always did. Most likely, it was the gravity of the occasion and all the accumulated pressure that served to slow down her mind. She studied Gianna's face, the first signs of wrinkles below the eyes and yet again, Erin found herself scarcely believing just who she was with, and this time, alone.

Gianna caught Erin's eyes and glanced down to the table. What was *she* thinking right about now? The silence protracted for a while longer and then the waiter returned with two pink cocktails in long glasses.

"I love these." Gianna sipped through the straw and made a delightful humming sound. "It's made from peach and Prosecco. I hope you enjoy."

Erin brought the straw to her lips and sipped. "Oh, Gianna, it's very tasty." For a second, Erin wondered if she noted a small squint from Gianna's eyes as she said the full version of her name. It wasn't the first time Erin had called her *Gianna* since their re-acquaintance. Perhaps the squint was from the sourness of the Bellini?

"Rowing..." Gianna smiled and leaned forward, "tell me, did you ever make it to the Olympics?"

"Um, not exactly." Erin took another sip from her drink. She worried the cocktail would soon disappear and she'd have nothing remaining to occupy her hands.

"The crazy professor would have been disappointed with that."

"He was!"

"And how about the Henley Royal Regatta? Surely you'd have qualified with ease? Please tell me you did."

"Same."

"Ouch, what was his name?"

"The professor? Andy Atkins. Yeah, he was pretty disappointed over a number of things." Erin hadn't meant to sound snide but there was no other way it could come out. Besides, the old prof was hardly the only person Gianna had left disappointed. Erin sighed, "the thing is, or *was*, that without a rowing partner, I couldn't really continue to compete in the *double* sculls." This subject had been touched upon at dinner earlier, but now, without Ben being around, Erin felt more able to discuss it.

Gianna blinked. "Why didn't you just find a new partner? You had a Fairbairns' medal. How hard could it have been?" Ugh, either she didn't get it, how much her departure had effected Erin, or Gianna was fishing for just how much damage her leaving had caused.

"Well, looking back, I could have found a new partner. It would probably have been quite easy considering..." Erin realised she'd hardened her facial features and tried to soften them, "you remember what I was like. I'm a very different person now. But back then ... I just gave up on rowing. Too many hard memories." She spoke the last sentence quickly and went straight into the next. "The Downing Boathouse needed structural repairs," Erin laughed.

"Well, it was bound to happen eventually..." Gianna trailed off, Erin guessed because she wanted to fish a little more but for whatever reason, didn't. "Your fiancé," she began instead, "he seems wonderful."

It would have needed an extremely *wonderful* person to act as a sufficient distraction from the girl sitting opposite. "Thank you, he is wonderful..." Erin trailed off. Though it just wasn't the same with Ben as it had been with the damn Italian. But where was the interrogation from Gianna? Was this the same girl she'd fallen in love with? Erin sighed, "you don't remember him, do you." It came out more as a statement than a question. That Gianna didn't remember Ben was hardly surprising given the only contact they had were angry glances over Erin's shoulder and across a crowded Starbucks a little over ten years ago.

Gianna shook her head. "No, did we ever meet?"

"Not really." Erin had since satisfied within her own mind that Ben didn't even recollect Gianna himself, which would have been more likely than the vice-versa. "I do have vague memories of you staring daggers at him on a few occasions." It still wasn't clicking. "He was that guy who worked at Starbucks, the one you said always stared at me."

Gianna's eyes flicked up as she went into thought. "Nah, it's not computing."

Erin flapped her hand. "Well, I don't suppose it matters. We started dating a few months after you left." Perhaps that latter fact was the more important of the two.

Gianna exhaled through her nose and hunched her shoulders forward. "Was he some sort of a rebound?" Finally, a glimpse of the old Gianna, the fearless, inquisitive girl she was remembered as.

Though perhaps that topic was better left for later, when they'd both had a little more alcohol, Erin answered anyway, after all, it was the reason she was in Napoli. "If you want my complete honesty, Gianna, at the time, I needed to do *something, anything*." Erin had just never intended for that *something* to stretch on for ten years. In the moment, she felt terrible and could see the reaction on Gianna's face; that she'd pulled a poor man into some sort of an abyss of love, which could never have been returned in kind. No, that wasn't quite true, because like with everything else, things were never as straightforward as *that*. Erin felt deeply for Ben and perhaps, yes, it *was* even love. But her very presence in Napoli was confirmation enough that she wasn't *in love* with him, at least not in the way Ben was for her. Erin moved her glass from one spot to another and then back again. "You hurt me! You were the only person in the world who had the power to hurt me like that."

Gianna's eyes dropped down as she began fiddling with a napkin. "I know I did." After several seconds, it became clear she wasn't going to push further on that subject. Perhaps more alcohol would be the answer.

As if by magic, the waiter appeared and took orders for more cocktails.

"The Spritz is very popular around here," Gianna said, breaking the tension.

"What exactly is it?" Erin asked with fascination.

"Prosecco again, carbonated water and a mixture of bitter liquors."

"Sounds yummy, I can't wait to try it." Erin had been intrigued by something Gianna mentioned earlier. "What is this Camorra you mentioned before?" Changing the subject to something a little lighter, at least for a short while might be welcome.

"The Camorra? Oh, they're pretty much a group of families who run the city. Much like the stereotype of us, it happens to play out pretty true in Napoli."

"They run the city?"

Gianna waited until the waiter placed down the two bright orange cocktails and walked away. "Each family controls a zone within the city. They keep businesses, tourists and residents safe. They make their money from local business and suppliers, and I'm not going to lie, they also engage in the usual stuff you associate with gangsters." Gianna frowned as she tore into the napkin. "They're not perfect, but on balance, they're a good thing for us."

"They keep you safe? What about the police?"

"The police?" Gianna laughed. Nothing else needed saying.

"I suppose it's a bit of a culture shock. These days we're all supposedly a part of Europe, but it's nice we all at least try and keep our old cultures and traditions." Erin sipped her Spritz, which was preferential to the Bellini.

"It's for that very reason Italy is such an important tourist destination." Gianna straightened in her chair as her face sprang to life. "Ooh, that's what I was meant to ask you..."

Erin grinned from Gianna's infectious sudden change in zeal. "What? What were you meant to ask me?"

"Everything. I'm still getting used to seeing your little face again, and I haven't even asked what you're doing. I mean, I'm pretty sure you're a successful physio, but ... Ok, I'll shut up, you talk now."

Erin could only smile. Small glimpses of the friend she'd once known occasionally glanced through and it was the most comforting thing in the world. She studied Gianna's eyes for a moment but there seemed a necessity to look deep. Something was missing and it bothered Erin because she couldn't put a finger on it. The hawkish intensity she always possessed, like a superhuman power, still remained, which was a wonderful comfort to Erin. Yet conversely, it was almost like something had been taken away. Then once again, it was Gianna who broke eye contact and looked down to the table.

Erin exhaled slowly and spoke. "Well, after my undergrad I took my masters and graduated in 2008. Then I spent two years working for a large physiotherapist in Peterborough, not too far from Cambridge, whilst taking my doctorate. I saved up enough money, secured a bank loan and opened up my own surgery just a short walk from my old student accommodation. Four years on, I'm doing quite well and having fun doing it."

"Quite well? You're far too modest. Don't think I haven't read all about your recent accomplishments. I was ... *am* very proud of you."

"Ah, you're probably referring to the Relief for Heroes thingy. It was nothing. Just forget about it." Erin looked down and span her glass. "As you know, a physio's work is never done, especially when you're dealing with war injuries and prosthetic limbs."

Gianna narrowed her eyes and pressed her lips together

before again looking down toward the table. She took a few deep breaths before tilting back up.

"Are you ok?" Erin asked.

"Well, I should be."

"Should be?"

Gianna exhaled again. "It's a couple of things, I suppose, but I don't really want to get into one of them right now. It'll put a total downer on a wonderful evening."

Erin guessed she was referring to her brother. She wouldn't push that any further for now. It would be best if Gianna found her own moment to confide in Erin, and Erin truly hoped she would indeed confide. "What's the thing you can get into?"

Gianna spent a moment gazing out into the square. "We followed such similar paths. Why do you think that was?"

Erin knew the answer to that. "It was *you* who gave me the idea to start my own practice." It was, after all, meant to have been the both of them.

"But the injured soldiers?"

Erin opened out her palms, "now that was a coincidence. They kind of came to me. Lots of them. Too many of them. I guess I've kind of specialised in that area now." Was it truly a coincidence? Or had it been something else?

Gianna stared for a few seconds, her head tilting to the side, a smile holding for the duration. "I'm very proud of you." She reached over, grabbed Erin's hand and squeezed it tight. "That's my girl."

The mutual comfort between herself and Gianna obviously wasn't yet quite how it used to be, but to Erin, it was still remarkable. In all her life, she was never able to communicate with another person quite as easily as with Gianna. Even after a ten-year gap, despite a few inevitable bumps, she sensed a rapidly building rapport. This could only be a good thing.

The faint trills of a violin drifted over from somewhere in the square and then a red-faced opera singer began bellowing beautiful words from beside the violin, drawing in an instant a few hundred heads in their direction.

"Ah, I've met him a few times." Gianna shook her head with amusement. "His name's Mario, he does this thing for a living."

"He's very good." Not that Erin thought she'd be able to tell the difference between a good and a bad opera singer.

"He is. It can be tough catching a break, so in the meantime, he makes a living doing what he loves. Better that than working behind a bar, right?"

Erin turned back from the singer to Gianna. "Absolutely, if you have a gift then you should use it."

"How are our Scottish twins?" Gianna asked.

Erin took a second to adjust to the sudden change of subject, then took an even longer pause. "Um, Gianna..." she saw Gianna straighten as she pulled her hands in across the table, closer to her body. The Italian at least had not lost the ability to read Erin. "I'm very sorry to have to tell you this..."

"What?" Gianna braced herself.

"Mikey died around six months after you left." Erin watched as the creases appeared across Gianna's forehead. "His brother said it was due to depression."

"He took his own life?" The disbelief was in her voice.

Erin nodded, stood and slid her chair around the table, closer to Gianna. Tears flickered in her eyes and Erin pulled her into an embrace.

"So much stuff I've missed." Gianna's words came out muffled against Erin's shoulder.

Erin felt the drops and the moisture building on her flesh. "There was nothing anybody could have done. We all thought he was happy. He seemed it on the outside."

Gianna pulled away and wiped her eyes with the napkin. "Are you sure this had nothing to do with either of us?"

Erin rubbed Gianna's arm. "I was certain to ask his brother that same thing but he insisted. If anything, you were a ray of sunshine in his life, just like you were in all of our lives."

"And all this time, I had no idea." Gianna dabbed at her eyes again. "I always envisioned that one day the four of us would have one big reunion party."

"And then together we'd all row along the Cam." Erin saw the corner of Gianna's mouth rise from the mention of the familiar river.

"The Cam! It was a dream I really wanted to see." She blew her nose. "One day, we'll all be together again and that's what we'll do." Gianna took a sip from her drink and shivered. "And his brother? Please tell me he's alright."

Erin laughed, "Scruffy? Yeah, he's perfectly fine but still a pain in the arse."

For whatever reason, Gianna's eyes flicked up at the mention of his name. "Well, at least *Scruffy*," she said, placing emphasis on his name, "is still around to cause everybody a few problems."

Erin thought back to her engagement, "he most certainly is. He's doing very well for himself, still single and being a pest, but I can see him becoming a true friend to me in the future."

"Becoming?" Gianna asked with narrowed eyes. "You met that man the same day you met me."

Erin paused, trying to find the words. "We went a long time without speaking. I used to walk by him on the odd occasion but I never went out of my way to speak with him."

"Why not?" Gianna saw Erin's stern, warning look. "Oh."

"Too many hard memories." Erin's face softened. "It was only more recently we've been making an effort." A change of subject to something lighter was called for. "How is business? I stopped by your surgery the other day."

"I know, I couldn't believe it when I missed you. I felt completely crushed ... devastated even."

"How on earth did you manage to find me?" Erin leaned forward and relived that magical moment in Pompeii.

"I was lucky, I know that much. Thinking about it now, it was a thousand to one chance. I knew how much you wanted to see Pompeii and so it was as simple as that."

"Well then, it wasn't really a thousand to one chance because you knew me so well." Erin smiled and held her gaze before, again, Gianna broke it and looked down to the table. "Maybe fate played a small part though." Erin laughed. "Seeing you again, for the first time ... now, *that* was a surreal moment, a total blur."

"It was wonderful and I'll always remember it." Gianna finally managed to smile back at Erin.

"And business?" Erin asked, referring back to her original question that got side-tracked.

"Business? Business is good, yes. It has its ups and downs like any other but I'm happy to say things are looking good." She tore into her napkin again.

Erin nodded and didn't follow up with the boring subject of work. Instead, she allowed the silence to protract for a while. Gianna still hadn't volunteered the information Erin sought. Sure, it would most likely be painful, but if anybody deserved to know, it was Erin. She cleared her throat, "Gianna," Erin watched as the Italian gave her full attention, "why did you leave like you did?"

Gianna took a deep breath and opened out her palms. "Erin, the reason was..." she stopped as a shadow loomed over the table.

Erin was so engrossed in the moment, it was several

seconds before she noticed the feminine presence hovering over them.

"Chi e' questa troia?" The familiar, tall brunette pointed a ringed finger an inch from Erin's nose as she spat the final word.

"Stai zitta, non e' una troia!" Gianna shouted back, leaning sidewards and moving a protective arm over Erin. "I'm sorry about this," Gianna's eyes were wide, like a frightened child's.

"Who is she?" Then it hit. It was the woman Erin had seen holding hands with Gianna the day before, the same woman who drank coffee with her while Erin watched from a distance. Erin had assumed at the time that this woman was in a relationship with Gianna, it really had looked that way. Erin hadn't really asked much about the woman and there seemed no need since Gianna had dismissed the woman as 'nobody' back in Pompeii.

"Who is this English whore? You told there was nobody else." The scary woman, switching languages, stood threatening above them both, one hand propped on a hip, the other clenching and unclenching repeatedly. Several people from other tables had turned their heads to steal glimpses at the unfolding drama. The waiter remained by the counter but kept a close eye on the intruder.

Gianna rolled off a string of fast Italian to the woman, which bothered Erin. Gianna had no need to hide anything. Erin understood she had no right to bounce back into Gianna's life and expect everything to be as it was ten years ago. Obviously, Gianna would know other people, women, lesbians. The bigger issue for the moment was, if as it seemed this woman was not 'nobody,' then why had Gianna lied about the fact?

The unwelcome guest seemed not placated in the slightest by Gianna's words. "You go now, English whore." She edged closer to Erin and made shooing motions with her hands, like

Erin was some common insect. The woman might even have been attractive if not for her overbearing and threatening nature.

"She is not a whore. How dare you speak of her that way." Gianna leaned even closer to Erin.

The woman didn't move and now her hand shook as it slowly balled into a fist. "You think me stupid? You disappear all day. You switch off phone. I see you sat close with English whore."

Gianna closed her eyes and squeezed the flesh at the top of her nose. Then, unexpectedly, she leapt from her seat and stood up to the woman who was quick to take a surprised step back.

Erin pulled at her hand. "Please, Gianna, there's no need."

The woman's eyes were drawn by the physical contact and in response, picked up Erin's drink and threw it over her. Erin recoiled from the sudden chill as orange liquid dripped down her face and neck, over her white summer blouse.

Two waiters appeared either side of the woman, "Vattene adesso." They took hold of her forearms and dragged her from the canopy. Thankfully, she left with minimal resistance, but Erin felt the palpable burning glower from her eyes, a look of sheer hatred she'd never before experienced.

Gianna slowly retook her seat and faced Erin, taking ahold of her hands. She exhaled a deep breath and blew hair away from her forehead. "Welcome to the lesbian lifestyle, this is how we roll in Napoli." She grinned, then lowered her eyes to Erin's orange stained blouse. "Erin, I'm so sorry about all that. She had no right to do that to you."

To Erin's surprise, she found herself chuckling, "it's alright."

"What? Why are you laughing?"

"I know how she feels." Erin squeezed Gianna's hands.

"She's not the only girl who's been sent bat shit crazy over you."

TOGETHER, THEY TOOK SMALL STEPS IN THE DIRECTION OF Erin's hotel, both wanting to extend the evening as long as possible. Even now, at eleven at night, the roads remained crammed with vehicles, scooters especially adding to the noise.

"You really don't need to walk me all the way to the hotel," Erin said, hoping Gianna would ignore her and continue.

"Oh shush you, I keep saying, Napoli is completely safe. I'm fine walking back on my own. You, on the other hand..." Gianna's arm brushed Erin's as they strolled along the pavement. "Besides, I don't know when or if I'll ever see you again."

Erin's heart beat faster as she looked down to the ground to hide the grin that stretched wide across her face. Gianna wanted to see her again! The feeling was more than mutual. Besides, they still had much unfinished business.

"Well, I'm happy to say, we're not leaving until Monday, so we have most of tomorrow to catch up." Erin saw the hotel in the distance. Major bummer. "You promised to be my tour guide, remember?"

"That's right, I do remember and I never break a promise," Gianna said quickly. "So I expect to see you for brunch tomorrow morning."

"Of course." This time Erin did not bother hiding the grin. "I just hope your little stalker friend doesn't find us. I'm not sure how well that would go down."

Gianna tugged down the cuffs of her blouse, Erin noticing a few dots of orange from the cocktail that must have splashed over her as well. "Don't worry about Agata. I've been meaning to break things off with her for a while."

"Agata, hey ... so you are seeing her?" Erin asked, lowering her head, feeling her shoulders drop.

Gianna's head swivelled to Erin and then back to the street ahead. "Yeah, yeah, kind of." She rubbed the back of her neck. "I probably should have said something but I really was meant to be breaking up with her."

Erin twisted around and placed a hand on Gianna's arm to stop her. "Hey, you don't owe me any explanations. You have your life, I get that, of course, I do." Regardless, she really hoped Gianna meant what she just said. They continued strolling closer to the hotel.

"I'm calling her just as soon as I get home." Gianna declared in a rush. "You have no idea about some of the crazy shit I've suspected her of. Speaking to you like she did really was the final straw."

Erin thought to ask just why the heck she was even with such a woman but then thought better of it. Gianna deserved so much better, at the very least, she deserved to be ecstatically happy with a girl who thought the world of her, who wasn't overcome with jealousy simply because she was enjoying a drink with another woman. Why had Gianna settled for someone who clearly wasn't that person? Then again, Erin could hardly judge Gianna harshly on that score, considering her own predicament. Not that Agata and Ben could be compared in any way. "I just want you to be happy."

The reception lighting of the Grand Hotel Santa Lucia shone in the twilight and then Erin stood facing Gianna, only realising after a few seconds that their fingers were lightly tangled together.

"I want you to be happy too," Gianna said soothingly, her eyes just slightly rising above Erin's.

The traffic seemed to have evaporated without Erin

noticing, which was remarkable for Napoli. For once, the world was silent.

This was the part where in the movies, Erin would lean forward and kiss her. And in the moment, she knew, she wanted nothing more than to experience Gianna's kiss like she had all those years ago. Things were perfect back then, but now, life was very much different. This was no movie, but a very difficult reality, and Erin's heart felt conflicted between doing what she wanted and doing what she knew to be right.

Erin touched the side of her neck, "I'll see you tomorrow, Gianna." The last word came out as a whisper.

Gianna swallowed, a hint of disappointment in her eyes, "yes."

And then Erin watched as Gianna walked away, a nervous twisting building in her stomach. Erin touched her belly. There was only one person in the world who could do that.

Erin made her way up the stairs toward the fourth floor and unlocked the door to her room.

Ben was sitting on the edge of the bed, leaning forward, his hands clasped together. His head darted up to Erin as she entered.

"Ben? Are you ok? Why are you sat in silence?" Erin swallowed.

His eyes were momentarily distracted by the orange stain down her top. "Hi, Erin, what happened to your blouse?"

"Oh, nothing, a bit of an accident with a cocktail. Are you alright?"

"Did you have a nice evening?" He asked, again not answering Erin's question. Ben had earlier said he intended on spending a few hours in the hotel bar with a couple glasses of wine and a good book. A copy of Oscar Wilde's The Importance of Being Earnest lay untouched on the bedside table.

Erin began rubbing a hand up and down her arm. "I had a wonderful evening, how was yours?"

"I've been thinking," he said, finally standing and walking toward the window with a slight wobble. "I've been thinking about us and how we are and how we were and a few other things." Having reached the window, he turned back to Erin and leaned back against it.

"Yes?"

"I need to know..." he twisted the watch Erin had bought him for Christmas around his wrist.

Erin took a step toward him, "yes? Go on..."

"Was there ever anything between you and this friend of yours?" He asked, barely managing to look Erin in the eye, and unable to say Gianna's name.

This was it. Erin had to give him credit for figuring it out. The only way he could have done so was if he'd remembered Gianna from when she was in England. It was also possible he'd picked up on a few cues Erin herself had missed, her lack of socialisation from a young age making it harder for herself to read people and the subtle signs they often transmitted. Or maybe it was as simple as taking one look at Gianna and knowing. Either way, Ben deserved to know the truth.

"Ben..." as soon as she said his name, he knew it. She saw it in his eyes for the brief moment before he averted them to look across at the wall. "She was the best friend I ever had." Erin swallowed, "and yes, she was so much more than a friend." Her hand shook as she pinched her bottom lip. There was nothing in the world she wanted less than to hurt Ben, but with the present trajectory, it was probably inevitable. "And yes, I did love her ... once." She hoped that would be enough and would spare them both from her having to go further into the details.

"Were you a couple?" He asked, briefly managing to meet Erin's eye.

256

She sighed, perched on the edge of the bed and placed her hands flat on her legs. "We never got round to that." Erin continued to explain what happened, how Gianna disappeared, how they'd lost contact and how she'd met Ben, all whilst staring glassy-eyed at the wall.

"Did you sleep with her?" He asked with a croak.

"Yes," Erin hissed, unable to look at him, "the night before she left." Then she turned to him as she fought and failed to hold back the tears.

Ben straightened and guffawed as though it'd been obvious all along. "So, you're running around Napoli like a headless chicken, no, like a lovestruck teenager, dragging us down here in the first place." He threw up an arm. "This is all because you want to rekindle things with *that* woman, isn't it?"

Erin had told Ben the truth of what they had been ten years ago. *That* in itself was a huge revelation. She felt no obligation, at least at this stage to admit what she didn't even know herself. If she denied Ben's accusation, she'd be lying to him. If Erin told him she came to seek out the love of her life after ten years in the hope of being with her, she'd lose Ben. The truth, as so often, was somewhere in the middle ground, which she wasn't even sure of herself – That Erin wanted to see if there was anything still there between herself and Gianna. The middle ground, the truth, would also, most likely, result in her losing Ben.

"Ben," she finally spoke, "I had to come to Napoli to find out why she left England and to make sure she was safe." She hesitated whilst she thought about the next words. "And yes, I missed her."

"You're a liar!" He spat. "You haven't let me touch you in weeks. Have you never heard of a phone call?"

Erin wiped her eyes as she watched Ben grab a pillow from the bed and throw it to the floor. "There's nothing going on between us," she regretted saying that as soon as the words left her mouth.

"But there will be if you have your way. Do what you have to do tomorrow. Just don't expect things to return to normal between us when you decide this ridiculous fantasy of yours is just that ... a fantasy." He lowered himself to the floor and turned away to face the wall.

Chapter Sixteen

PARCO VIRGILIANO

On Sunday morning, Erin waited for Gianna outside a café bar on one of the crossroads of Spaccanapoli. Much of the short wait was occupied by a church procession marching down the road complete with ringing bells and choir boys. The spectacle at least provided something interesting to watch.

Even now, at not even ten in the morning, the sun baked down like nothing England was capable of producing. Erin rubbed her chin as she watched Gianna approaching fully clad in a long red skirt and yellow shirt that again covered everything. "Do you Neapolitans not overheat in your own city?" When Gianna didn't get what Erin was implying, she continued. "Why are you covered up so much? It's going to burn like bloody hell today."

"Because I don't look as good as you anymore," Gianna said, sticking a thumbnail between her teeth.

That so wasn't true. "Hey, I don't care what you look like. You'll always be my Gianna." Not for the first time, Gianna appeared hurt from the use of the full version of her name. Erin rubbed Gianna's arm, feeling the bulk that ten years ago wouldn't have existed. "Besides, who says you don't look good anymore?" Erin most certainly did still find Gianna attractive, after all, the heart loves what it has to work for and God damn, she'd never worked for anything or anyone harder than the damn Italian.

Gianna ignored Erin and pointed inside. "Let's go in." Wow, her confidence really had taken a thrashing over the years.

They ate a breakfast of espresso with a selection of croissants and other pastries. Erin remarked how different breakfast was on the continent compared to England, where porridge oats was the staple.

"I remember and good luck finding that oat rubbish in this city," Gianna remarked just as a collision from somewhere close almost made Erin spill her espresso. Gianna laughed as Erin regained control of her cup.

"It's not funny." She set her cup down on its plate. "This bloody city..." Erin said with a sigh.

"You get used to it."

"But don't you miss Cambridge? The peace, the quiet?" As well as Erin herself being there.

"Of course I do," Gianna said without even needing to think. "It was the one place I was happiest and I could have stayed there forever, but things got in the way."

And Erin would endeavour to find out about those *things* today, she thought, staring a hole in Gianna's face, who then averted her eyes to the bill that rested on the table. Could she tell what Erin was thinking? She so often had in the past.

Within five minutes, they were both in Gianna's battered Fiat 500, careering west along Via Nuova Marina. Erin dug fingers deep into her thighs as Gianna drove within feet behind the knackered old car in front at ninety kilometres per hour. Erin had been curious about being driven around by Gianna but now she was actually experiencing it, she could not remember anything more terrifying.

"It's called Parco Virgiliano," Gianna said, turning to look at Erin with bright eyes.

"Right, ok, yes." Erin stretched up her neck and stared down with terror at the crumpled front end of the car. "And it's close, yes?"

Her eyes shifted upwards in thought. "Hmm, I'd say about seven or eight kilometres, but not all on this shitty city road. You'll get to see some coastal roads too."

"Are these coastal roads windy?" Erin asked, feeling her muscles tense.

"Windy?" Gianna asked with an uncertain tone. "No, it's a hot and sunny day."

"No, I didn't mean..." Erin clenched her fists as Gianna, along with the car in the other lane drove straight through a set of red lights, "I meant *bendy*. Are the coastal roads bendy?"

"Of course." Gianna leaned sideways and bumped Erin's shoulder.

Ok, no more questions, just let her drive.

Parco Virgiliano, actually an islet southwest of the city, was connected to the mainland by a manmade path built into the water. The islet, almost circular and largely rocky with dense tree cover was a welcome oasis of tranquillity away from the never ceasing noise of Napoli. Erin also felt relieved to be out of the car.

From the almost empty carpark, it required only a couple of minutes to cross the pathway built from rocks in the sea and then they were on the islet. It would be a steep walk up to the top, where Gianna promised incredible views, but thankfully the trees offered plenty of shade for the trek.

Gianna found the walk difficult and visible beads of sweat shone upon her cheeks but she laboured on without complaining. From somewhere high above, birds that Erin could not identify chirped their pretty tunes and the moment was so tranquil that she couldn't help extending her hand across the small gap and taking hold of Gianna's, while paying close attention for her reaction. It had been bold of Erin, she knew, but immediately, Gianna squeezed her hand to let her know the gesture was not unwelcome and for the next few minutes, every time Erin dared glance across, she was sure there was only happiness upon her old friend's face.

They walked lazily but eventually, they reached the lookout point. Several benches were positioned by the rails, which gave way to some of the most incredible views Erin had ever seen.

"Looks like we have the place to ourselves, which never happens, I can promise you that." Gianna zipped open her backpack and removed a large bottle of water.

"I've never seen anything like it." Erin slowly shook her head and pressed her palms to her cheeks, wiping away the perspiration.

"Here," Gianna passed Erin the water and stood close, pointing southwest, "that small island right there is Procida. And the larger one beyond is Ischia." She opened out her arms to encompass the entire view to their fore. "This is the Gulf of Napoli."

"And over there?" Erin pointed south.

"That is the northern coast of Sorrento and on the south side is the Amalfi Coast."

The mention of *Amalfi* reminded Erin of Ben, where he'd be travelling alone today. "I have some figuring out to do and I strongly suggest you do the same." He'd said as he kissed Erin on the cheek before heading out. The plan was to have dinner together tonight, where they would have an honest discussion about the state of their relationship.

"What's Amalfi like?" Erin asked.

"It's magical. They're famous for making a special kind of liquor. Have you heard of Limoncello?"

"I have, it's delicious."

"Well, you can also try chocolate, mint, Meloncello and many others." Gianna pointed northeast, back over the direction they'd come. "There are also some wonderful views of Napoli from up here but they're better seen from the other side of the islet."

Erin took Gianna's hand and pulled her down onto the closest bench. Directly in front, the sea shimmered from the sun. "No more stalling Gianna, it's just the two of us now, no opera singers, no ex-girlfriends, no distractions." Erin turned to face her, taking hold of her other hand as well. "I've waited ten years and crossed a continent to know why, right when we were on the brink of something quite special, did you run away from me, from us." Erin spoke without blinking and was almost amazed Gianna had held her gaze throughout. "Tell me."

Gianna inhaled deeply, closed her eyes and nodded. "Ok, I'm ready to tell you." When she opened her eyes she gave Erin's hands a light squeeze. This was it, finally. "Do you recall I had a brother who served in Afghanistan with the Italian army?" She asked with sadness.

"Of course."

"Well, part of the responsibility of Marco's battalion was guarding the opium crop from the Taliban, which is exactly what he spent most of his time doing. My father told me he'd phone home and complain about having to do such an immoral duty when they should have been torching the whole goddamned crop. They were told by higher command that they were protecting the crop because if they were to burn it, the farmers and the local population would be left poor, would turn against the alliance and then many would be forced to join or assist the Taliban. But as the months went by, my brother began getting wise to them." Gianna sighed then took a large intake of air. So far she was holding up good, her eye contact shifting between her lap and Erin. "With the general discontent within the battalion and by talking to the farmers, Marco and his sergeant discovered that the International Security Assistance Force were in fact harvesting and guarding the poppy crop for safe passage to the west.

"What?" Erin's mouth gaped ajar, unsure just how much of this was believable.

"It's true! Ask yourself this ... why, after all these years is heroin still flooding into Italy, into England and every other Western country from an Afghanistan that's had tens of thousands of foreign troops there for years? I mean, how hard can it be to burn the lot? Heroin is one of the most lucrative exports, why wouldn't governments at the highest level get involved? And let's not pretend your own country, Erin, didn't start two wars in the past over opium. There are precedents for this."

Erin nodded, vaguely recalling reading the words 'Chinese Opium Wars' on a rather long list of past British conflicts. "Right, ok, I believe you." Though she really hadn't put much thought into the subject and certainly hadn't looked into it in any detail. And why would she have? Erin never had Gianna down as a conspiracy nut, an eccentric, definitely, which was no doubt a product of growing up in this city, but she wasn't crazy. But since the topic was close to Gianna, Erin would listen and try to understand, even though at this point it wasn't clear what any of this had to do with her brother Marco. Erin assumed that part was coming.

"Then one day, the 20th of May, 2004, Marco and part of his company were ordered to base to collect supplies." Gianna averted her eyes from Erin, who realised that date was only a couple of days before Gianna left Cambridge. "We were *told* an improvised explosive device had detonated below their vehicle. At least, nobody has ever been able to prove otherwise." Gianna reached into her bag for a tissue and dabbed at her eyes.

Erin, at a loss for words, ran a hand through her hair, then took hold of Gianna's hands again.

Gianna exhaled and looked up in a small token of defiance. "In the years after, we had visits from some of his friends who'd since left the army. They said Marco was feeling increasingly unhappy with his duties and that he tried to spread discontent amongst his comrades by preaching the real reasons why they were there." Gianna tilted her head. "You remember when I told you the kind of person he was? He was exactly like you, Erin. He was a wonderful yet shy, socially awkward person. It would have been so hard for him to stand up and speak out like that and he wouldn't have done it unless he was absolutely sure." Gianna seemed to wait for Erin to say something. "I know what you're probably thinking ... was it murder?"

How did she do that? "I was ... I was thinking exactly that."

"I remember getting word from my father about Marco's death only a few minutes after you left my flat on that wonderful morning." Gianna squeezed Erin's hands tight. "My life went from perfect to agonising within a single second." She nodded and seemed to stare into nothing. "I had to be there, to be with my family, so I pretty much just grabbed my passport and money and dashed for the airport. I knew I was throwing everything away, but at that moment, I didn't give a shit." Gianna pulled her hands away. "Can you believe that's why he died, so the British and Americans could maintain their heroin monopoly?"

"I'm so very sorry," Erin croaked and felt an overwhelming sadness and loss because she would very much have thought of Marco as her own brother, had she known him.

"Looking back, sure, I could have contacted you but two things stopped me," Gianna said as anger brewed in her voice. Erin thought she could guess what those two things might be. "For a long time afterwards, I harboured a grudge against your country."

Erin shrank back against the bench. She'd be angry herself if what Gianna said turned out to be true.

She continued, "but eventually I realised I can't hold an entire nation responsible for the actions of its corrupt government."

"No, of course not." Erin sniffed. "What was the other reason?"

Gianna smiled, which surprised Erin. "Remember the first day we met?"

"Oh, only as if it were yesterday." Erin tilted her head to match Gianna's and grinned.

"You were so terrified of all those people, you looked like you wanted to sink into the floor."

Erin laughed, "I was in a bad way that day."

"It was the reason I wanted to be your friend. I guess I sort of felt responsible."

"You did? I never knew that."

"I used to try and help Marco, by introducing him to my friends, by insisting he joined in with us whenever there was an opportunity, even though he was a year older than me." She gazed for a moment toward the sea. "It was hard for me to contact you because you reminded me so much of him."

There it was – Right there. After ten years, Erin now had her answers.

After ten years, she finally knew why her life had changed in an instant when the best friend she ever had abandoned her. "I understand now and I accept it." Erin nodded, but she knew there was more.

"My father spent the following year trying to prove Marco was murdered by his own side, all while the press covered it up." Gianna looked away again and closed her eyes. "After that first year, things had improved a lot and I thought about returning to England to find you and restart my degree." She paused.

"What happened?" The ache and longing within Erin grew. The entire story was filled with many an *if only*.

"I promise you, Erin," she rubbed Erin's arm, "I was writing out the email to Downing College when I heard from my mother that my father had died."

"I'm so sorry," Erin whispered, feeling her heart beating exceptionally fast.

"He passed away from heart complications but my mother always said he died from a broken heart."

Erin blinked as a tear rolled down her cheek. Great! She'd wanted to stay strong for Gianna's sake and pretty soon doubtless there'd be blubbering too.

"So, there you have it." Gianna rocked to-and-fro from the hips, something Erin remembered she used to do on the rare occasion she was anxious. "I needed to support my mother, so I moved back in with her. Then I took a bar job to pay the bills, which meant I could no longer return to Cambridge. The following year I enrolled at the University of Napoli and graduated in Physiotherapy a full three years later than intended." She laughed at the last part of her story. "I finally achieved my *dream* a couple of years ago when I opened my surgery," her smile waned at the last part, which confused Erin.

"So, why did you not get in touch after graduating?"

"Erin, there were so many times, especially later on when I came close to contacting you but things always got in the way." She sighed, "I found that the longer I left it, the harder it got though the honest truth is that I was about to surprise you with a visit around a year and a half ago."

"What happened?" Erin dreaded asking but thought she knew the answer.

"My mother died." Her mouth trembled and her voice came out as a croak. "Clearly, something was trying to tell me not to bother, so it was at that point I finally decided to give up."

Erin pulled Gianna close as they both cried in each others' arms. Erin closed her eyes and tried to imagine how hard the last few years must have been for her friend. It was understandable that she'd worked herself to the bone, aged beyond her years, put on weight, neglected her health and in the meantime, Gianna had also lost all hope. More recently, in her loneliness she'd made poor decisions and settled for bad relationships; that crazy madwoman, Agata, who threw the cocktail over Erin sprung to mind.

There had once been a time when at her most vulnerable, Erin had been saved by the very girl who now clung to her, crying. Now, Erin had it in her power to return that favour and try to make things right with Gianna, to rebuild her just as she had once helped forge Erin into the person she had become. Where Gianna had once been protective over Erin, Erin now felt that same protective instinct over Gianna. Erin wanted to make everything right again, to repay the debt and see Gianna return to the happy, confident girl she used to be.

Erin pushed herself to arms' length and waited for Gianna to look her in the eye. "You should come back to Cambridge. We can work together, just like we always dreamed. I have room at my practice and I'd love to have you there with me." Erin would make damn sure Gianna regained her confidence, her love of life and even her love of rowing. But best of all, they'd be together.

Gianna's eyes glazed over. She opened her mouth as if to say something but no words were forthcoming. She shook her head several times as Erin felt her heart sink into her stomach. This was so meant to be, just the two of them. It was always meant to be this way. All Gianna had to do was say '*yes*.'

"Erin, I just can't."

"Why not?" Erin asked with hard eyes.

"Please, I just can't do it." She shook her head again.

Erin pulled her hands away. "Excuse me, but I've just asked you to come work with me in my own surgery. The least you can do is give me a real reason."

"Please, Erin, you'll understand one day ... maybe."

Why did life always have to be so fucking unfair?

All these wasted years and, as it turned out, they were all for nothing. Of course, sometimes events, life situations and tragedies interfere with the normal running of things; like everything that'd happened to Gianna, like that damn poem fluttering back into existence.

"Fate can only take a person so far. After that, it's up to you to show some courage and account for the rest." Erin had made a conscious decision to look for Gianna. It had been Erin who'd made the first move after ten years, put *everything* on the line and now Gianna needed to show some courage herself and meet her halfway. Erin could do no more than she already had.

"I'm not sure what you mean," Gianna said, averting her eyes once again.

Erin sprang from her seat and struck with her fist the railing that prevented her from tumbling into the sea before whipping back around on Gianna and exploding. "Damn it! Ten fucking years and not even a word to let me know you were alive. Gianna, what the fuck?" Erin's entire body was shaking but this time there were no clouds blotting out her vision.

Gianna stood and faced Erin but kept her distance. "I may have disappeared for ten years but you've been pretending to be in love with Ben for just as long. What are you planning on doing, Erin? Are you really going to marry him?" Gianna shouted the last words.

Somewhere far below a large wave smashed against the rocks. Erin moved forward, wrapped her arms around Gianna's body and pulled her close. Their lips met as they wilted into each other, their tongues clashing, heavy breaths from their noses loud as they struggled for air, Erin grasped the flesh on Gianna's back as she felt a hand clasping chunks of her hair. Erin lost herself in the kiss, ten years forlorn, and she remembered the first time she'd experienced Gianna's lips by the Cam, when she was innocent and life was so perfect. Nothing had ever been the same since. Why did things have to change?

Gianna pulled away, her eyes glassy. "No! You're not doing this." She took a step back. "You're engaged. The sweet Erin I always knew did not hurt people. Does your fiancé deserve this?"

And then Erin realised – Gianna was not the only girl out of the two of them who'd changed for the worse. "Gianna..."

"No! You go back to him now. Get married, have kids, live happily ever after. It's what you deserve." Gianna turned away, unable to look at Erin.

Erin panted and took a few seconds to regain composure. Gianna was correct. How could Erin have even thought to make such requests of Gianna when she herself was in no emotional state to make them. Erin *was* engaged to be married and that had to be fixed before anything else, even if in the end it still wouldn't make a difference with Gianna, she still had to make things right. "Gia?" Erin said, waiting for her friend to turn around.

Gianna slowly turned to face Erin over her shoulder.

Erin breathed, "I always regretted that I never said … that I loved you."

They began the descent, back to the car.

ERIN WAITED AT THE TABLE IN THE RESTAURANT OF THE Grand Hotel Santa Lucia, already on her second glass of wine. It was unlike Ben to be late, but she could allow for it this evening.

She would do it tonight, no stalling, no excuses. Erin was in love, still, even after all these years, with another woman. That Erin was a *lesbian* didn't really register on her mind as she glanced absently around to the other diners and at the people who stepped through the lobby. Deep down, over the past ten years and probably beyond, she supposed it was there all along, even if she never put a label on herself or declared it to her family. She pictured *that* conversation with her mother and shuddered. But first, she had to make things right with Ben. And that would be horrific, but probably not unexpected.

Ben strode into the restaurant and nodded to Erin as they caught each others' eye from across the room. "Hi." He walked around to Erin's side of the table and kissed her lightly on the cheek before taking a seat at the other side.

"Hello," she tried to smile but the knots in her stomach prevented any kind of happiness from showing on the outside. "How was Amalfi?"

"Fantastic. I stocked up on the Limoncello stuff. They'll make great gifts for everybody back home." Ben crossed one leg over the other and leaned back in his chair. "Sorry I'm

271

late, by the way, but you really do have to see the drive. I probably made a half dozen stops just on the way back ... all those small towns ... really stunning."

"Really?" Erin rubbed her hands down her dress in a vain effort at drying away the clamminess. Obviously, Ben had been in no rush to return.

"It's a real shame you've decided barely to leave Napoli, you have no idea what you're missing." He shook his head as he spoke, almost with a hint of condescension.

"Are we eating? I'm not really all that hungry." But a few more drinks wouldn't go amiss.

"You can do what you like, dear," he said, stony-faced, barely moving any muscle that didn't control his mouth.

"Ok, well then, I think I'll skip food this evening." Erin leaned forward. "We need to have a chat, about *us*."

"About *us*? Oh, don't worry about it, Erin. It's over between *us*." He reached into his pocket and pulled out his phone.

"Ok, I expected this."

"Quiet! Don't think I don't know what you've been doing today." He tapped his fingers against the screen and spoke without looking up.

Erin's head swirled, her feet tingled. "What I've been doing today?" She asked almost with a hiss.

"Imagine my *real* surprise," he said with sarcasm, "when I'm enjoying the views of the Amalfi Coast when I get an email from some Italian dyke by the name of Agata Castelli." He must have seen Erin's mouth plunge as she lost control of her facial muscles. "Ah yes, name ring a bell, does it?" He continued, reading from the screen. "'To the boyfriend of *English Whore*. Be a man and tell your woman to keep away from mine girlfriend.'"

Shit. Throwing a cocktail over somebody in anger was one thing, but going out of the way to seek out Ben was something else. "Ben, I'm so sorry you had to read that. I was going to tell you today that..."

"...Did you kiss her?" He asked, for the first time his eyes betraying what was going on inside.

What would be the best thing to say? The truth? That yes, while they were still technically engaged, Erin had kissed another woman. Or should Erin spare his feelings, as well as his pride, which would make it easier for him to move on with dignity when this whole thing was over with. After all, it wouldn't be easy for a guy to lose his fiancée to another woman. Either way, Erin had little time to decide. "Ben, we did *not* kiss." In hindsight, it would probably turn out to be the wrong decision.

"You're a bloody liar!" He threw the phone down in front of Erin.

She picked it up and gaped at the screen, the photograph showing herself in a tight embrace, kissing Gianna at Parco Virgiliano. She bowed her head, what could she say? "Ben, I'm so sorry."

He held up a hand, "save it," retrieved his phone and left.

THIRTY MINUTES AFTER BEN WALKED OUT, ERIN RECEIVED a note from the concierge informing her that he'd taken the car and left the city, gone up north somewhere and that he suggested Erin made her own arrangements with regards to the rest of the trip, or flying home, either way, he didn't give a shit.

Oh why, oh why, oh why had Erin lied to him? Now he'd have the worst of both worlds, knowing she'd been dishonest and that he'd lost his fiancée to another woman. Ugh, that wouldn't be easy for him to take. A thick excess of saliva built in Erin's throat, the skin of her face tightened. She felt disgusted.

Erin, halfway through her third glass of wine, knew the truth of the matter. She'd fucked up big in Napoli. "And that fucking bitch," she spat, not caring about the elderly couple enjoying a meal at the next table. Agata. That bitch had followed them to Parco Virgiliano and spied from the shadows, taking photos. Well, she had her wish now. Not only was it over with Ben in the most horrible of ways, but things had also been damaged with Gianna.

"What is with her?" Erin asked herself, taking another gulp of wine.

Why did she not want to return to England, back to the place she herself admitted was where she'd been happiest? Maybe the answer was in the very question. Was Gianna afraid that things might not be the same the second time around? It was a possibility. Or maybe it was because Erin had been engaged. Had Erin herself been as much a barrier to her own happiness as was the circumstance of Gianna running away? Perhaps if Erin hadn't spent the last ten years pretending to be happy with Ben then she would have been free to search for Gianna much sooner and things could have been so very different. Damn it, but Erin could have been there for her, to help Gianna through all the incredibly hard times.

"Or maybe you really are a coward, Gia ... Gianna." She downed the wine, pushed herself out from the chair, threw some money to the table and shuffled in the direction of the lobby.

The concierge was leaning against the counter as Erin approached. "Good evening."

Erin propped herself up against the desk. "You couldn't talk for a few minutes, could you? Anything to delay going back to my empty room."

The concierge straightened, raised a trimmed eyebrow and spoke with a hint of amusement. "You know, there's something about Napoli that makes or breaks relationships. There's something about Napoli that makes or breaks people."

"Well, I think it's broken me." Her eyes were drawn through the window, to the battered heap he called a car. He'd been right about everything he said. "Do you have any more wisdom you can expel for my benefit?"

He smirked, "if you ask me, it's better you know now than in say..." he shrugged his shoulders, "ten years."

Chapter Seventeen

VESPA

Gianna ran her finger down the day's diary entry, which didn't take long. "One fucking client." Signora Castelli wasn't due until late in the afternoon, which would give Gianna most of the day to stew over yesterday and how things were left with Erin. "How am I supposed to run a business with no fucking business?" The damn economy. When would things improve?

At least now she'd finished with Agata, one erratic and unpredictable aspect of her life was now out of it. Agata hadn't taken it well, not at all. What should have been a twenty-minute phone call had dragged on for nearly two hours as she pleaded with Gianna to change her mind. "It's that English whore isn't it?" She had asked, and Gianna responded in the negative, which had been the truth, not that it was believed.

Gianna just hoped Signora Castelli would not turn out to be another phantom client of Agata's. "Why did I ever get involved with her?"

She pottered about the surgery then fixed up another espresso in the kitchen. She sank the thick dark liquid in one, the powerful and bitter taste doing its work. Then she traipsed to the bathroom and studied her reflection, searching for signs of the ever-increasing and soul-destroying grey. She plucked one out, then another.

"Erin," she whispered. What a weekend that had been. Gianna would require days, weeks even, to process the events of the last two days. She had no idea what the hell had happened, it all flew by so fast. She remembered pretty much every last detail, in the most vivid of ways, from the sounds of the birds and the smell of Erin's flesh to the exact specifics of their conversations and Erin's facial expressions; a mixture of love, happiness, hurt and pain. "Oh, Erin, why did we leave things like we did?" She regretted that and how badly Erin had taken the refusal of her offer. "You'd be much better off without me, Erin, and I will not impose my overweight, fat self on you. I'm cursed and you deserve much better."

Gianna replayed in her mind, that surreal moment when Erin told her she'd loved her. "Does she still love me?" Did real love ever truly die? "Why would she say she loved me if it wasn't still so?" But more to the point, why couldn't Gianna bring herself to say the same? "I will always love you too, Erin." She held on to the sink and stared deep into her eyes. "But I'm too pathetic to say it to your face." The old Gia would have been far more likely to let her feelings known.

But Gia had died with her family.

What did any of it matter now? Erin was today checking out of her hotel and was probably even now heading north to Tuscany or wherever the breeze took her, along with her fiancé. It was doubtful she'd ever see Erin again.

Vedetta's voice, urgent and panicking shrilled through the opened door of the surgery. "You can't go in there."

A masculine voice followed, trying and failing to sound reassuring. Gianna left the bathroom to find a creature of the night, Vincenzo, pushing his way into the surgery.

"It's alright, Vedetta, I've got this." Gianna watched as Vedetta hesitated but closed the surgery door behind the large man, white bandages with heavy flecks of red wrapped tight around his head. Two large eye holes gave way to bloodshot irises, barely a trace of white visible, his eyes seemed to protrude at least an inch from their sockets, like some organ harvester had tried removing them and given up halfway through the job.

"Good morning, Dottoressa," Vincenzo croaked, his voice was hoarse as though there were glass fragments stuck down his windpipe.

"Vincenzo, how may I help you?" She already knew, of course, even though the urgency of the situation had largely bypassed her mind due to the events over the weekend.

"How are you today, Dottoressa?" He asked, pacing about the surgery.

"I've been better."

He really did look like a character from some bad horror movie, all bandaged up like that, whilst trying at the same time to look respectable in those polished black shoes, white shirt and tie, even if his girth forced the hems to untuck at the front. "You know why I'm here, Dottoressa. Don Sabbatino requires his payment. You owe him five thousand Euros."

Gianna could, if she'd made a real effort, have secured the money. She had a small sum left from her mother's inheritance but her dear mother would turn in her grave if that money were to be used on paying off the Camorra. "That money is for your future," she'd said, a few days before she died in a hospital bed as Gianna sat by her side.

"Don Sabbatino wishes to see you succeed, Dottoressa. Please tell me you have the money," he stepped toward her.

"Vincenzo, I don't have the money so do what you have to

do." Gianna took a step back toward the wall and hoped the retribution would not be physical upon herself.

Vincenzo sighed and reached around his back, pulling out from his belt what looked like a baseball bat, only shorter. Unlike the iron cosh he'd used three days before, this was made from wood. He'd clearly learned his lesson. He pointed to the skylight above the treatment table, the same light that had caused him so much agony. "I must be more careful this time." He pulled it down on its arm and turned to Gianna. "You should take a step back." After he was satisfied she'd moved far enough away, he said, "I want you to know that this pains me deeply." He held an arm over his eyes and looked downwards as he struck the light, the high pitched smash rattled around Gianna's skull. This time the shards landed safely over the floor, with some spreading out over the treatment table. Vincenzo had had a score to settle with that damned light and he breathed with relief at having achieved the simple yet mindless task unharmed. He then moved on to his other foe, the electrotherapy short wave diathermy, the monitor still smashed from before. He raised the bat and brought it down repeatedly over the equipment. That device alone had cost Gianna almost four thousand Euros.

Gianna backed further into the corner and covered her ears as he moved onto the radial pressure wave unit, all ten thousand Euros of it, demolishing it, followed by the recumbent cycle ergometer before he brought out a knife and slid it down the entire length of the treatment table's leather exterior, another one thousand Euros. He then approached Gianna's laptop and took several swings at the screen, his bearing more than a little off balance, doubtless from the effects of being nearly blinded.

How had it come to this? All Gianna had ever wanted with her life was to help people. People who'd found themselves most vulnerable, without the proper use of their limbs, and now all her most precious possessions were being trashed and all because, in her chosen career, she'd decided to forego the money and work instead for something that truly mattered to her. She thought about her brother, father, her friends in the army, those same people who'd inspired her to enter the field of physiotherapy. What would they think if they were around to see this?

Gianna used her hands to cover her face, closing her eyes in an attempt at blocking out the smashes and Vincenzo's grunts as he put his full force into destroying her precious surgery.

After untold minutes, only when the cracking and shattering noises finally abated did Gianna dare look up. Using a handkerchief, Vincenzo was wiping the sweat from his forehead where the bandages did not cover his flesh. "Don Sabbatino considers your debt paid, Dottoressa." He panted and stuffed the damp rag inside his shirt pocket. "It pains me deeply that it had to come to this."

Gianna wobbled over to her chair, at least that had remained untouched. "Are you finished now?" She asked, collapsing into the soft leather.

He nodded sadly, "I hope you're able to get back on your feet. Don't let this destroy you." Vincenzo turned around and stepped toward the door.

Gianna's chest heaved, her shoulders shook, the tears of hope lost streamed down her cheeks as she covered her face, enveloping herself in darkness – And then – A feminine gasp.

Gianna glanced up just as Erin entered. She was frozen to the spot as Vincenzo stepped quietly around her in the threshold. When Vincenzo disappeared, Erin dashed inside, taking a moment to scan the room before running toward Gianna and pulling her tight into a protective embrace.

Gianna attempted to speak, to explain, but the words left her mouth only as palpitations.

"Hey, shush, it's alright," Erin gently rocked Gianna to-and-fro while her mouth pressed against the top of Erin's breast, "it's alright, I'm here, I'm here."

There was nobody else in the world Gianna needed more than Erin right now, yet at the same time, she hated being seen like this, blubbering like a child with a destroyed livelihood, the mask and pretence obliterated. Gianna was supposed to be the strong one of the two and Erin, for all she knew about Gianna, had only ever seen her cry that one time on the punt back in Cambridge many years ago.

After several minutes, Gianna finally managed to speak. "You came back?" The sound came out muffled and for a moment Gianna wondered if Erin had understood.

"I came to say goodbye. How could I not?" Erin spoke with soothing tones. "My flight leaves in a couple of hours. Bloody hell, Gianna, what happened here?"

"The Camorra. I owed them money ... too much money ... and I didn't have it." The words sounded slightly more coherent now.

"Why didn't you tell me you needed help? I would have gladly helped you out. Heck, I would have sold my soul to help you."

Gianna closed her eyes and sank into her. Erin was leaving and this would be their farewell. She inhaled Erin, all natural Erin in her essence. Gianna sobbed, "I just couldn't tell you." Was it because she had too much pride or that she had become too much of a coward? Conversely, it was probably a lot of both. "I don't deserve your help and I don't deserve you." Cursed. That's what Gianna was.

Erin brought her to arms' length. "I used to think the exact same thing but you helped me anyway. You've helped me more than anyone else in the world."

Why did she persist? Gianna shot to her feet suddenly, startling Erin. All along, there had been one thing that had bothered Gianna. "Why did you really come here, Erin? Was it to boast about how well you're doing now? Or was it to show off your lovely fiancé? Perhaps you came to make me feel even more guilty for walking out on you." Gianna saw Erin step back, her eyes widen; she hated doing it to her.

Erin covered her belly. "No, of course not, none of those things."

"Then why are you here? You told me you were merely *passing through*." Again, Gianna saw the hurt upon her friend's face but took no pleasure from it.

Erin threw down her hands and stamped her foot. "Damn it, you bloody stubborn Italian, I came because you were the most important person I ever knew, because I missed you. I came because I needed to know you were alright but..." Erin kicked a shard of plastic that lay on the floor following Vincenzo's handy work, "but most of all, Gianna, I came to find you because that bloody poem fluttered back into existence."

Gianna laughed and stepped back herself, her eyes narrowing. "What? What are you talking about, a poem?"

Erin flushed the same colour as her hair, "never mind, it's nothing. I shouldn't have said anything about *that*."

Gianna moved forward, her arms folded. "Show me."

"Ooh, no way! Not you, definitely not *you*."

"I think that if you wrote a poem for me then you should at least show it to *me*."

"It wasn't *for* you, it was just *about* you," Erin said, her defiant words not matching her softening demeanour. And she made no attempt at running or shredding the poem before Gianna's eyes, which was probably a mistake.

"Blah, blah, blah, Erin, I want to see it." And she did too. She really, really did.

Erin hesitated but then delved into her bag and brought out an envelope. "I don't suppose it makes any difference now anyway." What did she mean by that? "I should have burned it when it dropped out of that bloody book, or even better, straight after writing the bloody thing." Erin gazed at Gianna, eyes full of pain; for an instant, it looked as though she was trying to burn Gianna's image into her mind – Oh shit – This was it. Erin gently placed the envelope on the table and whispered. "Maybe you'll burn it for me?" Before she turned away, Gianna thought she saw a single tear fall from her eye.

"Erin?" Gianna froze. Now the moment had arrived, she didn't want it, she wanted anything but for Erin to walk out of her life when she'd just found her again. But what could she do? Her English rose was better without her. The state of her surgery was evidence to that.

Erin took a step toward the exit and stopped. "And just for your information..." she said without looking back, "Ben and I split." Her shoulders lifted an inch before falling again. "You could have everything, if only you had the courage to take it." Erin turned her head and looked for the final time at Gianna. "Goodbye, Gia, wherever you are."

And then she was gone, floating away on the same breeze on which she'd arrived.

Gianna found herself frozen to the spot, unable to move her feet, unable to breathe, unable to think. The envelope. It lay there, next to her. Gianna reached for it, her arm tingling and numb. Prising apart the glue, she pulled out the worn sheet of paper, words smudged with teardrops ten years past. Gianna braced herself, breathed and read the poem.

Where Are You

You entered my life when I needed a friend,
Bright eyes meeting mine from through the crowd.

I didn't know then you would change my whole life,
In only a year we had, more anyone else allowed.

You entered my life and showed me new ways,
My perfect companion, you breathed me new life.
The things we did, the memories we made,
Just so much promise and future so bright.

You entered my life when I needed you most,
Over my own heart, the power you held.
But like all good things, they must one day come end,
Then that day you left me, you felt compelled.

You entered my life and tore out my soul,
So now I write this as a final farewell.
Will I ever love again, bright eyes through the crowd,
Will I ever be whole, can I break your spell.

.

The poem flailed to the floor as Gianna kicked a large piece of her former traction unit against the wall.

A shadow flashed across the room, temporarily blocking out the natural light from outside and Gianna found herself fixed to the spot, the only thing that moved were the tears that streamed down her face.

A sharp screech, a dull thud, a long scrape, an even louder smash.

Gianna's skin went cold.

Whatever that was, had been no ordinary collision.

Heart pounding through her mouth and finally finding the ability to move, Gianna ran. She didn't know how, but she already knew – This was bad, she sensed it.

Gianna threw open the door to the outside. A small crowd was gathered around the curb as more drivers exited from vehicles, hands covering mouths. Gianna looked around frantically for Erin. Where was she?

Further down the street, against the wall, a feminine figure lay sprawled and trapped beneath a scooter, an arm flapping about her face as though in a daze.

Gianna gasped. She recognised the Vespa. It was Agata.

She pushed through the crowd and everything became a blur. Erin lay crumpled on the road, blood masking her face, head nestled on a man's lap, foot facing the wrong way. Not breathing.

Chapter Eighteen

BETWEEN

"Erin, let's have a word," Mrs Reed whispered, standing a few short paces from Erin as she sat on the floor in a gap, away from most of the other kids.

Erin stood and followed her teacher to a quiet corner of the classroom, taking a seat.

"Erin, we need to have a little chat about Nancy, ok?" Her voice was even more soothing than usual.

Erin nodded, not quite knowing what to think. Where was Nancy today anyway?

Mrs Reed leaned closer and smiled, but her eyes said something different. "Erin, I want you to know that Nancy is not coming back to school."

"What?" A scary grey cloud whirled around in Erin's vision, blocking out everything other than herself and Mrs Reed. What was that? "Where is she?" Erin sniffed.

"Erin, sometimes, people need to move due to work or family reasons. Nancy's dad has moved the family to New Zealand. Have you heard of New Zealand, Erin?"

"No," Erin sobbed. What would she do without Nancy?

"Well, Nancy would like you to know that she's alright,

she's happy and that you should try to make more of an effort with some of the other children from now on." Mrs Reed tilted her head. "Do you think you could do that, Erin? It would make Nancy very happy."

"No," Erin wailed, collapsing into the table and shielding her face from the world. "I want Nancy."

THE BELL CHIMED FOR THE END OF SESSION AND ERIN HUNG back as the classroom emptied. Grabbing her bag, she held her gaze to the floor as she trudged past the teacher and pulled the door open, exiting the classroom. She headed in the direction of the computer labs as there were usually fewer kids hanging around there at lunchtime.

Slinking inside the labs, she entered the toilets. Empty. Erin breathed and opened the door to the solitary cubicle. She entered, closed the door, applied the lock, pulled down the toilet lid and sat.

Erin concentrated on maintaining a slow and steady breathing rhythm. After a few minutes, she opened her backpack and pulled out her lunchbox. Mum had made tuna mayo with thin slices of tomato today, exactly how Erin liked it. She took a bite and savoured the flavour. Erin checked her watch. Another fifty-five minutes of lunch to go.

She pulled out her magazine, "I've read this already," she muttered before delving further down, searching for the Game Boy Advance.

The door to the toilets opened and footsteps struck the tiles; two, three people perhaps? Then one of them rapped their knuckles against the cubicle door and Erin straightened in fright, holding her breath.

"We know you're in there, freak." Came the feminine

voice, though Erin couldn't tell who it was; Jazmine, Dominique, Lorna perhaps?

They banged louder so Erin pulled her feet away from the gap at the bottom of the door and brought them closer into herself.

"Why don't you open up so we can all have a smoke?" Laughter.

A different voice said, "you'd like that, wouldn't you, ginger freak? We can all spend lunch huddled together in a stinking, shitty toilet." More laughter.

"I bet she'd *really* love that. She probably gets off on thinking about other girls, knowing her." More banging and Erin feared they'd try climb over the top of the cubicle.

"Are you a fucking dyke, ginger freak?"

"I've never seen her speak to any boys."

"I've never seen her speak to any girls either."

THE BOAT CUT ITS ELEGANT PATH THROUGH THE DARK water while Erin concentrated on matching Gia's stroke rate as she slid back and forth along the track. Sweat glistened on her back, catching the sun as well as Erin's eye.

Erin noticed the large oak tree on the port side and how the boat's progress against it was diminishing. Sure enough, as Erin matched her rhythm, Gia was barely bothering to pull on her oars.

"I'm not sure this is how we'll win Fairbairns." Erin said with amusement. "Are you ok?"

Gia let go of her oars and the paddle ends dunked into the Cam with a splash. She leaned slowly back, her shoulders coming to rest on Erin's thighs. "It's almost as if there's nobody else alive on the planet." Gia stared straight up at

Erin, who suddenly feared her nostrils would be on full display.

"Well, it is Sunday." Erin glanced around and sure enough, there's was the only visible boat on the Cam, a rare thing. And neither were there pedestrians, cyclists or dog walkers close enough to make noises and spoil the rare harmony. "The advantage of training early, I suppose."

"We deserve a break. Stop with the oars and chill."

Erin did just that then raised the hem of her t-shirt and used the material to dry the sweat from her forehead. It was a beautiful, warm morning, considering it was mid-April in Cambridge. "I suppose it would make a nice change to enjoy the river for once." And there was nobody in the world better to enjoy it with.

Unlike Erin, Gia did not seem to care at all about the sweat pouring off her flesh, even as she lay back on her friend's legs. Clumps of long brown hair stuck, plastered to her forehead, the faintest hint of natural odour from a deodorant failed drifted between them. Her breasts gently lifted and fell with her breathing as the boat made the last of its purchase from their strokes before stopping. She closed her eyes and began to hum. What was she thinking?

Erin enjoyed the sensation of having her friend so close, resting on her lap. Her fingers flexed around the oar handles before letting go and allowing her arms to hang by her flanks. There was nowhere to put her hands now, limp as they dangled by the sides of Gia's head. Oh, but how would it feel to run her fingers through that thick dark mane as it flowed over her thighs. Far more than that, but Erin was filled with the urge to lean forward and show her what she'd wanted to do for a while. But instead, her hands just grabbed onto the side of the boat as the current slowly encouraged it downriver.

Gia opened her eyes, catching Erin's stare. How

embarrassing. But Gia didn't seem to care. "Have you ever been in love?" She asked instead.

Erin's hands gripped the wood hard in some uncontrollable nervous reaction. "What?" How the heck was she supposed to answer that?

Gia grinned as she pulled some errant strand of hair from her mouth. "It's a simple enough question. We shouldn't be hiding stuff like this from each other."

"Um, I guess you're right." Yes, Erin had been in love. Once. Or rather, she *was* in love now with a certain someone. But that person would never notice her, at least not in *that* way. And why would she? But Gia had asked the question and Erin never lied to Gia. She wanted to tell her. She really did. "I, um, I don't think I've ever been in love. No. Sorry." She was sorry too. But what else could she have done? It would have taken courage Erin did not possess to admit her feelings for Gia.

Gia remained without reaction for a long while as she just lay there, breathing. Then her eyes lowered and she blinked several times.

"Well, how about you?" Erin asked, ending the uncomfortable silence.

Gia's eyes shot back up as she reached back with her arms, trying to link her hands around Erin's torso. Her arms weren't long enough so instead, they seemed to settle for clasping around Erin's flanks. "Oh yes, I most certainly have." She said with energy. "And I can tell you it's the greatest feeling in the world." She squeezed Erin's fleshy sides. "But not so much when it's not returned." Her eyes flicked down again and then her hands slipped away and back toward her own stomach.

Erin closed her eyes, soaking up the feeling of her friend's head against her hips. Gia *had* been in love and Erin felt a pang of envy shoot through her. But, Erin thought, at least

Gia possessed the courage to be honest and truthful with such a question, which was more than she could say for herself. For Erin, the disappointing thing was that she found herself wanting to ask just *who* this person was. But she lacked the courage even for that.

A kingfisher, beautiful in its orange and turquoise finery, flew over the boat and dived into the water, plucking out a fish with its beak before soaring into the air to disappear in the trees.

Gia's chest maintained its steady rhythm. She'd gone quiet, which wasn't like her and there appeared genuine sadness in her eyes. Whoever Gia had been in love with must have been truly special. Finally, she sat up and as though the conversation of a few minutes past had never taken place, she said, "like you said, *this is not how we'll win Fairbairns*."

They grabbed the oars and the boat slowly began moving along the Cam.

Chapter Nineteen

WITHDRAW

Erin shook.

A slit of light seeped through a crack in her eyes until the pain forced them shut again.

Then nothing.

ERIN SHOOK.

Then somebody, a female perhaps, gasped from somewhere close.

Then nothing.

ERIN'S LEG JERKED. THEN A SHARP SCREECH, LIKE A CHAIR leg sliding back against tile.

She sensed somebody close and opened her eyes to a slit, just enough so the light wouldn't sting. It did anyway. Something dark loomed over her and then a hand brushed her forehead.

"Who?" She croaked.

"Shhhh." It was definitely a woman.

Then nothing.

ERIN OPENED HER EYES. THE BLINDS WERE DRAWN SO THE sting was barely noticeable.

"Welcome back to planet earth." Ben took hold of her hand. "You can feel me, I assume?"

"I can," Erin scanned the room. Just as she thought, a hospital. "What happened?" A more than noticeable twinge around her ribs announced itself every time she breathed, but it was her right ankle that hurt most even though she could tell she'd been sedated. Her ankle would hurt like bloody hell when that wore off.

"You were hit by a scooter crossing the road but don't worry about that now." He stroked his thumb over her wrist. "You've been in and out of consciousness all day."

"Didn't we..." her last memory of Ben was of him walking out.

"Yes, we did. Don't worry about that. We don't need to talk about that right now. I came as soon as I heard. Obviously, I had to be here for you." He hooked a foot around a chair leg and pulled it under himself as he took the seat. He came as soon as he heard? How had he heard?

"How did..."

A smiling doctor entered and spoke some broken English about Erin's condition. So she was still in Italy, which came as a surprise since she knew she was supposed to catch a plane. She'd most likely missed that and would need to catch another; the banal things that went through her mind as the doctor spoke, along with the meandering design on the ceiling. That would be sure to mesmerise her later. "But we need to keep you in for observations for some nights at least." Some of the doctor's words made it through to Erin's conscious, but not all.

She tried to nod, which wasn't easy from her supine position. "Thanks," she grunted instead.

"I be back in an hour and then your visitor leaves." The doctor smiled and left the room.

"I didn't catch any of what he said," she asked Ben, raising the tone of the last word to make it sound like a question.

He smirked, "you have a cracked rib and your ankle took a knock. He's not worried about those but you'll be remaining here for observation due to the head injury." He pulled his chair closer and spoke in a low voice. "They said you stopped breathing when you cracked your head on the road," he rubbed her arm, "which is why they put you in a medically induced coma to stop the swelling to your brain."

Erin's eyes had glazed over. "How long was I out for?"

"Three days. You ... we're all very lucky you're still with us."

When the doctor returned, Ben politely left, promising to come back the next day. The doctor carried out a number of tests, asked a bunch of questions about how she felt, then mentioned something about returning later.

A while after Erin drifted off to sleep and didn't wake until morning. Ben arrived holding some flowers, which he placed on the table to Erin's side. "How are you feeling this morning?" He asked, taking a seat.

She thought for a second. "Actually, if I could just take a shower, I might even feel human right about now." Erin felt alert and considering the sedation had waned, the pain could have been a lot worse. "It'll be nice to get out of this place." She sat up against the pillow. "I've been thinking about things."

"Oh?"

"Well, there's not a whole lot else do to around here." She took Ben's hand, gave it a squeeze and inhaled deeply. "About me and Gianna ... I'm so very sorry you found out how you did and the way we left things. You have every right to hate me right now."

"Erin, we don't have to talk about this now," Ben whispered. It meant a lot that he still cared so much to have returned from wherever he'd managed to reach.

She shook her head, "I think I'll feel a lot better once I've said what I need to say and I kind of prepared a little speech for you, so here goes."

"You have my full attention." Ben leaned forward as his ears pricked.

Erin took another deep breath, then began. "Let me start by saying that after ten years, I'm devastated we ended in such a horrible way. I should have told you what was going on in my head. I'm sure you've pretty much figured it all out by now."

Ben nodded in affirmation. "Well, most of it, but I still have a few questions."

"Of course. I *have* had feelings for Gianna for a long time and yes, she was the reason I wanted so badly to come to Napoli."

Ben sniggered, "well that much is obvious."

"I really, really should have said *something* about it to you. But the truth is that I wasn't totally sure myself about exactly what was going on in my head. That was why I needed to come here and discover for myself. It's just a damn shame you were dragged into it but I couldn't figure out any way around it."

"You needed a fall back option in case it went tits up with Gianna." His face remained expressionless as he spoke.

"You're not so silly are you." She held his eye contact,

which wasn't easy. "And I know, I'm the most selfish woman in the world."

Ben sighed, "if it makes you feel better, you're hardly the first woman in history to do that. In my case though, it doesn't make it easier that I was second best to a woman."

"I'm sorry," she said again.

"So you and she are now..." he trailed off, leaving the insinuation.

Erin sighed, "I still have that to figure out, Ben. I hadn't seen her in ten years, so I guess it's no surprise that things haven't been *exactly* how they were." She flinched, "it's very awkward, I just don't know. But one thing I've come to realise is that it was wrong of me to string you along for so long, for ten bloody years, when..." she hesitated, "when I wasn't truly in love with you. I'm sorry, but you deserve somebody who worships the ground you walk on. It was wrong of me to waste so much of your time."

Ben's voice was calm and measured. "Again, you're hardly the first woman, or man, in history to settle for what's comfortable. Sometimes it's just nice to be in a relationship, even if it's not going anywhere. Besides, you're not the only one responsible for *that*. I played my part too. How many times did we break up over the last ten years? Was it six or seven?"

"I think probably more than that," she chuckled.

"Exactly. And if I was being totally honest, I may have had an idea, at least back in the early days that you might have been ... you know..." he said, clearing his throat.

Erin's eyes flicked upwards. "So you *did* remember Gianna in Cambridge?"

"Oh, I wasn't one hundred percent certain it was the same girl but I was sure enough. So you see, I cannot allow you to take full responsibility for how we culminated in this bloody city. It was probably on the cards for a long time. Too long, in fact. And I really shouldn't have proposed ... as if doing *that* would make everything better." He smiled and waved his hand in front of her face as if he was exorcising her of some evil spirit. "I hereby nullify you of one half of the blame." He leaned forward and kissed her on the forehead. "And now, you need to recover and figure out what you need to do." He kicked back the chair and stood.

"You're going *now?*" Erin asked, alarmed.

"I have a trip to return to. I was halfway to Venice when I got the call. You know how much I hate this bloody city," he winked, "and it seems that no matter how hard I try, I just can't seem to escape the bloody place."

Erin giggled and felt the shooting pain from her rib. "I hope we can remain friends? Or at least somehow be friends in the future." Erin felt her voice crack.

"I hope so too but it'll be tough fixing my heart after this. It may not be possible. I hope you understand if that's the case."

Erin sniffed, "no."

Ben smiled and pulled the door open before turning back to her. "Get well and enjoy the rest of your life."

And then he was gone.

THE DAY PASSED SLOWLY. OTHER THAN WHEN THE NURSES stopped by Erin's private intensive care room, there was nobody around to talk with. The TV was all in Italian and Erin had no reading material. All she could do to occupy her time was to think which, considering the circumstances, was probably a blessing, or not. So she thought about her future and about the damn Italian as well as the fact that the two would most likely never be linked.

Erin closed her eyes as she pictured the Gianna of old and the happy times they shared.

An hour later, Erin's eyes opened with a start. She hadn't meant to fall asleep again.

"Erin," the voice hissed from the corner.

Erin turned. "Well, this is unexpected."

"I'm so glad you're ok. I thought I'd lost you." Gianna pulled the chair closer. Her eyes were puffy and red, her hair unkempt and wild.

"Hi, you, oh, the doctor isn't too worried and I'll likely be out of here in a few days. I have a concussion and an ankle that hurts like crazy." She gave a small nod in Gianna's direction. "In fact, I'd say you look worse than I do." Erin smiled and was glad when Gianna smiled back.

"I've been here every day. I spoke to you. I told you how sorry I was." Gianna wiped at her eyes, the skin beneath was sore.

"You're sorry?" What was she apologising for exactly?

"I feel responsible. She did it out of jealousy, because of me." Gianna looked down into her hands where they were fiddling with the edge of Erin's blanket.

"Who did?" Ah, then Erin guessed *who* after she asked the question. Surprisingly, Erin's mind hadn't yet been occupied with the culprit, what with everything else. If she'd seen the rider at the time, she certainly didn't remember it now.

"Agata," Gianna spoke with an unfamiliar scorn. "The police think she tried to kill you, which is probably the truth. If it makes you feel better, she's hurt pretty bad too. Not that I give a shit." It was the first time Erin had heard such hatred from Gianna, though probably justified.

Erin sat up against the bedhead. It was then that she noticed the damn poem clutched in Gianna's hand, the paper more crumpled and tear marked than ever. "I don't wish bad on the girl. Like I said before, I know what she's going

298

through." Erin grimaced. "Though I think I would probably have stopped short of attempted murder."

"Well, it's with the police now." Gianna reached for Erin's hand, who slowly pulled it away and hid it under the covers. Gianna dropped her gaze. "That poem was the most beautiful thing I ever read."

Erin laughed and covered her face with her free hand. "I'm a physiotherapist, you can sort of tell I'm no poet. It was beyond amateurish."

Gianna cupped her hands together and dropped them to the bed. "I understand now how much I hurt you. I hope you can forgive me?"

Erin looked deep into her eyes, those beautiful, intense and hawkish pearls that had the power to captivate, even now. But still, there was something missing, something that words could never describe. "There is nothing to forgive." Erin said, "I understand your reasons. Besides, you are not the same person I knew ten years ago." Erin saw her eyes glaze over, her lips part. "Gia is gone! Replaced by a person who I don't even know, some girl who's given up, some girl who can barely even look me in the eye anymore. You're not the same Gia who I won a rowing medal with, who pushed me to be better no matter how uncomfortable it was for me." It was the other speech Erin had prepared in case she ever saw Gianna again and it pained her to say it, as much as it pained Gianna to hear it, evidenced by her eyes that shimmered with the early formation of tears. "I offered you a chance to return to England, that place where you yourself said you were happiest, to start afresh, but you're too cowardly to take it. You'd much rather see yourself ruined by a gangster and date people who'll only drag you down with them because for some stupid reason you've come to the conclusion that's all you deserve. Well, you're wrong! It used to be that *I* was the coward ... but now it's *you*. At least I had my reasons. What are your reasons for letting yourself down so badly? I know you've had your setbacks, but guess what Gianna ... life goes on!" Erin turned her head away. "What do you think Marco would think of you now?" Erin squeaked. God, how she hated what she'd just said but it was more than necessary.

She heard the breath catch in Gianna's mouth.

Now that speech took courage. The courage to be honest with the person most loved, regardless of how it would make them feel. The truth! The same truth she only wished she could have told Ben many years ago.

What Gianna didn't know was that Erin's motivations for the speech were different to what she most probably thought. It was Gianna, who all those years ago, pushed Erin to be better. Although Erin's approach was different, she now tried to return that favour, in her own way. Deep down, Gianna was still that girl who grabbed life with both hands and shaped it to her own liking, rather than allowing out of control events to dictate life to her. Erin knew she was being cruel to her, cruel to be kind, for lack of a better expression. It was tough love, sink or swim. Erin had another chance to try and achieve what she had attempted at the surgery, when she had said her *goodbyes* to Gianna. What would Gianna do now? Would she descend back into the abyss she was headed, permanently beat down because, like many others, life had dealt her a few bad hands. Or would she, after hearing the truth from Erin, try and turn her life around? Either way, because of the shitty circumstances, not to mention living in a different country, Gianna would have to find the strength to do it on her own.

Sometimes friendship, as well as love, meant knowing when to allow them to make the journey alone, even if it would be painful for both.

Gianna's arm shook. "I'm so sorry and you're right. I'm a

huge disappointment, not just to you and everybody else, but to myself."

Erin reached over and pulled the poem from her hand. "I'm glad I wrote this and I'm glad I found it again. It's enabled me to deal with problems I've repressed for too long. What did *you* learn? Are you Gianna or Gia?" Erin tore the tattered piece of paper down the middle, doubled it over, then tore it again and again as she winced from a shooting pain in her ribs.

Gianna stood from her chair, to Erin's surprise, there were no tears. "I think I should go." She held her chin a touch higher than before, clenched her fists and rolled her shoulders back. "I hope this is not the last time we see each other." She even held Erin's gaze before leaning in to embrace her lying down.

Erin opened her arms and clasped them around Gianna's back. Did she get it? Had she taken the bait and understood everything Erin had said? More importantly – Would she act? "I very much hope so too."

After a few minutes, Gianna slowly pulled away and kissed Erin softly on the lips. Then she gently brushed a few strands of loose hair from Erin's eyes, smiled and straightened up.

Then Gianna turned around and without looking back, she was gone.

SPACCANAPOLI WAS NEVER AS DESERTED AS THIS. WHERE were the dense crowds of locals and tourists that constantly enforced an annoyingly slow walking pace? Instead, as Gianna pottered along the ancient street at her own, self-enforced painfully slow walking pace, only a scattering of people lingered. They seemed just as surprised as Gianna, for they all to the man or woman had some unearthly blank countenance.

Gianna approached the espresso bar where only days earlier she'd spent time with Erin. Outside, a beautiful woman sat at a table, sipping her coffee. Three tables along, a man stole glances at her while he dried his palms on a napkin. He should just go over and talk to her, Gianna thought to herself. How hard could it be? Gianna pottered by them and looked with interest at the man. He didn't notice her. What was with his eyes? It was almost like he was sleepwalking, or sleep staring.

Spaccanapoli remained eerie and silent as she continued. What was with Napoli today? Then a handful of people emerged at the crossroads ahead, walking across Gianna's fore from both directions. An elderly woman, hunched over at the shoulders, appeared as if from thin air. She shuffled along the street a short distance in front. A man, close to the old woman, made a move for her bag, attempting to tear it from her grasp. The bag strap was wound tight around her arm and he struggled to detach it. Gianna glared at the other men, in expectation they'd intervene and help the poor woman. Three of them watched on, torn over what to do. One took a step forward but then halted. Another glanced around him, as if searching for assistance. The third man reached out with an arm but took no steps closer.

Then the thief, with bag, scurried off into the dark as the old woman tried to come to terms with being robbed. Gianna stared evils at the three men, their eyes blank - Shame perhaps? They'd have to live with that for the rest of their lives.

Gianna turned back to the old woman, to offer her help and a walk home. But just like that, she was gone. "What is going on?" Then the three men continued along the intersection and soon, they too were out of sight.

Gianna took a few deep breaths before continuing, maintaining a tight grip on her bag.

Ahead, in the area where street performers usually gathered, a solitary man stood by a table. On it, boxes were lined out, crammed with DVDs; knock offs, of course. He smiled at Gianna as she neared him – Finally. Gianna was beginning to wonder if she was invisible this evening.

"Business not too good today, huh?" She asked as she came to a halt in front of the stall.

He raised an eyebrow, "I've never seen anything like it. One minute, it was like any ordinary day and the next, people were vanishing in all directions. Even Mario, the opera singer, took his collection and left. You're right, business stinks today, but what can you do?"

"I'm sure it'll pick up soon." Gianna turned her feet in the direction she was headed.

"Well, how can I interest you in Pompeii? Have you seen it? It's got that 'you know nothing Jon Snow' guy in it. The recording is actually pretty good, only a couple of people blocking the picture at around the eighteen-minute point. Only five Euros." The man didn't blink.

"I'm ok, but thank you anyway." Gianna took a step away.

"Not into post-apocalyptic stuff? I don't blame you. Too depressing. How about the new Jennifer Aniston film? I'll let you have it for five Euros." The man's voice, animated before, had now become almost monotone.

"Thanks, but no. I have to go." Gianna moved down the street, hitching her shoulders as a cool gust of wind sent a shiver down her spine.

The man shouted after her. "Well then, how about the Italian classics? Have you seen Malena?"

Gianna froze. Did he just say what she thought he said? She turned around. The man stared blankly forward. "What did you just say?" Gianna shouted, striding back toward the man.

"What?" The man asked, almost with a whisper as Gianna arrived back at the stall.

Gianna studied the man. Wavy brown hair with flecks of grey, sun-weathered and almost leathery skin, the rough hands of a grafter. She'd never seen him before in her life, yet it was as though she'd known him a long time.

Of all the things Erin had said over the last few days, of all the conversations Gianna had yet to analyse within her own mind, there was one thing Erin had said at Parco Virgiliano that came to the fore. *'Fate can only take a person so far. After that, it's up to you to show some courage and account for the rest.'*

At the time, Gianna had not known what she'd meant. But now Gianna understood everything.

"I'll take a copy," Gianna said, handing over ten Euros, "and keep the change."

Part Three

CAMBRIDGE II

Chapter Twenty

VALLENSBAEK STRAND

H e'd left Italy as fast as he could, driving straight past the great towns and cities he'd intended on visiting. Well, all except for Venice where Ben spent a few lonely nights; after all, he couldn't pass up the opportunity to see *that* place, even if circumstances dictated he couldn't enjoy it.

After Venice, Ben finally completed the lifelong ambition of travelling around Austria. The Alps were everything he expected and more. After three weeks, and still not ready to return to England, he continued. Switzerland, where he spent two weeks, was particularly beautiful and although there was probably no place on earth more expensive, nine Euros for a Bigmac, Ben didn't give a shit. Not on this trip.

From Switzerland he took the car into the southern French Alps, spending considerable time in the many picturesque villages where he took a fancy, too much of a fancy, to the local wine.

The thought crossed his mind to return home after France, but instead, he just carried on going, and why not? After all, Barcelona wasn't that far away. After falling in love with the entire Catalan region of Spain, Ben then headed into southern Spain, reaching as far as the clifftop castles of Granada and Cordoba. Cadiz was like somewhere on a different planet altogether, as was Seville, which possessed the most incredible plaza. From there, he headed north through Portugal where he considered boarding a ferry back to England.

But no, he wasn't done yet. And even though he received calls from his company, politely enquiring as to his state of mind, Ben simply told them he'd be home when he was ready, so leave me alone. He was thirty-one years old, had never travelled, and now he was doing what he should have done many years ago.

Ben took the car north through the vineyard regions of western France where he spent Christmas and New Years, before turning east, deciding on skipping the *city of love*, Paris, and ending up in Belgium where he toured all five major tourist cities; Bruges, Ghent, Brussels, Antwerp and Liege.

Since the Netherlands never really interested him, he skipped over it and instead drove straight into Germany where he became particularly fond of Cologne. After a month in Germany, he made up his mind to go even further and head for Norway, after all, he'd always wanted to see the Aurora Borealis. This meant that on the way, he'd have to drive through Denmark and Sweden. Oh well, it was a rough job, but somebody had to do it.

He took his time, enjoying the wonderful Danish culture and impressively long bridges that spanned the western Baltic Sea.

Copenhagen, now only twelve miles ahead, Ben had heard was one of the most beautiful cities in the world. The only problem was that darkness was upon him and Ben did not wish to see the city for the first time in the dark and so he made the small, supposedly inconsequential decision of booking in at a medium-sized, outwardly unimpressive looking hotel in the middle of a small boring town he'd never heard of. He squinted again at the sign on the roadside, "Vallensbaek Strand," he doubted he'd pronounced it correctly.

And so, almost six months after he last saw Erin, and with a heart on the road to recovery, he booked in for three nights at the unpronounceable Scandic Hvidovre. He figured it'd make a good base, being so close to Copenhagen.

It was five in the evening when finally, Ben dumped his bags in the room and sat on the edge of the bed whilst, for several minutes, contemplating the blank wall to his fore. "Bugger this, let's get a drink."

He nodded politely to the hotel concierge as he bypassed the front desk and headed for the lounge area, ordered some local Danish beer he had no idea how to pronounce and took a seat in the corner of the lounge, as far away from all other people as possible.

Opening his copy of Oscar Wilde's The Importance of Being Earnest, he flicked to page twelve and continued where he'd left off in Napoli. He grunted at the memory, "what a shit hole." He'd never return there, even if it wasn't that bad a place once you learnt to deal with the traffic and errant former fiancées. Whatever she was doing now, he wished her well.

He closed his eyes, breathed and then finally managed to bring his eyes to concentrate on the text.

After less than a minute feminine sobbing from somewhere close interrupted his flow. Ben pinched the bottom corner of page thirteen as his eyes neared the final paragraph on the page. The sobbing was joined by the high-pitched squeal of a young child. "Chapter one, I will vanquish you one day." He turned the page but concentrating on large blocks of text in ye olde English proved a task too difficult with distractions in such close proximity.

Ben began tapping his fingers against the chair's armrest and hoped the encroacher would notice the heavy rhythm, as well as his annoyance, and cease the noise without the need to be told. They didn't and in a fit of frustration, Ben snapped the book shut...

And saw the source of the distress.

A mother arched over her son, maybe six years old, as he rubbed his knee. She was facing away as she held the boy's *below the knee* prosthetic, her long blonde hair that flowed down her back stealing Ben's attention from the boy. Her slender waist gave way to slightly broader hips and slim legs, which to Ben, was the epitome of Scandinavian beauty. His attention was stolen away when the boy cried again and revealed a knee suture raw from discomfort. The mother fumbled with the prosthetic leg but seemed unsure of what to do. When she straightened and placed the limb on the table, Ben saw the big blue eyes, the perfect symmetrical features, long thin lips and crystal clear skin. Fuck!

He blinked several times and rubbed the back of his neck before tossing the book to the table in front but he'd misjudged the power needed and it slid off the far end and onto the floor. His fingers tingled as he cleared his throat and he found himself having to rub the sweat from his palms against his jeans. His body, he knew, was undergoing the stimuli of the ancient *fight or flight* mode, a feeling he hadn't experienced like this in nearly eleven years.

Ben stooped for the book, plucked it off the floor and came to a decision; back to the hotel room for him.

As he walked past the mother and son, the young boy looked up, smiled and wiped a damp sleeve across his face. Ben stopped, for whatever damned reason he couldn't say, breathed and crouched down. "Hello, young man, are you ok?" He hadn't planned on doing this, he didn't know why he did, and his voice came out at an embarrassing high pitch that he hoped was because he was speaking to the boy and not because his entire body was shaking with fear.

"He doesn't speak English. He's only six." The woman stared down, hair coming to an end somewhere around that tight fucking midriff. God, but she was beautiful.

Ben smiled at the boy and straightened up, thankfully having a couple of inches advantage over his mother, despite her height. "Do you mind if I..." he gestured toward the limb on the table and took hold of it before the woman had chance to reply.

Her eyes softened but only slightly and doubtless she'd be used to having men try it on with her.

"The problem is that your young man has outgrown the limb." He rubbed his finger along the titanium. "This is designed for ages four to six and," Ben checked the screws, "there's no more length to extend it any further." He crouched again and spoke to the boy, even though he couldn't understand. "It only takes a millimetre; one leg longer than the other and you're distributing your weight unequally onto the other leg. *That* is what causes the soreness. It builds up over time, you see?" He tilted his head upwards toward the mother, who then came to crouch beside Ben. He spoke softly to her, "you need a new limb or the boy could suffer severe bone problems." He gave her back the prosthetic. "What's his name?"

"Tobias," the woman whispered, "I can't afford another leg for him. I'll have to sell the car," she said, looking away.

When Ben returned to his room, he phoned Malcolm, his Director of Supplies. The only problem was that at six in the evening, what could be done?

Regardless, after a fourteen-hour drive, which included

311

SALLY BRYAN

passage through the Channel Tunnel, Malcolm arrived in
Vallensbaek Strand just in time for breakfast.

"You're fucking insane!" He declared, bringing a package
out from the back seat. "Six months, I don't hear shit and
then you drag me out here with a moment's notice."

"I'm sure you enjoyed the drive," Ben held out his arms
and took the box. "You sticking around for breakfast?"

"Fuck that, I'll eat in Copenhagen. May as well while I'm
here and yes, I'm taking the rest of the day off and you're
fucking paying me," Malcolm proclaimed as he clambered
back into the driver's seat.

"Shouldn't you at least stretch your legs before getting
back behind the wheel?" Ben joked, "perhaps I'll ask another
favour later on."

"Fuck you." The engine fired up. "I hope she's worth it."

"I'll see you in the city, yeah? Perhaps we can brunch
together?" Ben shouted as Malcolm drove away, flipping him
the finger.

Ben returned to the hotel restaurant and filled his plate
from the buffet. At a little before nine, the beautiful blonde
and her son Tobias entered. Ben watched with interest as the
boy, with crutches, expertly manoeuvred himself between the
tables towards the buffet, where his mother helped fill his
plate. She then carried both plates to an empty table at the
other side of the restaurant.

No man. No husband or father. How could that be?

Ben sipped his coffee and watched as the pair ate
breakfast by the window that overlooked the car park. Not
the best of views. She did this thing where she flicked her
hair back before every sip of orange juice, whilst barely ever
taking her attention from him. The boy kept his head down
and concentrated on his platter.

Ben placed a hand on the box that sat on the chair beside
him, breathed, and carried it in their direction. Tobias

noticed him first when Ben was only a few metres away, followed by his mother who took her cue from him. She leaned back and half turned her body toward Ben, her eyes catching his for a second, before being drawn down to the box.

"Good morning," Ben said, "I don't wish to intrude."

"You're not intruding," the woman said. Her teeth were perfect, straight and white.

Ben breathed and consciously controlled his voice, speaking slowly, keeping it deep and masculine. "I have a present for you," he said as he turned to Tobias. The box was too big to hand him, so he placed it on the table at his side. "Open it."

He grinned at his mother, silently asking for permission. She said something back in what Ben assumed to be Danish but in reality, it could have been any Scandinavian language. "What is it?" She asked, narrowing an eye, but raising a smile. Shit! Ben was in deep shit.

He patted the lid, "open it and find out."

The boy leaned forward, placed his hands on the lid and tried to lift it off. It was a tight fit, so his mother held down the base with both hands. The satisfying sound of friction filled the small space as the lid slowly parted from the box and then there was a whoosh of air as it came away.

Tobias inhaled when he saw the *below the knee* prosthetic and then his expression changed to one of sheer joy. It was a rare feeling, Ben thought, making a child smile like that and it was a good few seconds before he even noticed his mother wiping at her eyes.

Ben motioned for Tobias to unfasten the pins on his jogging bottoms and roll the hem up his leg. Ben took the limb and flexed the foot. "This is the only design you'll see with split toes ... for extra balance and shock absorption."

The boy couldn't understand his words but seemed to

313

understand the improvement in quality of life the limb would offer, for the foot looked as human as any other, and Tobias leant forward, hands either side of his face as he watched Ben's demonstration.

Ben ran his hand along the titanium where it came to stop on the latex clasp at the origin end. "This is the only system in the world that offers air cushioning at the stump. So there'll be no more soreness or itching where your knee connects to the cup." Ben held the small hand pump and showed where it connected into the latex.

"How can I ever repay you for this?" The mother said, delving into her bag.

Ben held up a hand. "Just make sure Tobias lives his life to the full ... that's all I ask."

Ben spent around half an hour teaching the boy and his mother how to attach and maintain the limb. He watched Tobias wearing it and Ben calibrated the length and foot angle accordingly. "You'll still need to see your specialist every six months, of course, he's a growing boy," he spoke to the mother whose voice had long since become a faint hiss.

"Thank you," Tobias said in English.

"You're welcome," Ben ruffled his hair then turned to the mother in finality. "Well, good luck. I'll say goodbye then," he began stepping in the direction of the exit.

"Wait!" She almost shouted. "You can't just go."

Ben turned back and jerked his head in the direction of the carpark. "I have a long day of sightseeing ahead of me, followed by a drive to Malmö. I hear the city is beautiful." Wait, would that be Copenhagen or Malmö? Though surely, neither would compare to the beauty of this woman, because she was precisely the type who struck fear into the hearts of men, the very vision of the old Norse Goddesses.

She took a step closer. "Well, we can join you. We're also here to visit the city ... Copenhagen, that is."

He nodded, it mightn't be a bad idea, and held out his hand, "I'm Ben."

She moved another step closer, reached out and took his hand, her warm flesh melting into his. "I'm Freja, you already know my son, Tobias."

Ben beamed at them, obviously she wasn't a lesbian. A good start.

"Let's go."

Chapter Twenty-One

HAPPY BIRTHDAY

E rin watched and monitored Glen Prudhoe's gait whilst taking the occasional glance at his weight distribution on the monitor as he pounded away on the treadmill. His prosthetic took an equal share of the load, which wasn't common during treadmill running so soon after receiving a below the knee replacement.

Erin made a note on her clipboard. "Ok, I think we're done."

Glen held down the button to decrease the speed and brought the tread to a steady walking pace. "We're done with the running?" He asked after taking a sip of water. "It's only been ten minutes."

Erin glanced at the monitor. "We're done forever. You just need to see your prosthetic specialist every six months but as for the physio side ... it was a pleasure knowing you."

He jumped from the machine and embraced Erin in a hug. "Thank you so much, doctor."

"That's quite all right, it's my job." Her words came out in a single restricted breath. He released her and Erin pottered over in the direction of the spare desk whilst trying to find an empty spot to dump the clipboard. There wasn't one so instead she dumped it on a nearby shelf. "If only I didn't have to see so many of your fellow army buddies. Only this week, I had two new clients with no legs below the knees."

"And all for nothing," Glen remarked as his jaw visibly clenched. "Tally'll only retake the shit hole the very second we're out," he pulled his hoody over his head, "and all to protect the government's bloody heroin stash."

"What?" Erin had a sudden flashback to that beauty spot just west of Napoli almost a year before; the birds, the heat, sitting on a bench with a stunning view and a beautiful woman.

Glen waved a hand in dismissal, "ah never mind me. It's best you don't get me started on the subject, trust me."

When Glen left, Erin surveyed the heaps of boxes, records, equipment and consumables that had assembled on top of the spare desk. Even the chair had become the spot Erin kept the medicine ball. "Not professional, Erin." She removed the clutter and placed it in the storeroom.

After she'd given the spare desk a dusting, she sat down at her own desk and relaxed back in the seat. She picked up the photo of her and Gianna in the boat and smiled at the memory. "It's probably time to start looking." She didn't want to be single forever. "I'll be thirty tomorrow." There was nothing like turning thirty to give a single girl a kick up the bum.

The phone rang, Erin checked the caller ID and grinned stupidly. "Hi, Scruffy."

"Hi, just checking we're still on for tomorrow?"

"Of course, it's not like I have a hot girl to spend the day with or anything."

"Hey, don't beat yourself up and enough of that defeatist attitude crap. We'll help you get laid for your thirtieth, ok? Scruffy's got your back."

Erin shook her head, "I'd settle for having some fun with a few friends."

"Aye, and that's what we're doing, but should a hot girl happen to take your fancy then I want you on top form. So dress your best."

Erin had already been shopping for a new dress with Holly, Scruffy's new girlfriend, after they all but dragged her out the other day. "I wouldn't dare do otherwise."

"Good. I'm sending Holly over to yours at six and then we'll head to the restaurant." Sounds like he had it all planned out.

Erin sighed, "I really appreciate what you're doing but this isn't going to be some sort of a massive thing, is it?"

"Of course, not," he sounded hurt, "and I'll be on my best behaviour. No handshaking. In fact, no party tricks of any kind whatsoever."

"Somehow I don't believe you."

Erin spent the majority of her birthday with her parents, who'd well and truly, in the flesh, made the trip south for the second time in as many years. Impressive. Together, they spent time at King's College and the adjoined chapel with the world's largest fan vault, had lunch at Trinity College and finally engaged in a long walk along the Cam where her father took a keen interest in the birds, or lack of.

Holding a pair of binoculars, his head shifted from left to right as he scanned the river. "Where the bloody hell are all the Kingfishers?"

"I told you, dad, I haven't seen any for a long time."

"What? The bloody things are supposed to be native to this bloody river." He lowered the binoculars and bizarrely, glanced around the nearby path, as though expecting to see one at his feet. "Where are they, Erin?"

She couldn't help but feel partly responsible. "I'm sorry,

dad, but they're gone now." It was a great pity; they truly were beautiful, majestic birds.

"Well, this is no good. No, this is no bloody good at all."

After the rather disappointing river walk, her parents departed for Alnwick and Erin headed home to get ready for the evening.

At six, the striking figure of Holly, with her rower's figure and long brown hair approached from along the driveway. Erin opened the door and gestured nervously to the very large holdall she was carrying.

"Well, we're getting started now," Holly said, pulling out a bottle of champagne. "I'll bung it in the freezer for ten minutes, but after that, we're popping it."

Erin clasped her hands in front of her neck. All day she'd been nervous for the evening and appalled at the stupid milestone she'd reached but now, for the first time, she actually allowed herself to feel excited. She'd be spending a few hours with some lovely friends. Holly too, was fast becoming her buddy and she was so thrilled Scruffy had found her. "How did you two meet again?" Erin asked after they popped the cork.

Holly rolled her eyes and placed a hand on the kitchen counter, as if gesturing she needed support from recollecting the memory. "He caused a bit of a scene shaking hands with the Minister for Energy and Climate Change. Don't you remember seeing it on the news?"

Erin laughed, "I do remember hearing something about it, but I didn't believe it." She took a sip from her glass and straightaway felt it go to her head. She was in for a long night.

"When he did that, I thought to myself, *I just have to have him*, and we started dating pretty much immediately," she stared into blankness with a dopey besotted look. "I guess I was just in the right place at the right time."

"But then you did something about it, right?"

"Yes, I guess I did. Oops, we forgot..." Holly held her glass up to Erin. "Happy birthday."

Erin clinked the glass. "And thanks for not mentioning my age."

Holly placed her glass on the counter. "Don't start. You look fantastic for thirty and we don't even have you in your new dress yet."

Indeed, Erin was still clad in the sports gear she'd been wearing for the walk. "I suppose I should get changed then."

"And I'm doing your make up," Holly asserted as she followed Erin into the bedroom.

"Really?" Erin turned her head as she walked. "What kind of a restaurant is this again?"

"Oh, just a regular restaurant. Scruffy says you like Italian, so that's what you're having." Holly grabbed the beautiful long white dress from the wardrobe and inspected it, for God only knew what.

"Scruffy said that? I haven't had Italian in a long time." Not since being in Italy, actually. And how would he know anyway? He'd never asked and probably wouldn't remember even if he had.

Holly watched intently as Erin slipped the dress on, staring at the floor. "The mirror is in front, you know."

"I know." Erin brought her eyes up and gave a shy smile, more for Holly's benefit.

She gasped, "you look absolutely amazing. I hope you know that." Holly smoothed out the dress at the bottom and stepped back. "Wow."

The dress was an all-white halter, tight to every inch and curve of Erin's body; her slender arms and shoulders were on display, placing an emphasis on her collar bones. The dress covered all her legs, giving an overall impression of elegance and sophistication, like what she might wear if she had exclusive theatre tickets, which she didn't. Regardless, she'd be turning heads tonight, which wasn't necessarily what Erin wanted. She sighed. What could she do anyway? The whole thing was out of her hands.

For the next hour, they drank champagne and giggled whilst Holly took care of Erin's hair and makeup. When the taxi honked from the street, they headed out the door.

"We're meeting at a pub first," Holly confirmed. "I assume you've heard of The Baron of Beef?"

Erin jerked her head at her. "Um, yeah, I've heard of it ... a few, um, interesting memories of that place." Eleven years and counting since her last visit. Was this really such a great idea? "And it was *Scruffy's* idea to meet there, you say?" Which was the difficult thing to believe.

"Yep," she said as though there was absolutely no significance to it whatsoever. Erin had always assumed Scruffy had the same phobia of that place as herself but one could never be quite sure where he was concerned.

When they arrived, Scruffy happened to be sitting alone at a large table directly below where Erin remembered the infamous *beer on a pole* incident had taken place. It was funny that even now, she could still remember the exact spot and a rush of memories began flooding her head.

"This is very brave of you," Erin told him. The pub was quiet for a Saturday night, though the few existing patrons were most definitely scrutinising Erin in her dress. She didn't mind as much as she might have in years gone past, though she most certainly did feel overdressed compared to everybody else.

"Aye, I figured it'd be good healing, not just for you but for the both of us." He stood and embraced Erin. "You look fantastic." He turned to Holly and kissed her. "You did a bloody fantastic job on her."

She stared Erin up and down with admiration, "she makes easy work."

Scruffy brought the drinks over and then spent the next half an hour regaling memories from The Baron of Beef. Holly seemed enchanted by the guy. With a bit of luck, this could be the real thing for them.

Though there was one thing that thus far had confused Erin. "Where's everybody else? Shouldn't they be with us?"

Scruffy checked his watch. "Aye, we should probably get a move on and meet them."

"What? We're leaving?" Erin frowned and felt totally confused.

Holly stood and took Erin's hand. "Just leave it to him."

They left the pub and the three of them clambered into a waiting taxi, which started moving without any commands. Erin scratched the back of her neck. "How does he know where we're going?"

"It's probably one of those new magic taxis they've been working on," Scruffy said without turning his head from the front passenger seat.

"Oh shut up!" Erin said, wanting to punch him. She hated surprises.

Holly slid closer on the back seat and for whatever reason, she possessed a mischievous grin that was bordering on being unsettling.

Erin looked outside as the taxi drove slowly past Downing College, a route that wasn't even necessary to get to... "hey, where are we going anyway?"

"Didn't she tell you?" Scruffy asked.

Erin found herself leaning forward between the two front seats. "She said we were going for an Italian."

"Aye, and yes you are."

La Mimosa, which would most likely have been Erin's preferred choice, was in the other bloody direction. Perhaps they were going to La Margherita instead but as soon as she thought that, the taxi slowed and came to a stop by the river.

Erin scowled outside the window, to the punts lined along the bank. "This isn't what I think it is, is it?" Her mind was assailed by the memory of Scruffy operating one of those things as a tour guide, those stupid stripy tops and straw hats.

He exited the car and pulled open Erin's door. "What thirtieth would be complete without a nice paddle down the river?"

Probably most of them, Erin thought, but kept it to herself. Bless him, he was trying hard tonight. Then it hit her, "I see what you're doing..." Erin stepped out from the taxi to find Holly already at her side, patting out the creases from her dress before continuing to ensure her red hair was flowing freely down her shoulders, for whatever reason, Erin couldn't fathom. The whole evening was beginning to take on a bizarre hue.

Scruffy's attention jerked to Erin and for a beat, it seemed there was a touch of apprehension, fear even, that flashed across his face. "You do?"

Erin smiled and straightened in defiance, hands on hips. "Of course. This is some kind of *trip down memory lane* theme for my birthday, ain't it? And I assume you're about to punt me downriver whilst refusing to look up and acknowledge me like the last time you did this, right?" Well, she'd go along with it out of politeness, after all, he'd clearly put a lot of effort into the whole thing and she didn't want to seem ungrateful, which she wasn't in any way.

Scruffy dropped his head in defeat and held up his hands. "There's no fooling you is there, Erin." He jerked his head toward the nearest punt that bobbed precariously on the water. "Now get in!"

Before Erin had chance to answer, Holly was taking her hand and pulling her toward the rickety old boat, an almost demonic grin permanently plastered upon her face.

Scruffy grunted as he used the oar to push away from the

bank and then the punt was slinking its way down the Cam, ducks spreading apart from its advance.

Holly sat opposite Erin, several times picking from her dress bits of fluff and fairies from dandelions that drifted through the air.

"You really want me looking my best don't you?" What was going on?

"Just looking after you."

Scruffy stood on the bow as he continued pushing the oar against the river bed and propelling the punt forward. The Bridge of Sighs was now visible, along with the usual clusters of tourists admiring the architecture.

"Really, Scruffy, what is going on?" Erin stuck her thumbnail in her mouth and bit down before Holly pulled it away.

"You'll ruin your nails." Holly chided. Really, what did it matter? "Just enjoy, but don't sit back." She reached over and held her hand against Erin's shoulder blade. "No creases."

Erin rolled her eyes and clasped her hands together on her thighs. Was that allowed? What were they scheming?

They drifted under the bridge and instead of stepping off the punt at one of the usual tourist stops, they continued down the Cam in the direction of King's and Clare Colleges and the Back Lawn.

"It's very pretty, isn't it," Erin remarked to Holly, more as a statement than a question as she gazed at the beautiful setting downriver. The perfect weather and last few hours of summer sun all combining to make an idyllic scene.

Holly didn't answer, or even seemed capable of replying with that permanently plastered smile that had apparently rendered her mute.

"Ok," Erin said. "How you doing up there, Scruff? You getting tired yet?"

He ignored her but did make the occasional glance back

to give some unearthly grin. What was wrong with everybody today?

Erin leaned forward and squinted. "What is that?" There was something on the Back Lawn. A marquee perhaps? "Honestly, to whom must you speak to rent *that place* out for a party?"

Scruffy continued pushing his oar against the riverbank to propel the punt and as they approached the Back Lawn, the faint chimes of an orchestra, aided by the small breeze, slowly began building in volume.

Erin leaned so far forward that she almost bumped foreheads with Holly, who in turn was now splitting her attention between the Back Lawn and Erin. The large white marquee came better into view, revealing a bar and then a trumpeter, trombone, violinist, as the classical music became louder with every passing second.

But where were the people?

The punt was still sufficiently far away so that the trees were restricting Erin's line of sight but she could indeed see movement between the weeping willows. "Is this a graduation event?" The timing seemed about right for it.

The punt glided closer and then a solitary feminine figure, stepped, almost appeared to float, down the Back Lawn toward the river. She was tall and athletic, had the deep tan of a Mediterranean with long, silky dark hair that flowed down her back. Erin squinted and placed a hand against her heart. The woman wore a long all-white halter identical to Erin's, the material clinging tightly to every inch and curve as her approach appeared to increase in speed the nearer she came to the riverbank, before coming to a stop at the edge, the breeze blowing and lifting her hair with the hems of her dress.

Erin's mouth fell open, she stood, her heel tapped the wooden bottom of the punt uncontrollably. Erin didn't notice the music, the sun, the ducks, the water, Holly, Scruffy, the other guests who were gathered far away from the girl. What Erin did notice was the girl's beautiful smile, her eyes that even from a closing distance possessed so much power and intensity. The damn boat could not move fast enough.

"Erin," the girl shouted as the boat drew closer.

Dare she even think it? Was this real? "Gianna," Erin shouted back, holding onto the boat's side to steady herself. "Gia!"

And then the boat came to a stop against the grass verge and Erin leapt onto the Back Lawn straight into Gia's arms. Erin felt the air driven from her lungs as tears poured down Gia's shoulder.

"You came back." Erin's voice, hoarse, came out muffled against Gia's flesh.

"I came back." Gia brought her mouth to Erin's ear and whispered, "and I'm back forever."

The breath caught in Erin's throat. "You promise?"

"I promise."

"Happy birthday," Scruffy said to Erin as he hopped off the punt and held out a hand for Holly. "We put a lot of work into this so you'd better bloody enjoy it."

Sometime during the last few minutes, the orchestra had started with Vivaldi's Four Seasons.

"Yes, happy birthday, Erin," Gia said, placing an arm around her back and squeezing her so tight, quite a thrill.

It was one of those surreal moments that sent a rush of blood to the head, heightening the senses to such an extent that tiny insignificant details came to the fore; the ripples of the water, the quacks of the ducks, birds in the sky and the shape of the glasses which the guests, who were slowly making their way toward the bank, held in their hands. Erin began to pick out those faces; her parents, who were even now supposed to be driving back north, brother, several former Cambridge friends, professors and rowing club members who'd doubtless be curious to hear Gia's story.

Erin twisted around to Scruffy, wanting badly to give him that much needed punch to the arm, but she'd let it go on this occasion. "Thank you for everything." She turned back to Gia, tears causing a temporary blurring of her vision. "And thank you for making this the best day of my life." Erin stepped back and gave her a proper look up and down and back again. "You look bloody fantastic."

"And don't I know it too," she propped her hands on her hips, "and you'd better appreciate the work I've put in these last few months." Gia stared hard and defiant into Erin's eyes, just like she always used to do. Could this really be the old Gia? Or as close to the old Gia as was humanly possible considering everything that had changed. The early signs were so good.

Erin shook her head. "How?" She knew she didn't make any sense right now. With a little luck, she'd regain some level of coherence eventually. Instead, she led Gia toward the marquee. "I think I really need a drink."

The rich smell of barbecue, serene music and friendly company together tempted several ducks out from the Cam, where the setting sun glistened and punts glided.

Gia, caught by movement in her periphery, turned to watch Professor Andy Atkins chasing after one of the ducks, drink in hand until finally, outrun and outwitted, he gave up. "At least he hasn't changed."

"No," Erin agreed, "in fact, I think he's worse now than ever." Erin gazed again at Gia, still barely believing she was here, in Cambridge, on her birthday. Not only that, but she'd be staying. "We obviously need to talk about stuff."

Gia nodded and smiled. She'd lost several of those faint wrinkles from before and her skin looked smoother and more vibrant. She'd obviously improved the quality of her diet and regained her love for exercise as the softness that a year ago was her shoulders, arms and stomach was now toned flesh with a hint of muscle. "We do but there's plenty of time for all that. I want you to have fun tonight. I'm here for good now, but we need to take things slow."

Erin nodded, matching Gia's own head movements. "That would probably be a very good idea."

"But I'm taking you up on your offer. I know I'm a little late but I assume it still stands?"

Erin laughed, "of course it still stands. My God, Gia, I need you at the surgery." She stared through a group of guests to where Glen Prudhoe on his prosthetic leg was standing with his wife and children. "I've never been busier," Erin said with a touch of sadness.

Gia gave a sympathetic smile. Even now, she understood Erin's thoughts. "I'd be honoured to join you then."

Erin grazed Gia's arm with the outsides of her fingers and wished she had a large mirror to see them both, in matching dresses. By the end of this, there'd better be a tonne of photos. "Where have you been staying anyway? I mean, surely you didn't just arrive today?"

"I've been here about a week," Gia smirked most adoringly, "bunking up at Scruffy's whilst we concocted our evil plan. I was terrified we'd bump into each other in this small city, which would have been just my luck and might probably have taken some explaining." Gia's fingers sank into Erin's waist and it was a thrill beyond description. "Can you imagine that? Our eyes meeting at the supermarket checkout? I've been going around wearing a tent and what Scruffy described as a tea cosy on my head ... the bastard. But the truth is, there's nothing left for me in Italy. Everything that's important is here." Gia stared beyond Erin toward the Cam. "And it still feels like home, even now. This place ... I can't tell you how incredible it feels to be back."

And Erin couldn't yet describe how it felt to have her back. "So all your stuff must be at Scruffy's house then?" Erin wanted to suggest she move in with her immediately but realised that might probably be taking things a bit too fast, but damn it, Gia belonged with Erin.

"It is and you know, he gets kind of grouchy at having my stuff spread all over his floor." Gia nodded in his direction. "Despite his name, that man's actually quite a neat freak. He'll be ecstatic to see the back of me."

Erin laughed at the memory of just how messy she used to be. "You'll be bucking up your ideas if you're coming to live with me." Whoops, the cat was out of the bag.

"Is that an invitation?" Gia asked with a wide grin.

Erin blushed, "so much for taking things slow."

Erin introduced Gia to her parents and despite her mother's initial reservations, she seemed to like Gia instantly, which was truly saying something considering she'd so recently been expecting a wedding and grandkids. "All this was a wonderful idea, Gia, quite an effort to pull off, I bet." By far the biggest surprise was that they were almost able to understand each other.

"Is this the big reunion party you always imagined?" Erin asked Gia, as they lined up together with Scruffy and Holly for photos.

"Almost but it's as perfect as possible."

"I'm sure Mikey is here in spirit," Erin thought about how brave Gia had been returning home to Cambridge with her head held high. "He'd be very proud of you."

EPILOGUE

Two days later, Gia arrived for her first day at work. They'd once spoken about being partners, but instead, Gia was technically an employee. It wouldn't matter in the long scheme of things as Gia took to the job immediately and proved to be a wonderful person to work with. Erin didn't tell her but she planned on making her a partner as a one year anniversary gift.

Their close proximity during the day proved quite a challenge and distraction, especially at first, as they repeatedly stole glances at one another from across the lab. Erin couldn't tell a lie, but Gia looked damned hot in her lab coat.

"I know you're doing it deliberately," Erin muttered under her breath, staring hopelessly at Gia's curves as she worked with a patient at the other end of the room. Although *taking things slow* had been a good idea, Erin hoped it was torturing Gia just as much as herself.

"I have a surprise for you," Erin announced after Gia's first two weeks were over.

Half an hour later they were both standing on the edge of the Cam beside a two-man scull.

"Erin, you have no idea how many times I've dreamed of this," Gia remarked as she hesitated but then finally stepped inside with a slight wobble.

"You're not the only one." Erin clambered in behind and together they pushed off the side with their oars. "Nice and easy to begin with, then we'll see how fit we really are." It had been eleven years since either girl had rowed.

Gia gestured upstream and squinted. "Where are all the other boats?" She shivered, even as she exerted herself on the oars. "Looks like I'll need to adjust to this cold again."

"Well, you really shouldn't have left me then, should you?" Erin joked. "Besides, it really isn't *that* cold. We've done it in worse."

After ten minutes, Gia threw down her oars and leaned back in the boat, her head coming to rest on Erin's thighs.

"This is not how to get back in shape," Erin said, enjoying Gia's touch and hoping she wouldn't move.

"Shhh, I don't care. I want things to stay just like this ... forever, if possible." Gia rubbed Erin's calf, which she felt deep down inside.

Erin closed her eyes and concentrated on Gia's hand as it brushed light strokes up and down her leg. "Yes," she whispered, finally.

Gia tilted back her head. "Yes, what?"

"The answer is *yes*." Erin ran her fingers through Gia's thick mane. "I always regretted not telling you, but you know what I was like back then."

Gia's chest rose and sank, in rhythm with Erin's own breathing. "Why am I getting a very strange yet beautiful déjà vu right now?"

It wasn't so déjà vu for Erin, who'd always regretted letting herself down when that perfect opportunity to change her

331

life had been gifted to her. This time she'd do things differently because if fate was to gift her a second chance, it would not return for a third. "I *have* been in love Gia and you're right, it *is* the most incredible feeling in the world." She leaned forward, brought her lips to Gia's ear and whispered, "I've never stopped loving you."

Gia brought herself to face Erin. "I love you too."

Erin's heart soared. She felt whole, like she'd finally made some sort of peace with herself and her past, with Gia and whoever was watching out for her. "You should move in with me right now. I don't want to wait another minute to be with you." Although she'd suggested it the other week, Gia had remained living at Scruffy's, technically anyway, just to be on the safe side, despite the fact she'd been sleeping over at Erin's most nights regardless, and more so especially recently, which kind of defeated the whole bloody purpose. Whenever Erin closed her eyes, she could see and feel Gia's tongue swirling inside of her.

"I'm there," Gia hissed, her fingers sifting through Erin's hair. "I've missed this, my English rose."

Erin leaned forward, her lips stopping an inch from Gia's as she whispered, "I've missed this too, my damn Italian."

And then their lips came together as somewhere high above, two Kingfishers flew over.

ALSO BY SALLY BRYAN

Novels

Euro Tripped

A Petal And A Thorn

Novellas

Trapped

My Summer Romance